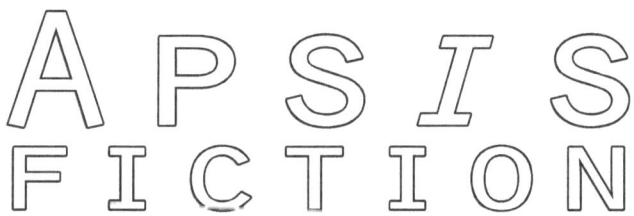

APSIS FICTION

The Semi-Annual Anthology of Goldeen Ogawa

Volume 6, Issue 1 • Mesohelion 2018

CONTENTS

I0642701

author • illustrator • editor • book designer
GOLDEEN OGAWA

a HELIOPAUSE PRODUCTION

Apsis Fiction: The Semi-Annual Anthology of Goldeen Ogawa
Volume No. 6, Issue 1, Whole No. 10 (Mesohelion 2018).
Published semi-annually by Heliopause Productions.

FICTION/Science Fiction/Short Stories

FICTION/Fantasy/General

First Edition 2018

ISBN: 978-1-945781-11-7

STATE OF THE ORBIT

W<small>E LAUNCHED</small> *Apsis Fiction* because I had no less than three separate series, and we didn't know where to start. Doing a semiannual anthology forced us to get the stories edited and published with the least possible fuss, and allowed each series to be moved along without having to prioritize any one.

With this issue one of those series has come to a close: "The Peculiar Case of Professor Odd" marks the end of the *Adventures of Bouragner Felpz*—at least as told by Corianne—and with its completion any future issues of *Apsis* would have been found wanting, in my opinion. There will be more (a lot more) of *Driving Arcana*, and indeed *Professor Odd* proper, but as "Cerberus Retired" provides the finale for Season Two, and with the next stories to be published being fully fledged novels in their own right, this seemed a fitting place to retire *Apsis Fiction* . . . at least for the time being.

Readers who have been keeping apace with the stories in *Apsis* need not fear: the three novellas which constitute the third volume of Felpz adventures will get their own publication in *The Aubergine Spellbook*, which will also include a new short story which is the very final word on the matter. Episodes 7 through 12 of *Professor Odd* will again see light in *The Complete Season Two*, complete with new illustrations, and forthcoming episodes will be immediately published as singles, and later similar collections. New spokes of *Driving Arcana* will arrive in batches of three until there are three such published, at which point they will get their own omnibus release.

And what of the novels I spoke of? First and foremost of these is *Lucena in the House of Madgrin*, which features characters both new and familiar, and while it is a story independent of the three series already mentioned, serves to fill in those gaps which Corianne has artfully scattered throughout her own narrative. Neither a sequel nor a prequel to *The Adventures of Bouragner Felpz*, it is a related work, and one which I originally wrote simultaneously with the early Felpz stories.

So really it is high time I put current projects to bed and got a move on it.

This issue will be going to press in early fall, around the same time the first issue came out, which is fitting. Like that issue (Mesohelion 2013) this one also has artwork inspired by photographs from the Hubble Space Telescope. Specifically the "stellar nursery" of the Horsehead Nebula, though somewhat upstaged by the chaos demon Fairig, shown here in her more benevolent aspect as a creator-goddess. Though she does not appear directly in any of the stories herein, as an entity that inspires creative chaos she can be thought to influence all writers who work in the fantastic and the extraordinary, especially this one.

—Goldeen Ogawa
Oregon
August 2018

Here is the finale of Professor Odd *Season Two. Best read after all the previous episodes, and especially the first, "The False Student," the seventh, "The Dogs of Canary Island," and the eleventh, "Davebot," all of which are available as singles from* Heliopause. *The first also appears in* The Complete Season One. *Though "Cerberus Retired" is the last episode of Season Two, it is not the last episode of Professor Odd, and will be followed by "The Angels of Tyson 4" sometime next year. It was originally published as a single from* Heliopause *in August 2018.*

CERBERUS RETIRED

Prologue

TO AN OUTSIDE OBSERVER, the hijacking of Heliotrans Run 4413—better known as the Cerberus Express—began when it was boarded by a group of aliens who took control of the engines, causing it to stop in the middle of the Denallian Passage. In truth the story began a little before that, when four passengers appeared out of the galley's air lock and proceeded to sit themselves at the front of Coach 20 where they took up an entire row. By their conversation they were quickly determined to be aliens, and a conductor was sent to deal with them. They promptly produced tickets, signed and stamped and perfectly in order—save that they had been issued *after* the exotrain had left Amphitrite, and there was no record of the four strangers having boarded there or anywhere else.

Still, they were perfectly within their rights to be on the train, and the conductor whizzed away after a brisk reminder that they were in coach class, and that their conversation should be kept below forty decibels. One of the strangers—a tall male human with pale skin, short, dark brown hair and eyebrows like a pair of eagle wings—hunched in his seat, looking embarrassed, but his companions—an equally tall humanoid woman with fluffy, cherry-pink hair in a green trench coat, and a pointy-eared anthropomorphic dog with gold fur wearing a navy denim jumpsuit—seemed hardly contrite at all. The fourth member of their band was a barrel-shaped robot, and though its expression was impossible to discern, its reaction to the conductor's request was clearly audible for the entire coach to hear:

"THIS IS NOT A DANGEROUS LEVEL OF NOISE," it began before the dark-haired man shushed it. "IT'S NOT LIKE I SOUND ANY MORE PLEASANT WITH THE VOLUME DOWN," it finished, but only to the ears of those in the nearer rows.

"I believe it is the thought that counts," said the pink-haired woman, stretching comfortably in her seat. "I am sure everyone appreciates the effort, Dave. Don't let it bother you—come on now, you're missing the show."

Part One: Talking to Strangers

ALISTER BANE LET OUT A SIGH OF RELIEF as he watched the small metal orb that served as a conductor whizz into the air lock and then on to the next coach.

It had been strange enough just trying to imagine the train they were on, never mind actually riding in it.

"An *exotrain,* Alister," Professor Odd had said to him, her jaguar eyes sparkling from between strands of pink hair. "It's a *train* that runs through *outer space.* Eighty coaches long, this one's got a triple engine at the front—that's why they call it the *Cerberus* Express—and it's the fastest way to get from Amphitrite to Typhon at sub-light speeds."

"And just how long does that take?" Elo had asked, dryly.

"Eighteen kadents," Professor Odd had replied, then rolled her eyes up, did some internal calculations, and added: "Or, about four years."

"Four *years?*" Alister had gasped. "People sit on a train for *four years?*"

"Most of them spend at least some of it in suspension," Professor Odd said with a shrug. "But everyone gets up for the Denallian Passage, which only takes four *hours* and is the *best thing.* We'll hop on just before it enters the passage, enjoy the show, then hop off again. We can get tickets at Amphitrite—the Premier knows me—and then jump over to the train."

She grinned at them, bright and a little bit manic.

This, Alister had thought, is what happens to you when you live in a place that can open doors anywhere in the multiverse. See that train? That train moving through *outer space?* Wanna ride it, but only for a little while? Have your ship—place, home, *whatever,* (it's called the Oddity for a reason)—just open a portal joined to a door inside the train and *ta-da!* You were there. To be honest, Alister had been surprised when Professor Odd insisted on buying tickets. But after they had been accosted by a conductor barely five minutes after sitting down—and not even a human-shaped conductor; a robot even more unfriendly looking than Dave's panvironment suit!—Alister understood her precaution.

Lightly belted in and hovering over his seat ("They keep the gravity at a minimum, to conserve energy," Odd had explained) Alister had dared to glance at their fellow travelers, trying to gauge the impact their interaction with the conductor had had.

This was difficult. Not everyone on the train was human—or even human-shaped—and for those that were, many were strange colors or had slightly altered facial characteristics. Their expressions were as alien to Alister as were the long-necked, bird-faced people, only even more unsettling for all their familiarity in other respects.

"Technically, *we're* the aliens here," Professor Odd had been explaining. "Humans in general, I mean, not just transuniversal travelers like ourselves. Amphitrite and Typhon are both part of the Aquarian system, you see, which was colonized by the Sollan Commonwealth—that's native humans—about three hundred kadents ago. It's become something of a melting pot, however, since this universe became multiplicity-aware."

"YOU CAN THANK THE DENALLIAN BELT FOR THAT," Dave said.

"How does the Denallian Belt have anything to do with this universe being multiplicity-aware?" Elo asked.

"Just what *is* the Denallian Belt?" Alister chipped in, whispering fiercely. "And . . . does multiplicity-aware mean what I think it means?"

"One question at a time," Professor Odd laughed, then looked elaborately around at their coachmates. The seats had been designed for four to sit abreast, then a narrow aisle, and then four more. They were a little wider and taller than the train seats Alister had ridden in back home—before he'd fallen afoul of the Canary Company and been whisked away to the relative safety of adventures with Professor Odd—but it still made for a packed environment, and some of the other passengers had sensitive-looking ears, and were already glaring at the Professor.

"THEY ALL TIE TOGETHER," Dave told them, his harsh voice muted, but no less abrasive and distinct. "THE DENALLIAN BELT IS A BENIGN PARTICLE FRACTURE IN THE FABRIC OF THIS UNIVERSE, HELD IN BALANCE BETWEEN THE GRAVITATIONAL FIELDS OF THE STAR AQUARIA AND THE GAS GIANT TYPHON. IT FACILITATES TRANSUNIVERSAL TRAVEL WITHOUT THE AID OF ODDITIES OR OTHER METAPHYSICAL TECHNOLOGY. THE INEVITABLE RESULT BEING THAT SPECIES FROM ACROSS MANY DIFFERENT UNIVERSES HAVE CONVERGED HERE, RENDERING THIS UNIVERSE AWARE OF DEFINITE OTHER UNIVERSES—IN OTHER WORDS, AWARE OF THE MULTIPLICITY OF WORLDS, OR 'MULTIPLICITY-AWARE.' DOES THAT ANSWER YOUR QUESTIONS?"

"Ye-es," said Elo, nodding slowly. "Thank you, Dave."

"The Denallian Belt is absolutely fascinating," said Professor Odd in an eager wheeze. "I've ridden the Passage at least a dozen times, and I always discover something new. All that aside, I wanted to show *you,* Mr Alister, simply because it is the most brilliant thing."

She pointed as she spoke, and turning to follow her direction, Alister found himself looking out the long, rectangular window that filled the wall nearest to them. Because they were sitting in the front of the car they also had a clear view out a smaller window that faced forward—through which Alister glimpsed a corner of the next coach—and by these windows Alister saw exactly what the Professor meant by "brilliant."

From this distance the starry blackness of outer space was cut across, like an arbitrary sort of horizon, by a band of smoky light that put Alister in mind of long-exposure photographs of the Milky Way. Clots of darkness, like ink suspended in water, drifted across like clouds over a desert. They were lit from behind by a profusion of magenta light, which shot shafts through the inkiness like rays of red sunshine. The red haze itself was pierced by bright points of gold, which came and went in a twinkling dance that left Alister mesmerized.

"Why go through it?" Elo asked in a piercing growl. "Sounds awfully unstable, and if it's a *belt* and not a *sphere* you can easily avoid it."

"Not if it's on the same plane as the planets you're traveling between," Professor Odd said in a patient tone. "Which it is, if you're going from Amphitrite to Typhon. You *can* go around it, yes, if you're in a conventional spaceship which can move above and below the plane of the ecliptic, but the exo-trains can't do that. They're infinitely more fuel-efficient— which is why they are so affordable and popular—but part of that comes from running on tracks, and you can't *build* exolines strong enough to support that kind of variation: they've got to be as flat as possible, which means if you're running a line between Amphitrite and Typhon, you've got to go through the Denallian Belt. Which is what makes the Denallian *Passage* so remarkable—they couldn't build a track around it, so they built one *right through it,* using all sorts of clever tricks to manipulate the space-time fluidity, and allowing everyday passengers the chance to observe a truly amazing phenomenon up close. It is *wonderful.*"

"Hold on," said Alister, whose grasp of interplanetary travel, while limited, included the knowledge that planets did not just sit in one place, like an island, and this clashed with a fixed line on which a train could run. "How does the line even *work?* Like, what if Typhon's on the other side of the star? You can't just go in the same direction every time—the planet wouldn't *be* there."

Professor Odd was nodding enthusiastically. *"That's* where four-dimensional thinking comes in handy," she said with a grin. "And orbital resonances. Amphitrite and Typhon are in a two-to-one orbital resonance—that is, Amphitrite orbits the star Aquaria *twice* for every *once* that Typhon goes around. And Typhon's year is *exactly* the same length of time it takes for the Cerberus Express to travel between the two when their orbits synchronize. So you've got the line, right, which is anchored to Amphitrite on one end—it's moving *with* that planet—until it hits the Denallian Belt, at which point it changes tracks to the Denallian Passage (which is anchored to the belt itself and does *not* orbit the star) and once it gets through *that* it's just in time to get picked up by the Typhon side of the line as that comes around for its half-year. The train spends the second half of its journey traveling on a line anchored to Typhon, and reaches that planet just in time for the return trip to set off for Amphitrite, which then repeats the entire journey in reverse. The *key* is that, thanks to the space-time fluidity of the belt, it takes long enough to go through the Denallian Passage for Typhon's orbit to bring it around, while to the people *inside* it actually goes by much faster. It's a puzzle of moving parts, one which the people of this system solved by turning a disadvantage into an asset. It is really most remarkable. The only difficulty is that the trains have to be kept on a strict schedule, otherwise the pieces don't line up and nasty things can happen. It's never pretty when a train runs out of track, but it's particularly bad when it's a train running through *outer space.*"

Alister nodded, and though he felt like the picture in his head of what Professor Odd had described was a little blurry, he got the idea well enough to try nervously searching what he could see of their way ahead, in the hopes of assuring himself that the Denallian Passage was where it should be, and that the exotrain was not going to run out of track and go careening off into space.

"You can't actually *see* the passage unless you're up in the con," Professor Odd said, seeing him look. "Great view, but it's very tiny and cramped and the people there don't appreciate sudden visitors. Besides, the passage isn't as interesting as the Belt itself, which we can see perfectly well from here."

"Just so long as it's *there,*" said Elo, who was clearly having similar thoughts as Alister.

"THIS RUN IS ON TIME AND SHOULD NOT ENCOUNTER ANY SPLIT-TING," Dave assured them.

"In fact," said Professor Odd, "we're in the process of shifting at this very moment. Hard to tell, because they've engineered it so well. Remember there's a lot more *space* in space, so it's not like changing tracks with a terrestrial locomotive. It's more like a gradual relay. But you'll know when we get into the belt. You'll start seeing . . . things."

Obediently Alister turned and peered out the window. The wisps of ink and magenta haze looked the same as ever, but had the golden lights *moved?* He watched, fascinated, as the backdrop of ink and haze and light *shifted* around them, and then it was like looking at the cross section of a geode.

There were . . . Alister couldn't help thinking of them as *fractures* in space; places where one part had slipped sideways from another, leaving an angular golden scar. They formed a rough pattern, which was what put him in mind of a geode, he thought, but now he looked, the pattern was constantly changing. Sometimes it was a spiral, other times it was crystalline—all sharp corners—and sometimes it was in smooth waves.

Then his view was washed out by a cold, blue light, which filled all the windows for a moment, and left his eyes stinging.

"First marker!" Professor Odd cried in a restrained voice, but now their fellow passengers were also peering eagerly out their own windows, and no one bothered to chastise her. Once he rubbed the afterimages out of his eyes and could see properly again, Alister realized why.

The crystalline patterns had come alive, bleeding in and out of each other in mad swirls. Then, like clouds shedding off a rising airplane, a whole new vista appeared outside the long, rectangular window.

It was like mountains made of crimson clouds, with blue shadows in their depths, rising in billowy crags as far as Alister could see. At each peak was a shining, golden light, and for as many mountains as appeared right-way up, there were just as many that hung down, like huge stalactites, anchored in the streaks of purple-and-pink clouds that stretched, lazily paralleling the ecliptic. Far away the mountain shapes blurred into heaps of crimson mashed potatoes, their stars stained rosy with distance.

It was breathtakingly beautiful and amazing, and then, climbing out from behind a particularly large mountain, the round curve of a planet hove into view.

"Is that . . . ? Is *that* . . . ?" Alister couldn't bring himself to finish the question.

"A glimpse into another world," Professor Odd said in an excited whisper. "Windows, you know, like what the Oddity sees from the space between."

"But we're *in* a world!" Elo exclaimed. "How is that *possible?*"

"A MORE PERTINENT QUESTION WOULD BE, HOW IS IT *STABLE*?" Dave said, forgetting to lower his volume. A few of the aisle-seated passengers looked around in annoyance.

"They are both *fascinating* questions," Professor Odd said happily.

Outside, the planet was coming fully into view. It looked like a rocky, pock-marked world, dry and yellowish, like an ochre version of Mars. A splotch of white near its top suggested a polar ice cap, and it was ringed with a faint line of black, which bled into the cloudy, red spacescape of the Denallian Passage like the ragged edge of paper in water.

"It's *possible* because of a delicate balance between gravity and escality created by the same orbital resonances that make Heliotrans Run 4413 possible, as well. It's *stable* because . . . well, because it *is*. To be honest even *I* don't know why it doesn't collapse or blow apart—or do both at once—which is one of the reasons I keep coming back. That, and I would like to see a manaflot."

Alister blinked, wondering if his ears had tricked him into thinking the Professor had broken down into gibberish. But then Elo was asking, in clear, enunciated words:

"What is a *mana-flot?*"

At his elbow, Alister could feel Professor Odd vibrating with excitement, and he peeled his eyes away from the amazing sight of a planet eclipsing a star pinned to the top of a cloudy mountain, to find the woman grinning madly at them.

"*Nobody knows,*" she said, sounding positively delighted. "That's literally what they're called: when some Sollan Commonwealth settlers asked a Rikilinni what they were, the fellow replied with '*A'ya Manaflottl,*' which basically means 'blowed if I know,' and it stuck."

"And the Rikilinni?" Alister asked.

For answer Professor Odd pointed with a long, elegant finger to a passenger two rows behind and opposite them. They were tall, even sitting down, with two scaly legs that ended in three-toed, taloned feet. They had a plump body covered in black-and-blue feathers, and a round face with a beaky mouth similarly wreathed in feathers, stuck at the end of a long, thin neck—whose longness and thinness were accentuated by the stacks of metal necklaces that were the creature's only clothing.

"The closest thing Aquaria has to natives," Professor Odd whispered. "But only because they got here first."

The Rikilinni twitched, as if sensing their gaze, and Alister tore his eyes away from the alien to stare out the window some more. The ochre planet had disappeared, but now he could see, faded in the distance, more ragged windows into darkness, and more planets through them. Some of these were small and rocky, others huge and streaked with bands of clouds. Still others were dark and glittered strangely. They were not all lit the same; some of them were visible as full discs, while others were crescents of varying fatness, and still others were only discernible by the ring of illuminated atmosphere around the edges.

Alister stared, feeling his mouth slowly open, as more and more windows came into view. Then they passed through another flash of bright blue, and he squeezed his eyes shut just in time.

"Don't tell me, that was the second marker," he heard Elo say, and when the blue had faded from behind his eyelids, he chanced another look.

Back was the misty, half upside-down landscape of mountains and gold stars, but the only window was a single circle, floating between two opposing peaks. It showed a gibbous blue world, streaked with white clouds, under which brown-and-green continents lurked, like whales under the surface of the ocean. The clouds, though thick around the poles, were thin enough that Alister was able to recognize the landmasses beneath, and he felt a lump rise in his throat as he realized what he was looking at.

Several of the human passengers had also recognized it, and a faint murmur echoed around the carriage.

"Isn't that . . . Earth?" Elo asked in a small voice.

"*An* Earth," Professor Odd said. "No telling which universe it's from, except that it's not far off the temporal median. See, there is India, Africa, your Mediterranean, a bit of Europe . . . "

Alister watched as the window to a version of his homeworld slid by, craning his neck to follow it through the windows of the seats behind him. By the general leaning among the humans aboard, he was not the only one.

They had probably studied maps of Earth, he realized. Seen pictures of their planet of origin in history books—or whatever passed for books here. Which was how Alister had seen his world, to be fair, but he fancied he was probably the only one— outside his companions—who had actually set foot on any of the continents just visible beneath the clouds.

Just as the window was slipping entirely out of sight, Alister thought he saw something bright—like the tail of a shooting star—go streaking across the blue-and-white sphere. But then the window passed outside his field of vision, and he was distracted by a subtle shift in the cloudy landscape ahead.

Where before, the mountainous clouds had been uniformly magenta with blue shadows, now the blueness was spreading, seeping out in a glow of pale aqua that rose like steam from the red peaks. Stars of silver were interspersed with those of gold, and a few of them had broken free from their cloudy peaks to hang in the pink-and-purple mist.

It was utterly enchanting and beautiful, and Alister felt a warm glow of appreciation rising in his chest, forcing out the pangs of lonely homesickness.

Beside him, Professor Odd sighed impatiently. "I *do* hope we see a manaflot," she began, and there was a sickening lurch.

The train didn't stop, and it didn't come off its tracks; it felt more like the whole machine had *shivered,* deep in its metallic bones. All the passengers who were not securely strapped in (including Dave) were shaken off their seats, though Dave stabilized himself immediately with a few careful bursts from his anti-grav plates.

"What was that?" Alister exclaimed, all the pleasant, dreamy feelings jolted out of him.

"*Not* a manaflot," said Professor Odd, unbuckling herself and standing up.

Dave extended one cloth-covered tentacle-arm and pushed himself back against the foot of his seat.

"THAT," he said, loud enough for the whole coach to hear, "IS TROUBLE."

At first it didn't seem like anything had changed. The train continued running, the spacescape kept sliding past, and after a time the passengers settled down again.

All except Professor Odd, who remained standing, her eyes narrowed, gazing intently around the coach, as if the answer were hidden in the metal joints and seals of its walls.

Eventually she frowned and said "Hmm," in the same way doctors did to keep themselves from saying "Uh-oh."

"What's wrong?" asked Elo sharply.

"I'm not sure," said Professor Odd, sounding annoyed. "Something, though. Just . . . wait here a minute. I'm going to see what it is."

"I'll come," said Elo at once, unbuckling herself and leaping over Alister's lap.

Alister hesitated. On the one hand he knew it was best to stick close to Professor Odd. On the other he knew that was also a good way to have your holiday derailed, and he *had* been having a rather good time watching the views of the Denallian Belt.

Dave, it seemed, shared these feelings, and hoisted himself back onto his seat so he could have a better view out the window. That decided him.

"Have fun then," he said, giving the Professor a wry smile.

She patted him firmly on the shoulder, and began making her way down the coach, with Elo at her heel, toward the air lock where they'd left the Oddity's portal. Alister turned back to the view, now dominated by a massive, rocky crescent of a planet, platinum-white and pockmarked with craters. He saw striations in its surface as well, which put him in mind of a grid of roads. Or fracture lines in quartz. He wasn't sure. He tried to distract himself by wondering, but couldn't shake the worry which nagged the back of his mind, and constantly threatened to nag the front of it too, if he didn't concentrate on enjoying the view.

The triple engines of the Cerberus Express bore only a rudimentary resemblance to their terran-bound locomotive namesakes. Specifically built for the Amphitrite-Typhon line, they were

huge, bulbous things, with three particle-intake manifolds—
tubular contraptions with spiky arms of metal reaching out
and forward, the depths of which glowed white-gold—arranged
with one on its own, a little ahead of the others, and the remaining two side-by-side a little ways back. Behind each manifold
was a small bulge housing the command pods; just large enough,
inside all the armor and radiation barriers, for a driver and tech-
nician to fit, packed head to toe. Struts of reinforced metal stuck
out to either side behind the engines: the con towers which
Professor Odd had found so crowded. They also served as communication antennae, though any messages they sent would be
a long time finding their recipients while the train remained in
the Denallian Belt.

Behind the manifolds, the command pods and the con towers, the body of the triple-engine stretched, rectangular and
windowless, housing both the fusion generator that powered
the impressive engines and the full complement of drivers, technicians, engineers, and staff. They lived in cramped, close quarters, and for the most part ignored the suspension bunks they
were technically required to use for at least one kadent per run.
Because the kind of person who chooses to work and live in a relatively small, fragile place, hurtling through outer space, directly
above what is essentially a tiny, well-contained star, tends to be
the kind of person who is very keen on keeping that place running smoothly, and taking four-month-long naps while someone *else* takes over your job was never an attractive idea.

So in practice the alpha crew was always active, while the
suspension bunks held a skeleton beta crew who could ostensibly be woken up and take over operation of the train in an emergency. It was common knowledge that the beta crew would be
pretty terrible at this if there were not enough members of the
alpha crew to show them what to do—on a voyage as long as Heliotrans Run 4413 the engines would invariably develop quirks,
patched in inventive but non-obvious ways, and routines became more and more elaborate and intricate, until someone just
coming out of suspension—no matter how much training they
had—would be as lost as a layman.

This was a glaring security flaw, but one which had yet to
cause the alpha crew of the Cerberus Express any trouble. They

had never needed their beta crew, which consisted of an ever-changing roster of junior technicians, engineers and drivers. Because even the sort of person who chooses to work in a small space above a tiny star hurtling through the solar system often decides that spending eighteen kadents in suspended animation for who-knew how much of their natural lives was a waste of time, and moved on to other, more interesting assignments. The result was that the beta crew would have been mostly useless, while the alpha crew became more and more proficient.

However, even the best crew can fail. Especially if their engine is hit by a capsule-like spaceship that latches onto the side of the reactor case, blasts a hole in the armor, and injects nitrous oxide into the atmospheric processors.

Alarms went off, and a few crew members managed to get masks on, but within minutes all the key areas of the engines were manned by people who were about as capable of operating an exotrain as a Pomeranian.

One affected member, performing as only someone who had spent a lot of time thinking about what they would do in a worst-case scenario could, sent off a boilerplate distress signal and engaged the auto-op, before passing out slumped over the controls.

The few remaining conscious crew members quickly found the source of their problems, and crowded around the breach in a concerned huddle. So when the arc of electricity shot through the aperture it was able to jump from one to the other, before terminating in a protruding lever handle.

The masked bodies—humanoid and exoavian—collapsed on the ground, twitching, and lay still. Smoke from the breach washed over them, obscuring their forms, but not enough to cause trouble for the lithe figure in a tight-fitting exposure suit stepping through the breach and into the engine.

It was joined almost immediately by two larger, bulkier figures, who lumbered forward and locked stabilizing braces around the breach.

"Get the translators working," said the first one, turning their helmeted head toward the larger two. "I want to talk to the passengers."

In the distance an alarm was blaring, and interspersed with it was a melodious, artificial voice that said: *"Class six engine breach. Alpha crew compromised. Waking beta crew . . . "*

"Never mind," said the lithe figure in a sharp, highish, no-nonsense voice. "Let's find the spatial locks. And for the love of god, get this thing *stopped.*"

The mountains had given way to gently rolling hills which put Alister in mind of sweeping ocean waves when the pleasant, white-balanced light that filled the carriage was abruptly replaced by emergency red. In an instant the clean lines of the interior were cast in red-and-black outlines, the passengers turning into surprised shadows, the lights of Dave's suit blazing beside him.

That was all the warning they had before they were suddenly thrown against their restraints, and Alister felt the familiar rising in his stomach as the artificial gravity gave out. He was vaguely aware, somewhere in his jostled mind, that several passengers had gone hurtling through the air and hit the front end of the coach with alarming *thuds.* There was also a synthetic voice, speaking above the blaring alarm that had started up, but both were drowned out by the horrendous screaming that was coming from all around them.

The Cerberus Express, like its terrestrial cousins, had an emergency brake. It did not stop the train all at once—the speeds at which it traveled made this comparable to an ordinary train running into fifty feet of reinforced concrete at sixty miles per hour—but reversed its engines and contrived to decelerate at the highest rate that its engineers had deemed both the train and its passengers could endure.

Even though it was *called* the emergency brake, it really wasn't. In fact, most emergencies would only be made worse by stopping the train. Keeping to the scheduled speed was critical to the success of the run—too fast or too slow, and the train could miss its connection with the Denallian Passage, or the Typhon line. Only when the consequences of *not* stopping were worse than missing a connection was the brake activated. Such as if the train's sensors detected a fault in the line.

In essence, the only thing worse than stopping was running out of line, and the *only* time the former would even be considered was if the latter were unavoidable.

Either way, it meant the train was going to spend more time in space than normal and so it began to implement energy-saving procedures even before it came to a relative stop. So all the lights switched to low-energy red, the gravity was shut off, and the temperature lowered to the minimum necessary to support life.

Had she been present, Professor Odd would have been able to explain all this to a confused and increasingly frightened Alister, but while he and Dave were enduring the rapid deceleration from thousands of miles per minute to functional immobility, she and Elo were encountering their own difficulties.

Namely, the difficulty of trying to reverse the emergency brake from the only place in the engines that was not currently flooded with nitrous oxide, all the while bracing against the inertia that was hurling the occupants of Alister's coach against their restraints, or, if they were unlucky, its walls.

At least, Professor Odd was trying to reverse the brake. Elo was in the Oddity, looking for their respirators.

"I left them on the table!" the Professor called over her shoulder, through the tiny circular hatch that was serving as the Oddity's door.

"That doesn't narrow it down much!" came the strained reply.

Professor Odd shrugged and turned back to the controls. They were for raising and lowering the long-range antennae, but since the emergency brake had to be accessible from every control node on the engine (and some of the coaches), it followed that one *should* be able to turn it *off* from any of those places as well.

Someone, it seemed, had thought this wasn't such a good idea, and Professor Odd kept coming up against security walls and messages requesting confirmation from the Master Con. Which, she knew, was located just behind the three actual engines. Which she also knew was soaked in an atmosphere that even she could not think straight in. Hence the workaround from the communication booth.

Inside the Oddity, Elo gave a frustrated growl. "Hold on," she shouted. "I'll be back in an instant!" And the portal vanished.

Professor Odd waited an instant, and when nothing happened but the train kept braking and the alarms kept blaring, she pursed her lips and turned back to the console, her priorities changed. Now, instead of trying to get the train going again, she worked on flushing the atmosphere.

Somewhere out there, Elo had tried detaching the Oddity from the local universe so she could look for the masks properly, and after finding them she could reopen the portal a split-second later in local time in the Master Con, where, if all had gone well, she would have reversed the emergency brake and switched off all the alarms.

Because nothing had changed, something had got in her way. And if something was bad enough to slow *Elo* down, it was bad enough that Professor Odd could not afford to be trapped in a tiny communications booth.

Agent Parthenon sat in the Master Con, surrounded by shipping and passenger manifests, and regarded the the beta crew critically.

They were not in the con with her—it was only large enough for two or three people, and then only ones who knew each other well—but their pictures were displayed on the banks of circular screens that took up the entire ceiling, and with a swipe of her finger she could bring up their names, ranks, ages, gender designations (the Rikilinni, it turned out, had three different genders, none of which correlated with male or female, and the practice had been adopted by some of the Sollans), and their experience records. She was pleased to see none of them had ever *actually operated* the train.

That was good. They would be frightened. Unsure what to do. People like that were much easier to manage.

Which was to say: they were easier for Agent Parthenon to bully.

"They shouldn't give us any trouble," she said, pushing the files off the screens. "Let me see the passenger manifest."

"Uh . . . " said Caruthers, wedged in the doorway. "There are over *eight hundred* of them . . . "

"So run a scan; see if it raises any flags."

There was the quiet clicking of fingers on buttons as Caruthers did just this. Agent Parthenon relaxed into her seat and began shuffling passenger profiles across her screen as Caruthers sent them over. That was the thing about Caruthers: he was obedient, which was a blessing in a commtech operative. He was also over six feet tall and could double as a bruiser when needed. Which Agent Parthenon needed rather a lot. He was almost as useful as Villafranka—her *actual* bruiser—with his remarkable aptitude for precision sniping and chemical warfare. It meant that Agent Parthenon could do with a two-man team what it took an entire unit of other operatives to accomplish.

Such as commandeer an alien space train and take it in for study.

Behind her, Caruthers let out a low grunt. It was as close as the man got to swearing, and it was like a pin going into the back of Agent Parthenon's neck—a tiny sensation that portended serious consequences.

"What?" she said.

"Got a flag," said Caruthers. A pause, then: "Two of them."

"Let me see," said Parthenon.

Two profiles were duly placed on her screens, and the agent felt her breath catch in her throat at the names displayed.

That was all they were. Names. No photos, no homeworlds, no preferred pronouns. But Agent Parthenon didn't need any of that to recognize them.

"Specimens ten-sixteen *and* ten-seventeen," she whispered, her eyes going wide.

"Is *that* who Alister Bane was?" Caruthers asked.

"You didn't hear that," snapped Parthenon. "But do a search for something matching the description of Incongruity M87."

More tapping.

"Not getting anything," said Caruthers, and Parthenon exhaled.

Too soon.

"Wait."

"What?"

"I have . . . something. I don't know. Look at who is traveling *with* ten-sixteen and seventeen . . . "

Agent Parthenon peered at the files as they came up on her screen.

"Marhütz Elo," she said, frowning. "And . . . Dave?"

"Dave's species is listed as robot," supplied Caruthers. "But from the parameters recorded by the conductor, it could just as well be an environment suit. Wasn't Incongruity M87 . . . "

"*Aquatic* . . . " finished Agent Parthenon. She pulled herself out of the captain's seat and squirmed around to look at Caruthers . . .

. . . who wasn't there anymore.

He wasn't there because the doorway wasn't there anymore. To be precise, it looked like the outer corridor had been replaced by a set of carpeted stairs, lit faintly by a confusion of multicolored lights.

A golden, furry paw appeared on the topmost stair.

Agent Parthenon sprang into action. Like all agents trained under Director Carver, she had been thoroughly briefed on what was referred to as The Great Breach—that unfortunate incident in which both Incongruity M87 and two alpha-priority specimens had inexplicably vanished. She had studied the security footage of the strange, anthropomorphic canine, and she knew she had to act quickly.

She barreled up the stairs, pulling her arc taser from its holster, firing almost blindly.

She would have missed, but the gun did its job, and on the second rebound the electric current found its target.

There was an earsplitting shriek, and Agent Parthenon found a pair of canine jaws locked on her gun arm. She looked into furious brown eyes, felt the deadly teeth as faint pressure under her armor, and calmly pressed the trigger again.

That only made the canine bite harder, but when she lost consciousness her jaw slackened, and Agent Parthenon pried the animal off her arm.

Taking a pair of restraints off her belt, Agent Parthenon secured the canine, chipped her, and for want of something more secure, tied her to the back of the captain's chair in the Master Con.

"Caruthers!" Agent Parthenon shouted.

There was no response.

Of *course* there was no response. Ten-sixteen had had portal technology. Whatever was on the other side of the doorway, it wasn't the outer corridor anymore.

After double-checking the restraints on the canine, Agent Parthenon charged her arc taser and began to creep, cautiously, up the carpeted stairs and into the lair of Specimen 1016.

The world went dark. Alister wasn't sure if he fainted or if it was just the emergency lights giving out temporarily. He felt dizzy and sick, like some of his brain had been forced out through his nose.

Someone had unbuckled him and bent him over his knees, and when he tried to straighten up he felt gentle pressure on the back of his neck.

"STAY DOWN," Dave ordered.

Alister stayed down.

"Wha-ah-appen'd?" he asked, thickly.

"OUR TRANSPORT HAS BEEN COMPROMISED."

"S-sorry?"

Behind them a Rikilinni had climbed out of their seat and was pulling blankets out of a hidden compartment in the ceiling. They paused, and out of the corner of his eye Alister saw their raptor-like feet turn toward him. They spoke in a harsh language made up mostly of clicks and a guttural sort of rattle. Alister had no idea what they meant, but he recognized that tone: the creature was frightened. Frightened and *angry*.

"THE TRAIN HAS STOPPED," Dave said—whether in answer to his question or in translation of the Rikilinni Alister wasn't sure.

For a bleary moment Alister wondered why this should be so alarming. A stopped train was no big deal. It just sat on its tracks until whatever was wrong was fixed—worst case scenario people could get out and find other transport.

But they weren't on an ordinary train, he realized with an addled jolt. They were on a train in outer space which had to travel at a set velocity otherwise its tracks didn't line up and . . .

. . . and they happened to be in a part of outer space where other space craft couldn't reach them. Deep in the Denallian Passage, and help coming along the line from Amphitrite wouldn't reach them any time soon.

Alister felt light-headed and cold, and a moment later realized this wasn't his imagination: the temperature *had* dropped, and the gravity had decreased.

The pressure behind his neck vanished—to be replaced with a softer, lighter sensation. Someone had draped a blanket over his shoulder. Or tried to. It was beginning to float away—as indeed was Alister, now he had been unstrapped.

He clutched awkwardly at the blanket and groped for Dave. He felt his ankle grabbed instead, and he relaxed incrementally as his mind slowly came up to full cognizance.

"Where's the Professor?" he asked, his first thought that of escape.

Beside him, Dave made an angry buzzing noise.

"I DO NOT KNOW," the creature replied.

"An' Elo?"

"THE SAME."

Alister let out a long breath.

"So what do we do?"

"GIVE ME TIME," said Dave, and when Alister glanced at him he saw all his lights had dimmed.

Nervous, but confident in Dave's problem-solving abilities, Alister chanced to sit up—the decreased gravity meant his brain was now fully supplied with blood—and looked around at their coach.

The Rikilinni that had spoken earlier was moving down the center aisle, distributing blankets. They had pebbly, gray legs and deep blue feathers that contrasted sharply with their orange-and-gold necklaces. Most of the other passengers were still strapped into their seats and looked even more dazed than Alister felt. He saw a dark-skinned woman with her shiny black hair pulled up in a tight, conical bun, accepting a blanket from the blue Rikilinni, and then falling back against her seat. Her eyes focused on Alister, and he looked away.

The few passengers who hadn't been strapped in when the train stopped were now lying in heaps near the front of the coach, where they floated low to the ground. They were all human, and there was a globby cloud around the whole area. Alister realized with a lurch that it was blood.

He made to stand up—whether to go and see if there was anything he could do or just to see better, he wasn't sure—and nearly sent himself careening up into the ceiling. Only Dave's tentacle-arm, which remained wrapped around his ankle, prevented him from cracking his head open on the bulging lower extremity of the suspension chambers.

These were round, pod-like shapes that lined the ceiling of the coach. Each one had a little window and a digital readout below it, and a light which glowed green, blue, or red. Most of the pods had their lights off—they were empty—a few were blue—their passengers were still in suspension—one had just turned green—its occupant was in the process of waking up—and two were red—something had gone wrong inside.

Alister's eyes had begun to adjust to the harsh red emergency lights. Light from the gold starlike things outside was still pouring in through the windows, and it helped to fill in the black shadows cast by the emergency lamps.

"Let me go," Alister said to Dave, once he'd got a good grip on the handle of his seat. "I want to see if I can help."

"NO," said Dave, and his grip, if anything, got tighter.

"But—" Alister began to protest, and then he stopped and realized Dave was perfectly right.

They were in a much more awkward situation since the Professor and Elo had taken the Oddity's portal off somewhere else, and the least Alister could do was not become separated from Dave. Considering how quickly the situation had deteriorated, the best way to be certain of that was to remain physically connected to him at all times.

And, glancing back, Alister saw that the blue Rikilinni from earlier had worked their way to the front of the coach, where they had been joined by a human in a black jumpsuit. The two barely looked at the motionless figures, but went to the third, who was moaning faintly. There was a conference of clicks and hushed voices, and the injured person said something along the lines of needing to recalibrate.

After a while the human in the jumpsuit stood up and came down the aisle, half walking, half pulling themselves along the backs of the seats. They stopped at each row and asked the passengers something, then moved on. Alister feared that when they reached his row he wouldn't be able to understand them, but the human—who had papery-white skin, flat, straight yellow hair, and appeared perfectly genderless—spoke to him in an accented but understandable form of English.

"Do either of you have first-aid training in bio-synthetics?" they asked, their large, black eyes flicking back and forth between Alister and Dave.

Alister had to shake his head, but Dave let out an uncertain buzz.

The white face turned to him expectantly.

"I HAVE NO OFFICIAL DOCUMENTATION OF EXPERTISE," he said.

The human smiled, thinly. They had a single gem set in the middle of their forehead, which twinkled faintly in the dim red light. Alister couldn't tell if it was a decoration like a nose ring, or a part of their body.

"Neither do we," they said. "But we don't know where to start with cyborns, and fer is badly injured."

For a moment Alister thought that "Fur" was the injured person's name, but then Dave replied, sounding even more annoyed than usual:

"I WILL ATTEMPT TO HELP FIHR," which made the word sound more like "fear." It was only after Dave had made his way to the front of the coach, dragging Alister along by the ankle, and he'd had a chance to listen to the white person talk a little more, that he realized that *fer* and *fihr* were actually second person pronouns, roughly equivalent to *he* and *him* or *she* and *her*—with *fiheren* being equivalent to *his* and *hers*—though Alister found he had trouble recognizing them as such, since the words were completely foreign to him.

He watched, feeling helpless and useless, as Dave went and sat beside the injured person—cyborn, whatever—and began examining them—*fihr*—with his free arms. The other two passengers had been wrapped in extra blankets and put carefully in a corner. He didn't bother asking if they were all right: it was obvious they were already dead.

The survivor was a human-shaped person with metallic, grayish skin, blank, black eyes, a barcode tattooed above their—*fihren*—right ear, and a stripe of pink lights running down the left side of fihren face. These were dim and flickering ominously when Dave and Alister arrived, and when they—*fer*—spoke, it was a croaking sort of rattle, halfway between a human voice and Dave's own, synthesized one.

Alister found himself floating over a conversation he only half understood, ("I AM GOING TO CYCLE YOUR CORE PRO-CESSORS," said Dave. "Advise against that," moaned the cyborn. "I'm on the Red Giant Oh Ess." "YOU REQUIRE A FULL SYS-TEM RESET. DO YOU WANT MY HELP OR NOT?"), but at least he had a better view down the length of the coach.

All down the rows people were active. A few, like the blue Rikilinni and the white-skinned person, were moving among the passengers, distributing blankets or small breathing masks. Everyone had an air of carefully contained panic, and they kept looking at something over the door at the far end of the car-riage. Squinting a little, Alister was able to make out a digital display that showed a series of numbers. These were in two sets: on top was a static 4.500.76, while below was a number that be-gan 0.005.4 and climbed to 0.006.1 in the minute Alister spent watching it.

It was a counter, he realized. Counting up to 4.500.76—whatever that was. His mind helpfully supplied several options, none of them pleasant: it could be the amount of breathable atmosphere they had used; the length of time the heat, light, and gravity could be maintained; or, and this was what Alister rather feared it was, it stood for the amount of time the train could spend still in its tracks before it would miss its connection with the last section of line, and the climbing number was how long they had been stopped.

At 0.007.8 Dave finally managed to convince the cyborn to let him power cycle their—*fihren*—core processors, and after a few moments there was a whir of motors and a small bolt of lightning jumped from Dave's suit to the chest of the cy-born. Their—*fihren*—body convulsed once, and then fer opened fihren eyes and said in a much clearer, almost musical voice: "Wow. It worked."

"CAN YOU RUN DIAGNOSTICS NOW?" Dave asked.

The cyborn took a breath to answer, and the door nearest them—the door that led to the next carriage closer to the engines—burst open, and a large humanoid in a dark, armored suit with a visored helmet strode into the room. Alister saw the gun, saw the burst of white smoke spew from its muzzle, and sucked in a short breath of clear air and held it, before his eyes began to sting as the smoke filled the coach.

Elo came around to the sound of angry beeping drifting down the steps from the Oddity. Her forelegs were twisted up in a cramped position, and there was something that felt like a burn all along her left one. The restraints chafed it painfully, but she bit back the automatic yelp to glare around at her environment in search of her enemy.

She blinked. She was strapped to the main seat in the Master Con, her wrists secured in metal and kevlar manacles, which were in turn linked by way of a thick cord that ran from one to the other and through a supporting strut of the chair on the way.

They were good manacles; strong and tight, and the cord, when she bit it, had the same effect on her mouth as aluminum foil. Not something she wanted to chew through if she could help it. The strut had been well chosen, too; no weakness there she could exploit.

No, she wasn't going anywhere any time soon, unless the person with the key to her manacles came back—which, by the sounds coming from the Oddity, wasn't in the near future either.

All of which would have been disastrous, except that she was *exactly* where she'd been trying to get in the first place. The Master Con and the master controls were, not at her fingertips, but, having the sort of body that bent in half rather easier than a human's, could be reached by her hind paws if she ducked her head just right.

It was slow going, typing on an unfamiliar keyboard when she couldn't see half the screens, with less-than-optimal appendages, but the small beeps and clicks of the train's Master Con were thoroughly drowned out by the noises the Oddity was making—it was sounding truly angry now, and Elo almost pitied the person stuck inside (*almost*)—and no one interrupted her.

There was no way to reverse the emergency brake. They were effectively stopped, and the train required authorization from a ranking officer to get it started again. It was something Elo thought she could have worked around, given full use of her limbs, but as it was she satisfied herself with getting the atmospheric processors working again, cleaning out the nitrous oxide, and as an afterthought cycling all the air in every coach as well. It was energy the train's algorithms didn't want to spend, but after seeing that Coach 20's atmosphere had tripped an alert, she overrode all the warnings (feet jerking roughly), and then lay back against the seat, exhausted.

There was a *ping* from somewhere below her seat—where she could not see—and then, like a muddy fuchsia sun, Professor Odd's wig rose into view. Her face was black with grease and smoke stains and her expression was angrier than Elo had ever seen it.

"*Who did this to you?*" she mouthed.

For answer, Elo jerked her left foot toward the Oddity's door. "Be careful," she hissed. "She's got an arc-taser, and I think she knows who we are."

"Who is *she?*"

Elo snarled, silently. She'd gotten a good whiff of the person, but her scent had been masked by her armor, which smelled mostly of nitrous oxide and hot metal. Still, there were only so many people in the multiverse that she had knowingly pissed off, and she had a hunch as to which group this one belonged to.

"I think," she whispered. "I think she's with that *Canary Company.*"

Professor Odd's face sobered at that, and she looked gravely at the door.

"Right," she said.

Elo thought for a moment that she was going to storm into the Oddity on her own, but instead the Professor went to work untying her. It was even slower going than venting the atmosphere had been, and by the time Elo was free, the noises from the Oddity were horrendous.

"Now what?" asked Elo, wincing as she flexed her forelegs.

Professor Odd turned the broken manacles over in her hands thoughtfully, then put them in the pocket of her coat. "Follow me," she said grimly, heading for the portal at last.

Alister had, when he was fifteen and very bored, timed how long he could hold his breath. He'd lasted almost a minute and a half, but that had been sitting in his room on a rainy Sunday with nothing more exciting than temperamental winds outside.

Clinging to the ceiling of an alien space-train-coach while a large armored person shot at Dave through the stinging white smoke made him need to breathe more, it turned out, and it felt like no time at all before his lungs were burning and his diaphragm was aching. He breathed out as a compromise, trying to at least get rid of some carbon dioxide. That eased the pressure for another couple of seconds, and then Alister's chest wanted to expand. It wanted to expand *now*.

A sharp wind sliced through the coach, blowing him back along the ceiling and taking most of the smoke with it. Alister was so surprised he took a breath before he could see clearly. The dizziness almost overwhelmed him, before cool, clean air flowed into his lungs and the fog lifted from his eyes.

It revealed a scene in disarray. Passengers were cowering behind their seats or clinging to the ceiling, like Alister, and on the ground near the door, Dave was wrestling with the armored person. He had all ten of his arms out and had managed to wrench the gun out of their hands, and was using it to hit them repeatedly in the neck, all the while keeping their other arm and legs from striking his suit. He was also trying to maneuver himself so that his anti-grav plates were pressed up against the person's chest.

Alister watched in dazed amazement as the flash of blue light went off, at the same time Dave let go of the person's arms, and the two bodies went flying apart in opposite directions.

Dave's suit went sailing through the center of the coach, but the armored person slammed backwards into the side of the doorway, where they went limp.

Dave fired his plates again and went coasting forward, spinning slowly, his arms guiding him over the seat backs or moving confused passengers out of the way. He reached the armored person before they fully recovered, and calmly began ripping chunks off their armor. Their helmet came off with a hiss of pressurized air, and Alister found himself gazing down into a grizzled, craggy face locked in an unpleasant expression.

The man—Alister was pretty sure the person was a man—had bright blue eyes that stood out strikingly from his olive complexion and dark hair. His cheeks were lined and his mouth was thin and his teeth, when he snarled at Dave, were yellow and a little crooked.

Dave curled an arm around the man's neck, and said in his loudest and most abrasive tone:

"TELL ME WHO YOU ARE."

There was silence in the coach now, since all the passengers except for Alister had gone to huddle at the far end—including the injured cyborn, who had been helped along by the blue Rikilinni—so when the man answered his voice was audible for all to hear.

"Villafranka," he said, gone a little red but still sneering at Dave. "Comma, Tony," he went on. "Operative number eight-four-eight, two-zero-six," and his mouth shut with a snap.

"Ask him who he works for," Alister called down from the ceiling, when it became clear that Villafranka wasn't going to say any more.

Dave didn't speak, but spared a couple arms to yank fiercely at the man's chest plate. It came away with an ugly snapping sound and the man winced but still didn't say anything.

Under the armor he was wearing a dark gray jumpsuit made of tough, canvas-like material, and across the chest had been printed a logo: two upper case C's facing away from each other, and under them a three-headed yellow dog, with wings.

"Sorry, didn't I say?" said the man, Villafranka, with an unpleasant grin. "*Canary Company* Operative, and you're not getting away from us this time, M-eighty-seven."

*   *   *

The buzzing was beginning to get to Agent Parthenon. It had started the moment she'd entered 1016's lair, low and insistent in the back of her head. She'd looked around for an insect or perhaps a motor to explain the noise, but eventually she realized that it was coming from the huge banks of screens and colored buttons that took up the near end of the ship. So she'd sat down in one of the jump seats and tried to switch the thing off, but she had been stumped by the controls.

This annoyed her. Agent Parthenon had been trained to quickly pick up many languages and control types, but those of the specimen's lair flummoxed her. They equally flummoxed her multiversal translator, which overheated and shorted out seconds after she'd jacked it into what she thought of as the mainframe. She'd been reduced to looking for the big, obvious lever or red button that would power the thing down. The problem was there were several levers, and many of the buttons were shades of red. Most of them did nothing, though one lever made the buzzing rise to an ear-splitting shriek. She put it back the way it had been at once, and thankfully the noise receded.

It was about that time she noticed that the buttons she had thought were red were now green, blue, or orange. She stared at them in consternation, and as she stared the colors shifted before her eyes.

Color was clearly not how you told the buttons apart. She scrutinized them for any other sign—something carved in their surface, perhaps? She switched her visor to display UV radiation, then infrared, but still saw nothing to indicate a difference in the buttons.

So she left the controls and went over to the huge table, which was laden with artifacts from at least a dozen different universes that she could recognize—and several more that she couldn't. It was stunning. Specimen 1016 looked to be a multiversal pack rat. There was even . . .

Agent Parthenon's gaze lurched to a halt at the sight of Specimen 004, laid casually over a solar-powered orrery from Alt 16. The temporal manipulator that had gone missing at the same time as 1016's inexplicable escape. With trembling hands Agent Parthenon reached out to take it.

Her hands were trembling because the buzzing was giving her a headache. She clenched her teeth, trying to keep her head clear, and that was when everything got knocked sideways.

That was to say, *she* got knocked sideways. Something hit her very hard in the side of the head, and she flew sideways, slamming into a chair and bouncing off the wall. Only her encounter suit saved her from a nasty concussion, and as it was the buzzing intensified to the point where she could barely see straight.

She could see well enough, however, to recognize the golden, furry face snarling down at her.

"I don't think that was *entirely* necessary," said a light, husky voice, and Agent Parthenon wincingly turned her head to see Specimen 1016, wearing a dirty pink wig, standing in the doorway with her hands on her hips.

"She tased me so hard it *burned*," snapped the canine, viciously knocking Parthenon's head back. She tried to get her hands up to defend herself, only to find them caught and bound in her own cuffs. Then the strange paw-hands were at her throat, and she felt the hiss of seals breaking as her helmet came free, jerking roughly over her head.

The buzzing stopped almost immediately, and Agent Parthenon blinked, breathing fiercely through her nose, and was surprised to discover that the interior of the lair smelled like her grandmother's kitchen—wool carpet and clean linen with an undertone of nutmeg. The clash of senses rendered her temporarily speechless, until she heard Specimen 1016 speak again.

" . . . yes but how are we going to get her to be reasonable *now?*"

When your opponent has the physical advantage, better to play your intellectual strengths. Which Parthenon had plenty of.

"I can be reasonable," she said at once, trying to keep her words clear, even though her head was still spinning.

"*Sure* you can," said the canine, sounding unconvinced.

"Can you tell us what you've done with the alpha crew?" asked Specimen 1016, coming over to the table and picking up

Specimen 004. She fiddled with it, and the machine made a plaintive hum. Disabled, Parthenon noted with interest.

"Stassed them," she answered, truthfully enough. "Beta crew easier to manage."

"Yes," said Specimen 1016, her eyes glittering uncannily. "*Why* do you want to manage them? *What* are you doing here?"

Agent Parthenon shrugged as much as she dared. "Collecting samples," she said. Which was true, but she decided not to let Specimen 1016 know that "samples" meant the entire train, or that passengers were expendable.

"Of what?" asked 1016, her tone bright and brittle and hard as steel.

Now some prevarication was in order.

"Fuel and raw materials," said Agent Parthenon. "Can I sit up, please?"

Reluctantly the canine drew back, and Parthenon eased herself into a defensive crouch. Her hands were still securely shackled, but she had full use of her feet, and with a little work she could tease the laser torch out of its hidden compartment at her wrist.

"What for?" asked 1016.

"Clean energy, of course," said Parthenon, and it wasn't even a lie that time. The Company *was* extremely interested in clean, sustainable energy, and the technology behind the engines had looked promising from initial observations. Hence Parthenon and her team being dispatched to collect a sample in the form of the train itself.

The tip of the laser torch was poking into the bottom of her palm. She almost had it.

"How many are on your team?" asked the canine.

Agent Parthenon smiled. She could tell the truth here and they'd never believe her, so she did.

"Two operatives plus myself," she said, as blandly as she could manage. The torch was in her hand, just pointed the wrong way. Parthenon adjusted her feet, to draw attention away from her hands.

The canine scoffed incredulously.

"No," said Specimen 1016 thoughtfully. "She was telling the truth there. That's bad. Elite team. Not concerned with native casualties. *Tsk, tsk, tsk.* And I suppose you saw us on the passenger manifest and thought we'd make a nice addition to your haul. *Really* your company is so . . . "

Agent Parthenon decided she didn't want to wait and hear what Specimen 1016 thought of the Company. Torch in hand she sprang forward, knocking over the canine—who predictably latched onto her leg. She swiped at the grasping paws with the torch, and the canine let go with a yelp. She turned on Specimen 1016, who stepped sideways, leaving the corridor to the stairs and the door into the train open.

"Hold onto something, Elo," she said, and tapped a nearby button, while bracing herself against a monitor.

It was like stepping into a wind tunnel. Agent Parthenon was knocked off her feet and tumbled toward the stairs. She thrust out a hand to stop herself, and found it knocked aside by 1016's foot. When she put out her own foot to steady herself, it slipped down the first stair, and suddenly the gravity seemed to increase. Combined with the wind this was enough to send her stumbling down the stairs and into the Master Con, where the wind stopped abruptly, and gravity returned to the gentle suggestion that it had been on the train.

Because she was *back* on the train, Agent Parthenon realized, and made to fling herself back into 1016's lair—only to find the doorway now led to the access corridor, and Operative Caruthers was standing in it, his shoulders tense.

"*There* you are," he said, the relief evident in his voice. "Villafranka has made contact with Incongruity M87 and Specimen 1017, but they've been giving him some trouble."

Agent Parthenon pursed her lips and pushed her laser torch back into its holster. She'd lost her helmet, but she had a backup respirator in their ship. She could manage.

"Then let's go give *them* some trouble," she said with a bitter snarl.

"WHAT IS YOUR MISSION?" Dave was asking for what felt like the tenth time, and Villafranka was starting to answer, as he always did, "Villafranka comma Tony, Operative number eight-four-eight, one-zero-six . . . " when the whole coach shuddered.

The dim red light blacked out entirely and ablative shields went down over the windows, sending the coach into complete darkness.

Alister gripped the latch of the nearest suspension pod, pressing himself back against the ceiling, as the coach erupted with shouts and, a little while later, screams. Dave was blaring, and in the blaring Alister heard words:

"EVACUATE. EVACUATE. *EVACUATE!*"

In the dark, Alister became aware of a dim orange glow pricking out on the wall, forming the shape of a rough circle, with brighter points of light at intervals all around it.

Something hard and round slammed into him.

"EVACUATE!" Dave blared in his ear, and Alister found himself propelled backward toward the far end of the coach. Judging by the softer things that thumped into his back, they were hitting some of the other passengers.

"What's going *on?*" he managed to ask, before the breath was knocked out of him.

"THEY ARE INCISING THE COACH," Dave answered, and behind him Alister glimpsed the ring of orange light, which had intensified and spilled out, like melting metal. Which it was, he realized with a jolt; someone was cutting into the side of the carriage.

Which, considering there was only the inhospitable environment of the Denallian Passage outside, would prove disastrous for anyone remaining in the carriage.

Cool, gray light from the air lock between the coaches flooded inside as someone got the far door open. It was quickly choked by dark bodies, packing in one on top of the other. But even with the gravity virtually nonexistent, Alister realized they could not evacuate all the passengers from their carriage into the following one. Sure enough, the doors closed—on screams of horror—long before Dave and Alister reached them.

Someone—probably the blue Rikilinni, Alister guessed—knew how to manage the air locks, however, and it was hardly four minutes before the door opened again, and another group of passengers crowded out.

Alister and Dave were the last—having been the farthest forward when the evacuation started—and just as Alister extended an arm in relief to pull himself into the air lock, he felt something thin and sharp and hard hit him in the center of his back.

It was so surprising, and so sudden, that he barely managed an inarticulate gasp, and then cold fingers dug into his sides, and he was yanked violently backward. He made a blind grab for one of Dave's arms—felt one brush his fingertips—then he was whizzing through the air until he slammed into a warm, hard body. An armored hand clapped over his mouth, and he heard Villafranka's rough voice whisper in his ear:

"Not again, ten-seventeen. *Not again!*"

"RELEASE HIM!" Dave blared, and Alister peeked over the hand to see the creature's panvironment suit, its lights ablaze, rushing at them down the carriage. Behind it, the air lock had closed for a second time.

There was a thundering *bang* as the piece of wall within the orange circle exploded into the coach, the force of it knocking Dave into the far wall.

Alister struggled, but Villafranka's grip on him was like iron, and he felt himself pulled toward the ragged circle of bright light beyond the newly created aperture. He heard his captor growl, "Give me atmo, Parthenon! I've got ten-seventeen!" And then something was snapped over his head. Surprised, Alister took a breath, felt dizzy, and then the world slid sideways around him, bleaching white as he was dragged through the hole.

The tiny ship attached to the side of Coach 20 remained long enough for the stranded operative to scramble inside, dragging his catch with him. The ship's air lock slammed closed just as the twining arms of Incongruity M87 reached it, and with a sharp blast it took off, leaving a ragged, gaping hole in the side of the carriage. The Incongruity had to change tactics and grip the sides of the hole to prevent itself being sucked out along with the atmosphere, and the ship powered away from the stricken train, through the boundary of the Passage and into the unstable medium of the Denallian Belt itself.

Behind it, still on the train, Incongruity M87 pulled itself back inside, spewing a collection of jarring noises that formed no words in any language in any universe, but which nonetheless managed to communicate frustration, disappointment, and fury.

Getting the beta crew out of the suspension quarters, where the Canary Company agent had locked them, was fairly easy. Getting them to get the train going again, wasn't.

"Why don't you calm down and explain to me, in detail, exactly who you are and why you think you should be giving the orders?" said their captain when Professor Odd suggested it would be a good idea to start the train. Soon.

"I'm not giving you any orders," Professor Odd said, with what Elo thought was admirable patience.

The beta captain was a pink, blond-haired man with watery blue eyes and a comfortable belly, which he was currently thrusting in the Professor's direction as if it were a third arm.

"I'm only *suggesting*," Professor Odd went on, "that you get this train started and perform the necessary repairs *en route*. By my calculations you can still make the Typhon line without overcranking the engines."

"Right," said the beta captain, stroking his shiny, pink chin. "And what makes you such an expert on Heliotrans Run 4413? Fancy yourself an exopilot, do you?"

Professor Odd turned away from the man in exasperation. "How are you doing defrosting the alpha crew?" she asked Elo.

"Coming along," Elo said from her perch in the Master Con. "That agent set all sorts of funny booby traps for whoever tried to wake 'em up. I think I just about got them all—"

A faint vibration went through the floor, spreading to the walls, the ceiling, and settling into a low background hum.

Professor Odd flew to the nearest con center and brought up all the exterior displays she could muster. The tower was yet unmanned, but from the Master Con she could control most of the cameras remotely. The screens showed images of the train, its coaches, and a view from the roof of the caboose.

"That feels like we're *moving*," Elo said.

"We aren't moving," said the beta captain smugly. "Engine's powered down, remember?"

"We're *definitely* moving," said Professor Odd, a thrill in her voice. "Oh, oh *Elo,* we need to fetch Alister and Dave—they'd *love* to see this!"

Elo pushed herself away from the controls and crawled over to peer at the screen. "See what . . . ?" she began, and trailed off into amazed silence.

Behind the last carriage, lying along the pearly, glinting line, was something that, to Elo, looked like a giant, semi-transparent kite. A hard, rocky head sat on top of nebulous, triangular wings that stretched out to either side, while sharp spikes, beaded with blue light, ran in a ridge down the middle, disappearing behind the swell of wings only to appear again as a forked tail that faded into the hazy, magenta distance.

"What is *that?*" she whispered.

Professor Odd turned to her, her jaguar eyes shining.

"I *don't know,*" she said, sounding absolutely delighted.

"Oh bugger all," said the beta captain, who'd been watching as well. "Not another bloody *manaflot!*"

"I rather think you should be thanking them," said Professor Odd primly. "It'll be easier for your to start the engines while the train is in motion—" she broke off suddenly, her good humor evaporating.

Elo didn't have to ask; she had seen exactly what the Professor had. Near the front of the train a coach was belching steam from a ragged hole in its side, and in the center of that hole, spread wide like a starfish, was the tiny form of Dave's panvironment suit.

"I think we've done all we can here," said Professor Odd, pushing herself away from the monitors while Elo was already scrambling for the Oddity. "Good luck, captain, and if you get a chance, thank that manaflot for me." She kicked her way past the bewildered man, nearly colliding with Elo as they reached the portal to the Oddity at the same time.

"If Alister was in that coach—" Elo began.

"Dave wouldn't let that happen," Professor Odd said, sharply, pushing buttons and pulling levers. The Oddity *bonged* plaintively, but the portal obediently shifted, leaving the Master Con behind, and opened abruptly onto the damaged coach—via the same aperture that the Canary Company's ship had created.

There was a rush of wind as the atmosphere of the Oddity flowed in to fill the vacated coach, nearly blowing Dave off his perch. Once it abated, Elo barely had time to unbuckle herself and begin saying "Are you all right?" before Dave was threading his arms into the Oddity and pulling himself inside. His suit fell sideways with a *clang* as soon as he made it through the portal, and to Elo's alarm it began venting steam. He was blaring a single, angry note through his translator, one that Elo couldn't be sure was his equivalent of a scream or simply a malfunction.

"DO NOT ASSIST ME. I AM FUNCTIONAL," he said when she went to tip him upright. Peering beyond him into their old coach, she saw that the place looked thoroughly destroyed. From what she could see of it, all the windows had shuttered, and the only light trickled in from the Oddity. It smelled of burnt metal and alien blood and was, as far as she could tell, deserted.

Then Dave was rolling sideways up the stairs on his tractor treads, helping himself along with his arms. There were scorch marks all over his suit, along with some gashes and dents, and one of his anti-grav plates had got a crack in it. He came to a halt with a whine beside Professor Odd, who was flipping through views of the other coaches on the Oddity's screens.

"THEY TOOK—" Dave began, at the same time Odd said, "Where is—" before they finished together:

"Alister?"

"ALISTER."

Elo felt like her stomach had dropped out of her abdomen. Her hackles went up, and she began to growl instinctively. She didn't have to ask who. She knew, beyond a shadow of a doubt, what Dave was talking about. Something had ripped a hole clean through the coach's wall, and the Canary Company agents had to have come from *somewhere*. *Something* had got them through the natural portals in the Denallian Belt and over to the train.

A small ship, probably. Just big enough for the push there and back again. Hadn't that one agent said something about taking the train for study? She pinned her ears back and strapped herself in again.

"Then let's go *get* him," she snarled. "Can you find their ship?"

"Already done," said Professor Odd, who had disconnected from the train. Now the Oddity was floating freely between universes, its door a blank black slab. That would give them the maximum amount of local time to reopen a portal into the Canary Company ship and grab Alister, which they would need to do before it reached its *own* portal. Elo had never seen the Oddity's portals dragged through another portal, but from what Professor Odd had said, it was apparently a very bad thing.

"THEY ARE MOVING EXCEPTIONALLY FAST," Dave remarked, pulling himself upright to get a better look at the screens.

Elo could see what he was talking about now: there was the little ship—hardly more than a pod with some rockets attached—and they were firing on all thrusters toward a ragged, black hole through which the crescent face of a familiar blue-and-white planet could be seen. Pulling back the view Elo quickly saw why:

Another manaflot was chasing them, and from this angle Elo could better see how its rocky, solid-looking head was really more of a skull. Or perhaps a helmet. It sat on top of the transparent, ghost-like body, glowing from within, its huge jaw gaping wide. At least, she thought that was its jaw. Though the creature was symmetrical, and she wasn't certain whether the apertures in the skull/helmet were eyes or mouths or something else entirely.

It was undulating through the medium of the Belt, the blue lights flashing along its spine, leaving a trail of fire in its wake, and no matter how alien it was, Elo could recognize that behavior.

"I think I know what the manaflot are," she said, hollowly. "They're the . . . they're the real natives of Aquaria."

"MUCH ASSISTANCE THEY ARE BEING NOW," Dave said.

"Actually—" Elo began, meaning to tell him about the manaflot that was currently pushing the exotrain out of its dead stop, but then Professor Odd began hissing like an angry pot.

"A block! An *effective* block!" she practically shrieked. She tore at her hair, which promptly came off and flew across the room to land on the table. Beneath it, her tentacle was coiled tightly, the pale tip writhing around itself in agitation.

"You can't get into their ship?" Elo barked. "Let me try . . . "

She tried, but to no avail. The little ship was battened down tighter than a diving bell. There wasn't even a square inch they could use to anchor the Oddity's portal.

"We could try it unanchored—" Elo began, but Professor Odd had pushed back from the controls, folded her arms, and was staring grimly at the screens.

"No," she said, after a long moment. "I know where they are going. We'll meet them on the *other* side."

Alister slammed into consciousness at about the same time the ship carrying him slammed into something solid. At least, it *felt* solid to Alister, but he seemed to be feeling everything in extremes at the moment. His clothes were too coarse and itchy; the air on his face was stingingly cold and dry, and whatever drug he'd inhaled was making his head pound like the pistons of a steam locomotive.

"You're coming in too steep!" a man's voice shouted. It sounded crackly, as though it were coming through a radio.

"No choice!" shouted a woman, much nearer to him and in person. Her voice cut through the fog in Alister's head like a knife, disrupting the piston engines, and he winced. "Have the retrieval team waiting at these coordinates—Parthenon out!"

After that the world went shaky and sickly yellow around the edges. Alister felt bile rise in his throat, but either he had already vomited or his stomach was otherwise empty, because nothing more came up. He didn't exactly pass out, but he lost time in clumps.

He was in a small space with his hands twisted behind his back and straps holding him to a stiff board. He was sideways, or upside-down, or standing on his toes. There were lights flashing everywhere, the shadows of three hunched bodies nearby.

There was fire all around them outside. It felt like his insides were floating upward into his chest. He was weightless again.

Then there was darkness, and the gravity was crushing. Something bubbled up in his agonized mind and came out as a sort of groan.

There was a *phuzzzzzzzt* of radio static, and then the woman from before said: "This is Agent Parthenon, the duck is in the water and we're all alive. Negative on the exotrain, but we recovered a specimen. No, you don't have clearance for that. Get the retrieval team here, now."

The roof came off the little black world Alister and his captors had been stuck in, and people in masked hazmat suits crowded around the rim. Black-gloved hands unfastened (but did not untie) him, and he was lifted clear of a tiny spaceship, its ablation plate burned away to almost nothing, while around him bobbed the bloated gray forms of life rafts. Beyond that was blue. A dark blue ocean and a pale blue sky, and in his nostrils the smell of salt and burned metal.

"Prep him for transport," the woman was saying. She had bronzy skin and thick black hair pulled back into a tight bun, and she was wearing a suit of close-fitting armor. She also had a headset microphone and a collar with the double C's and three-headed, winged dog of the Canary Company. "He's had recent contact with Incongruity M87. He needs to be quarantined at HQ."

The open air of the ocean was rushing into him, lifting away the last traces of the drug. The gentle rocking of the waves was soothing after that hellish ride, and Alister found his mind was clearing rapidly. With the lifting of his mental fog, there was no panic beneath. Instead, Alister found only a dull resignation.

They had got him. After countless worlds and who knew how many years, he was right back where he'd started with Professor Odd—in the hands of the Canary Company. It seemed, now he thought about it, an inevitability. It was something he'd spent so long worrying about happening that, now it was actually happening, it was almost a relief: the waiting, at least, was over.

Now on to the next bit.

As he was lifted into a hammock to be pulled up to a waiting helicopter, he found himself briefly at eye level with the black-haired woman.

"You won't keep me, you know," he said, his voice almost lost in the chop of the helicopter. "She'll come. She might already be here."

The woman met his gaze, and Alister was astonished to see outright hatred in her face. Then she smiled. It was a small, satisfied smile, and it frightened Alister more than anything he'd seen that day.

They pulled him up into the helicopter. There was another hellish ride, and then someone put a black bag over his head and he lost track of space.

The helicopter landed. He was pulled out, put on what felt like a gurney, and wheeled to another vehicle. Probably a van, just like last time. They drove him for a while, and eventually he was unloaded into a place that smelled of antiseptic. He was put in a small cell with a thin blanket and a hard pillow, and finally given use of his hands. When he pulled the hood off and looked around he found it was dark—the only aperture being a barred window with a metal grate behind it, shut fast.

Alister leaned back against the wall and waited. Professor Odd had come for him in far, far worse places. It was only a matter of time.

Alister waited there, in the dark, listening to nothing but the ringing of his own ears, for a very, very long time.

No one came.

Professor Odd had found the universe in a matter of seconds. Had found the entry point of the Canary Company ship in just a few more. She'd located the door nearest to the cell where they'd taken Alister, and was just about to drop the portal when Elo let out an inarticulate bark, leapt across the aisle, and yanked the Professor's hands off the keyboard.

"*Stop,*" she managed to gasp, in English, at last. Her paws were shaking.

"Elo? Elo, what is it?" Professor Odd's body was a rigid frame, her hands frozen with her fingers splayed over the keys.

"*Look,*" wheezed Elo. "*Look* at the temporal lock!"

Professor Odd looked—the time at which they would enter the universe was displayed in a series of blinking lights near one of the lower screens, at first glance no different from all the other blinking lights—"But I set it to . . . " she stopped. She looked again. Her eyes bulged.

With a few taps at the rack of buttons she released the universe and tried again. She set the temporal lock, with the utmost care, at the exact same moment as Alister's entry point. But when the Oddity tried to connect with the universe, the lock broke and the time of entry slid forward. A *lot* forward. Had she opened the portal, they would have come through almost a *year after* Alister arrived.

"No," whispered the Professor, and tried again—this time pushing the Oddity's portal even further back; three hours before Alister's arrival, which was as far as it would go.

The same thing happened. It jumped to a day in June, ten months after the pod from the Canary Company went through.

Elo was growling, deep in her throat, without realizing it.

"That agent," she said through the snarls. "She *did* something when she was in here!"

"It could be a natural temporal incongruity," Professor Odd said, but she did not seem convinced. "Or, they could be doing something from their end." She stroked a tube of light that ran up from the floor nearby. "The Oddity was blocking that agent. She couldn't have known what she was doing." She let her hand fall, her shoulders slumping with it. "I don't know *what* they know. They've had access to multiple universes, and there *are* things that can mess with the Oddity's doors. If they got hold of a portal destabilizer that might do the trick . . . " she trailed off.

Elo felt ready to crawl out of her skin. Her forearm was still hurting, she was beginning to feel sick with worry about Alister, and the Professor was just *sitting* there. She wanted to bite something, but instead she went back over to her own seat and tried to get a peek at what was happening to Alister. But though the monitors could track his progress through the universe's spacetime continuum, the information was of only the vaguest and most rudimentary kind.

There was a sloshing sound from the kitchen alcove. Dave, who'd parked his panvironment suit there and fairly writhed into the sink once he'd got the water going, blinked at them over the porcelain lip, his eye rising like a pinwheel orange-and-yellow sun. Then, slowly and deliberately, he crawled out of the sink and over the carpeted floor toward the Professor. He left a trail of water and slime in his wake, but Elo hadn't the heart to complain about it.

Dave reached the Professor and plucked at her coattails. The woman broke off frowning at the Oddity's controls and obligingly leaned over so Dave could crawl up onto her bare head, his green, octopus-like arms draping gently over her shoulders. One of them, trailing down her back, found her own tentacle, wound tightly at the base of her skull, and gently pried it open. In response, the Professor's tentacle wrapped around the arm like a creeping vine finding a hold on a tree branch.

Despite the invertebrate nature of the appendages, Elo recognized the gesture as a comforting one, and not for the first time she wondered how much of Dave's personality was lost in his monotone translator.

They stayed that way for some time; Professor Odd hunched over the controls with Dave wrapped around her head, speaking in a language that could not be heard save via the transmission of his psychoactive slime. They didn't communicate this way very often, because of the mess, and Dave never tried it with Elo or Alister. They had both heard his true voice, however, on the one occasion when he had to extricate their minds from a simulated reality. The memory of it brought a shiver down Elo's spine, and though she was dying to know what was being said, it was not enough to make her go over and stick her head under Dave's mantle.

Eventually the Professor's shoulders gave a little shake, and she sat up straight. One of Dave's arms had slipped, so it covered half her face, but her visible eye found Elo, and its gaze was steady and direct.

"Leave off that universe," Professor Odd said. She paused, spat out some slime, and went on. "We're not getting in *that* way."

"There is *another* way?" Elo asked incredulously. She had entertained the possibility of visiting some other universes first, to see if that jogged the temporal slip, but that was as likely to make it slip the *wrong* way as anything else.

Professor Odd blinked her single, visible eye, and a drop of greenish slime ran down the side of her nose. "There are lots of different ways," she said. "I just can't access them."

"So what good does that—" Elo began, but the Professor had held up a finger for silence, and she snapped her mouth shut.

"*I* can't access them," she repeated. "Well, I mean, *some* of them yes, but what would be the point? I stay with the Oddity; it's as simple as that. But there *are* other ways of getting between universes—as the system of Aquaria and our friends at the Canary Company have shown—and more importantly there are *other* people who can go places *I* can't. Namely," she rolled her eye upwards.

"Dave?" asked Elo, hardly daring to believe.

"How do you think he got into Alister's world in the first place? Walking? No, Dave here can jump worlds, given the right circumstances. He just can't take his panvironment suit with him. So, he'll go on ahead and we'll meet him there. And in the *meantime*," she went on, before Elo could point out the riskiness of such a plan. "In the meantime, we're going to find him some *backup*."

The right circumstances for Dave to get into Alister's home universe turned out to be a lake under a stormy sky on a planet whose atmosphere even Professor Odd couldn't breathe. They opened the portal just long enough for Dave to writhe out through a natural gateway formed by a jumble of rocks, over the wet beach, and to watch him disappear beneath the surface of the blackish water. Then the Professor switched the portal off and spent a long time staring at the glowing, colorful buttons of the Oddity's control panel.

Elo came over and stood at her shoulder, internally quivering with nerves while trying outwardly to remain stoic and calm.

"The rats will understand," Professor Odd said, after what felt like an eternity. "They will help. And the dogs—yes, the *dogs*—they might be willing. And of course . . . there is always *him*."

"Rats?" said Elo. "Dogs? Who's *him*?"

Professor Odd looked up, as if only just now realizing she was not alone.

"Elo," she said, her eyes very earnest and clear. "Apart from me and Dave, you know more about interdimensional travel than anyone I've ever met."

Elo sniffed. "Because I learned from *you,*" she said.

Professor Odd shrugged off the implied compliment. "Point is, getting between universes without the Oddity can be a little tricky. Even if your world has the way, doesn't necessarily mean travel is feasible. Would you be able to—I mean, if you had a willing team—do you think you could . . . "

"Give the natives a helping paw?" Elo finished, feeling her panic and frustration condensing, solidifying into a hard ball of grim determination, high in her chest. A solo mission, effectively, away from the relative safety of the Professor and the Oddity. But for the Professor—for *Alister*—she would do it. She didn't bother being surprised at the intensity of the feelings of protectiveness and responsibility that rose up in her when she thought of him. Alister had entered her territory like an abandoned puppy, and since then had become an important member of her pack. It was a small, unconventional pack, but Elo protected its members with a tenacity that would have done justice to her feral ancestors. She found herself grinning in the human manner, which she knew most people found unsettling, but then, this was hardly something to smile about.

"Tell me what you need me to do," she said.

Professor Odd beamed at her, briefly, like a flash of sun glancing off a mirror. "In just a moment. We should get the rats on it first, since they're closest."

Elo frowned. "What *rats?*"

Professor Odd smiled, tightly, and began recalibrating the portal. To Elo's surprise, she saw they were going back to the same universe with the exotrain and the Denallian Belt. Same solar system, too, but instead of latching onto the train, Professor Odd had the portal open into a space station orbiting a bright blue gas giant. Elo caught a glimpse of it out of a huge observation window that filled one side of the promenade of gracefully curving arches of silver steel, with little pearly lights strung along their length. Small, bright ships moved between them, and beyond the blue swell of the planet she could just make out other space stations, falling in orbit with them.

"Is that . . . isn't that *Amphitrite?*" she asked, following the Professor out onto the promenade—which had a floor of polished black stone and a number of people—human and Rikilinni—in the distance. Which distance was disappearing rapidly as they spotted Elo and Professor Odd, and began rushing in their direction.

"The very same," said Professor Odd, turning and striding toward the approaching group with fearless confidence. "I told you the Premier owed me a favor. Well, several favors. A perpetual favor, you could say. Did I ever tell you *why?*"

"Not that I recall," Elo said, dryly.

"I really should," said the Professor. "After this is over. Marvelous story, really. Good dinner conversation. But the short version is this: I saved her life. Her life, and the lives of some other, *extraordinary* people. Ah, hello my distinguished individuals!"

This to the group of people who had at last come within hailing distance. They were a motley bunch: a human man, two Rikilinni and a white-skinned cyborn of indeterminate gender. They were all wearing what was recognizably a uniform: blue tops with high, stiff collars, and an emblem embroidered on the sleeve. The humanoids carried low-profile pistols, while the Rikilinni had mean little batons under their stubby arms, but the weapons remained in their respective holsters as they came to a disorganized halt at the Professor's words.

"I'm glad to see you still recognize me," Professor Odd said—and without her dark glasses and wig, it would have been hard not to, Elo thought. "Not to sound cliché, but I do mean this literally: *Take me to your leader.*"

This was done, amazingly, with no protest whatsoever—though Elo caught the cyborn giving Professor Odd astonished looks, and whispering to the human in words they thought were inaudible, but which Elo's keen ears picked out easily:

"That's the—I mean, that's *the*—"

"Yes," said the man through gritted teeth.

"She actually *exists!*"

"Of course she does, now *shut up,* the wolf can hear you."

Both of them glanced at Elo at that, who, despite their desperate circumstances, couldn't help giving them a toothy grin.

They were led out of the promenade and into a roomy elevator which carried them deeper into the space station, through several thick doors that opened with hisses of pressurized air, and finally into a circular room richly furnished with wooden chairs and tables, which were in turn covered by embroidered cloths or thick, woven rugs. The place smelled of wool and wood polish, and reminded Elo of the contents of a Victorian sitting room from Earth transferred to an advanced space ship.

Which might very well have been exactly what it was.

At the center of the room was a huge wooden desk, covered with little stands holding transparent tablets aglow with words and figures. Behind the desk sat a hooded figure, their back to them, looking up at a wall full of monitors. These displayed a block of code that even Elo couldn't read, but whatever it was must have been important, for the figure didn't turn around until after the big, reddish Rikilinni—who seemed to be the one in charge—had coughed twice and said something in their clicking language.

Elo caught a whiff of something both alien and familiar and definitely *not* human, and that was all the warning she had before the figure turned around, and she found herself looking up into the long, pointed, pink-nosed, black-eyed face of a giant anthropomorphic rat.

Her fur was a rich, honeyed brown, and there was a subtle twist to her mouth and around her eyes that suggested a human spectrum of emotions and thoughts lay behind the murine façade. She looked at Professor Odd, twitched her nose, and with a motion of one pink, and undeniably *human* hand, sent their escort hurrying from the room.

"What's gone wrong *now?*" asked the rat-person. She had a raspy, gruff voice. Elo thought she detected an Anthropocene Earth Spanish accent, but it might have been something else. "You only ever visit when something's gone *wrong.*"

"Not true!" said Professor Odd. "I came here for dinner, once. Just for fun. Ask Kaklee."

"I *know*," said the rat-person, who Elo assumed was the Premier of Amphitrite. "And you didn't even stop to say *hello*—"

"There were *children* involved!" Professor Odd protested.

Elo coughed, causing the Premier to glare at her. It sobered the Professor, however, who clasped her hands behind her back, and went on, almost contritely.

"The fact is," she said. "And I *am* sorry about it. But the fact is, there is trouble. A lot of it. You'll want to get a message to the Premier of Typhon as soon as you can—the Cerberus Express encountered some problems in the Denallian Belt, and the beta crew was in charge when I left."

"The *beta* crew—" the Premier began, pulling down her hood so she could train both her round ears at the Professor. "Why did you *leave?*"

"*Because,*" said the Professor, and took a deep breath. "A friend of mine was kidnapped, and he's in even more danger than the exotrain. The people who took him are the bad sort of scientists, more interested in invading other universes and stealing their technology—and inhabitants—than in actually *learning* how the multiverse works. I'm going to rescue him, but I need help. I need the Rats of Alnitak."

The Premier's whiskers twitched, and she seemed to expand a little. "Give me the coordinates—for your friend *and* the exotrain," she said briskly. "Come back in a week to debrief the kids."

"You can count on it," said Professor Odd, and leaned over the desk to embrace the rat-person.

"A *week?*" asked Elo, while they were being led back to the promenade.

"We have time," said Professor Odd. "As long as I don't try to enter Alister's world, it doesn't much matter what I do beforehand. Now it's time to find *you* a team, I think."

"I think," said Elo, who'd been doing some considering in the Premier's office. "I think I know exactly where we should go next."

The huge power poles marched away across the windswept, gray-green plain. Drooping from their arms in graceful arcs were strands of thin cables, hardly visible in places against the bright sky packed with white clouds. They ended in a city of towers and metal boxes, built on a concrete platform which also supported domes of shiny, blue-black stone. A big black sign with white pictograms warned all approaching that dogs would be struck by lightning if they did not wear proper protective gear.

The tall, silver-and-cream dog with a face like a knife looked over at the conversion plant from where she sat in the little garden outside the bunker, sipping her afternoon broth. It wasn't that she *liked* looking at the conversion plant, it was just that it was the only thing *to* look at when you worked at NeoCanii Base North. Well, if you didn't want to bust your eyes watching computer screens all day.

And then, very suddenly, there *was* something else to look at. Someone had come out of one of the access doors on the side of the largest conversion box—a door which the dog knew led to a solid bank of wires and circuits—and they were assuredly *not* wearing proper protective gear: they were covered from ears to tail in a bulky suit laid heavy with bags and packs and the sharp, angular shapes of weapons.

The dog straightened up and watched in amazement as the person then *dropped to all fours* and loped through the conversion plant, scaled the chain-link fence surrounding it, dropped to the ground on the other side, and then continued loping straight for the base.

The dog's broth had gone cold in her paws. She stood and stared as the figure, having spotted her, altered course and made for the little back garden outside the bunker. When it reached the low stone wall that separated the carefully tended plants from the rough grass outside, the figure stood up, and the dog was astonished to see an intelligent yet *feral* face staring at her from amidst a swirl of rich, golden fur.

Memories of half-believed stories and unbelievable mission reports swelled up inside the dog's head, and she fumbled in her coat for her regulation comsys. She hardly needed it nowadays, but she couldn't know that this dog—wolf—*canine*—spoke their language.

Then the person spoke, both in audible Standard and in a form of *canilingua* that the dog could just about understand. They said:

"Is that you, Ksanos?"

The dog flicked both ears backward, then forward. *No.* Then she got her comsys turned on—its damn batteries were low again—and speaking as carefully as she could in both languages, answered:

"I am Natalyas, her daughter. Are you . . . are you the *golden wolf?*"

The stranger's face made an expression of mixed amusement and disgust. "I am no wolf," she said. "I am Marhütz Elo of the Black Thirteen Auxiliary, a *vroknaär* of Aratowan, and I have a mission for you."

And now, a conversation that may or may not have been recorded. Due to the specific circumstances surrounding it, aside from the two participants, no one else would have been able to hear it, taking place as it did across the void between universes, packaged in time and light and the motions of atoms.

But if someone had the power to unravel the code and sort the messages into the correct order, it would have sounded like this:

"Hallo?

"I know you're out there.

"I know you're listening.

"I tried contacting you before, and it didn't work. *This* is working now, I can tell. So why don't you answer?

"Are you cross with me? I hope you're not. I took care of some people who needed help. They were looking for *you*, but they got *me* instead. I think I managed to help them rather well. Just thought that, in the broad scheme of the multiverse, you might be willing to . . . er . . . well, take a call for *me* as it were. Now. Because I can't."

"You are referring to the Antimovian Incursion on Primo Terra BK thirty-eight seven?"

"Oh great hitch you've given them *numbers?* How dull. But yes, yes that would be the one."

"I've just come from there. You should know you left that world vulnerable to future incursions and some rather impertinent people took advantage. I was put to extreme inconvenience sorting it all out."

"Sorry about that."

"Yes"—a contrite cough—"I did appreciate the gesture."

"Those *impertinent people,* they didn't have multiversal technology and wear an emblem sort of like two Cs and a winged dog?"

"How could you possibly know that?"

"Because *I've* just come from a world where they were being *very* impertinent."

"Oh?"

"They tried to steal an exotrain."

"My dear, surely you jest."

"Don't you 'my dear' me, I'm not your Irene Adler."

"A multitude of apologies, Professor."

"Yes, well, anyway. That's not the worst of it. I got them off the train—well, I think mostly the manaflot did that *but*—the real problem is . . . they have my friend. You remember Mister Bane?"

"How could I forget?"

"They took him."

"What on all the earths could they want with *him?* Not that he didn't seem a nice, stalwart lad, perhaps a bit *plain* . . . "

"They belong to *his* native universe! He got mixed up with them entirely by accident, all because of me—well, me and Dave, *but*—for some reason they think he's got some special, secret knowledge of how the multiverse works, and I took him *away* from that world to keep him safe from them."

"And now that they have reacquired him, you fear for his well being?"

"Yes."

"And now he actually *does* have some valuable knowledge pertaining to the workings of the multiverse."

"Yes."

"And I assume, since you are asking *me,* that for some reason your . . . *usual* means of transport has been compromised?"

"Pretty much exactly right, yes. Look, I'll give you the whole rundown if you'll agree to help."

"And why would I do that, my dear Professor?"

"I'll even let you call me your 'dear,' see? I'm *hoping* you'll help because you are, against all first impressions, a *decent per-*

son, and that you actually do *like* helping people. Also, I think you dislike the Canary Company even more than I do—which is saying something!"

A silence filled the empty space, and anyone piecing together the conversation might have been fooled into thinking it stopped there. But a little time later the second voice—which was smooth and rich with an educated accent—came back.

"Meet me on Primo Terra FJ seventy—it's the one with the Icelandic Empire, you can't miss it—and wear a hat, it's cold in Reykjavík."

"*Where* in Reykjavík?"

"It doesn't matter. I will find you."

And after that there really was silence. It stretched on forever through the void, eating up the unheard conversation, until there was no trace of it left whatsoever.

The Oddity's lights were dim, and the darkness which usually hovered high under the ceiling stretched down and curled in the corners of the place like a black fog. It draped over the table and hung around the shoulders of the thin figure sitting at the controls. She sat very still, her back ramrod straight, and her olive-green trench coat fell in stiff folds around her legs. Her long, pale hands rested on the bank of colored buttons, their rainbow of lights reflected in her brown, feline eyes. She blinked once, causing the reflections to die and be reborn in between the swipe of her thin, platinum lashes. She wore a thick wool scarf wrapped around her neck, and a wig with cream-colored hair tipped in pink sat on her head. In the depths of the Oddity, the place hummed in soft anticipation.

A shift and a whisper of fabric announced movement: Professor Odd had reached into her pocket and removed a crumpled piece of paper. Spreading it open over the buttons, she ran a finger down the bulleted list of items, each of which had been marked off with a neat red tick.

When she had been down the list twice, making doubly sure each item had been accomplished, at last she stood up—pushing the list back into her pocket—and turned toward the door.

It was a matte, black rectangle, but with the swipe of a lever the Oddity *bonged,* and the door changed to a plain metal affair with a round handle in the center.

Professor Odd clenched and unclenched her fists, inhaled to the deepest extent of her lungs, and then let the air out in a long, measured breath.

She walked down the steps, grasped the handle firmly, and pulled the door open.

Clear, white-balanced light flooded onto the stairs of the Oddity; the portal led to a long hallway with a neat, linoleum floor and square lights bolted to the ceiling. There were no other doors.

Professor Odd walked down the hallway, her shoes making soft *clicking* noises on the clean floor. The place smelled faintly of cherry blossoms, making her wrinkle her nose.

At the end of the hall she consulted the map that had been nailed to the wall, and after a moment turned left, went up a flight of stairs—which had once been corrugated metal but were now covered with carpet—and then along another hall, this one with windows that looked out onto a central courtyard where there were fruit trees in bloom. Several of the windows were open, letting in wafts of fragrant air.

Professor Odd walked faster. The hall here was carpeted as well, so she moved in utter silence up to the big door with a frosted glass window.

The frosted glass had once had an emblem etched onto its surface, but this had been scratched out of existence and a sticker of a bird put in its place. Professor Odd frowned at it for several seconds, and then for several more where, on the wooden plaque below the window, someone had painted over the name that should have gone there, so it only said: "DIRECTOR ---------"

Professor Odd pursed her lips, took firm hold of the door's handle, and went inside.

The room beyond was clearly the deputy office—there was another door on the far wall with "AUTHORIZED PERSONNEL ONLY" stenciled over the scratched-out logo—and it was filled with bookshelves and one man-high computer. A small desk was squeezed between these, and behind it sat a small, plump woman with coppery skin, slanted eyes, and black, frizzy hair.

She stood up in surprise at seeing Professor Odd, her dark eyes going round in amazement.

"Director," she said, her voice high with nerves but otherwise pleasantly musical. "*Director,* you need to get out here *now!* It's *her!* I'm *sure* of it!"

Before Professor Odd could even open her mouth to respond, the door on the far side of the room slammed open and a man leapt out.

He was a tallish man, narrow in the way tall people are without really being thin, with dark brown eyes and dark brown hair that had been shaved back to a short fuzz all over his head. As if to make up for this, he had acquired a thick, full beard, neatly trimmed, which almost completely hid the lines of worry that had been seared onto that face since the last time Professor Odd had seen it. He was wearing a somber brown blazer jacket and trousers, but the shirt peeking through at his collar was a garish combination of orange-and-pink swirls that stood out like a poppy in a muddy field.

"*Professor!*" he cried, trilling both his Rs in excitement. "You're *back!* You're *here! Finally!* We've been looking all *over* for you! Even *Elo* was getting worried!"

He'd reached the woman's desk now, which stood in his way of advancing any farther unless he wanted to go around a blockade of bookcases. He got around this problem by stepping up onto the desk—the woman snatched a metal tablet from under his patent leather soles—and hopping down on the other side. Spreading his lanky arms wide he threw them around the Professor's shoulders and embraced her briefly, before pushing himself back—but not letting go of her shoulders—to grin at her.

Professor Odd blinked, her wide eyes going impossibly wider as she stared at the man in amazement and consternation.

"Mister *Alister,*" she whispered. "What on all the earths has *happened?*"

Alister Banc giggled at that. A happy, bubbling sound quite at odds with his formidable appearance. His swooping eyebrows wiggled at the ends as he shrugged.

"Who'd have thought *I'd* ever be *answering* that question?" he said, and then sobered up. He cleared his throat. "You're late, Professor. Almost two years late, by our best estimate. You can blame Dave, if you like, but I wouldn't. He was going to fix the interference they were running, but then . . . well, he never got around to it. Anyway, you're here now, which is the important thing. Raji, Raji," he said, half turning to the woman behind the desk. "Can you get a message through to Elo? Tell her the Professor has turned up at last!"

"I can try," said the woman, who was still staring at Professor Odd like she was a character out of a storybook come to life. "Might take a while to reach her, though."

"Better send it right away then," said Alister, and turned back to the Professor, still grinning hugely.

At last Professor Odd raised her own hands and clapped Alister on the shoulders.

"My reinforcements came through? You got my message?" she asked.

"Oh yes," said Alister, stifling another laugh. "Did they *ever.*"

Professor Odd's grip tightened a little, then she released him.

"Tell me," she said, pinning him with an intense, catlike glare. "Tell me what I missed."

Alister shrugged and looked around at the crowded office. He put his hands in his pockets. "It's a long story," he said.

Professor Odd went over to a chair that had been tucked between two bookcases and dragged it over to the desk, where the woman—Raji—was busy typing away at a small computer. Carefully she sat down, and then picked up her feet and rested them on a corner of desk. (Raji glanced at the intruding shoes, looked like she was going to protest, then looked at Professor Odd's face and thought better of it.)

"So tell me your story, Mister Alister Bane," said Professor Odd. "I have *time.*"

Part Two: The Good Man Bane

ALISTER SAT IN THE DARK. His body ached, he felt dizzy and sick, and he wanted more than anything for the Professor to pry open his cell door and take him home.

This didn't happen, however, and as he sat in the dark, growing cold and stiff and beginning to see funny colors swooshing around in front of his eyes, he realized what a cruel irony it was. Because he was fairly certain that he *was* home, in a horrible, twisted way. He was back in the universe he'd started in, however long ago *that* was. (A year? Two years? Ten? Time was different in the Oddity, and Alister had taken to only counting the time he spent in actual universes, not floating in the void between.) But home . . . where was home, now? Was home his college dorm? But that had been stripped and bare the last time he'd seen it, and anyway it had never felt like much of a home— not properly.

Home to Alister had been a rambling stone house in the Old Country near Loch Galross, with hundred-year-old roses climbing over its crumbling front and a big, warm kitchen filled with his grandmother's cooking. Specifically his seventh and eighth summers, when he had the place to himself and was old enough to really start exploring and noticing things. Then they'd renovated it, put in modern plumbing and heating, and turned it into a Bed and Breakfast. It was still the same house, still the same stony exterior, and even the same roses growing up the outside, but it never quite felt like *home* after that. It was warmer and brighter, but it was always filled with new and strange people, and Alister had to be very careful whenever he left his room, otherwise he'd be pounced on and fawned over. It had been a relief, really, moving away for university, though Alister still missed the old town, with its little bookshop that had special-ordered his astronomy books so he didn't have to bus all the way to Stirling, the tea room with its ever-changing array of oddly flavored sweets, and the fishmonger who was old friends with his grandfather and would let Alister sweep the floor for chips.

The problem was *that* home didn't exist anymore. The old fishmonger had retired, and though his son had expanded the business, it no longer had the same, welcoming feel. The bookshop had been forced to close—there had been a coffee house chain opening in its place the last time Alister had been for a visit, which the tea room had been eyeing nervously. The old house was still there, but *that* hadn't felt like home since the renovation.

Alister was a little surprised to realize, as he curled up in the dark and resigned himself to a long wait, that the home he was pining after was a tear-drop shaped room lit by dim, colored lights, where the windows with pink, lacy curtains looked out into the void between universes, and a huge table covered in amazing and interesting things sat in the middle. A place where he had to climb a ladder to get up to his room, but it was large and comfortable, and he got to pick out a new, colorful shirt each time he woke up.

Home was Elo cooking a giant pan of scrambled ostrich eggs in the kitchen alcove, or sitting around the table drinking a hot, chocolatey beverage that came from an isolated monastery on Niatano, or watching movies displayed across all the Oddity's screens.

Home was a safe, cozy, crowded place where he could retreat to after days on sunny beaches, or at the tops of mountains, or touring castles, or—occasionally—having hair-raising adventures.

He could imagine that home so clearly that after a time Alister began *seeing* the Oddity's lights shifting into view before his eyes, and he realized he was seeing things in the dark again, so he shut them.

His cell contained a thin blanket and a hard pillow, and a bucket which needed no explanation. After a while Alister wrapped the blanket around his shoulders, curled up on the pillow, and in his perpetual waiting, eventually fell asleep.

He was woken some time later by his bladder, so he made careful use of the bucket before lying back down at the opposite end of the cell.

The next time he was woken it was because his cell door had opened, and someone was shining a light directly into his face. He raised a hand to shield himself, but a moment later someone stuffed a hood over his head, and then he was marched out of his cell.

Even in his frightened, half-awake state, he knew that the wrong people had come for him.

*   *   *

Interview Room 7 at Canary West was a small, cold, window-less room with sound-proofed walls. Agent Parthenon liked it because it felt secure and she knew where all the cameras were. It had a table and two chairs and a lot of hidden microphones, but she could access all their feeds and that was the important thing.

Currently it also had herself, seated in the chair facing the only door, and Specimen 1017, who was handcuffed to the chair opposite her. Parthenon thought the handcuffs were not strictly necessary considering how bewildered and disoriented the man was, but better safe than sorry. Parthenon was con-scious of the privilege she had in conducting the initial inter-view, and she wasn't going to let anything ruin her day. Not even the Professor—Logistics had made sure of that.

Agent Parthenon narrowed her eyes at the man across from her, who blinked back out of red-rimmed, watery ones. (The only light in the room was angled so that it shone over her shoulder—not directly in the interviewee's face, just so that it made it painful for them to look at her.)

He was a young man, tallish and lanky, with short brown hair, strong dark eyebrows, and stubble over his chin. He could be considered handsome, Parthenon noted with professional disinterest, if he didn't look so much like a lost, half-drowned rat. He was wearing the same shiny blue jacket—now a lit-tle singed and stained—and bright yellow-and-white paisley button-down shirt as he had been when they collected him, and this Parthenon noted in her log.

Pulling up the specimen's file, she frowned at the name it showed at the top.

"Alister ... Galross ... *Bane*," she said, leaving imposing gaps between the words. "Strange surname, for an Albian. You're not a crossborder brat, are you?"

The specimen's face twisted in annoyance. "That's my mother's name," he snapped. "*Her* name was Bain—with an I N instead of an N E. Changed it because there was another actress in Glascal named *E Bain*."

He certainly had the accent of an Albian, Parthenon noted. But not a Glascallian. His accent spoke of the southern high-lands, but she wasn't enough of an expert to place him exactly.

"Yes, Evelyn Bane," said she said, making sure to sound as bored as possible. "Died of a heroine overdose at twenty-four. Disowned by her parents, her only child was then adopted by the father's parents, and raised in . . . Lochgalrosshead?"

Specimen 1017 sighed and slumped back in his chair. "My father's hometown. Grandmam said I got Galross as my middle name because Mum didn't care for *his* name."

"MacUpsaig," said Agent Parthenon, reading from the file. "Yes, I can agree with her there. And you were raised exclusively in Lochgalrosshead?"

"Sounds like you have my family genealogy all laid out in that nice file of yours," said the specimen. "It should be able to tell you *that* at least."

"No summer camping trips? No . . . inexplicable adventures as a child? You may only remember them as innocent, fun play-times."

Specimen 1017 looked at her mulishly from under one cocked eyebrow. He had good, strong eyebrows, perfect for cocking, and had the ability to raise one independently of the other—something Parthenon had yet to master, to her ever-increasing frustration.

"I nearly drowned in Loch Galross when I was eight," he said, his tone arch and sarcastic. "Do you count near-death experiences as innocent, fun playtimes?"

In truth Agent Parthenon did, but only if they were *other people's* near-death experiences, and only if they were *near-*death ones, not *actual-*death ones. She made a note in the specimen's file though, mostly because she thought the action would annoy him.

"Our census shows your peers chose to pursue university in Alba," she said, changing the subject in the hopes of getting the man to admit something that way. "What brought you so far south?"

Specimen 1017 rolled his head back until it hung off the end of his chair, and stared at the ceiling. She saw his throat work as he swallowed, and his eyebrows knotted. Eventually he said:

"Weather seemed nicer," and shut his mouth firmly.

Agent Parthenon set down the file and her log and folded her hands over them to give 1017 a direct stare.

"You know, Mr. Bane, I cannot help you if you do not help *me.* Now, we know—"

She was cut off, however, by Specimen 1017 raising his head and beginning to shout at her.

"Help me?" he said, a little hoarse. *"Help* me? After you *kidnapped* me—twice!—and stuck me in a dark room overnight, and handcuffed me to a chair? You could give me a *drink,* or maybe some *breakfast,* or even, I don't know, *let me go home!* That'd help a lot, I tell you, and you don't need to know my childhood history or the reasoning behind my choice in university to do any of that!"

Agent Parthenon sighed. It was not an ideal response, but she'd managed to get a little material to work with. Enough that, she was reasonably certain, Dr. Carver would keep her on the case. She certainly hoped so. Specimen 1017 was a harder nut than he looked, and she was curious to find out what would make him crack.

Pressing a hidden button on her wrist, she said: "Terminate interview in seven, please," and then sat back and watched as two custodians came in and dragged the specimen—still shouting—away.

They put Alister, none too gently, back in the same cell as before. Unless it was another, identical one. The bucket was empty, anyway, and the place smelled of disinfectant. He'd knocked his elbow on something hard between there and that horrible room where he'd been interviewed, and for a while afterward he had to sit curled in a corner, nursing it and trying not to cry.

If he started to cry, Alister knew, he'd lose any control he had left over himself, and would probably go insane.

It had been a mistake to shout at that agent. But she had looked so smug, so satisfied, and so . . . well, like she wasn't seeing him as a real *person* at all. It had made him scared and angry, and he'd lost his temper.

What had brought him south, indeed! Like he was going to tell her all about the stupid row he'd had with Granddad over not taking a job straight out of school and "wasting his summer" building a telescope in the attic and how Grandmam had found him in tears in his room and said that she'd sent his marksheet to Baybridge, which had an excellent astronomy course in Gill College, and only asked that he come back afterward and make the whole of Lochgalrosshead proud.

Then again, maybe he should have, much as it shamed him. Losing his temper had probably killed any chance of getting food or—more importantly—water.

Were they just going to let him wither away and die in here? Well, they'd certainly never know his story if they did that! Unless they were just waiting for him to die in order to dissect him. Then Alister remembered how, when they'd found Dave, he'd been missing the tips of his arms, and shuddered.

The Canary Company didn't wait for you to die before it started cutting into you.

He was jerked out of his downward mental spiral by the scrape of metal as a small hatch at the bottom of the door to his cell was slid open.

Hope flared in his chest for an instant, only to be put out again when he saw it was not the Professor. It was a tray containing two plastic boxes, a foil-wrapped package, and a tiny water bottle. It looked like the kind of dinner tray one might get on an airplane, except there were no eating utensils.

Then the hatch was pulled shut, and Alister had to grope his way over and feel around until he found the tray again.

He drank the water in one go, then cautiously opened the containers and ate their contents using his fingers. This turned out to be a salad with some fruit, a piece of dry chicken, and a small, hard, baked potato.

Eating the potato was a mistake. It dried out Alister's mouth all over again and nearly stuck in his throat. He was thirstier than ever, but at least his stomach didn't hurt as much, and he didn't feel as dangerously dizzy. He pushed himself back up against the far wall and tried to think, but all his mind would do was spin worse and worse scenarios of what would happen if he wasn't rescued, and he fell to hoping so hard that ever nerve felt on fire and he jumped at the slightest sound, the faintest hint, of a door opening to another place altogether.

* * *

Agent Parthenon stood in the director's outer office—which was as close as anyone got to Dr. Carver these days—and looked directly at the dark little eye over the display screen showing a grainy depiction of his face. It was, she knew, the camera that fed what he saw on his own screen, and she'd noticed how much better the man responded when the image of *her* face seemed to be looking directly at him. As opposed to what he himself was doing: his camera was up and a little to the side of his screen, so what she saw was an indirect view of the side of his face. It made gauging his expressions difficult, but not impossible. Agent Parthenon fancied she was good with expressions, and right now, unless she was very much mistaken, Dr. Carver was torn between excitement, satisfaction, and fear.

The fear was evident in the twitch of his eyes, though not in the cadence of his voice, which was as rich and relaxed as ever as it came rolling out of the speaker in confident waves.

"Has he given any information about the manner in which he and Specimen 1016 have been jumping universes?"

"No, sir," said Agent Parthenon. "But I expect it was by the same machine that I encountered."

"Yes . . . and, previously—has he given you any clue as to his earlier travels?"

"No," said Agent Parthenon, not liking to give two negative answers in a row, but truthfulness was the better option here. Dr. Carver wasn't the best at spotting lies, but he always found out eventually, and when he did you were lucky if you were only fired. The Canary Company had an extremely strict non-disclosure agreement, and the more sensitive information you were exposed to, the worse you had it if there came a reckoning. So she sighed and went on.

"No, he hasn't admitted to anything directly. But he has corroborated our own research pertaining to his childhood. I've started a search for his father, but would you like me to bring his grandparents in, now?"

On the screen, Dr. Carver stroked his chin with a long, brown finger, and eventually shook his head. "Not yet," he said. "But keep them under observation. I want to see if he tries to contact them by . . . unusual methods."

"We stripped him of all his tech," Parthenon pointed out. "Not that he had much to be going on."

"Like I said," said Dr. Carver, tapping the tips of his fingers together, in the way he did when he was pleased with himself but didn't like to show it. "*Unusual* methods."

"Will do, sir," said Agent Parthenon. "Anything else?"

Dr. Carver thought about this for a little while, then said: "If he continues to be uncooperative, you have permission to take more direct measures. Oh, and see that he's properly scanned and catalogued."

Agent Parthenon saluted, and held it until her screen had gone dark—signifying the end of the interview. Turning on her heel she marched past the director's secretary—a thin, pale-faced man that put Parthenon in mind of a fish—and exited the outer office. As soon as she was in the hall she pulled out her in-house phone and hit the button for operator.

"Get me accounting," she said when prompted. Then, when a bored voice announced this was what she had, she went on: "Got a specimen for you. A re-log. Number 1017. Yes, *that* one. Custodians will be on hand—he's a live one." She hung up and, pocketing her phone, walked down the hall with a spring in her booted step, whistling softly.

After a while Alister fancied he could see shapes in the colors that swirled before his eyes from the lack of all other stimuli. They put him in mind of large-finned, slow-moving fish, and one looked so real—so solid and detailed—that he tried to put his hand out and touch it.

Of course his hand met empty air, but that didn't disturb the vision, which hung before his eyes until he closed them.

"Just *don't* start talking to them," he muttered to himself, letting his head rock back against the metal wall. Talking to *himself,* he reasoned, was perfectly fine, as long as it really was *himself* he was talking to.

"You'll get through this, Alister," he told himself, firmly. "The Professor's having a wee bit of trouble with one thing or another. Maybe there was temporal slippage or something, but she'll be here. She'll come."

In truth the idea of temporal slippage frightened Alister. It could mean he was in for a long wait if it slipped the wrong direction. It was more comforting to imagine that Professor Odd was already in this world, and just having a hard time getting to him—the Canary Company seemed to know enough about how the Oddity worked to be careful of the portal anchors it left available.

The problem with that was Alister kept half-expecting the Professor—or maybe Elo or even Dave—to open his cell door and set him free. So it was especially disappointing when the door opened—Alister had the presence of mind to shield his eyes this time—and a pair of masked people in hazmat suits reached in and dragged him out.

They were not exactly rough, but they weren't gentle either. They handled Alister as though he were an animal, like a dog, and spoke to him only in short, simple words. Like he was a dog.

Alister managed to keep himself together until they led him into a clean, white, sterile-looking room with metal rings bolted to the walls and a drain in the center. Then the delicate net that had been thrown over his instinctual urges to fight and run was shredded, and he kicked and flailed and got one of the suited figures a solid hit in the midsection, but the other one clapped a plastic cup over his mouth and nose, and between one panicked breath and the next Alister's mind went fuzzy and vague. It felt like he was swimming in his own mind, caught in waves of a milky liquid that surged up and washed out his vision.

They were stripping him, spraying him with something warm and wet, then toweling him off and putting him in plain, canvas trousers and a pullover shirt. They sat him on a stool, and one of them held his head steady while the other one mechanically shaved off his hair with a pair of clippers. Alister was aware of the sensation like the distant brush of a prickly wind, but overall he was too focused on staying conscious, on remembering where and who he was, to pay much attention to what was actually happening.

His mind kept slipping sideways, remembering how the Professor had described the experience of being lobotomized: as if her brain had gone like a smashed kaleidoscope, and at the suggestion, Alister's mind helpfully summoned up images of broken color and light, which filled his milky vision and threatened to drown him.

A flash of light. A small red eye was staring at him, then it was removed, and he looked down to see his hands were covered in ink, and they were pressing his fingers to a strip of white paper.

That was wrong. He wasn't a criminal. He shouldn't be here.

He struggled. Someone said, "Specimen is responding."

"So give him another hit," someone else said.

Something was placed over Alister's mouth again, and the smell of sticky sweetness flooded his nostrils, and then he was sinking, dragged down under the rising tide of milky, broken colors.

Darkness fell. It was so complete it took Alister a moment to realize he was awake. He blinked against the scratchy surface his face was resting on, confused. He didn't remember going to bed. He didn't remember his room being this dark.

Then he realized he wasn't *in* his bed *or* his room. He wasn't even in the Oddity, and with that the crushing despair came back.

He was lying on his side on the cold, hard floor of his cell, one arm up to provide a cushion for his head, his higher leg crooked at the knee to prevent him accidentally rolling onto his face.

Coming fully awake now, with a slight, lingering nausea in his throat, he realized his head was freezing, and the arm that had been doubling as a pillow was completely numb.

With a groan he rolled onto his back, using his good arm to bring the numb limb down and across his chest, massaging it gingerly through the pins and needles. He could feel the floor against the back of his head, and when he explored that area he found his hair had been reduced to a short stubble. The clothes he was wearing were coarse against his skin; they felt too large, and seemed to be made of canvas. They had even taken his shoes; his feet were freezing.

He was beginning to shake. Whether from withdrawal from drug they'd put in him, or from the growing lump of panic in his chest, he wasn't sure. Once he regained feeling in his arm he pushed himself into a sitting position and curled into the nearest corner, bringing his knees up into his chest and wrapping his arms around them.

The darkness pressed in on all sides, like a physical force, and it was with a twisted sense of relief that Alister saw the fuzzy, indistinct shapes of colorful fish begin to emerge before his eyes. At least that was *something*.

"Mister Bane," said a female voice unnervingly close to his ear.

It was both like and unlike the Professor's, and Alister had spent so long hoping that for a split second he thought it *was* her. But a part of him recoiled, knowing the speaker was someone very different, and so he only grunted in response. Inside, however, he felt like a glass plate had broken under the momentary relief. He was all sharp edges, and it hurt.

He was glad it was dark; at least they couldn't see him cry.

"Mister *Bane*," said the voice, and this time he recognized it as belonging to the bronze-skinned woman who had interviewed him earlier.

"*What?*" snapped Alister, stifling a sniff.

"This could have gone much more pleasantly for you, if you had been honest with us from the beginning."

The voice sounded as though it was coming from somewhere up and to the right. A hidden speaker, Alister guessed.

"What do you *think* I've been doing?" he asked, spitting the words out.

"There's no need to take that tone," said the voice, reproachfully. "You know as well as I do how important our work is."

"No, I *really* don't," said Alister.

"Every precaution must be taken in the face of an infinity of threats," said the voice, as if quoting something. "*You*, well. We're not sure if you're a threat or not. Since you have behaved uncooperatively from the start, we must assume you are a threat. If you have information that implies otherwise, you can help yourself by sharing it with us."

"*Me*, a threat?" Alister said, stifling a hoarse laugh. If he started laughing, he knew, it would quickly turn to screams, and then he wouldn't be able to stop. And then, because he figured whatever he said could not possibly make his situation any worse, he went on: "I'm *no one*. I'm just a bloke from a nowhere town in Alba. I'm a . . . *was* a university student. I'm no one special. I had a completely ordinary and boring life until *you* lot came along and *erased* me. And since then I've done nothing—*nothing*—to harm this world! I haven't even been *in* this world!"

"Nothing?" said the voice icily. "Then it was *not* you who deactivated our operations on Canary 6?"

Alister swallowed. There had been the time he and the Professor had intercepted a party of genetically modified dogs who were attempting to ship research and tech to the Canary Company through a naturally occurring wormhole. It had certainly seemed like the better option for the dogs, whose society had been held back by the Company's interference.

"You'd no right to be messing about with them," he said instead.

"And you continue to refuse to share the technology by which you facilitated your prior travels," the voice went on, as if it had not heard.

"*What* prior travels?" moaned Alister. "I never went—" he broke off with a gulp.

He *had* gone off world before the Canary Company had first captured him. For barely half an hour, he'd been given tea in the Oddity, and then returned to his class moments after he'd left. And when the Company had scanned him, something had come up on their radar. Which was why they'd kept him, erased all evidence of his life and treated him like an object.

"Look," he said, taking a deep, steadying breath. "Something you've *got* to understand. I only ever *visited* the Oddity before you got me. And it was by *accident*. I *promise* you I'm nothing special."

Silence. It lasted so long Alister thought the voice had gone away, and was just beginning to see the colorful fish again, when it cut through his half-dreaming with a sound like a snarl.

"Your prevarication is telling," it hissed, sending a chill down Alister's spine. "The Dustings test doesn't lie. You *are* holding something back, and until you comply, your situation will continue to become more uncomfortable, Mister Bane."

Alister shut his eyes and leaned his head back against the wall with a soft thump.

"*More uncomfortable,*" repeated the voice. There was a faint click, and then nothing.

Uncomfortable turned out to be an understatement. Things went downright *unbearable* after that conversation, though it was such a slow build Alister didn't realize how bad things were at once.

The first thing that happened was they pulled him out of his cell, stuffed a bag over his head, and marched him to another cell which, once the bag came off, was pitch black. Feeling around, Alister found the expected bucket, which seemed to be bolted to the floor, and a small pile of bedding. The ceiling was lower— he couldn't stand up completely straight—and there were no windows at all, just a small ventilation duct with a heavy grill over it, securely bolted down.

Food no longer came in plates, but in thick, plastic bowls. It was the consistency of cold porridge, but tasted slightly meaty.

Out of curiosity more than anything else, Alister left his bowl on the far side of his cell one time, to see if someone would come in to get it. He hadn't seen a living person since the people in hazmat suits, and he hadn't seen a human face since the interview with the company agent. A part of him wanted to make sure that *people* still existed—even though he knew they must: the bucket periodically retracted through a hole in the wall and came back empty.

No one came, but instead the little flap cracked open, and something that scratched on the hard floor was poked inside. Curious, Alister felt for it, and just had time to close his fingers around the long, thin wire, when an electric shock burned his hands, and he let go with a yelp.

He heard muffled laughter from beyond the door, and someone said, "That'll learn ya," and then the wire found the bowl, hooked it, and dragged it out.

Alister left his bowls right next to the door after that. If the people outside were anything like the owner of the voice he'd heard, they could go disappear for all he cared.

Time stretched. Not in the tranquil, ageless way it stretched in the Oddity. This was the agonizing pull of monotony that went on forever and ever, spreading Alister's mind thin across it.

The colorful fish came and went. Sometimes he heard voices, and though at first he was careful to make a distinction between real noises and the voices in his head, when the latter turned out to be the *only* voices he heard, eventually he took to listening to what they said out of sheer boredom.

"Have you tried *talking* to them?" Professor Odd asked him. Alister could see her crouched, her pose a mirror of his own, against the opposite wall. And because he could see her, he knew this was all in his imagination. It was his brain trying to fill in the empty gaps by pure invention.

Well, maybe he could help himself help himself, as it were.

"Yes, I've *tried* that," he told the apparition. "They won't *listen.*"

"Not the agent," said the ghost of Professor Odd, with a shake of her head. She wasn't wearing a wig, and the green leopard spots that dotted her skull stood out luridly against the pale skin, while her tentacle curled lazily over one shoulder. It twitched as she went on: "The people in suits. The ones giving you *food.* Everyone here who actually knows what's going on will be too invested in what they're doing to admit that it's wrong. Try talking to the grunts. The custodians. The people who are feeding you. *They're* the ones who might actually listen. Listening to orders is what got them into their position in the first place; who says they won't listen to you?"

It was a mad idea. And as it came from Alister's own brain, he wondered if this meant he was also going mad.

But he was desperate. After who-knew how long in the cool, dark, lonely cell which was beginning to smell, with barely enough to eat and drink, dried not-porridge caked on his hands and his back cramping from not being able to straighten all the way, he was willing to try anything.

The next time he was fed, Alister took the empty bowl and put it in the corner farthest from the slot, and when the wire came, tapping and probing, he leant down by the opening and said:

"If you want the bowl back, just say *please.*"

The tapping of the wire paused, and then a man's voice, very close on the other side of the door, said: "Don't get cocky, son, or I'll open this door and take your brain apart myself, no matter what Parthenon says."

It was a overpowering sensation, hearing another human's voice again, and having it be so unfriendly. It made Alister's head pound, and he went and crouched beside his bucket while the wire fished his food bowl out and the flap slid shut.

He didn't have the heart to try again right away. But he started paying attention to the *manner* in which the food bowl was placed in his cell. He noticed how, on some occasions, there was a sharp *smack* of the dish hitting the floor; half the time the slop inside spilled. Other times it was slipped inside with more care. Almost *considerately.* When Alister moved his bowl out of reach after it had been placed in his cell, rather than tossed, it seemed the person behind the wire was a little less sure of themselves, and it took longer for them to find the bowl.

After the shock of the first voice had worn off, Alister tried again—this time after the considerate person had fed him.

He took his bowl and knelt at the far end of the cell. He waited. There was a whisper of metal as the slot slid open, and when he heard the tap of the wire he said:

"I can give you the bowl back, if you'd only *ask.*"

There was a gasp from the other side of the door, and a clatter that sounded like whoever was behind the wire had dropped it.

"Hello?" said Alister, his chest so full of hoping that he could barely speak.

The wire resumed its tapping, but more shakily, now.

"Just *ask,*" said Alister. "I'll put it down right by the slot, no tricks."

The tapping stopped. Very faintly, as though it was coming through a layer of steel and concrete by way of a narrow tube, a female, South-London voice said:

"Sorry. They didn't say you could speak . . . "

A joyful chorus rose up inside Alister's mind. Professor Odd gave him the thumbs-up from her corner of his cell, and he had to blink hard to dispel the hallucination so he could continue.

"Why shouldn't I?"

"Just didn't expect it, is all." The owner of the voice—which was light and pleasant and sounded like music to Alister's starved ears—coughed. "Er, *could* I have the bowl back?"

Alister didn't want to give the bowl back. Giving the bowl back would mean the speaker would go away, and he'd be alone with his overactive imagination again. But a part of him reasoned that this same person had been feeding him regularly, and would likely feed him again. And he *had* said . . .

Reluctantly he crept forward and slipped the bowl into the slot, wincing away when he felt his fingers brush the wire—but it didn't shock him this time.

The bowl retreated, followed by the wire, but the slot didn't close. After a while, the voice said:

"Thank you."

"You're welcome," said Alister, miserably.

"Er . . . " said the voice, and Alister held his breath. "Why do you sound Albian?"

"Because that's where I'm *from*," Alister replied.

"Oh," said the voice. Then: "I'm probably not meant to know that."

"Probably not," said Alister.

"Right, I should . . . er . . . be going."

"Come back," Alister called into the slot, before it could close. "I'll tell you more things you're not meant to know!"

But he said it to the closed slot; the person on the other side probably hadn't heard.

Still, it was good to have spoken to someone outside his own head. Alister went and curled up in his favorite corner, hugging the memory to himself.

"It's not much," said Elo, who had taken the Professor's place. "But it's a start."

Alister agreed.

The friendly feeder did not come back after Alister had spoken to her. It was all messily delivered food and angry, stabbing wires when Alister tried to hide his bowl.

"Don't worry," said Elo, when Alister was curled tightly in on himself, crying so hard he could barely breathe. "It'll get better soon, I promise."

She gave him one of her earnest, canine smiles, and Alister wished, with every fiber of his being, that she was real. How he wanted to wrap himself around that strong, soft, furry body, and feel the warm, wet gust of her breath. But when he crawled over to the corner it was cold and empty, and he had to scream for a while after that. He only stopped when his throat got so sore it hurt too much.

Someone must have heard him, though, because the door opened and another pair of masked, besuited people reached in for him.

It as worse this time. Monumentally worse. They did not drug him: they held him down while they clipped the short fuzz that had grown over his head and face, and then pushed him under a heavy spray of water that started too cold and ended too hot. They blasted him with hot air instead of toweling him dry, which left his skin parched and papery, and finally they stuffed him into another pair of simple, canvas trousers and pullover shirt. These were a tannish color, Alister noticed, and had PROPERTY OF THE CANARY COMPANY stenciled in black on the back of the shirt. He wondered, dully, if that referred to the clothes or to him.

At the end they sat him down in a chair, in a room that was both too bright and too dark at the same time. It had been so long, and Alister's brain had spent so long spinning out in the dark and silence of his cell, that it wasn't until the bronze-skinned woman with the long, aquiline nose and sharp, black hair walked inside that he realized he was back in the interview room. *An* interview room, anyway. It looked just like the last one, but for all he knew they had dozens, just the same.

The woman—whose name tag said Parthenon in neat, black letters—put a manilla folder on the table and began carefully arranging the papers in it so they were laid out in front of her. Alister tried reading them upside-down, but could only make sense of the headers ("Education" and "Previous Travels" jumped out at him).

Mostly, however, he felt numb and cold and a little itchy. After so long in the dark the light hurt his eyes, making them water. He found himself blinking up at Parthenon, humiliated and miserable.

"Mister *Bane,*" she said, in a voice calculated to rake on nerves already made raw by his rough treatment and sensory deprivation. "Now that you understand what uncooperative behavior entails, I am hopeful you will be slightly more . . . *obliging.*"

Alister wanted to upend the table and shove it into Parthenon's smug, pointed face, but they'd shackled him to his chair, and besides, he didn't think he had the strength. Something inside him crumpled, and he leaned back with a groan. He found himself staring at the ceiling of the room: it was metal with peeling, white paint. Alister thought he could make out landscapes in the sharp, angular cracks—mesas and buttes, with canyons and valleys between.

He blinked, trying to get his brain to anchor in reality, but it kept sliding off sideways.

"What do you want to know?" he asked, his voice sounding fuzzy and indistinct even to himself

"We just want to know about your previous travels, Mister Bane," said Parthenon, with the sort of sweetness that put Alister in mind of cold medicine.

"There've been rather a lot," mumbled Alister. "There was Niatano . . . and the bubble world . . . and the dragon world . . . and the one inside the machine . . . the Professor gets around, you know?"

"Yes," said Parthenon, her voice icy and brittle. "I know. But I was asking about your *previous* travels. *Before* you met the Professor."

With a great effort Alister raised his head to stare at the woman. He knew he couldn't read expressions the same way Professor Odd could, but she looked perfectly sincere to him.

"*What* travels?" he asked. "My summer trips to Glenfinnan?"

"No," said Parthenon. "I mean your previous travels to worlds other than this one."

"I didn't *have* any travels to worlds other than this one," Alister wailed. "Not before I met the Professor!"

"Then why did you register as a partially alien entity when you were first scanned?" asked Parthenon, her words pointed. They stabbed at Alister's soft, mushy brain like needles, making him wince.

"I don't *know*," said Alister, letting his head fall back to stare at the ceiling again. The landscape had changed while he was away: now it looked like the world with the lightning canyon, where he'd found the man chained to the rock. There was even a sharp zigzag of broken paint, where the metal showed through, reminding him both of the impossible stone formation, and the cracks of void that showed through later.

He jerked himself. He'd been asked a question. He needed to respond.

"Maybe it was because I'd already *been* out of this universe when your lot picked me up—*with* the Professor," he said, trying not to sound sarcastic. Getting Parthenon to believe him was his best chance at getting out of this with his wits, let alone his life. But it was as though his brain could no longer fully control his mouth, and the words flowed out like acid over his tongue.

"That's all there is: I was as monoversal as all of you! Then I meet her and *bam!* Hiya, this car door leads to a place between worlds! Heya, your universe isn't the only one. Oh, also the dog can talk and your substitute tutor is a strange alien lady with a tentacle growing out the back of her head! *That's all there is!*"

He looked back down, only to find Parthenon staring at him grimly.

"No," she said, quietly. "No that's *not*, Mr. Bane. We have incontrovertible evidence that you made extensive, unauthorized trips to other universes before you were abducted and brainwashed by the Professor—"

"I wasn't—!" Alister began, weakly, but Parthenon's words rolled over him like a tractor.

"—which was *also* a breach of our laws—"

"Who says *you* get to make—"

"—and leaves us with no recourse but to treat you as a Level 6 Priority Subject. Now, you can cooperate, and you will be given as much autonomy as we feel it is safe to allow—"

"I *am* cooperating!" Alister ground out.

"—but if you continue to hinder our work, you will be archived."

That didn't sound good at all, but Alister was so angry, frightened, and off balance by this point that he didn't care.

"What do you not understand about 'I did not go traveling to other universes before I met the Professor?'" he snapped, seeing spittle fly from his own lips. "What do you not understand about *I'm telling you the truth already?* Is it too much to admit that you were *wrong*?"

Parthenon's mouth pinched in at this, and she whispered something into her collar. A moment later two suited men stepped into the room and approached Alister.

At this point Alister's brain gave up its tenuous hold on rationality, and he began to kick and scream inarticulately. Adrenaline filled his veins. He didn't even feel the needle going in, and only knew he had been drugged in a distant way, as his vision clouded over and everything went black.

This time Alister dreamed. As the drugs loosed their hold on his brain he dreamed of cracked landscapes that fell apart under his fingers. He dreamed a new childhood for himself, in which the attic door in the old house outside Lochgalrosshead really did lead to another world. It was a world just like his, only everything that was normally silver glimmered with all the colors of the rainbow. The next time he went through the door, he was on an alien planet with a purple sky and tall, mint-colored plants like giant dandelions—puffy, spherical blossoms on long, thin stalks that reached up far above his head. He found one flower that had fallen down, and he was able to see that it was over three feet across, and the little flowers were actually the crinkled wings of moths. Moths made of petals, though. He later learned that they were not moths, but an alien species that grew from the flower at the top of the stalk. When they were fully developed they spread their wings, causing the flower to bloom, before flying off to fertilize other flowers, thus repeating the cycle.

Why had he never told Professor Odd about these memories? She would have loved to hear about the strange flower-insects. She might already know of them, and they could go back to that world. Alister dearly missed that world—it had smelled sweet, like honey and ice cream, and the ground had been soft and squishy.

It was only as he drifted closer to consciousness, becoming aware of the hard, cold metal under his cheek, the cramp in his elbow, and the faint smell of disinfectant, that he remembered that it was a *dream*, not a memory. Parthenon was *wrong*, no matter how much she seemed to be convinced otherwise.

Yes, said someone inside Alister's head. *You can still distinguish fact from fantasy. Things could be worse.*

Now he was hallucinating Dave, Alister thought, miserably. He didn't want to go from one dream to another. He wanted reality, but reality was so horrible he couldn't bear to face it.

I am sympathetic to your predicament. I was once put in a similar position. I survived, and so will you, said Dave—not in his harsh, abrasive, synthetic voice, but in the smooth, cool tones that Alister remembered permeating his mind when Dave spoke to him directly, through his slime. Alister felt something wet run down his cheek, and cursed himself for crying so easily. He was missing Dave—*Dave* of all people!—he must be in a very bad state.

You are in a suboptimal mental state, it is true, said Dave. *But it is less disintegrated than I had feared. I am also touched that you missed me, but mostly I am sorry. It took far longer than I had anticipated.*

Alister wondered what Dave could be talking about. What took longer than anticipated?

Getting here, said Dave. *But, as you humans say, better late than never, correct?*

Alister squeezed his eyes shut. If only Dave *was* here.

But, said Dave. *I am.*

It was only then that Alister came fully awake. He realized that his head was strangely warm at about the same time he realized the wet things running down his cheeks were not tears but drops of slime. Then his brain registered the smooth slide of little feelers wriggling across his scalp, dipping into his ears; he could not open his right eye because there was an arm with gently grasping suckers draped over it. More arms twined around his head, running down his neck (but not around it) to lie across his shoulders.

He shot up abruptly, pulling his knees up and crawling backward until he hit the wall.

Careful, warned Dave, and Alister felt his muscles go limp as the consistency of the slime changed subtly. *I am highly squishable like this, and it won't help anyone if I am injured!*

Still disbelieving, Alister raised a hand and slowly wiped the slime from his left eye. He felt the side of one of Dave's arms—comparatively cool and smooth and slick with slime—and rather than pull away, he let his hand linger.

Could you hallucinate a solid object? he wondered.

Quite possibly, said Dave. *Never underestimate the capacity of the human brain to delude itself. As it happens, however, I am* not *an hallucination: I am real and present in this narrative, as are you, and as such we are both in grave danger. I need you to listen to me, Alister Bane, but most of all, I need you to trust me. Can you do that?*

The wetness on Alister's face *was* from tears now, but this time he felt no shame. No matter whether Dave was really here, or if he was simply an extension of Alister's own brain, the answer was the same:

"Aye," said Alister, his voice a hoarse wreck. "Aye, I trust you."

Rajinder Ayoadé pushed the trolly laden with bowls down the narrow aisles of the high-security animal ward. The place had always given her the creeps, and now coming back after two months, it was even worse. The flat, metal doors with the food-flaps at the bottom, like mean little mouths, and the single peep-hole in the center—Rajinder hadn't dared look inside after what she had seen the first time; an animal that contorted should not be alive, she felt, and had been sick afterwards.

But the Canary Company paid their techs well, even if they were junior techs, and even if they hadn't got the best marks from university. The nondisclosure agreements were draconian, but they also didn't seem to care that her parents had come from the two regions on earth that were the most at odds with Greater Britain, and even though she was literally a black sheep in a sea of whites, on the whole her coworkers were decent people, and the work itself was interesting: searching for evidence of other universes *sounded* crazy, until you saw some of the artifacts that the Company had found.

It was just the high-security animal ward that got her down, especially after the time one of them had spoken to her. A talking dog or large cat was something Rajinder was not quite ready to accept, even at this point. Not, she told herself, because she didn't think they could exist, but because a part of her knew that, if an animal could speak like a human, that meant it could think like a human, which meant it could probably *feel* like a human, which meant it had no business being locked up in such a horrible little cell.

And they were horrible cells. Rajinder had to clean them out when they were vacated, and even though she jammed the door open behind her, so there was no chance of her accidentally being shut in, she still felt like the place was pushing in on her, like it wanted to crush her. They were so small and narrow and isolating. A human would go crazy in there.

So she'd asked for a transfer, which had been granted, but now her replacement had got the flu, and she was the only Jr Tech with the training to make the hi-sec animal rounds. It had been with a clench of her stomach that she noticed Specimen 1017 was still in his same cell, and when it came time to push the little bowl through the slot, she did it with her fingertip, and then quickly moved on before she could hear anything from within. She finished her rounds without incident, cleaned out the two newly vacated cells, washed her hands, and had her own lunch.

She was almost in a cheerful mood by the time she made her second round, picking up the empty dishes. When she reached 1017's cell she hesitated, but when she put her hand in she felt the bowl right away, and no voice spoke.

She straightened up, holding the bowl, and something exploded in her mind.

There were words—there must have been words—but they were wrapped up in emotions and feelings and hard to make out. Mostly, she was struck by a sense of desperate loneliness, of fear and despair and a little bit of anger. It was so sudden, and so strong, that she staggered backwards, knocked into her trolly, and fell down.

Her hands were tingling where they held the bowl, so she dropped it, but the thoughts and feelings continued to assault her, and now the words came through strong enough that she could make sense of them.

Help. Help. You must help. They are hurting me. Let me out. Let me go. Help. Please, help.

The message repeated, over and over again, like a tape on loop. The longer Rajinder sat there, however, feeling her heart thudding in her chest, the stronger it got. After a while, it began to change. The rush of emotions diminished, replaced by a growing sensation of numbness and cold.

Open the door, Rajinder, said the words. It was not a voice. She heard nothing, but the meaning appeared in her head out of the swirl of confused feelings. These words had a different flavor than the cry for help, as though they came from a different person. A person who was not scared or lonely, but was, in a distant way, deeply angry.

"I can't," she whispered. "Don't know the code."

The release sequence is eight, eight, eight at first prompt, twenty-seven at second prompt, one, zero, one, seven at third prompt, the security word is technetium, *like your chemical element, and the colors are red, red, green, red, blue, purple. The activation word is* clear.

"*I can't . . .*" Rajinder whispered, but the words went on: they seemed to be a recording as well, and had answered her implied question by accident.

The release sequence can only be entered by a native human. Open the door, Rajinder. The release sequence is . . .

And the words went through her head again. And again. And *again.*

Eight, eight, eight at the first prompt. Twenty-seven at the second prompt.

"*I can't,*" she moaned.

One, zero, one, seven at the third prompt.

"Please," said a voice on the other side of the door. It was hoarse and weak, but it was still recognizable as the one that had spoken before.

The security word is technetium, *like your chemical element.*

"I don't know what you are!"

And the colors . . .

"My name is Alister Bane, I'm a human from this world, just like you."

. . . are red, red, green . . .

"Then why are you locked up?"

. . . red, blue . . .

"Someone made a mistake. Please, I promise I won't hurt you."

. . . purple.

"How do I know that?"

The activation word . . .

"I gave you the bowl back, didn't I?"

. . . is clear.

The spinning in Rajinder's head slowed, though the words continued to repeat. Now she was beginning to feel nauseated, a cold sweat breaking out all over her skin and her breath quickening.

"If I let you out will you stop talking inside my head?"

. . . like your chemical element.

"Yes."

Shakily, Rajinder got to her feet.   This was worse—inconceivably worse—than simply talking to a high security specimen. But she could always say later that she'd been mind-controlled. It wasn't even a complete lie.

She felt torn up inside: Specimen 1017 was probably a dangerous alien. There had to be a reason he was locked up. There *had* to be, because if Specimen 1017 was a human, then what the Company was doing to him was unforgivable. It would upend everything Rajinder believed about the order of her life. She was one of the *good* guys.

Good guys didn't lock people up in dark cells and feed them dog food.

Good guys got people out of places like that.

Eight, eight, eight . . .

Rajinder pressed the key three times, and was prompted for a confirmation number.

Twenty-seven . . .

Then one, zero, one, seven. When the display switched to letters and asked for a security word she worried briefly that "technetium" might have been spelled with two I's, but her first guess must have been correct, because the panel switched to a color box, and she carefully tapped the screen on red, red, green, red, blue, and purple. A ding prompted the activation word, and in the steadiest voice she could muster, Rajinder said:

"Clear."

The heavy door let out a hiss as the lock disengaged, and Rajinder stepped back. The words were still repeating in her head, and she collapsed against the trolley, sliding to the floor and sitting there, trying not to be sick.

There was a whisper of movement on the other side of the door, and slowly it swung open—barely clearing Rajinder's feet—and someone came staggering out of the cell.

He was a man. A tallish man, skin so white it was almost translucent, with deep, sunken eyes and bony hands and wrists where they protruded from the end of his shapeless canvas shirt. He towered over her, yet leaned heavily on the doorframe, blinking against the light.

His head was covered by a bright green *thing* with countless tentacle-arms curling around his face and draping over his shoulders. Pale, greenish slime covered his skin, dripping from his nose and staining the neck of his shirt. Half his face was covered by a slimy green tentacle, and his one eye, when it found Rajinder, was red-rimmed and brown.

With a visible effort he unstuck his mouth and said: "'M sorry about this," and bent over her.

Rajinder cowered away, fearful of anything such a person might apologize for in advance. But the man only touched her lightly on the forehead, and the voice that had been on repeat in her mind abruptly vanished. The words *thank you* flashed briefly behind her eyes, and then all was quiet.

Save the groans of the man, who had stumbled into the hall and encountered the trolley, which slid sideways under his weight as he tried to steady himself. Rajinder grabbed it to keep from being run over, but couldn't muster the courage to help the man, much as she wished she could.

Instead she sat and stared as he staggered off down the hall. With his back to her, she could see that the tentacles converged on a round body the size of a pie pan, with a single, yellow-and-orange eye glaring at her from the center. She held the creature's gaze until the man dragged himself around the nearest corner, and the strange duo was lost to sight.

"I think 'm gonna be sick," Alister mumbled aloud, mostly out of habit.

Dave's arms tightened slightly around his shoulders.

You can make it.

"I *cannae* make it," Alister whined. His vision was blurry and the slime kept getting in his eye. He felt dizzy and weak, and feared that any moment men in hazmat suits would descend upon them. "We're in the middle of the *Canary Company*," he pointed out. "We can't just *walk out.*"

No, we cannot. But you must continue to walk for now. Walk to the end of the hall, then turn right up the stairs.

Alister nearly broke down crying at the thought of stairs, but he somehow made it to the end of the hall, and there *were* stairs, with a railing he could clutch and heave himself along. He had to stop every third or fourth step and lean his head against the wall.

We are losing time, Dave told him, and Alister felt an arm slipping down the back of his shirt. It tickled a little, making him twitch. *Your escape has been noticed. You must climb.*

"What's the *point?*" Alister moaned. His saliva felt thick and he was having trouble catching his breath.

Freedom, said Dave. *But you must summit these stairs.*

"I *can't . . .* " gasped Alister.

I can, said Dave.

This confused Alister. In his confusion he raised his head, and at the same time heard voices shouting in the hall below them. He had to move.

He *couldn't* move. His atrophied muscles and weak body were being strained to the breaking point, and he felt like he was about to crack.

Trust me, said Dave, and though his voice was silent, spoken in thoughts and feelings and images, Alister thought his tone had taken on a hint of desperation.

"Y'can't mean . . . " he began.

I can if I must, said Dave. *It appears I must do so, for both our sakes. I have no wish to go back into that tank.*

Belatedly Alister realized that Dave had just as much to fear from the Canary Company as he did. Perhaps more. That made him feel terrible all over again, for forcing Dave into this situation.

But Dave had come. Dave had come *for him.* It seemed the least he could do was cooperate.

"Do what you have to," he wheezed. "I'll try to help."

Just continue to breathe, said Dave, and all his arms clamped down at once.

For Alister, his body went fuzzy and distant, as it did when he was falling asleep. Except now it was in violent motion, running jerkily up the steps. He felt his toe stub against the metal with numb detachment, saw the two suited figures waiting for them at the top and could do nothing to stop his charge or change his course.

His muscles tingled from whatever Dave was covering him in, and he ran, so fast he did forget to breathe, barreling into the figures and tearing past them.

They let him go, because all that lay beyond was a solid wall. Alister saw the scraped metal surface rushing at him, and closed his one eye in preparation for the impact . . .

. . . and fell softly into darkness, landing on something which gave under him, like a net. His mouth opened, and he had the surreal experience of hearing Dave use his own head as a slime-to-audio translator.

"We have pursuers!" Dave announced through Alister, somehow managing to sound synthetic and irritated, even when using a human voice.

"Shifting the portal 90 degrees," said a voice with a heavy Slavic accent.

There was an expectant silence, then the Slavic voice said: "Not pursued anymore, my ten-armed friend. I take you are our man Bane?"

"Yes," said Dave through Alister, and then receded, his arms loosening, and Alister felt the sensations from his body become more immediate. His toe smarted something terrible. He groaned.

"Cut it a wee bit close there, dint ya?" asked another voice. A voice with an unmistakable Edinburgh brogue, but a slight lisp that suggested some unconventional teeth.

Alister blinked his one available eye open, and found that this darkness was nowhere near as complete as that in his cell. It was only the dimness that came from having a few racks of red LEDs as a light source. They were more than enough to illuminate the crowd of people who were leaning over Alister, their whiskery faces twitching in interest.

He was surrounded by half a dozen large, bipedal rats, each wearing a slightly modified version of a silver jumpsuit with a wide, metal collar—as if there were helmets somewhere that sealed on over them—and each with a small metal box strapped to their necks. In size they were only as big as a large cat, but that was still far bigger than any rat Alister had seen. Their faces, though perfectly murine, held a similar level of intelligence and character as Elo's, and their expressions of interest, concern, and amusement (in one) were all eerily human.

I will leave you with the Rats of Alnitak, said Dave. *I require rest now.* He curled his arms under himself, leaving only two looped around Alister's shoulders, so he could cling to the back of his neck, and Alister felt his presence recede from the cold slime that still covered his head. And with it, much of Alister's own consciousness fell dormant as well.

Things took on a dreamlike quality after that, even though Alister knew this time it was no dream. He was aware of sights and sounds and physical sensations, but they had become detached from meaning.

He saw one of the rats—a smallish, brown one with a mangled right ear—come forward and extend a small, pink paw.

"Good to meet you, Alister Bane," a voice said in his ear, and even though he didn't see the animal's mouth move, he knew it was the rat which had spoken. "The Professor has told us much about you; it is an honor to meet you at last."

"He's got a chip," said the Slavic voice from earlier.

"No time," said the Edinburgh brogue. "We'll deal with that after we rendezvous with Retrieval Bound."

"And you'll let *me* do it," said another Slavic voice, deeper and angrier.

"Then let's get him in the sling and move out!"

Alister felt himself nudged and prodded gently, and he rolled along as best he could. He was wrapped up in a heavy cloth, then dragged laboriously onto a hard surface which rolled under his weight.

"I hope ye have a strong stomach, laddie," said the Edinburgh brogue, and a weight settled on his chest.

Alister tried to answer, but his mouth had gone thick and he couldn't get it open.

"He's shutting down," muttered the big, Slavic voice, and something sharp jabbed into Alister's arm. He groaned.

"That should keep you from crashing on us until we make rendezvous . . . "

"Everyone aboard?" someone called, and another answered, from around his feet:

"Good to go, Leader!"

Then there was a lurch and they began to roll.

What came next was almost worse, in a way, than everything that had come before. Alister was aware only of a mad plunge through darkness, of a smell like old sewage, and a few places where it felt like they went upside-down. A cool, damp wind scraped at his face, chilling the places still covered by Dave's slime.

Alister didn't know much. He didn't know the rats, or how they'd gotten here, or where they were taking him. But he also knew he was no longer in his cell, and that this wasn't a dream, and that was enough to keep him awake, keep him aware, and most of all keep him present.

Agent Parthenon sat in her office, the lights dimmed to the faintest glimmer, the screen of her monitor casting her face in harsh blue. The only sound was the faint click of her fingers skittering over the keys, and occasionally the whisper of outgoing breath.

The case of 1017 bothered her, like an itch she couldn't reach. She'd had stubborn subjects before—more stubborn than Alister Bane—and they had broken. They had revealed all. That was part of why she could wear the little, golden, dog-head pin of a Company Officer.

Alister Bane—*Specimen 1017,* Parthenon had to remind herself—was not that stubborn, really. True, she'd *thought* he was because he hadn't admitted to his extra-universal travels right away, but the more she had observed him the more she got the feeling he wasn't strong enough to lie for this long.

And that was wrong. The truth *couldn't* be what he was saying (correction: it *wasn't* what he was saying), and yet he seemed to think he *was* telling the truth.

Could the Professor have wiped his memory of his previous travels? Parthenon wouldn't have put it past her, though the thought didn't strike her as being quite right.

Nothing struck her as being "quite right," and that bothered her. It bothered her because Parthenon liked being quite right. She liked it enough that she could admit she was wrong and change her opinions in order to keep on being right, or so she liked to believe. But now all these conflicting facts were giving her a simmering feeling of unease. As though there were a bigger picture she was somehow missing, and no matter how far she pulled back from the situation, she still couldn't see it.

So she went over the data they had collected again and again, while she waited for her next chance to interview the man Bane.

Alister Bane was between 22 and 24 years of age, depending on how time had passed for him since he escaped from the Company. He had had some unknown level of extra-universal experience before being abducted and brainwashed by Professor Odd—Specimen 1016—and since then had traveled to at least one of the Company's subject worlds. He had been involved in the abortion of Loyal Dog, and had also likely been present—along with the Professor—on universe F34. He left little birds made of folded paper as his calling card, and was thought to have the ability to pilot the Professor's strange ship.

Agent Parthenon shuddered at the memory of that place. It had been so alien, so incomprehensible, and she'd gotten the inexplicable feeling—which she hadn't felt since she was six and snuck into her grandmother's bedroom to go through the old woman's jewelry case—of being somewhere she wasn't supposed to be. It was almost an accident that what little data she had managed to collect had allowed Defense to generate a temporal block on spontaneous portals—but who knew how long that would last.

She'd had Alister—*Specimen 1017*—for almost six months. It was only a matter of time before the Professor came for him, she was certain. And while he was cracking, what she could glimpse of his insides didn't tally with what she'd been told to expect.

Somehow, that troubled her more than it should have.

Round and round she chased her feelings of discomfort, until she dug in her heels and put in a request to see the director. This was unusual, but Parthenon had spoken with Dr. Carver more than any other operative since she'd brought Specimen 1017 home, and she felt it was likely her request would be granted. She was in the middle of sending the forms when her comm went off in alarm.

Parthenon jumped at the sudden sound, then spun around in her chair as she recognized the tone: it was a breach alarm. Someone, somewhere, had gotten out of containment—and in her paranoid mindset she knew exactly who it was.

She paged Caruthers and Villafranka, then dispatched a unit of custodians to the hi-sec animal ward, all while in the process of putting on her encounter gear.

If Bane was out, it meant he'd had help. Which meant the Professor. Agent Parthenon could feel the blood pounding in her ears, her heart racing at the thought of meeting Specimen 1016 again, the adrenaline of the chase joined by the adrenaline of anticipation.

In a way, this crisis was a relief: there was no question of what she should do, and Parthenon threw herself at it with a will.

Events passed before Alister's eyes like the images of a video on fast-forward: jumping and jerking from one scene to the next, sometimes with large chunks of time missing in between.

They were sliding through the darkness. They were stopped. Someone put a rope in his hand and said "Hold fast to this . . ."

He was pulled along by the rope, crawling on all fours with small, warm, strong bodies on either side of his head. His hands and knees were so cold he could not feel the pain in them, though he knew it was there.

Then they were stopped. Someone said:

"Tau, Vec, get me some eyes."

A little while later, the first Slavic voice said, "Patrol pattern has changed."

"It's going to be tight getting through the orange corridor," said a new voice. They had a jagged, angular accent Alister didn't recognize.

"We'll take the next rotation—and get that chip out of our man, Dostor."

Small hands on Alister again, pulling at his shirt and feeling over the skin on his back. He tried to protest.

"Here, subdermal," said the big Slavic voice. "You might feel a small prick."

Alister wondered what it said about the state of his brain that he didn't feel a thing.

"Good man," said the big voice. "Tau, give me the runner."

Another jerk. The Edinburgh brogue said, "In the hole . . . "

"Positions," snapped the voice that seemed to be in charge.

"On deck . . . "

Movement around him.

"Click one, go," said the brogue, and they were in motion again.

Alister found himself thrust up through a circular hole. There was a corridor beyond lit by dim orange lights. The walls were made of ribby-looking iron, and wouldn't stay still.

They made him walk, somehow, though Alister had to drag himself along the wall. They got to a wall, turned a corner . . .

. . . and he was nearly knocked off his feet by a flood of information from Dave. It was the creature's way of shouting, and it left Alister's inner ears metaphorically ringing.

"Danger, danger," he gasped. "Someone coming . . . danger . . . Dave's says . . . danger . . . "

"We got a terrier," hissed the brogue, and then the dream turned into a nightmare as they were surrounded by people in white encounter suits.

Alister was shoved to the floor. The next thing he knew he was looking up as a fierce battle was fought in the space above him. Rats in silver suits shooting at the humans in white. One of them was caught in a net.

A gloved hand reached for him.

An entirely new sound ripped through the air. It was a sound Alister knew, but from a world so long ago and far away it felt like it was from another life. Yet he knew it, knew it with every fiber of his being, and in the shocking rush of joy and relief that coursed through him he began to laugh.

The hand hesitated.

And the howl came again.

The rats were joined by dogs. A big one with a flying mane of white hair tackled a human, bringing them to the floor, from which they did not rise. The dog turned, unsheathing a giant knife, and fell on the person holding the netted rat.

Weapons were fired.   Someone yelped.   Other people growled.

Large, paw-like hands grabbed Alister by the shoulders, lifted him, and began to drag him away.

"*Elevators,*" said a canned voice in his ear. "Level 12!"

"We'll not make it!"

"Oh *yes* we will," said a blessedly familiar, husky voice, and another pair of paws landed on Alister.

He was collapsing into the small, square box of an elevator. It was packed with rats—one still cutting their way out of a net—and dogs on two legs. One of them was golden with alert, triangular ears, and wore a purple jumpsuit.

The elevator stopped. They rushed out, Alister now supported by two large, humanoid dogs. Each wore a headset with a little LCD screen.

Their way was blocked by a dozen or so people in dark encounter suits. One of them was small, lithe, with an aggressive set to her shoulders. She was holding a gun trained on the golden wolf.

"You will surrender," she said, her voice amplified. "Or I will execute you *immediately.*"

Alister felt himself falling. Physically, as the dogs on either side laid him down, and mentally as well. He was falling back into the dark place, into his cell. He was there already, curled in a corner, alone. The rats were gone. The dogs were gone. Dave was . . .

Dave was still wrapped around Alister's head.

He wasn't in his cell. He was on a cold, tile floor. The rats and dogs were all around him, laying down their weapons.

Wait, said Dave.

Alister was confused.

Just wait.

Voices above him.   Someone was speaking to Agent Parthenon in a smooth, cultured voice. A dangerous voice. Peering up, one-eyed, Alister saw a tall person in a long, black coat.

Parthenon argued. The person in the black coat spoke soothingly. Eventually she threw her hands up and marched away.

Human hands took Alister, put him on a gurney and strapped him down. He'd lost track of the dogs and rats, but Dave was still with him, telling him . . .

Wait . . .

He was being pushed through hallways with bright yellow lights in the ceiling. They hurt to look at, so he closed his eyes.

He was in darkness. A gentle darkness with a faint, blue glow. Someone was peeling Dave off his head.

Alister struggled and realized he was unbound. But his arms were weak and they only flailed, uselessly.

"Easy there, Mr. Bane," said a deep, northern voice. "Your friend here is in almost as bad a state as yourself. I'm just putting him in some fresh water, and then we'll get you cleaned up."

Shakily, Alister rubbed the slime out of his eyes and blinked up at the figure leaning over him.

A broad-shouldered, dark-haired, dark-skinned woman swam into focus. Her hair was cropped in a no-nonsense cut, and she had kind lines around her eyes.

"*Watson,*" Alister whispered.

"People keep getting my name wrong," the woman sighed. "But considering the circumstances, I suppose you can be forgiven."

Alister managed a weak laugh at that, which exhausted the dregs of his strength, and promptly passed out.

* * *

He became aware of the voices before he was aware of anything else. He floated in warm, pleasant darkness, and listened.

"Is he still all there, do you know?"

Elo. That was Elo. The golden wolf in the purple jumpsuit. That had been Elo.

"Too early to say, I'm afraid," said the hearty northern voice. *Watterson,* that had been her name. Not *Watson* . . . Dr. Watterson, who'd scraped him off the pavement in the Professor's home world, when he had been on the run from the . . .

"I have high hopes, considering he was able to remain conscious for as long as he did," said a smooth, cultured, English voice. It was the kind of voice one could imagine performing Shakespeare, or announcing on the radio. It gave Alister shivers, even though it seemed the Detective was on their side this time.

"Yes, but he was stewing in your green friend's juices most of the time," said the big, Slavic voice from earlier, and this confused Alister.

Dave made sense. It was improbable, but it made sense. So did Elo's miraculous appearance. Even the Detective and Dr. Watterson, surprising though their presence was, could be believed.

But the rats? Where did they come from? And there had been other dogs, surely—and *dogs,* not *vroknaär* like Elo.

"Don't you dare blame Dave," he heard Elo snap as he struggled to open his eyes—his lids felt unbelievably heavy. "You'd never have gotten him as far as you did without his help."

"I do not think," the Detective cut in smoothly, "that exposure to Dave's, er, *presence* would make much of a difference either way, considering the mental strain he was already under."

"In any case," said Dr. Watterson, "it's no good speculating; we'll just have to see how he is when he wakes up."

At last Alister got his eyes open. He was lying in a bed with blankets up to his neck. Pressure around his left arm suggested a cuff of some kind, and there were tubes disappearing under the covers leading toward it. Following them up, he saw a bag of clear liquid suspended from what looked like a modified coat hanger.

Fluids, he thought, though his mouth was still dry and tacky.

Beyond the coat hanger the room was dim and hard to make out, except for where a group of people were clustered around a large, wooden desk. He recognized the shape of Elo's shoulders—she had her back to him—and across from her the smooth, dark head of the Detective. Beside him sat Dr. Watterson, and between them, filling in the sides of the desk, were an assortment of rats and three more dogs. Alister didn't recognize any of them, save the big white one who he'd seen tackling a man in a suit earlier. This one was leaning back and appeared to have its right foreleg in a sling.

There was no sign of Dave.

Strangely, this was what that spurred Alister into speaking. He tried to ask where Dave was, but what came out sounded more like: *"Burrvis hay-ve?"*

The crowd around the table surged into motion, all save the Detective who simply lifted his ink-black eyes and looked at Alister with a satisfied expression.

Elo was at his side in an instant, joined shortly by Dr. Watterson, with the rats crowding in curiously between and around them.

"Alister? Alister?" said Elo, nosing at him urgently. "Do you remember me, Alister?"

"Of *course* I remember you," Alister tried to say, but it came out more like, *"Occurth a revembuh ye."* He curled his lips in frustration. "Needth *water,*" he said, as clearly as he could.

"Drink slowly," said Dr. Watterson, producing a small bottle with a soft, rubber straw.

It was difficult, as Alister discovered he was very thirsty. The fluid got sucked up by his dry mouth as fast as he could suck it in, and he worked his free hand out from under the covers so he could nurse the thing more comfortably.

"Where's *Dave?*" he asked again, once his mouth felt more like a mouth and less like sandpaper with a dead slug in it.

"What? Dave?" said Elo, blinking in surprise. "He's just on the other side of you. Put him in a bucket of water, but he insisted on staying close by."

Rolling his head Alister found that there was indeed a bucket on the other side of his bed, filled to the brim with dark water. A single green tentacle with a delicate yellow tip emerged, formed itself into an equilateral triangle, and then disappeared beneath the surface again.

So Dave was all right. Alister lay back with relief.

"How do you feel?" Elo asked.

"I feel *great,*" said Alister vehemently. Now that he'd watered his parched mouth, he felt better than he had in ages. "I'm just fine."

And promptly went back to sleep.

He slept a lot for a long time. Weeks, it felt like, though it was probably only days. He would wake, drink, and sometimes eat the little yogurts and warm cereal that Dr. Watterson put before him. Elo helped him get out of bed and totter over to the bathroom when he needed to, and the sight of a proper, porcelain toilet nearly made him burst into tears.

"I'm so sorry," Elo said, one time when she was tucking him back into bed. "I had no idea it would be so long for you. We all came as fast as we could."

"It's all right," said Alister, falling back against the pillows with relief. "'m just glad ye *came.*" He slept, and if he dreamed, he didn't remember.

After a while, he began spending more time awake. He was able to sit up in bed and eat proper meals, and get to and from the bathroom on his own. The IV drip was taken out, and he got to bathe. Afterward he sat in a comfortable, squashy armchair, and listened as Elo told him some of their story.

The rats, he learned, were the result of a genetic engineering experiment, and came from the same world as the exotrain he had been on when he was kidnapped.

"Our prime member," explained the leader of the rats, who was scruffy and brown with a mangled ear and was called Autoclys, "is the Premier of Amphitrite. All seven of us swore to help Professor Odd in any way we could after she . . . uh . . . well, after she helped us out of a tight spot." He fiddled with the collar of his suit. Alister noticed that the rats, rather like the dogs, spoke through little microphones—in the rats' case, these were incorporated into metal collars that seemed imbedded in their skin. Autoclys had a pleasant, vaguely Bostonian accent, while his second-in-command, Rapsidora (larger and golden-brown) spoke with an even heavier Albian brogue than Alister.

"We were meant for assignments too dangerous for humans," explained a small, white rat who was the owner of the Edinburgh accent. Her name, it turned out, was Astatrix, and she seemed to be in charge of logistics and planning. "Professor Odd found us working a research satellite in a decaying orbit around Alnitak. We would have all died if she hadn't intervened."

In addition to Autoclys, Rapsidora and Astatrix, there was also Tauclavian (dark brown, and the Slavic voice Alister half remembered), Dostor (by far the largest of the rats; twice the size of Rapsidora and pitch black, he was the deep, Russian voice who had told Alister he was a good man. Apparently, he was their medic), and Vectarine (small and unassuming and light brown, with the jagged, angular accent Alister didn't recognize). Most of her silver suit was covered in straps and holsters for weapons, and he didn't ask what her job was.

The Rats of Alnitak, as they called themselves, had had to come to Alister's world by way of one of the naturally occurring portals in the Denallian Belt, which had taken a good deal of preparation and been incredibly dangerous.

"Don't tell your Professor we did it that way," Astatrix told Alister confidentially. "She'll blow her wig right off. There were safer ways, of course, but the Denallian Belt seemed the fastest.

"It was," said Elo. "You certainly beat us here."

Elo's group, it came out, were the descendants of the dogs they had met on Canary 6. Natalyas Boraznes-Swissgard was the youngest daughter of the medic Ksanos Boraznes from Discovery Intent, while Siimo Sant-Akit was the son of Omu Akit. Both dogs were obviously mixes—Siimo had definite St. Bernard features—while the huge white dog with the injured arm, Bursang Samoy, Alister guessed descended from a Samoyed. She seemed embarrassed to have been injured, and mumbled something about how it was an honor to meet the Good Man.

In addition to Elo, however, there was one familiar face. It greeted Alister when he woke and there was no one but Dave for company, springing into view from where its owner had been curled beside Alister's bed. Keeping watch, he realized.

"Hel*lo* there!" it grinned at him, rusty red and round with perked ears, the LCD display on its comsys making a :D.

Alister would have known that voice anywhere, even though it technically came from a computer.

"Reiji?" he asked.

"Of *course* Reiji!" said Reiji Shibo, his tightly curled tail wagging. "Couldn't trust a wolf to lead this mission all on her own! Knew we needed at least *one* original member from Discovery Intent on Retrieval Bound. Shani would have come, but we needed her on the other side to stabilize the Link, and the rest are too arthritic."

"But they're still alive?" Alister asked.

"Of *course* they're still alive!" said Reiji, rolling his eyes. "It hasn't been *that* long. And Neo Canii's got some ideas about what to do with the arthritis, too. Actually, that's partly why we're here: mostly it's for *you* of course, but if we can hunt down some of the packets our previous teams delivered to the Canary Company, well then, all the better!"

The "Link" which Reiji had so casually mentioned turned out to be the main reason that the rats had beaten the dogs: Elo and the dogs of Neo Canii had built a special ship capable of towing the comet bearing the wormhole into a stable orbit of Earth, which they managed to catch on its outward journey from the sun. Then it was a matter of making a vessel capable of traveling *through* the wormhole to Alister's world, and making sure they would come through at the right place on the other side. Luckily, they'd had someone waiting there, ready to help out.

"It was a fascinating problem," said the Detective, leaning back in a rickety wooden chair and crossing his long legs. "Calibrating the portal with such limited technology, I mean. Infiltrating the Company, pah," he rolled his eyes. "They are, it pains me to say, more paranoid than clever, and more interested in developing weapons from their stolen technology than actually studying what is out there. Disappointing, but easy enough to manipulate." He shrugged.

"Yes," said Alister, uncertainly. "But how did *you* get here?"

"Professor called us, didn't she?"   said Dr. Watterson. "Couldn't say no, not when it was for you."

Alister blinked at her. The woman looked down at her shoes.

"Dr. Watterson has been assisting me in my cases for the past year or so . . . local time, of course." The Detective told Alister, with a small, wry smile. "But I believe she would have come anyway, when she learned you'd managed to get yourself into trouble again."

Alister opened his mouth to protest, and then caught the amusement in the man's dark eyes.

The Detective was *joking* with him. Horribly, but he was trying. Alister shut his mouth, and began to reevaluate the man in front of him.

They never said exactly how they managed the jump across worlds, and neither did Dave—though no one bothered to ask. Dave, it seemed, had been obliged to leave his panvironment suit behind, but the rats managed to construct a slime-to-audio translator which, though it was accurate enough, sounded even worse than the last one.

"WOULD YOU PREFER I USE YOUR HEAD?" Dave asked, when Alister remarked on this.

Alister fell silent. He did not like to think about the time when his mind and Dave's had been so closely linked. The way it had opened doors to places beyond his comprehension made him feel dizzy. At the same time, it had given him no lasting trouble. Certainly nothing compared to the confinement and sensory deprivation he'd suffered at the hands of the Canary Company.

Which, it turned out, they had not entirely escaped. Yet.

"Technically we are still within their headquarters," said the Detective, knitting his fingers together. "However, as those are bloated and sprawling, they provide exceptional hiding places, and this way we remain close to the Link, through which we will evacuate our happy band, once Dr. Watterson deems you strong enough to make the jump."

The Link, Alister eventually found out, was the Company side of the wormhole through which the dogs of Reiji's world had been sending information, technology, and—horrifically—*other dogs* for several years. It had a rudimentary set of controls that allowed it to be harmonized with other universes that contained compatible wormholes. It was nothing compared to the Oddity, however, and Elo explained it would be like jumping blind if you didn't have someone on the other side to manipulate the receiving end.

"That's part of why Ksanos had to stay behind," she said. "She's become something of an expert on portals."

The reason they had to wait for Alister to recover was not because going through the wormhole itself was particularly traumatic—that took no time at all—but because they had to do it in a tiny ship that would then plummet to the surface of the planet, with all the associated physical strain.

The rats would join them, even though they had come from the natural portal to the Denallian Belt. This opened in high orbit around Earth as well, and though their ship was capable of making launch, it had been difficult enough landing without being noticed. They doubted a rocket taking off would go undetected.

This was explained to Alister briskly, cheerfully, as if it were not the maddest idea he'd ever heard. To get to the Link at all they'd have to sneak through the heart of the Canary Company, and though the Detective seemed confident this was possible, Alister doubted it would be so easy.

He'd been having ideas, so strange he could not have voiced them, but they lodged in his heart and grew. Then, on the first day when he was strong enough to get up and do things on his own, he was invited to sit at the large desk as they went over their grand plan of escape. The Detective had barely begun when Alister cut him off.

All he said was, "No," but it caused the entire room—humans and dogs, *vroknaär* and Dave—to go silent.

No one interrupted the Detective, except for Dave, who interrupted everyone. The rats respected him grudgingly as a peer of the Professor. The dogs because he was a human. Even Elo and Dr. Watterson let him say his piece before contradicting him.

Now all the eyes at the table turned to Alister, who was sitting across from the Detective, leaning back in his chair. Though he was aware of their combined gaze he felt no pressure or fear of judgment. A dead certainty had settled in his stomach, weighing down the doubts, and with them most of his fears as well. He had always been afraid of not knowing what to do. Now he knew what he had to do, and more importantly, he knew it could be done.

"No," he said again, shaking his head. "We can't leave, not yet."

"Pray, why not?" asked the Detective. His voice was sweet but his eyes were hard. He leaned forward, resting his elbows on the table, and laced his fingers together.

Alister was not intimidated, but he did hesitate.

During his escape he'd been so addled that he'd lost track of time, and even the things he remembered had been divorced from meaning. He'd seen *Elo* and not immediately recognized her.

Now, however, he was beginning to remember meanings without the images to go along with them.

There had been a girl. No, a *woman.* She had a kind face and she'd let him out. She'd been frightened of him, but she'd let him out. *Rajinder* was her name, he remembered because Dave had told him, and he remembered everything Dave had said like a tingle in his brain.

At the time he'd only been aware of the events as they were happening, and everything else had been pushed to the background. Now he realized he'd left a kind, compassionate person in a place where her act of heroism was more likely to be punished—and punished horribly—than rewarded.

She'd not only let a specimen escape, she'd come into contact with *Dave.* And if simply stepping outside the universe was enough to get them interested in Alister, what would contact with Dave entail?

No, Alister couldn't leave things as they were. Not with Rajinder possibly suffering a torture as bad as his own. Not with the Canary Company as it was: a huge, inhumane organization that spread its disruption across multiple worlds. Not when it would chase him—now more fiercely than ever—for the rest of his life.

Something the Professor had said came back to him in meaning and intent, though he could no longer remember the exact words. It made him smile, though, because he knew now how to explain himself.

"You remember how we came back?" he asked the Detective. "That time you were hunting the Professor? After we'd got clean away from you, remember how we came back?"

"I could not forget even if I wished to," said the Detective with a sigh.

Alister nodded. "The Professor said it was the only thing to do. Because otherwise you'd just keep chasing us. So she had to go back and explain."

"Alister," said Elo, and the warning tone in her voice told him she knew what he was thinking. It didn't faze him.

"Well," he forged on. "This is like that. Only bigger. Even more important, because the Canary Company has been making life miserable for a lot of people, across a lot of different worlds."

"What are you steering for, Mr. Bane?" asked Autoclys, his whiskers twitching.

Alister looked around the table and said, quite simply: "We're not running away. We're going to take the Canary Company apart, and *then* we'll leave."

"Are you *mad?*" Elo barked, but Alister saw how Reiji perked his ears, how Rapsidora and Tauclavian looked at him almost hopefully, and how the Detective got an expression of surprised respect on his face.

"Yes," he said, mildly. "I am a little angry. *Listen,* Elo. The Canary Company's been stealing from other worlds—things and knowledge and *people*—for who knows *how long.* And what are they doing? Turning their knowledge into weapons. They're not just getting ready for this universe to become multiplicity-aware—they're getting ready to take it to *war.*"

"Yes, I *know,*" said Elo, pinning her ears back. "But here? Now? We are not *prepared!*"

"Aren't we?" said Alister, looking around at the table. "Because it seems to me we've got *two* crack strike teams, the cleverest, most dangerous man I've ever met, a *very* good doctor"—Dr. Watterson snorted but did not interrupt—"*you,*" he jabbed a finger at Elo, "and *Dave,* and we're *already inside.* I'd say if anyone can do it, *we* can."

He sat back, folded his arms, and looked defiantly around the table. A small acorn of terror had lodged itself in his dead certainty, but this was squashed when he saw the way the Detective was smiling at him.

It was Natalyas who spoke first, her clear, comsys voice cutting into the silence like a sword.

"I did always wonder what happened to Discovery Intent's predecessors," she said, her mouth curling into a slight snarl.

"Never liked bullies, of any species," said Autoclys, and all the rats nodded.

"I do not customarily accept a new commission on top of one not yet completed," said the Detective with a shrug. "But I suppose in this case we may consider it an *extension*."

"Oh for—" Elo threw up her paws. "Alister, this is *not* what the Professor sent us to do!"

"The Professor sent you all to rescue me," Alister said. "Which you *did*. Thanks. And this is what I think we should do, because it needs to be done, and we've got a chance to do it."

Elo gave him an exasperated look, but Alister was only halfway paying attention. Dave had slipped a single, cool tentacle over his hand, and he felt the word appear soundlessly in the back of his head, giving him all the assurance he would ever need.

Yes.

For Rajinder Ayoadé the following two weeks were the most upsetting she'd ever had—including the bad spell after she and Damien had broken up and the time her cat had gone missing.

It turned out the specimen she'd let out had been of even higher priority than she first imagined, and far from getting fired—though she was certain that was just a matter of time—she was given interview after interview. These culminated with an actual agent coming down from Acquisitions to put her through the meta-scan, which was a machine that was said to be able to read your mind. It gave Rajinder a headache, and the uncomfortable feeling that they had not got what they wanted from her. This was borne out by the fact that she was not allowed to go home, but was escorted to "guest quarters" just a floor above the hi-sec animal ward. Rajinder knew she was essentially a prisoner, and worried herself to sleep every night over what her fate would be.

There had been whispers about what the Company did about security breaches, internal leaks, or plain old incompetence. Rajinder had always been low enough on the food chain she'd thought herself below such punishments, yet now the possibility of being "stripped" and tossed back into the world without a penny or a memory to her name—if they bothered to give her a new one—was a distinct possibility.

Rajinder lay in bed, her mind running circles around all the terrible possibilities her future held, when she heard a skittering from the ceiling, and the light fixture above her bed began to unscrew itself.

She watched it curiously, wondering if she'd gone mad. Then something small and metallic was lowered on a thin piece of wire, until it hung at what would have been eye level if she stood up.

"Well, go on, *take* it," said an annoyed Russian voice.

Automatically Rajinder glanced around to see if she was in view of the surveillance cameras. She couldn't see any, but she assumed she was. Privacy was something only the Director of the Canary Company could afford. (No one had seen him in years: Rajinder thought he must be using up all the privacy allowed in their area, which was why no one else had any.)

"I haven't got all day," said the voice, and the small, metallic thing—which looked a bit like an earplug—began to retreat toward the ceiling.

Rajinder pushed herself up off the bed and snatched it off the wire with a small *pop.*

"Now what?" she asked the light fixture. It wobbled, as if being screwed back into position.

"Put it in your ear," came the voice, now rather muffled. "Do what the good man says."

It sounded a little sarcastic, but Rajinder obediently put the little bud into her ear, where it settled comfortably. She was aware of a faint hum of static, and then a familiar, Albian voice said:

"Hello . . . *am* . . . Rajinder?"

"That's me," said Rajinder, her heart pounding in her chest.

"Right. Good," said the voice. "Okay, give us a wee moment, Rajinder, and we'll have you out in no time. Are you wearing sensible shoes?"

"I—what?" said Rajinder.

"Sensible shoes," repeated the voice, patiently. "And trousers, preferably. You might have to do a spot of running."

Rajinder looked down at her Company-issued canvas trousers and thick, leather boots which she hadn't bothered to take off.

"Yes," she said, still uncertain.

"Good," said the voice in her ear. Then it went on, apparently speaking to someone else. "I have contact. Let's blow those comm lines."

Agent Parthenon sat in her office, replaying the reel from the Jr. Tech's meta-scan over and over again. It didn't tell them much they hadn't already been able to guess, or see from the security cams: Ayoadé had clearly been the victim of a chemical attack and had been coerced into opening the door. How she had gotten the release code was still a mystery, but Parthenon suspected it had something to do with Incongruity M87, which had inexplicably accompanied Specimen 1017 when he exited the cell.

Parthenon chewed on the end of her braid. It was moot now. Agent Barrow had taken them into custody, and from what she knew of the man, she didn't envy them. Far from it.

The truth was, Agent Parthenon kept replaying the reel purely because it was the most recent recorded images she had of Alister Bane.

Alister Bane, who was strong and weak at the same time. Who broke, but cleanly. Who was, when you peeled back his extraordinary history, just a plain, decent young man thrust into a situation far beyond his grasp. Who had made a spirited if ill-thought-out attempt at escape, only to be recaptured.

Agent Parthenon had not been permitted updates on his status since he'd passed out of her jurisdiction, but her thoughts kept going back to him, and with these thoughts her feeling of uneasiness grew.

The Canary Company was necessary. It did good work. It did not make mistakes.

Then what was Alister Bane? Was the fault with Parthenon? No, she had performed her duties perfectly. The fault lay further back, further up, with the person who had first labeled Alister Bane as Specimen 1017, High Priority Asset.

Agent Parthenon shut off the reel and stood up. She left her office and got on the lift up to Administration. She didn't make an appointment. Making an appointment would give her a chance to change her mind. Better to do it now, and get it over with.

Whatever else could be said of her, Agent Parthenon faced her problems head on with all guns blazing.

Two minutes after Rajinder put in the earbud her door sprang open a crack.

"You're clear," said the voice in her ear. "Go through it. Turn left."

Rajinder did so, and was just past the lifts when one of them chimed arrival.

"Corridor on your right, take it," came the instructions, and Rajinder darted down the indicated passage. She'd barely gone ten feet, however, when she ran into a locked door.

"Be ready to enter the combination," said the voice in her ear. "Do you have access to the control pad?"

"Yes," said Rajinder. "But it's bio-locked."

"Bio-locks are overridden. You just need the command code. Ready?"

Rajinder's fingers hovered over the glowing panel. Behind her, she could hear a pair of custodians getting out of the lift. They were speaking together, but quietly.

"Yes," she whispered.

The voice in her ear gave it to her, and she entered it as quickly as she could. The door *dinged* happily, and slid open.

It revealed a tall, brown-haired, pale man with a gaunt, bony face and a close-cropped beard. His hair was a dark fuzz covering his head, and his eyes had not lost the wide, haunted look. He was just in the act of removing a small, silver earbud—the mate of the one Rajinder still wore—and slipping it into the pocket of the neat, black shirt he was now wearing.

There was a shout from behind her.

The man leaned forward, took her lax hand, pulled Rajinder through the door, and slammed it shut behind her.

"Hallo," he said, not letting go of her hand. "Gotta run now."

They did. Down the hall, around a corner, and through another door that sprang open at their approach. It led to a maintenance-access stairwell, and together they started climbing. Despite huffing like a steam train, Rajinder couldn't stop the flow of questions that streamed out of her.

"Who are you—really?"

"I'm just a bloke—*really*," the man replied, tugging her around a landing. "My name is Alister Galross Bane, I'm from Lochgalrosshead, Alba, and this has all been a huge mistake."

"What are you doing *now?*"

"We're trying to stop them making any more mistakes."

By "them" Rajinder assumed he meant the Company, but that didn't explain who he meant by . . .

"Who is *we?*" she demanded.

"Me, the rats—they've infiltrated security control—the dogs, Elo, and the Detective and Dr. Watterson, of course. Oh, and Dave!"

He cut himself off, as if listening to some unheard voice. Rajinder guessed he had another bud in his other ear, because a moment later he cursed, and said—to apparently no one— "What do you *mean* Dave's vanished?"

A short beat.

"Well, did he get the bloody thing shut off?"

Another beat. The man Bane groaned.

"Best thing to do is finish it quickly, then—I'm halfway to Rajinder's extraction point, where is Retrieval Bound with the Director's office?"

They had slowed their climb as they spoke, and were almost at a sedate walk. But Bane's hand was like a metal clamp on Rajinder's wrist, and his eyes darted about the stairwell, so wide the whites showed all around the dark brown irises.

Below them a door banged open. There was shouting.

"South stairs are compromised," he informed his unseen allies. "I'm aborting the climb. I can make it to Retrieval Bound if you open the blue passage. Just *do* it Tauclavian—*now!*"

They reached another landing while the man spoke, and the door out of the stairwell sprang open for them. It revealed a passage that Rajinder had never seen before in person, but she knew it from studying surveillance footage when she was in training.

They were in the upper levels of the Company's main tower, where the senior agents and the Director himself kept their offices. They were pelting along a corridor lit by actual daylight from actual windows. They came to an intersection, where the man turned left and continued running.

"Meant to get you out, first," he panted as they ran. "Sorry 'bout the detour. But I figure safest place for you is probably with the dogs. They'll take care of you while the Detective and I deal with the Director."

A door along the corridor banged open at their approach, and a long, furry arm reached out. Alister grabbed its paw-like hand and swung them both through the door, where they nearly collided with an almost human-sized dog with a bushy, white mane, holding something that looked like a submachine gun slung under one arm.

Here, at last, they stopped, and Rajinder had to double over panting, but she still managed to stare at the people who filled the room.

They were, she was certain, *people*. Even if they looked like dogs. They walked on their hind legs, their feet flat on the ground, with square shoulders and fingers on their hands. Their faces were completely canine, but they all wore headsets with microphones and liquid-crystal displays perched over one cheek.

There were four of them: the big white one, a smaller reddish one, a jowly tan one, and a slender white-and-cream dog with a narrow, knifelike face. And there was a fifth one who walked on her toes, who did not wear a headset, and whose fur was a brilliant gold. Something about the keenness of her face and the length of her ears suggested *wolf* rather than dog, but Rajinder had no time to ponder the details. An agent walked into the room at that point, followed by a burly woman in a neat, tweed suit.

"What happened?" the man Bane asked, letting go of Rajinder at last.

"Who is *this?*" asked the agent—who, Rajinder began to realize, probably wasn't *actually* an agent. Even if he *was* wearing the Company uniform, all black with a silver badge, and a cold, cruel expression.

"This is Raji—Rajinder," said Bane. "The one who let us out. What *happened?*"

The man who was not an agent shrugged. "Dave infiltrated Defense, and was about to start work on their exterior manipulator, when he abruptly cut contact with us and vanished. I can assure you he was *not* captured, but other than that, he could be anywhere."

The man Bane sighed heavily. "Where are we with the director's door?" he asked.

"Ninety-percent cracked," came a voice from near the floor, and Rajinder blinked down at the largest rat she'd ever seen. A rat in a silver jumpsuit with an assortment of bladed weapons strapped to its back, and a peculiar tablet clutched in its paws. "This would be going faster if I didn't have to keep him from noticing. Do we really have to surprise him? At this point?"

Bane pursed his lips. "Yes," he said, grimly.

They were picking the lock on the Director's inner office door, Rajinder realized, stunned. The not-agent came and stood to one side of the door, while the man Bane took up position opposite him. The golden wolf came and crouched by his elbow, while the burly woman in the tweed suit stood behind the not-agent. She had a small, silver pistol, pointed resolutely at the floor.

"You might want to have a seat over here," said a pleasant, clear voice at her shoulder. Rajinder jerked around to find the pale dog with the narrow face looking at her earnestly. She let it guide her over to the secretary's desk, where the dog briskly picked up the chair that had been knocked over, and settled Rajinder into it.

From where she sat she had a good view of the outer door— the dogs had set up a sort of barricade in front of it and taken up defensible positions behind overturned cabinets and chairs— but she had to crane her neck around to see the door to the inner office, and so she heard more than saw what happened next.

The little rat by the floor said: "Got it. Any time now, gents."

The not-agent looked across at the man Bane, at the gold wolf, and finally over his shoulder at the burly woman with the gun. He nodded once.

"All right then," said the rat, hitting a button on her tablet. "Have at 'em!"

There was a faint *pop* and the door jerked open a crack. The not-agent reached out and pulled it open the rest of the way, just in time for the golden wolf to dive inside, out of sight. It was followed closely by the not-agent, the burly woman, and finally the man Bane.

There were raised voices inside. Rajinder heard the Director's voice—higher and squeakier than it had sounded in public announcements—shouting for someone named Parthenon to *do* something.

Bane gave a startled shout, quickly cut off. The wolf growled. There was a quiet exchange of voices, a muffled struggle, and then the hiss of a door opening and closing. After that there was silence, and Rajinder heard a deep, northern voice say, quite distinctly:

"Bloody *hell.*"

Parthenon's mind was a blank slate, wiped clean of everything but the sudden need for action. The situation still seemed surreal to her, even as she felt the man's neck under her hand, the weight of his body pressing into the muzzle of her gun, the drag of his feet as she walked him backward into the Director's bolt-hole.

It had been dreamlike, gaining entrance to the inner office, seeing the Director face to face, and then *arguing* with him of all things. Agent Parthenon had never, in all her years of service, ever imagined disagreeing with the Director, let alone taking him to task over a difference of opinion. Yet this she had done, and done with a glad agony, like the lancing of an infected wound, and then . . .

. . . then the door had burst open, and in the manner of dreams there was Specimen 1017—along with Agent Barrow and his assistant, and the golden wolf from the train.

She'd heard the Director's commands only distantly, for her mind had already assessed the situation and her body was taking action.

Specimen 1017 was the most physically vulnerable, so she'd gone straight for him. Got him in a choke hold and used him as a living shield while the Director opened the door to his bolt-hole, dragged him in after him, and only when the door was sealed did she reassess her actions.

The bolt-hole was small, but well fortified—an oblong room with a bunk and a control station, a ration cabinet, a first-aid cupboard, and a small shower stall. Clearly, it was prepared for long-term use, but only by a single individual. The three of them would not be able to remain here for long.

The Director was raving, pulling at his short, curly, black hair. Shouting something about traitors and the Professor. The *Professor,* he was certain, was behind all of this.

"Oh *sure*," said Specimen 1017, dryly. *"Now* you ask about the Professor."

Director Carver looked like his eyes were going to pop out of his head, he was so furious and frightened.

"Of *course* the Professor!" he practically screamed. "That's why we're interested in *you,* of course! You're the only one we've got that has had prolonged contact with her!"

"Really?" said Specimen 1017. He sounded unimpressed. "I thought you wanted to know about me nonexistent extra-universal travels as a child!"

Parthenon let the conversation wash over her. The blank slate of her mind was filling with urgent thoughts, all jostling for position, all demanding her attention.

Wanting Specimen 1017 for his contact with Specimen 1016 was understandable, but it did not explain why he'd been listed as *partially* human at the very beginning. The only reason that Parthenon could see, if he had not, in fact, been a multiversal traveler at the time, was that listing him as partially human would have made it easier to process him for archival.

And if he had *not* been a multiversal traveler at the time, it meant that the Canary Company, the guard dog of her world, had turned on one of its own.

Agent Parthenon had done a number of things, she knew, that were not entirely nice, all in the name of the Canary Company, with the understanding that everything the Company did was for the benefit of its home world. To protect the innocents still living under the assumption that their universe was the only one, safe and unassailable from the vast multiplicity.

Of which, she felt now with creeping certainty, Specimen 1017—*Alister Galross Bane*—had been.

Her hand tightened unthinkingly on his neck, and the man broke off what he had been saying with a cough.

"I am going to ask you one more time," she whispered in his ear, ignoring the Director, who was practically steaming. "What were your extra-universal travels prior to meeting Specimen 1016?"

Alister Bane rolled his eyes around and glared at her. His face took on a resigned expression, and he said, in a bland, dead tone:

"Once, I found a magic door that led to a planet with huge dandelion flowers, only instead of seeds they had these moths that flew off and pollinated the other plants. *There.* Happy now?"

Agent Parthenon didn't move. Her body felt frozen, her mind like a river rushing beneath a frozen surface, as she stared at his face in horror.

Agent Parthenon could read a person well enough to know when they were lying, provided she had references to work from. It had been difficult to read Alister Bane on account of the fact that she hadn't been able to catch him in a flat-out lie. And now she knew why: up until that moment, everything he'd said had been the truth.

This new bit about going to a planet with giant dandelion flowers, *that* was as plain a lie as Parthenon could ever hope to see.

And if everything else he'd said had been the truth . . .

In the distance she could hear the Director shouting, but he—and whatever he was saying—suddenly seemed unimportant. What was important was the man currently trembling under her grip, brave and frightened and weak and strong all at once. One of theirs. One of *hers*. One of the people she'd signed on to *protect*.

"I am *not* a villain," she hissed at him through gritted teeth, whether for the man's benefit or her own she was uncertain.

Alister Bane dared turn his head to gaze back at her, anguished and sad and so *disappointed* it made Parthenon furious.

"Then stop *acting* like one," he whispered. He sounded more annoyed than anything else.

It was really as simple as that, Parthenon realized with a mix of relief and horror.

The ice inside her mind broke, and thoughts and feelings came pouring through. It shook her, and she ripped her hands from the man, pushing him away while she tried to grapple with the sudden surge of emotions.

Director Carver was shouting at her, and reluctantly Parthenon spared enough attention to translate the noise into words.

"*Parthenon!*" he bellowed, "I *told* you to terminate Specimen 1017! He's more trouble than he'll ever be worth!"

Parthenon froze, anger and betrayal and despair warring with her cold training, leaving her suspended. In that instant she was neither Agent Parthenon nor the girl who had signed up to be a superhero so many years ago. She was a complicated tangle of history and feelings blown sky high and now falling, tumbling, toward a new person she wasn't quite sure of yet.

She felt the impact of the projectile before she felt the pain. It nearly knocked her leg out from under her, and she staggered, just as another hit her square in the stomach. The next thing she knew she was on the ground, her entire lower half alive with pain, and worse, the particular knowledge that an artery had been lacerated. She stared blankly at the Director, who was re-aiming the hand rifle he'd pulled from the rations cabinet so that the muzzle was pointed straight at her head.

Wait, Parthenon thought. *I'm not me yet . . .*

It was a strange feeling, going from having a gun pressed into his spine, to seeing the owner of said gun getting shot. There was no explosion of blood or flesh, just the loud *bang* of the weapon firing, and then Agent Parthenon was staggering. Another *bang* and she doubled over, collapsing to the floor. Alister could only stare in mute horror when the blood finally came, pouring alarmingly from the wound in her left leg.

Only when he saw the Director raising his gun a third time was he able to act, and then it seemed only natural to charge at the man, grab his gun hand and turn it to the wall, sending the third shot into the first-aid cupboard—which was a grotesque sort of irony, Alister thought—and try to wrestle it from his grasp.

Neither of them were trained fighters, that much was clear, and Alister had the advantage of height. The Director still held the gun, however, and it went off twice more while Alister tried to twist it out of his grip. It was a miracle neither of them were hit.

Then, in the sudden way things seemed to be happening, the man went limp in Alister's arms, and he looked up to find himself nose to nose with Agent Parthenon, her dusky face gone greenish and stretched with pain, and then the three of them were slowly crumpling to the floor, collapsing in a messy pile of limbs and blood.

At last Alister managed to wrench the small, evil rifle away from the Director, and he threw it blindly across the floor.

There was no need. The man—the neat, dark-skinned man who had once led him through the bowels of the Canary Company, into an office not unlike this one—lay limp and motionless under him. Even before Alister could check for breath or pulse he knew he must be dead: there was a mean, thick knife sticking out the back of his neck near the base of his skull, and Parthenon's gloved hand still clung weakly to the handle.

The woman lay back against the floor, and though she still breathed, it was with quick, shallow breaths, and her lips had gone bluish.

Alister tried to get up, and nearly slipped in the puddle of blood that had spread under them even in that short time. So he shoved the late Director aside and crawled over Parthenon, feeling clumsily for the wound in her leg, which seemed to be the source of the blood.

"I'm sorry," he found himself saying, for lack of anything better. "I'm sorry. I'm sorry." Sorry for not knowing how to stop the bleeding. Sorry for not being able to take a gun away from a crazy man. Sorry for . . . well, sorry for getting her shot, really.

S'all . . . s'all right," said Parthenon, her voice weak and slurred. She batted limply at Alister's shoulder. "Don't . . . don't bother."

"I have medics on my team," Alister said. "One of 'em's a really good doctor. She'll patch you up no problem. Let me put something on this, they'll get that door open in no time."

He crawled around, trying to reach the first-aid cupboard while still keeping pressure on the leg wound, and found he couldn't reach. He paused, momentarily stumped, and Parthenon gave him a pained smile.

"You're a good man, Mr. Bane," she said, unsticking her mouth with visible effort. "Anyone ever tell you that?"

Reluctantly Alister crawled back over to her and placed both hands on the leg wound. Blood kept seeping up through his fingers, but he tried not to think about it.

"They might have mentioned it, yeah," he said.

Parthenon blinked at him, her eyes coming briefly into focus. They were a remarkable tint of hazel, Alister realized. He'd never noticed before.

"You've gotta . . . gotta promise me something," said the bleeding woman, clearly fighting to stay conscious.

"Aye?" said Alister, figuring he probably owed it to her.

"Take care . . . take care of the Company," she said, regarding him with dim gravity.

"Sorry?" said Alister, certain he hadn't heard right.

"S'important, what we do. What we've been *s'posed* to be doing. Guard dog. Watch dog. Like Cerberus. Canary Company, like *canii*, like dogs. Important that . . . that we're here. Big multiverse. Not friendly."

"Not all of it," Alister protested.

"People here need looking after," Parthenon went on, ignoring him. "You got to look after my boys. Caruthers, Villafranka. Can't let people like Carver lead them. They go . . . go wrong in the head. Wrong like me. Lose themselves."

"That's not what I—" Alister began, and then stopped. Agent Parthenon's eyes had unfocused. How long would it take Vectarine to unlock the reinforced door?

"Okay," Alister said, gratified when Parthenon seemed to focus on him. "Okay, I'll . . . I'll look after them. I'll take care of it. All of it."

Parthenon smiled blearily at him.

"Know you can do it," she said, letting her head fall back. "Know you can . . . the Professor . . . she taught you things. Taught you good."

"Aye," said Alister, sliding himself up so he could keep eye contact, but Parthenon had shut hers. "Parthenon?" he tried.

A flutter. A flash of hazel.

"Name's Octavia," the woman mumbled.

"Octavia? Please, you've got to stay awake."

Octavia Parthenon blinked up at him and frowned. "I'm sorry, Mr. Bane," she whispered. "Tell her . . . tell her I wish we could have met . . . in a different life. Different circum . . . stances . . . "

"Well, it is an infinite multiverse," Alister said with forced cheer. "Perhaps, in some other time and place, you will."

"That'll be . . . nice," said Octavia Parthenon, her eyes drifting shut and her face going lax. And though Alister called her name, shouted, even gently shook her shoulders, she never opened them again. Her breath slowed to a gurgling hiss, so faint that when the door came open at last (with a small *bang*: Vectarine had had to resort to slightly more violent methods) and Dr. Watterson hurried inside, the first thing she did was put on a plastic mask and breathe into the unconscious agent's mouth. She handed one to the Detective, who took over alternately blowing air into Parthenon and pressing firmly on her chest, while Dr. Watterson inspected the leg wound. At the look on her face, Alister knew it was all over. Still, they called in Dostor, and between the three of them they worked for another fifteen minutes, before Dostor sat back on his haunches and shook his head.

"We are literally beating a dead human," he announced. "Call it."

"Who was she?" Dr. Watterson asked Alister, tired and concerned.

Alister could only shrug.   "Her name was Octavia Parthenon," he said. "Beyond that, I'm not really sure."

He got up and walked over to the control console. It was bio-locked, but a little help from Dr. Carver's body soon had him accessing all the man's files—and the communication system for the entire Company's complex.

"Security," he said, and was gratified when he heard Tauclavian's voice respond immediately.

"Don't scare me like that, Bane!"

"How are things with you?"

"All good and quiet over here. Still in control. But Vec says you had some excitement?"

"You could say that," said Alister. "Look, do me a favor, I'm going to make a Company-wide announcement. Can you, like, do a little something, make sure everyone's listening?"

"*Da, da,*" said the rat. "Easy."

"Mr. Bane," said the Detective, looming over Alister's should like a tall, disapproving shadow. "What are you doing?"

Alister pursed his lips, took a deep breath, and squared his shoulders. "The right thing, I hope," he said.

Crouched under the secretary's desk, Rajinder was surprised when she heard the musical cue signaling a public announcement. It surprised the dogs, too, who had temporarily relaxed when Elo reported that Alister was alive and unharmed, and that Carver was dead.

Rajinder was still reeling from that, even though she had no love for the man, when a voice that was not the Director's spoke where before only the Director's had been heard.

"*Employees of the Canary Company,*" it said. "*This is your director speaking. I would like to apologize for any disruption our recent security exercise might have caused in your work. You will be glad to hear that it was a success, and things will now return to normal. However, in the coming days I plan to execute a complete overhaul of this company, to better facilitate our ultimate mission: to protect our universe. Please use this time of change to reassess your own goals and work habits, as we work together to right old wrongs, and clean out the corners which have become unfortunately cluttered with unnecessary projects. Thank you.*"

*   *   *

Alister leaned back from the microphone and let out a deep breath. His hands were shaking, but there was a lightness in his chest, and a certainty in his gut, that told him he was doing the right thing. Then there was a weight on his shoulder, and he looked up to find the Detective gazing down at him.

"Well done, Mr. Bane," he said quietly. "Well done, indeed."

Alister rubbed the fuzz on the back of his head. "I hope so," he said.

There was a startled gasp, and they both looked around to find the woman, Rajinder, peering in at the mayhem and gore with a look of horror on her face.

"Sorry about the mess," said Alister, and her eyes jerked toward him. "You're not in any trouble, though. In fact," he added, with a burst of inspiration. "Would you like a job?"

It was a frighteningly easy process, taking over the Canary Company. The Director had become so much of a recluse in the time since Alister and Professor Odd had made their improbable escape—which had been *five years* of native time, Alister was stunned to discover—that it was possible for Alister, who neither looked nor sounded like the late man, to slip into his shoes with only a modest amount of deception. Tauclavian set up a voice filter for him that made him sound like Dr. Carver when he made his company-wide announcements, and for everything else he needed done in person he sent the Detective, whose false identity as Agent Barrow turned out to be invaluable. Then it was just a matter of sorting through the frightful mess that the Company had become, pruning off the bad bits—like Dr. Carver's old secretary, who had been absent for the entire confrontation thanks to a little trickery by Astatrix and so could be safely reassigned without having his head meddled with—and promoting good, new growth.

One of the first things Alister did in this regard was make Rajinder his new secretary, though the woman refused that title.

"Call me your Executive Assistant," she said, her dark eyes glittering. "I like that."

It turned out she also liked organizing things even more than Alister, and soon he left her on her own to sort through the Company's rosters. She had, after all, first-hand experience with most of these people and was a better judge of their characters than he.

This left Alister free to settle some pressing unfinished business—namely, what had become of Dave.

The creature had last been heard from on his way to Defense, which was a wing of the Company devoted to extra-universal protection, and where they suspected the machine interfering with the Oddity's portal was located. Dave, it appeared, had found the machine, locked down the room it was in, and then disappeared. When Vectarine finally managed to get the door open the room was deserted save for the machine, which Dave had smeared with slime that said *Do not touch*, and a small puddle of slime in the middle of the floor.

Alister knelt there, in front of the black, button-studded face of the machine, and cautiously dipped a finger in the puddle.

Dave's voice—his real voice—crept into his mind, but faintly. As though he were listening to a recording left on someone's answering machine.

Apologies, Alister. And Odd, when she arrives. I am unable to complete my mission, and it may be a long duration before we see one another again. Unforeseen complications have arisen which require my presence elsewhere. I will find you later. I exist . . .

. . . then there was a complicated bundle of feelings and tastes that Alister could not put into words. He stood up, feeling dizzy and a little heartbroken. He had the slime scooped into a small jar, sealed, and ever after carried it around with him, since Dave obviously meant the Professor to hear it as well.

He was laid surprisingly low by the loss of Dave, even though, as Elo pointed out, *no one* on their team had *actually* died. This was true, Alister realized with a stunned sense of relief. Aside from Bursang's strained shoulder, the dogs of Retrieval Bound had suffered no injuries, and all the rats had come through unscathed. Alister clung to this comforting fact, since the more he delved into the workings of the Company, the more depressing it became. When they found the vault that housed the previous reports and artifacts from the dogs' world, Reiji threw a fit. There, alongside his world's best technology, were the preserved corpses of his predecessors. Many of whom, it was clear, had made it through the portal alive, only to have died as a result of the experiments later performed on them.

Less disturbing, but even more troubling, was what Alister found when he had all the cells in the high-security animal ward opened up: animals from other universes, many of whose species he did not recognize. The Company had kept scrupulous records of where each animal had come from, but since most were in no condition to be sent back, this was of little use to Alister. He had to train up a new batch of techs to care for them properly, while he and the Detective set about recalibrating the Link so that, once rehabilitated, they could each be returned to their respective universe.

One specimen, however, they did not return. They found it in the robotics wing, and Alister immediately set Tauclavian and Vectarine the task of dismantling it and destroying the components. He then had to go and rage at Elo about it.

"An *Antimovian!*" he gasped, burying his face in his hands. "They'd got a bloody *Antimovian* locked up in there! Sure, it was deactivated—*or so they thought*—but really, that's just asking for trouble!"

"This whole place was asking for trouble," said Elo, darkly. She was still angry on the dogs' behalf over what had become of their previous Canary 6 teams.

Some things they found, however, were more amusing than disturbing. Alister went through his own file with a wry grin on his face. Someone—probably Dr. Carver—had worked very hard to make him look a lot more dangerous than he was. There he found both of the folded paper birds he had left for the Company—the one he left in his abandoned dorm room, and the one he'd sent with Discovery Intent's modified package—and these he kept on his desk in the Director's inner office, while the seed of an idea sprouted in his head, cautiously unfurling delicate, new leaves.

The dogs went home after the last of the alien animals had been returned. Alister accompanied them to the Link—which was an arc of metal and wires over a worn concrete slab with a giant red X painted on its surface. He hugged each dog before they climbed into their little space pod—since their side of the portal opened in high orbit around Earth—but Reiji gripped his hands and made him promise to come for a visit.

"You'd be something to show my great-grandpups," he said. "Which is something I'll actually get to do, thanks to all the lost tech we're bringing back."

Alister smiled but made no promises. They retreated a safe distance while Elo activated the Link, and in a flash of blinding light, the ship vanished.

The rats stayed on for almost six whole months after the surprise coup. Alister needed their help running the security system, which controlled every aspect of the physical buildings the Company inhabited. Once he and Rajinder had picked out a trustworthy team of new recruits and got them trained up, however, the rats went home as well. They didn't leave through the Link, but on their own ship, which as Alister now had full control of the Company and could tell the governments of Earth not to mind the rocket they were sending into orbit, they were able to do.

"If we see the Professor, we'll let her know what's happened," Autoclys assured him, and Alister had to be satisfied with that.

To someone working at the Company the shift from militant to scientific, from defense oriented to *study* oriented, came about gradually and, it seemed, naturally. Few people were actually fired, but there was a lot of reorganization of personnel. Many of the operatives found themselves assigned to boring tasks, while many techs got surprise promotions. A lot of the custodians left of their own accord, disappointed in what the Company was becoming but too disheartened to start up again somewhere else. They drifted back into a world that had been kept ignorant of their work, and found themselves under appreciated and unbelieved. Meanwhile, new blood kept flowing in, until the roster of employees at the Company was almost unrecognizable from what it had been a year before.

It was at that time that the Director announced a small cosmetic change. The Company's name remained the same, but their logo got an overhaul. The two Cs stayed, but the three-headed, winged dog was removed, and in its place appeared a small bird, its wings outstretched. In metal it was simple relief, but on the Company stationary, and anywhere else it appeared in color, the bird was bright yellow.

The Detective left shortly after that, along with Dr. Watterson. It was a small relief to see him go, Alister had to admit, even though he would miss the doctor. The Detective was invaluable as an ally, but Alister could never shake the feeling that he was planning something else. That he was altogether *unsafe* to be around. Yet he was perfectly amicable when they said their good-byes, and Alister found himself thanking the man wholeheartedly.

"And, if you see the Professor . . . " Alister began, and trailed off.

"Yes, yes, of course," said the Detective. "I will, of course, relay the glad news. I fancy, however, that the next time my path crosses hers will also be the next time my path crosses *yours*. Good day, Mr. Bane."

Alister watched on the security video as the Detective and Dr. Watterson walked out the front doors of the Company, got into a waiting cab, and drove away.

Then it was just Alister and Elo—and Rajinder, who took over more and more of the day-to-day running of the Company. She and Alister had many long talks about this, while Elo got more and more impatient.

It had *been* a whole *year.* The Professor *should* have turned up by now. But the days crept past, and no magic doors opened. In his heart, Alister began to fear that they never would. Nevertheless he made arrangements that, should any magic doors happen to open, and should a person resembling the since-deleted description of Specimen 1016 come striding into the halls of the Company, all would be ready for her.

Epilogue

PROFESSOR ODD LOOKED AROUND THE OUTER OFFICE with new appreciation once Alister finished recounting the events of the past two years. She got up. She walked across and bent over Rajinder's desk, squinting at the main monitor. She went to a window and peered out. Then she turned around, clasped her hands behind her back, and inhaled deeply.

"Well," she said, and seemed not to know what to say next.

"*Well,*" she repeated, her forehead creasing.

"We-ell . . . " she said, chewing on her lower lip.

Alister began to feel nervous. He thought he'd matured a lot in the two years since last he'd set eyes on the Professor, but seeing her again—and so clearly *just* as he remembered her—had brought him right back to the exotrain and the moments before everything went to hell. Suddenly, it was dreadfully important that *Professor Odd* thought he'd done the right thing, never mind what anyone else said.

"I know it's not . . . " he began, and had to stop and swallow, nervous as the first time he'd seen her without her wig on. "I know it's probably not what *you'd* have done . . . " he tried.

Professor Odd looked up at him, sharply.

"No," she admitted, and shrugged. "It's not what I'd have done. But you know something, Mister Alister?" Now her face brightened, and she smiled, thin and delicate. "I don't think I could have done any better."

She was grinning wholeheartedly now, and Alister felt himself returning the expression. He stood there, stupidly happy, as she walked over and clapped him on both shoulders. "No," she said, her smile wide and white. "I couldn't have done better myself."

A small kernel of discontent ruptured Alister's balloon of joy. His smile faltered.

"I'm sorry," he said. "About Dave."

Professor Odd shrugged and shook her head. "We'll find him," she said. "Or more likely, *he'll* find *us.*"

"I still have his message," Alister assured her. "If you'd like to . . . *am* . . . listen to it?"

"Yes," said the Professor, thoughtfully. "Yes I think I should."

Alister produced the jar and handed it to her. While Professor Odd dipped a cautious finger into the viscous liquid Alister went over to Rajinder's station.

"Any word from Elo?" he asked.

"You *know* what sending messages through the Link is like," she hissed at him. "It could be *weeks.*" She glanced at the Professor, her eyes wide.

"So that's . . . ?"

"Yes," said Alister.

"Should I invite her to dinner?"

"I don't know if she'll stay that long," Alister admitted.

Professor Odd was thoughtful as she wiped her finger on the front of her coat and handed the jar back to Alister.

"Keep it," he said. "He meant the message for both of us, and I've got my own copy. I mean, portion. Whatever."

Professor Odd rolled her lips between her teeth and nodded, tucking the jar away inside her coat.

"I've been meaning to ask," Alister said. "What was it he said, there at the end? After the bit about '*I exist . . .*'"

"Hmm?" said the Professor. "Oh, that was sort of a sign-off. Like the way you or I would sign a letter. A multisensual signature, you might say."

"You mean *that* was his name?" Alister sputtered.

Professor Odd grinned at him. "Pretty much. Now you know why I called him Dave."

Alister had to admit she had a point.

In the tentative lull in conversation, while Rajinder looked like she was working up the courage to ask the Professor to join them for a meal, Alister heard the unmistakable sound of claws in the hallway, and a moment later the door burst open for the second time that morning, and Elo exploded into the room.

"*Finally!*" she howled, throwing herself at the Professor, her tail working like a propeller.

"Elo!" Professor Odd cried, flinging her arms wide as she was knocked off her feet by the charging canine.

"That was fast," Alister remarked, surprised and pleased, watching the two collapse into a happy pile at his feet.

"Got your message right before I left," Elo panted, and it was clear she had: she was still wearing her pressurized spacesuit. It must have been uncomfortable for Professor Odd, being pressed against it by the *vroknaär's* embrace, but she was grinning and laughing and stroking Elo's neck. "*Lucky* thing!" she said, her voice an excited yap.

"This whole incident has been a lucky thing," Professor Odd said, raising herself onto her elbows and grinning up at Alister.

He had to laugh, and in that moment, when they were all happily disarmed, Rajinder stood up, straightened her coat, and said:

"Don't you even think of disappearing on us now, Professor. You must stay—at least for dinner." She seemed a little consternated when, far from arguing, Professor Odd agreed at once.

They ordered in—which was standard procedure whenever Elo was around for meals—but gathered in the tree-lined courtyard in the middle of the complex, where many employees went to eat their packed meals. Everyone knew Elo, by this point, and though Professor Odd got a few curious glances, her proximity to Rajinder rendered her safe from any probing questions.

"They don't know who I am," Alister explained quietly, around his plate of curried potatoes. "I mean, ostensibly I'm a friend of Rajinder's who sometimes joins her for meals. They call me Alex. But as far as they know it's still Dr. Carver in the inner office. We decided it was best that way."

"I think he should retire soon, though," said Rajinder, helping herself to another serving of braised carrots.

They ate and chatted; Elo had to tell her portion of the story all over again, and had the Professor fill them in on her actions since last they'd seen one another. Eventually they walked back up to the director's office, but Professor Odd paused, glancing down the hallway that led to the Oddity.

"It seems, Mister Bane, that you have handled things so well here, you hardly have need of me anymore," she said.

Alister rounded on her.

"*What?*" he exclaimed. "After all the time I spent *waiting?* Oh no, Professor Odd. Don't you think about scurrying off—not without *me.*"

Professor Odd blinked at him.

"But," she said. "You only came away in the first place because you were running from the Canary Company." She gestured at the empty hall. "They're not chasing you anymore: *you* took care of that. You can go *home* now."

"Yes, yes, I thought about that," said Alister, waving a hand impatiently. "I even went for a visit to the Old Country. Sent my grandparents into fits, but they're all right. House is still the same. Village still the same. But it's not *home,* not anymore." He looked very hard at the Professor, since it was important he make her understand.

"Look," he said. "Last time I left—the first time—it was because I dinnae have a choice. Well, now I *do* have a choice, and I've decided I'd like to keep traveling with you . . . if that's all right," he added, suddenly uncertain.

But Professor Odd was grinning at him, a huge smile of amazement and disbelief. It gave him the courage to go on.

"And . . . and I feel I owe it to him, to find Dave."

Professor Odd nodded, understanding, but then frowned.

"You'll need some time, I expect," she said. "To tidy things up here, I mean. You're not just a university student anymore, Mister Bane. You're the director of the Canary Company."

"*Yes,*" admitted Alister. "As to that . . . give us a wee moment?"

He left Professor Odd in the hall and dashed into the Director's office, and then into the inner office, and finally into the bolt-hole. He pulled open the first-aid cupboard, and from that removed the bulky, blue carpet-bag and the slim, black briefcase that he'd kept at the ready for the past eighteen months. On his way out he was stopped by Rajinder, who was twisting her hands nervously together.

"Do you want to read over Dr. Carver's retirement announcement?" she asked.

"I trust you've done a masterful job of it," Alister assured her. He gave her an awkward bow. "Congratulations on another promotion, Director Ayoadé."

Rajinder rolled her eyes at him. "Get out," she said, then added: "But come back occasionally, yeah?"

"Count on it," Alister assured her, and walked out into the hall.

He had half feared that the Professor would have vanished on him, but she was still there, with Elo at her side, looking mildly surprised.

"You *have* given this a good think," she said.

"Eighteen months," Alister said, grinning. "Rajinder and I planned to make the switch ages ago, but then we got stuck, waiting for you."

Professor Odd looked around the hall. She put her hands behind her back and rocked forward on her toes.

"Just one question, Mister Alister," she said. "Why keep the place going at all?"

Alister blinked at her, surprised at how readily the answer sprang to mind.

"Because Parthenon was right," he said. "You can't just snap the head off a thing like the Canary Company. There's enough people here with questionable ethics that they need a good place to work, to keep them from making trouble. And besides, there *really are* things in the multiverse to be afraid of. Killer robots, for example. A world needs someone watching out for things like that. But not a violent guard. Not a Cerberus. It's like what you said when you first learned this was called the *Canary* Company."

"The canary in the coal mine?" Professor Odd asked.

Alister nodded. "Something that can detect a danger before it's a danger. Something to warn people if trouble is coming. And something to work on a solution, if trouble does come. *That's* what this world needs, and that's what the Canary Company is now."

Professor Odd smiled. It was brief, but bright.

"Don't worry, Professor," said Rajinder, leaning on the door to the director's office. She'd grown, if possible, somehow larger all over in the course of the last year. More confident, assured. Even if she was a little starstruck at the moment, she managed to look perfectly calm as she said: "I'll make sure we stay on track. And if there's any trouble, be sure you'll hear from me."

Professor Odd regarded the round, serious woman, and nodded. "Yes," she said. "I expect I will."

"If you've all quite *finished*," said Elo, putting her paws on her hips. "*I'm* ready to go home. So long, Raji. It's been swell. We'll be back for Christmas."

Rajinder laughed, and walked them down the hall to where the Oddity waited. To Alister it looked like any other door, but when Professor Odd dragged it open there were the familiar, carpeted steps, the salmon wallpaper, and beyond that the dim, colored lights.

"Wow," said Rajinder, peering up at them. "I almost wish I was going with you. Maybe we could spell each other? After you find Dave?"

Alister agreed that this sounded like a fine deal. He hugged Rajinder, said a last, internal good-bye to the halls of the Canary Company, then followed Professor Odd's bright green coat up the steps and back into the Oddity at last.

It was exactly the same, and new all over again. Alister found that he'd remembered some things wrong and forgotten others entirely: like the delicate spiral pattern on the lace curtains, and the particular smell of wood and tea and spices that seemed to come from everywhere and nowhere.

The musical sounds of the Oddity disconnecting from his home world were as familiar as before, and he stretched out with glad relief into the nearest cushy armchair.

"Well, Alister?" said Professor Odd, spinning around in her seat at the cockpit. "After all this, I think you have earned the right to call our next destination."

"Oh please," groaned Elo. "Can't we just *drift* for a while?"

Alister thought he agreed with her, then he thought of something.

"I had a dream once, while I was waiting for you," he said. "At the time it seemed almost like a memory, even though I knew it never happened. There was this world with these huge, dandelion-like flowers. Only instead of fluffy seeds, they had moths. Moth-seeds, you know? And when they bloomed all the moths flew away. I don't suppose you know of a world where that's real?"

Professor Odd shook her head. "Can't say I do," she admitted. Then she perked up. "But then, we do have an almost infinite number of universes left to explore. They might very well exist somewhere . . . out there. *You never know.*"

"But not now," Alister added, hastily. "I want a nap first. *In my own bed.*"

"Seconded," agreed Elo. "Sleep first, then adventures."

And, for the moment, Professor Odd had to be satisfied with that.

Professor Odd and Company will return in
"The Angels of Tyson 4"

"Half Lives" is the third spoke of the second wheel of Driving Arcana, *and the twelfth spoke overall. The first draft was written in the summer of 2015, when I was myself reeling from the loss of a loved one. It is preceded by "Out of Space" and will be followed by "Critical Magic," which leads off the* Rotation Five *collection, coming soon from* Heliopause.

HALF LIVES

Northeast Texas
February

THE GIBBONS HOUSE HAD BEEN EMPTY for almost ten years, and as far as anyone in the area was concerned it could stay that way for another hundred. Songbirds had colonized the attic and mold had taken over the walls. Spending a night in the crumbling master bedroom had become a rite of passage for local adolescents, who insisted the place was haunted by old Martha Gibbons and her three children. Which local legend said she'd killed, before her husband, Fred, had her shipped off to a sanitarium in Dallas. Fred had denied all of this to his dying breath, which had begun the long period of quiet neglect as the house settled into ruin and the bottom of the already-stagnant real estate market.

The shake roof was mostly moss and the ancient Century 21 sign completely covered in wild grapes when Charlie Hickins and Roger Barnes slipped through the sprawling barbwire fence and crept up the main drive.

The sun had not yet set, but it was already shaping up to be a viciously cold night. Charlie had prepared for this by borrowing his older brother's down parka and stuffing a thermos of hot cocoa into the inner pocket. Roger had a thick wool blanket wrapped around him like a shawl, but could only envy Charlie the cocoa.

The crumbling porch, with its peeling, whitewashed boards, creaked under their light feet as Charlie hopped up and shoved open the window beside the door—which remained locked as a final nod to the house's official status as a bank-owned liability—and scrambled inside.

"It's *really* dark," Roger said as he followed, wiping a thick layer of dust off his hand and onto his blanket.

"Yeah," said Charlie in tones of tolerant condescension. "That's kinda the *point.*"

It was dark, too. Not the spooky dark of a horror movie, where there was just enough light to see the terrified expressions of the actors, but the pure pitch of a closed closet on a moonless night. Roger immediately tripped over something that nearly sent him sprawling.

"*Ow!*"

"Quiet!" hissed Charlie. "You don't want to make old Mrs. Gibbons angry!"

"But I can't *see!*" Roger protested, groping around until he found Charlie's arm. "What's the point of a haunted house when you can't even see to see the ghosts?"

"Oh, you'll *see,*" said Charlie ominously, and Roger felt him moving away, further into the house. It suddenly occurred to him that being in a place where you couldn't see a thing was even worse, in a way. Suddenly every brush of air against his cheek could have been the hand of a dead child, and old Mrs. Gibbons could be standing *right behind him,* her cleaver raised, and he couldn't look and see.

Muffled in the distance, something growled.

To his shame, Roger yelped.

"Did you hear that?" he gasped.

"Yeah," said Charlie, his bravado betrayed by the waver in his voice. "It's prob'ly . . . prob'ly the dog."

"The Gibbonses had a dog?" Roger asked.

"'Course they had a dog," said Charlie knowingly. "Big, monstrous, Saint Mastiff thing. Ate babies whole."

Roger swallowed. "It sounds like it's gettin' closer," he whispered.

Charlie didn't answer. Under his hand, Roger felt his arm was shaking. It was enough to send a wild fear down his spine which struck him mute and still. So overcome were they with imagined horrors coming at them out of the velvet dark that it wasn't until they heard the unmistakable crunch of tires on the gravel outside that they realized the growl had been that of an engine, and that its owner was now parking right outside the front door. The yellow beams of its headlights shone in through the busted window, showing Roger that the room they stood in had once been the kitchen, and that what he'd tripped on had been a corner of the ancient refrigerator, which had been pulled away from the wall and disconnected.

"Who is—" he began.

"Run!" hissed Charlie, and grabbed his hand.

This was easier said than done. The kitchen also held two broken chairs and a flimsy table, all of which managed to get in their way as they made for the back door. In their clamor they didn't hear the thump of footsteps on the porch, or the scrape of a key in the lock. The next thing they knew the room was flooded with light as the overhead flickered on, and an affronted, feminine voice said:

"What the *hell* are you doing here?"

The boys blinked up at the young, fat woman who was looming over them. She wore jeans which clung to her meaty legs almost desperately, and a lavender cardigan under a down jacket even puffier than the one Charlie wore. She had a purse slung over one shoulder and a set of keys in her right hand, which was just descending from the cobweb-covered switch for the overhead. She had a pinched, white face like an angry kitten, and dark brown hair swept back around her ears that, had her face been a good deal more gaunt, would have made her look like a movie star.

They stared, caught and helpless, saying nothing. Then, as the woman did not take physical hold of them, Charlie took the opportunity to complete their dash for freedom, and a moment later the back door was banging behind them and they were pelting out through the overgrown garden, into the comparative brightness of the night-blue sky and distant stars.

In the kitchen the woman put her chubby fists on her ample hips and shook her head.

"Well," she said to herself sarcastically, *"that's* a promising start."

The house south of Texarkana (Texas side) was not as much of a wreck as she had assumed. Most of the lights still worked, and so did the water. Of the three toilets only one could be persuaded to flush, but that was enough for Kati Maliska. The drive from Mount Vernon had taken almost eight hours, and that was seven hours longer than she had ever driven in a day before. But here she was, alive and relatively well, and as free as the limited resources she'd been able to cram into the little Fit would make her. The rest would be coming via UPS in the next week, and then . . . well, it was too much to think more than a day ahead at a time, so she busied herself with setting up the little kerosene stove she'd bought at the local mercantile, put on a bowl of noodle soup to heat, and opened a can of sardines. Not trusting the table or the broken chairs, she picnicked on the floor and looked around the sorry room with skeptical optimism.

It was the pits, she had to admit. The advantage of being in the pits, however, was that there was nowhere to go but up. At least, she hoped so.

The entire house was dark and cold, and after one look at the cavernous master bedroom (cloaked in dusty white sheets like so many sleeping ghosts) Kati decided the kitchen would remain her base of operations. The ancient furnace was unresponsive—not surprising—so she put on her hat and gloves and two pairs of wool socks before crawling into the sleeping bag she'd laid out on her inflatable bedroll.

In the night she dreamed of Bren, so vividly that within the dream she forgot he was dead. She woke in darkness with the touch of his lips still tingling on her own, but the air was cold and empty when she reached out. In the dark she heard someone crying, and it took her sleep-fogged brain several moments to realize that that someone was her.

At least she thought it was her. It seemed numb and far away, and went on long after she shut her eyes and rolled over on the narrow, little bed.

She woke again in the frigid chill of dawn to a silent room lit by uncertain gray light, and the urgent need to use the one working toilet. It was worse, somehow, now that she could see the mold and algae coating the tiles and the thick calcification in the toilet bowl. The room was little more than a closet anyway, and she got in and out as quickly as she could, all the while trying not to touch anything.

The hall outside connected the kitchen to a massive living room, the huge, oak table still sitting solidly in the middle of it. Beyond this table, visible through the doorway, was a broken mirror—hung with the intention of reflecting daylight into the otherwise dreary corridor.

There was a shadow in the mirror staring intently back at her, but when Kati turned to look it was only her own reflection. In the partial dark, however, she looked more like a ghost than anything else, and she shivered and turned away.

Maybe she could convince the camp stove to toast poptarts, she thought hopefully. Then there was instant coffee, and a whole lot of unpacking.

The poptarts got burned, the coffee was clumpy, and the house resisted her attempts to colonize it. Literally. It turned out that the front door, kitchen door, bathroom doors and master bedroom door were the only ones she could convince to open. The rest remained stubbornly shut, even after she climbed in through the broken window of what turned out to be a den-like room and unlocked its door from the inside. Inspection of the door frame revealed what looked like an alien fungus grown over the lintel, creating a thoroughly effective jam. It resisted all of Kati's best efforts, and when cautiously prodded, proved as hard as concrete.

Temporarily defeated, Kati backed down and looked around at the closed-off room.

She didn't much like it. There was an old sofa in a loud Native American–style pattern, and sheets covering what turned out to be mounted heads of various animals over the hearth and on the walls. An empty gun rack stood on the mantelpiece, between two dusty shooting trophies.

There was also a cabinet of old and varnished wood which, once Kati wiped a few inches of dust off it, turned out to be a rather fine object. Nevertheless, the thing gave her the heebie-jeebies. Perhaps it was the house, or the bad dreams, or the un-settling experience with the mirror, but Kati was beginning to suspect the house of harboring something nasty. Somewhere. And for some reason she was convinced that that something nasty was in the cabinet.

She was standing there, working up the courage to open the thing—because the rational part of her mind told her it would be empty, and then she could forget her misgivings—when she was nearly frightened out of her skin by a loud knock on the front door.

It was simple surprise, that was all. It had not sounded at all like a skeleton hand rapping on the inside of a coffin. Kati shook herself, went for the door automatically before remembering the alien fungus, and instead stuck her head out of the window to shout, "Be right there!" before climbing through it.

Her shirt caught on a splinter in doing so, and she came into the kitchen woefully examining the hole it had caused. There was another knock on the front door. It didn't sound impatient, per se, but rather expectant. As if the knocker knew she was there, but wasn't in a hurry. They could wait. They could wait all day.

That only made her hurry forward to open the door, eager to see another living face.

At first glance it might not have been. It belonged to a large, round woman—not as fat as Kati, but a good two inches taller—and looked dark gray in the overcast morning light. A pair of curious hazel eyes squinted at her from under a bright orange knitted hat, while a fuzzy brown scarf obscured every-thing below the puckered, brownish lips. She was wearing an argyle sweater vest over a moss-green cardigan, and over that a fur-lined parka. She had on a long denim skirt, out of which protruded two rubber-boot-clad feet. She had a bottle of Jack Daniels whisky under one arm, and a mop in the other.

"Hi?" said Kati, uncertainly. "Can I help you?"

The woman shrugged. "I don't think so," she said, in a voice that, even to Kati's untrained ear, clearly didn't originate anywhere in the Lone Star state. "My name's Alma Bonifaunt, I'm here to help you get settled in."

South Carolina? Kati wondered. *Maybe Georgia*? It was someplace southern, but all she could be sure of was that it wasn't Texas and it wasn't Arkansas—even if a nonnative might have mistaken it for such.

"That's . . . uh . . . that's mighty kind of you," Kati said. "But I don't need any help."

"You get 'er opened up?" asked Alma Bonifaunt.

"What?" asked Kati.

"The house," said the woman, running the two words together so it sounded like '*Thee-ouse*.' "You get her opened up?"

"Um . . . " said Kati, thinking of the alien fungus.

Alma Bonifaunt sighed, her huge shoulders heaving. "That's what I thought," she said, and started walking into the house.

It was move or be run over by the big, rubber boots. Kati chose the former. She followed Alma Bonifaunt into the kitchen, where the woman leaned the mop against the wall and set the bottle of Jack Daniels on the table. She shrugged off her parka and began unwrapping her scarf.

"You're not from around here," she was saying, draping scarf and jacket over one of the broken chairs.

"Neither are you," Kati shot back before she could stop herself. It was borderline rude, and she didn't want to offend the woman, but after everything, her well of tact was running close to dry.

All the woman did, however, was turn around to fix her with a level stare, and anything Kati could have said to ameliorate her words evaporated.

Alma Bonifaunt had a ragged, white scar running from under her left ear, slanting down across her throat, before jerking up and ending below her right. That part had healed roughly, leaving a fold of skin that wobbled a little, like the wattle of a rooster, as she spoke.

"This house been shut down for over ten year," she said, as if Kati hadn't spoken. As if she didn't have the fully healed scar of a mortal injury there on her neck. "Bad things grow when air don't get in. You, you sit yourself down there, girl, have a drink, and you let me handle this."

Kati eyed the bottle of whisky.

"A little early for that," she said. She might be a grief-stricken madwoman, she thought, but she wasn't an alcoholic. Not yet anyway.

"That ain't whisky there," said Alma Bonifaunt, raising a pair of wispy brown eyebrows. "You just try some and if you don't like it say so, and I'll take it away again." Then she turned, picked up the mop, and waddled away into the house. When Kati automatically moved to follow, she found herself confronted with the business end of the mop as the woman turned around and forced her back toward the kitchen. "Go on now," she said, as if Kati were an overly attached dog. "*Get.*" Only because of her accent it sounded more like "*Git.*"

Kati was forced to stay in the kitchen, sitting on the counter because all the chairs were broken. Maybe she could make a run to town later and get some of those folding camp chairs. If there were any that could fit her. And if the weird old lady didn't stay all day. She sighed. She could hear Alma Bonifaunt clattering around in the depths of the house, with now and then the occasional grunt. Kati fancied some of them were disapproving, and some of them satisfied, and some of them the result of hauling open doors that didn't want to be opened.

After a while she dug out one of the little plastic cups that had come with the package of camping utensils she had bought the day before, and gingerly poured half an inch of the contents of the bottle into it.

It smelled strongly of lemon and honey, which was promising, and when sipped, even though the liquid was cold, it warmed her throat and sat in her belly like a comforting fire. Kati frowned at it, wondering if it did in fact contain some alcohol. She rinsed it down with a glass of water for good measure, and then gave up on waiting and went to find out what Alma was getting up to.

The house was much lighter now. And colder. The woman had torn down all the curtains and opened the windows, letting in a frigid, winter breeze. Kati wrapped her coat more tightly around her as she progressed across the living room and through the door she assumed led to the ground-floor bedrooms—which was now standing wide open.

It did lead to more bedrooms, by way of a narrow hall which opened onto the back porch. The rooms themselves were dusty and damp, strangely desolate in the gray light flooding in through the open windows. There were pale patches on the floor, evidence of long-ago beds, and one still had a battered old wardrobe in it. It was not the kind that invited exploration, however, no matter how big a *Chronicles of Narnia* fan you were. Kati shuddered at its water-stained front, and decided it looked more likely to house skeletons in bloodstained nightgowns than a portal to a magic world.

Everything was old and dead and forgotten. Even with the fresh influx of air there was a heavy scent of mold, and Kati wondered about setting up some fans to help clear the house's atmosphere.

There was a *bang* from upstairs and a horrible screeching. Kati jumped and then ran, down the hallway and up the bare, wooden stairs, at the top of which she was attacked by something black and angry the size of a small cat.

It was a lucky thing she didn't go tumbling right back down and break her neck. As it was she threw up her arms and dropped, and the thing flapped away, still screeching. Gripping the edge of the banister for support, Kati looked down and saw a huge, black bird—a raven or a crow, she couldn't tell—perched in the open window. It cawed at her reproachfully, ruffled its feathers, and flew off.

There was the thump of feet, and she twisted around to find Alma Bonifaunt standing over her. She had tied a white rag over her hair in place of the knitted cap, and carried a broom whose end was full of cobwebs.

"Now what you doin' up here?" she asked. She didn't sound angry, but then it was hard to tell if she was feeling anything at all.

"I-I-I . . . " Kati stammered, her heart still racing. She swallowed. "I heard a bang . . . "

Alma Bonifaunt nodded. "That happens. Why'd you come up here?"

"To . . . uh . . . help?" Kati offered.

"Don't need no help," Alma Bonifaunt said. From this angle her scar looked especially ghastly, and she was so pale she seemed to melt into the dingy, stained walls. "Go downstairs now. Get something to drink. Then you'll want to go into town and order some propane. Furnace still works, is just out of fuel."

"But," Kati began. *But you're a stranger and this is my house,* she was going to say, and then realized that everything of value that she owned was still locked in her car. What could Alma do while she was gone? The house was already a wreck.

"Okay," she said instead, and hobbled off down the stairs.

It turned out to be the right thing to do. As soon as she was out of the house Kati felt her spirits lifted, and she spent an almost enjoyable day driving up to Texarkana to do some much-needed shopping. Camp chairs she found, as well as a refrigerator which could be delivered the following day. In anticipation of this she refilled her cooler with ice and a few essentials (milk, eggs, baloney and peanut butter, bread, more poptarts), and stopped at a café for a piping hot mocha latte and some internet. She found a propane service and set up an account with them, and also made arrangements for satellite internet to be installed at her new property. A landline she could live without. Netflix, not so much.

She picked up dinner-to-go at Denny's on the way out of town, and arrived home just as the sun was sinking redly behind the line of trees to the west.

Alma Bonifaunt was smoking a cigar on her front porch, blowing bluish rings into the evening air. She stubbed the thing out and threw it away as soon as she saw Kati approaching, for which Kati was almost regretful. She didn't like cigar smoke any more than the next nonsmoker, but the rings had been impressive.

"I brought dinner," she said, raising the plastic bags of takeout.

Alma Bonifaunt sniffed. "That is kind of you," she said. Not like she was grateful, just stating a fact. "But I ain't hungry. Come inside and see what I done."

What she had done, Kati found, was completely clear out the house. The windows were shut now, and the rooms were bare and *clean*. Alma had destroyed the alien fungus, scraped away the mold and cobwebs, swept the floors and wiped down the walls. All the broken pieces of furniture (which was most of them) had been chopped into kindling and piled next to the woodstove in the living room, which was burning merrily. All three toilets flushed, and Alma had found a bed frame from somewhere, moved it into the living room, and laid Kati's roll out on it.

"Sleep here until you get the furnace working," Alma said by way of explanation. "Bedrooms not clean yet. Also, ah, don't go into the attic."

"Why not?" Kati asked, feeling a flicker of alarm.

"Not clean yet," said Alma, with a shrug. "I'll be back tomorrow and get it opened up. Do the basement too. You get propane?"

"They're coming this week," Kati said.

Alma nodded. "That's good." She turned to go.

"Wait," Kati reached to take her arm, then thought better of it. But Alma paused and turned cumbersomely to look at her, and she went on: "I brought food. It's Denny's, but . . . I thought you might—as a thank you for all your help."

"Ah-ah," said Alma, looking awkwardly out the nearest window. "Naw, I don't need nothing from you. You just sleep well tonight. I'll be seeing you in the morning."

"Oh," said Kati, feeling unaccountably disappointed. She had begun, she realized, to actually *like* this strange old woman. And the house was so very big and empty when she was alone in it.

"Good night then," said Alma Bonifaunt, and shuffled off through the kitchen door.

"Good night," said Kati, hearing it close behind her.

It was not a good night. Despite the warmth from the woodstove a chill settled in the room, and around midnight Kati woke to find a thin layer of frost on the outside of her sleeping bag. As the fire was still going she stoked it up and moved her makeshift bed closer. All this did was make her stove side too hot, while the other side froze.

She was skimming the surface of sleep when there was a rat-tling, scratching sound from the attic. Faintly at first, and so intermittent that Kati had enough time to doze off before being jerked fully awake again. It was probably a tree branch scraping against an upstairs window, but she couldn't help remember-ing the big black bird that had nearly hit her in the face earlier that afternoon. And Alma Bonifaunt's warning to stay out of the attic.

It was all so very cliché haunted house horror that Kati would have laughed at it. Had it been daytime. And had she been among with other, living people. Not stuck in a big drafty house that was literally freezing, with funny mirrors and alien fungi and a creepy wardrobe.

What was her alternative, though? Go back to Mount Ver-non, with all its painful memories of Bren and the life they had dreamed of?

Kati hunkered down more deeply, and managed to pull a fold of her sleeping bag up over her head. Like a child hiding under the covers. Well, it had worked for her as a kid, why not now?

And perhaps it did. It certainly kept her face from freezing, and sufficiently muted the noises coming from upstairs that she was able, at last, to get some proper sleep.

She dreamed of Bren. He was kneeling beside her, still in the paper hospital gown, and he was stroking her shoulder.

He was trying to say something, but though his lips moved, no sound came out. Kati tried to ask him what was wrong, but in the way of dreams she couldn't speak either. It made him sad. After a while he got up and went away, trailing his catheter tube across the floor. His feet, though bare, sounded loudly on the freshly swept floorboards.

Then Kati opened her eyes and realized the footsteps were real. She sat up to discover Alma Bonifaunt standing in the doorway to the kitchen, a fresh bottle (Southern Comfort this time) in one hand.

"Get on up there, girl," she said, her scar-wattle shuddering under her chin. She raised the bottle. "Made you a new brew.

Come along and I'll pour you a stop. Looks like you need the chill off. Dun't the stove work?"

What are you doing in my house? were the first words through Kati's mind. She dismissed them, however, since asking probably wouldn't get her any reasonable answer. Glancing around she discovered that the stove was cold and dead.

"It was," she said, pulling the neck of the bag closer around her shoulders. "Must have gone off in the night."

"Mmm," said Alma. She went back into the kitchen, leaving Kati to wonder whether the guttural utterance had been sympathetic, disapproving, or ominous.

It must have been sympathetic, because Alma came back a few moments later with a lighter in hand and a rolled up newspaper. She herded Kati into the kitchen while she got the stove going again, and true to her promise Kati found she did feel much better after a cup of the strong, lemon-ginger brew. Tea, maybe, she thought. With just a dash of whisky? It didn't matter. She made herself a baloney sandwich and went into the living room to eat it while Alma fussed with the stove. She was muttering something about "Dern ghists," (whatever a *ghist* was) when Kati came in, but fell silent from then on.

The refrigerator was delivered as promised, and though the delivery man cheerfully wheeled it into the kitchen, once off the trolley he made a speedy departure—throwing up gravel behind his van's tires as he sped away. It left Kati frowning on the front porch, a manual the size of an old telephone directory in her hands.

She spent the rest of the morning getting the thing set up. It was an exercise in frustration, mostly, but by noon she was able to move the contents of the cooler into the newly operational fridge.

She made peanut-butter sandwiches to celebrate, and took them upstairs on a paper plate to share with Alma.

The attic of the house was reached, not through a trap door, but by an additional staircase accessed by a narrow wooden door which looked, from the outside, like a broom cupboard. It was standing open when Kati reached the landing, revealing the planks of wood which passed for steps leading up into the drafty dark.

She barely noticed them. The door opened outward, and she could see that its inner face was covered in gashes—as if an animal had been trapped inside, clawing to get out. They looked fresh. Night-before fresh.

Kati nearly dropped the sandwiches when there was a loud *crack* from below her.

Leaving the disturbing sight she fled down the stairs and out onto the front porch, where she discovered the author of the disturbance was one of the spotty kids she'd shooed out of the house on her first night. A pockmark in the wall beside the door and a new rock on the porch answered the rest of her questions.

Furious, she set down the sandwiches and picked up the rock.

"Does this belong to you?" she asked, hefting the rock meaningfully.

A sandy head ducked behind a handy blackberry bush.

"Are you a witch?" the boy called, brazen in his curiosity.

"What?" shouted Kati, so angry she doubted her ears for a moment.

"Do you worship the devil?" the boy called. He sounded genuinely curious, and that somehow made it worse.

Before she could answer she heard Alma's voice reverberating from the depths of the house.

"Charles Anthony Hickins," she called, her voice growing louder as she approached, rubber boots clomping ominously. "You get yourself on home now before I calls your momma an' tellin' her you be destructing other folks's properties."

A daring head poked above the bush. Two curious blue eyes regarded them.

"She livin' in a haunted house!" the boy called, pointing at Kati. "Ain't she a witch, Mrs. Bonifaunt?"

"Go away!" Kati screamed, and hurled the rock as hard as she could.

It fell short—which was probably just as well—but the boy shrieked and took off for the drive, ducking behind her car and sprinting for the road.

Kati watched him go, chest heaving, heart pounding—not just from indignation, but the fear that he might very well be half right.

"Aw, now there you go, Miss K," said Alma, patting her gently on the arm. The old woman stooped cumbersomely and picked up the plate of sandwiches. "Here you are. You have yourself a nice lunch, and I'll go get the attic aired out. Houses are much better with clean attics."

Kati sat on the porch and ate both sandwiches, then went back inside and made herself a third. She drank the entire bottle of Alma's brew—which, despite the warmth it gave her, didn't get her even a little buzzed. She considered going upstairs and asking Alma about the scratch marks, but in the end decided what she needed was contact with the outside world.

So she packed up her laptop and charger, climbed into her car and drove to town. She ordered the café's biggest mocha latte and sipped it while she checked her feel-good blogs and sent a short email to her mother, assuring her that everything was fine.

But everything *wasn't* fine. Hauntings and ghost stories had always been something Kati laughed at, but now . . . and after last night . . .

It could all be in her head. She could be imagining things. What she needed was someone to talk to who wouldn't judge her either way. Someone who could *find out* whether it was a ghost or not. The problem was all the people who came to mind were either skeptics or deluded ghost-hunters.

Still, it couldn't hurt to ask the internet.

As she expected, most of the hits turned up paranormal fetishist sites and people claiming to speak with the dead. It also turned up a lot of posts about St. Louis, and the weird things that may—or may not—have happened there.

At the bottom of one of those articles, there was a name mentioned. It had a phone number, and a contact at UC Santa Cruz.

Kati frowned at the name and number for a long time before saving it to her phone and closing down her computer.

Alma was gone by the time she got home, but there was a note on the kitchen table.

Attic safe. Will be back for basement tomorrow.

Kati crumpled it into a ball and hurled it into a dark corner. But she didn't have the courage to go up into the attic and see it for herself. She pulled an extra blanket out of her car and went to sleep with it draped over her head.

The additional blanket kept out the chill and any disturbing noises the house might have produced, but it couldn't stop the dreams. This time, she dreamed that Bren had cooked dinner, and they were eating it together off their knees, on the sofa. Rook Parliament was playing in the background, and though there was a happy warm glow in her stomach, a cold breath hissed along her back and made her shiver.

When she asked Bren if he felt it too he looked unhappy. He leaned over to take her empty plate away, and she realized the coldness was coming off of him. When he left to wash up, it retreated with him.

Because Bren was dead. That's why he was cold. Then how could he be in the kitchen, washing the dishes? And not just any kitchen—the dingy one in the old Gibbons house. Bren had never been here. The only reason she'd bought the place at all was because he'd—

Kati woke up to the sound of running water. The light from the woodstove was a low, orange glow, and there was frost on the outside of her sleeping bag again. Clutching her blanket around her shoulders she sat up, trying to locate the sound.

It was coming from the kitchen.

Half of her wondered if she'd left the faucet on. The other half, still in the dream, thrilled at the thought that Bren could be *here*.

But if he was here . . . then he'd have to be . . .

Kati still couldn't think it. She was a rational adult. People died all the time. The world would be far too crowded if everyone left ghosts wandering around after they were gone.

She sat there in the dark for what felt like an hour, listening to the water run. When it became clear that was all she was hearing (no click of dishes or stomp of feet), and the last of the dream shredded away, she dragged herself off the bed and stumbled into the kitchen.

The tap was going full blast. It squeaked as she turned it off.

Afterward, she stood at the sink for a long time, her skin prickling, wondering if she should just leave now. Go jump in her car and drive back up to Illinois, memories be damned.

If she was going to do that, however, it might as well be on a full night's sleep—or, failing that, daylight. She turned to go back to bed.

Bren was standing in the hall.

Kati didn't scream. It wasn't that she couldn't, it was that first she had to inhale, and the sharp rasp of her breath made her that realize she was awake. She was *awake* and Bren was *there* and if she made any more noise he might vanish.

He was only a shadow as it was: a dark silhouette against the dim glow from the woodstove. But she knew him by the set of his shoulders and his stooping neck—as if he was constantly apologizing for how tall he was.

Kati held her breath until her lungs burned. Then she let it out in a shaky whisper.

"Bren?"

Bren didn't answer. The shadow took a step forward, one arm reaching out—Kati felt a blast of cold air, like opening a freezer—and then he recoiled as though something had zapped him. The shadow folded up on itself and crumbled away to nothing.

In its place was a much smaller shadow. The size of a child, it regarded Kati curiously, and then a voice spoke out of its dark face.

"Where's mama?" it asked.

It was a child's voice—small and frightened and fragile—but the shock of it sent Kati stumbling backward out the front door, across the porch, and then tripping barefoot over the gravel to her car. She got in and locked the doors before she remembered that both her keys and her phone were still on the kitchen counter. Then she cursed and thumped her forehead on the steering wheel, shaking and crying from a mixture of sadness, fear and frustration.

The house sat there in the dim starlight, dark and empty and still, and remained that way for the rest of the night. Kati knew it did, because she watched it until the sky turned from black to gray to faintly pink in the east, and finally a cold winter dawn spread over the tops of the trees and flooded the world with light.

By then Kati was feeling enormously silly. Her eyes ached and her head throbbed and how had she hallucinated Bren? And why did the kids here think it was a fun idea to spook their new neighbors? That was obviously what it had been. Maybe the boy from earlier had a younger brother or sister.

Kati cursed as she tiptoed back into the house—now perfectly quiet and empty, of course—rebuilt the fire and made herself breakfast. She was just debating whether or not to make a third cup of coffee or try for a nap later that day, when there came the predictable stomp of boots, and Alma Bonifaunt let herself in the front door, the by-now-expected bottle tucked under one arm.

"Mornin' Miss K," she said, setting the bottle—Jack Daniels again—down on the counter beside Kati. "Go ahead and make yerself comfortable. I'll be down in the basement until noon most like."

Kati frowned at the bottle. She was feeling increasingly suspicious of Alma Bonifaunt—not her brew, necessarily, since Kati had felt no ill effects—but of what she was doing helping her out with the house so much. The boy from before had said it was haunted. It certainly *felt* like what she always imagined a haunted house to feel like. Maybe there was something else—some reasonable explanation—for why it was that way. She hadn't learned much of its previous inhabitants. Perhaps it was time.

"I'll give you a hand," she said, getting to her feet.

"Ahh-hh," Alma began, but Kati cut her off.

"No, really. You've done so much. I should help," Kati insisted. "Besides, I wanted to ask you about the Gibbons—the people who lived here last. Did you know them?"

Alma Bonifaunt looked disappointed. "Can't say I *knew* them, knew them," she said dubiously.

"Well, you can tell me what you know while we work," Kati said brightly, taking the tote of brushes and spray bottles Alma had brought out of her hands. The basement was accessed by a door in the laundry room at the back of the house, and Kati started for it, swinging the tote merrily.

Alma made a sound like *"Ermmrr,"* and clomped disapprovingly after.

After everything else the house had thrown at her, Kati was surprised to find the basement mostly benign. There was an ominous-looking tank which turned out to be the water heater, sagging ducts wrapped in fiberglass insulation, and a bare, concrete floor with a single battered chair in the middle of it. It wasn't even that full of spiderwebs—there were a few in the corners by the ceiling, but other than that the main inhabitant of the place was a thick coat of the pervasive mold, which grew in fuzzy gray streaks in the floor cracks.

Alma said nothing, merely pulled out a hoary brush and got to work scraping away the fuzz.

"So . . . what was it with the Gibbons?" Kati asked, after they'd been working in silence for almost ten minutes. The only other sound being Alma's brush, and Kati's broom—which she was using to knock down cobwebs.

Scrape, scrape, scrape, went Alma's brush, but no reply.

"That kid—Charles?—he said this place was haunted. Did it have something to do with them?"

Scrape, scrape . . .

"House got a long hist'ry," said Alma at last. "I can't as say."

"Why not?" Kati was becoming certain Alma knew, and it aggravated her. Following a trail of spiderwebs around behind the water heater, she heard Alma reply:

"I only come here a few year ago. House was empty then— folk thought as it was always gonna *be* empty."

And there were plenty of mundane reasons for *that* to happen, Kati reassured herself. There was a reason she'd been able to buy the place in cash, and it wasn't because of the life insurance payout from Bren. Which she hadn't gotten any of on account of them not actually being married. (First they had wanted to wait until he was better. By the time it was clear he wasn't getting better he went downhill so fast it was like a plane crash, and before she knew it he was gone.)

Kati stopped and stared at the gritty wall in front of her for several minutes, grappling with the hollow, dry grief that had been repressed by the general weirdness of the house.

She felt a rush of cold air on her back and turned around to find Bren standing at the foot of the stairs.

In the better light—though it still wasn't very good—she saw he was wearing a stiff, white shirt and trousers. Like a hospital gown crossed with real clothes. His face had an odd look as well: it had the puckered, hollow cheeks and eyes from the last time she'd seen him, but overlaid with a warm glow that spread to fill his old outlines. Like the healthy Bren and the dying Bren had been pushed together into the same space.

"You don't belong here," Alma said quietly, and Kati jumped.

"Why not?" she asked, and then realized Alma was talking to Bren.

The ghost of Bren, she now had to admit.

Bren looked at Alma indignantly, his mouth screwing up the way it did before he said something unpleasant. But when his lips parted, no words came out.

Alma glanced at Kati, shrugged, and then walked forward.

It looked like she would just pass through Bren, but instead she grabbed him around the waist and hauled him back up the stairs.

But shouldn't ghosts be insubstantial?

Nothing made sense. Kati dropped her broom and ran up the stairs after them. She arrived at the top out of breath, and could only gasp in horror at what she found.

Alma was beating the living daylights out of Bren. If he had anything living left, that was. Kati didn't know. All she knew was that he had his hands up defensively, and Alma was calmly punching him in the throat, over and over. With every hit she landed, he went a bit more transparent, but it didn't stop her blows from connecting.

"Alma—*no!*" She screamed, and that distracted Alma long enough for her to stumble forward and grab her arm.

It felt like an iron bar under her hands, but Alma froze—and Bren took the opportunity to scramble away.

"Get *out,*" Kati gasped, pushing Alma toward the door.

"You don't want me to go," Alma said, warningly.

"Yes, yes I do!" shouted Kati, bracing her feet and shoving.

"His sort only make trouble," Alma said, when they were in the kitchen. "Ain't right, them being here!"

"*His* sort?" Kati screeched. Alma's body was cold under her hands, her breath felt like ice. "What about *your* sort?"

She had no idea what she was talking about, but she was certain—if she was certain of anything—that Alma had something to do with the hauntings.

She'd never seen Alma eat. Or drink. Or use the bathroom.

Maybe *Alma* was a ghost?

Kati's thoughts had gotten this far when she nearly fell on her face as Alma abruptly turned and walked out the front door.

"Be sure to drink the brew," she said, her gnarled hand on the doorknob. "Otherwise they *will* kill you."

"*What?*"

The door slammed. Kati was alone.

Really alone. When she turned around and scrambled back toward the basement, Bren was gone. And no matter where she looked or how loud she screamed, he didn't appear again.

Kati crawled into the makeshift bed, clutched a pillow to her chest, and broke down crying. Later, emotionally and physically exhausted, she fell asleep in the wan winter light filtering in through the front windows.

Kati made herself poptarts for dinner and sat up late in the kitchen, half hoping Bren would appear—and half dreading it.

She missed him so much it hurt. The raging black grief that had driven her out of Mount Vernon had returned full force. As if seeing his face had opened up all her old wounds.

She *missed* him—but not this strange, mute vision of him. She missed her real, warm, infuriating, charming, *alive* Bren. The ghost—for lack of a better word—scared her.

She didn't know what she wanted, but in the end it didn't matter. Her phone said it was one in the morning and nothing had happened. She went back to bed and curled up under the blankets.

And woke up what felt like a minute later to the sensation of something cold prodding at her shoulder.

She flailed awake, and it felt like her hand passed through a cloud of ice crystals. It stung and tingled, like pins and needles, but evaporated when she yanked her hand back.

There was a small shadow crouched over her, and cold air poured out of it. Kati felt her teeth begin to chatter.

"Where's my mama?" asked the shadow.

Kati was so terrified she could barely move, but her chattering teeth proved that she could, and she managed a hoarse, strangled scream and flailed for her phone. With shaking hands she turned on the flashlight and shone it straight into the place where the shadow's head was.

It illuminated the wall on the other side of the room, and no matter how she swept it over the stove and the floor and the bed and the couch, the only shadows she saw were the normal kind and gave way before the beam of light.

She needed help. She almost wished Alma was there.

No, no she didn't. She didn't want Alma. But she needed *someone.*

Kati had never gotten over her childhood nerves when it came to calling strangers on the phone. It took her days to muster the courage, and left her feeling awful afterward.

But when she looked up the number for the contact in California, she didn't hesitate to dial it.

Mescalero Indian Reservation
New Mexico

THE NIGHT AIR WAS COLD AND DRY AND BITING in the high desert hills. The stars shone like an army of diamonds in a sky so clear it was not black, but a deep, almost iridescent blue. Sparse pines strutted on the horizon, guarding the dark earth from the hordes of shining soldiers above.

The huge red truck—just another black shape in the black landscape, presently—and the even bigger trailer—a slightly paler object the size of a small house—were the only guests of the Twin Spruce RV Park, parked in the lee of a sloping hill, up against a cliff which, in daylight, had been a rosy beige.

It was getting on midnight, and Clara was lying stretched on top of the trailer, ostensibly keeping watch, but since everything felt miraculously peaceful, was keeping herself awake

by star gazing. Not properly, by identifying known constellations, but by trying to see new pictures in the present arrange-
ment of stars. She had managed to find a rabbit, a dragon, and a
sword, and was puzzling over a conjunction of bright stars directly overhead which could have been a frying pan or a broken
egg when the phone bleeped at her.

Not her phone. *The* phone. The phone Jill's professor friend
had insisted she get. Unlike their personal smart phones (insisted on and sponsored by Jill) this was a basic brick that could
do little more than make and receive calls, and—if you were very
patient and had nimble fingers—texts.

Jill called it a burner, and gave its number out to anyone and
everyone who she thought might have useful information for
them. As a result, it tended to get pranked a lot, at odd hours,
which was why Selene and Clara had taken to trading it between
them for their watches. Just in case something serious came
through.

"This is the Arcana Crew, Clara speaking," Clara answered
dutifully. She listened in silence as the panicked breathing on
the other end resolved itself into a high, frightened voice with
a pleasant, midwestern accent. She listened to the words it said,
a frown gathering across her smooth, hairless brows.

What she heard did not make any sense, not even in light of
her own extraordinary experiences. That could be put down to
pure fear, however, which was the one thing she was clear on.

This was not a prank.

"Listen—what is your name?" she asked, when there was
a break in the torrent of words. "Catty? Listen, I need you to
breathe. Yes, keep breathing. Are you still on the property?"
She waited. "Are you able to leave?" Another wait. "Then do so.
Do you have access to transportation? Yes, a car is excellent. Do
you have friends you can stay with? No, no it's okay. If you can,
go get in your car. Get *off* the property. I'll stay on the phone
with you."

She listened to the sounds of a woman, very scared and
breathing in heavy, labored breaths, searching for her wallet
and keys and blundering out the door. Feet crunched on gravel,
and a door opened and slammed shut. A car's ignition came on,

and then a rumble of engine and a crunch of wheels in gravel. Eventually this stopped, and the woman's voice returned.

"Now you need to get away," Clara told her. "What is your general location? Where is that—oh, North Texas. Understood." Clara closed her eyes and summoned up her mental map of that state. It was sadly vague. "Drive . . . southwest. Mostly west. At least fifty miles. Find a motel, then call me back with your exact location. We will meet you there. If anything happens—if you see anything or experience mechanical difficulties, call"—she pulled out her main phone and looked up its number. She told it to the woman on the other end. "Yes," she said in answer to a question. And then, a little surprised, added: "Yes, you're welcome."

She hung up. She swung her legs over the side of the trailer. There was thirteen feet and change between the roof and the packed dirt. Over twice her own impressive height.

She dropped casually, almost lazily, and landed with a soft thump, her knees almost touching her chest. Unfolding herself she stepped lightly to the door of the trailer, and gave it a gentle rap.

"No way is it three AM yet," Selene said by way of greeting as she pulled the door open. In the dark she was another shaggy-headed black shape, a fold of her flannel shirt illuminated briefly as she checked the time on her own phone.

"It isn't," said Clara. "Go wake up Jill. We have a haunting."

"Haunting, great," said Selene dryly. She heaved a sigh. "Well, after angels I suppose a few ghosts will practically be a vacation."

Somewhere outside Douglasville
Texas

THE MOTEL OFF OF 77 had cracked asphalt in the parking lot and the kind of flickering VACANCY sign that had always reminded Kati of a camp horror movie. After the cold eeriness of the house, it was practically heaven. She checked into their last nonsmoking room wrapped in her spare jacket and black socks, to hide the fact that she was in her pajamas and didn't have any shoes, and turned on all the lights as soon as she was inside. It had been a good thought, grabbing her wallet on the way out the door. Now she just wished she'd thought to bring her laptop as well. The place had free wi-fi (of course it did), and some internet and a proper screen would have gone a long way to keeping her company for the rest of the night. Because there was no way she was getting back to sleep.

When she called back to inform the owner of the dreadfully calm voice she had spoken with earlier—what *had* her name been? Something like Carrie, or Carla—where she was, it promptly joined her in with another woman who, by the sound of it, had her on speaker phone in a moving vehicle.

The new woman's name was Jill, and she sounded so competent and awake that it soothed Kati's sore nerves, and she didn't mind at all spending the rest of the night—as her benefactors drove from somewhere in New Mexico right across the breadth of Texas—explaining everything that had happened in the last three days.

Jill proved to be a good and sympathetic listener, only stopping her to ask small, clarifying questions, and waited patiently through a long diatribe against Alma Bonifaunt, creepy kids, and bossy neighbors.

When that finally ran out it was almost dawn, and the crew—which appeared to consist of the calm voice (*Clara*—that was her name!) the patient Jill, and a low drawl that belonged to the driver of the vehicle: a woman named Selene. Selene didn't speak much until after Kati had told them about her confrontation with Alma Bonifaunt and the encounter with the childshaped ghost which had prompted her to call in the first place. Then she asked,

"This Alma Bonifaunt . . . she give you anything to eat?"

Kati blinked, staring up at the ceiling of her motel room and puzzling over the non-sequitur question.

"No?" She said. Then, "Hang on—wait, she did give me this funny tea to drink. Tasted kinda like booze, but it didn't even get me buzzed. What?"

At her words Selene had let out a long, pained sigh.

"What, why is that bad?" Jill asked sharply, taking the question right out of Kati's mouth.

"It depends on what Alma Bonifaunt is," said Clara, her voice as ever an even, calm monotone.

"Alma Bonifaunt's not *really* my problem," Kati admitted. "It's the *ghosts.*"

"Yeah, yeah we'll get to that," said Selene. "But this Alma . . . you say she *touched* this guy's ghost?"

"Bren's, yes," said Kati.

"That's dangerous," said Selene, sounding as though she was explaining something to Jill. "Not many people can see ghosts, and even those that *can,* can't interact with them physically."

"Because they're dead?" Jill asked.

"'Cause they're *ghosts,*" said Selene. "Ghosts aren't real things. Um . . . I mean, they're real in that they *exist,* but . . . uh . . . they're not primary objects, if you know what I mean."

"I don't think I do," said Jill, again speaking for Kati. Kati decided she liked Jill.

"Ghosts are like shadows, or echoes," Clara supplied helpfully. "By-products of a life, a person, or even a memory. To see a ghost requires only a specific form of supernatural sensitivity—it occurs naturally, if rarely, in all animals—to merely sense their presence can be achieved through the right training. But to touch one—to essentially reach out of this world and interact with them on their own plane—that means you'd have to be . . . "

"You'd have to be not quite alive yourself," Selene finished. "Or, at least, alive in a different sort of way. I don't think even vampires can touch ghosts—different levels on the same plane, or something like that."

"Vampires are real?" Kati gasped.

"As far as I can tell," Jill told her, while in the background both Selene and Clara groaned, "pretty much everything you've ever heard about in fairytales or horror stories actually does exist—but it's usually different than popular media."

"So . . . so what?" Kati gabbled, half joking—but only half. "D'you think Alma's a *zombie* or something?"

She was expecting them to laugh. Instead there was a thoughtful silence and then Selene said,

"*Maybe?* I'm not sure, sister. I'd have to see her myself. But she don't sound like a zombie."

"She could be a witch," Clara suggested. "I can ask Faraday if she knows the name."

"You do that," said Selene, and a moment later there was a *boop, boop, boop* and Kati thought maybe she'd been hung up on. Then she realized they had been on a shared call with Clara, who'd just cut out.

"In the meantime," Selene said, confirming her suspicions, "getting back to this ghost matter. You've seen two different ghosts, yeah?"

"Yeah," said Kati, faintly. It felt strange, being taken so calmly seriously by complete—and completely *sane*-sounding— strangers. It was like describing a bizarre wildlife sighting, or talking to her dentist about a troublesome tooth. Thinking about it like that somehow made things easier. "Yes," she went on. "There's this kid—I can't even tell if they're a boy or a girl— who's only ever been like a shadow. They ask for their mom— but, like, in a really *creepy* way."

"Ghosts generally *are* creepy, when they talk," Selene said. "Doesn't necessarily mean they want to hijack your soul."

"Is *that* what ghosts do?" Kati yelped.

"Sometimes," said Selene.

Kati remembered how Clara had so vehemently instructed her to leave the house and took in a shuddering breath.

"Yeah, well . . . the other one is . . . was . . . " she stuttered to a halt. This was harder. By orders of magnitude.

"Bren, you said?" Jill prompted her, unexpectedly gentle.

"Bren, yeah," said Kati. "He was my . . . he was my fiancé. And I saw him, like, full on. There. Looked solid and everything."

"Yeah?" said Selene. "What did he have to say?"

"Nothing," said Kati. "I mean, I got the feeling he *wanted* to, you know? Say something, I mean. But he couldn't."

"Huh," said Selene. "If you don't mind my asking, how did he—" she stopped abruptly, like someone getting a nonverbal cue from someone on the other end. "Uh . . . " she said. "How long has he been dead?"

This required more thought than Kati expected. She knew the date, of course—she could never forget—but it had become detached from the rest of her life. How much time had passed since then? It had been summer when he went into hospice, and he hadn't lasted long after that. The summer seemed like a million years ago . . . or just last week.

"About five months," she said.

"I'm sorry," said Jill. She didn't sound like she was just saying the words because they were what you said to someone whose fiancé had just died. She was saying them like she really was *sorry,* deeply sorry, in every way possible.

It still left Kati at a loss for how to respond, so she just said "Thanks," and tried not to sound too hollow.

"And this is the first time you've seen his ghost?" Selene asked, her tone strictly business.

Kati began to say "Yes," and hesitated. Hadn't there been something else? Before the ghost? But those had just been dreams.

But if ghosts were real, then maybe dreams were more important than she thought.

"Yes, I mean—I never saw his ghost before. But there's also been dreams—kinda weird dreams—ever since I got here."

"Can you describe them?" Jill asked.

Kati tried. She thought she didn't do a very good job, but Selene and Jill listened patiently and at the end Selene *hmmm*-ed like she was a doctor and Kati had just related some troubling symptom.

"And—oh right, I can't believe I haven't mentioned this," Kati said. On the other end of the line the silence took on a charged quality. "It's been cold—*really* cold—in here. There. Like, the heating is just this woodstove and I'm camped out in front of it, but every night I've been waking up with *frost* on my sleeping bag."

"Oh," said Selene, with so much meaning packed behind the word it stretched on for several beats.

"What's that mean?" Jill asked promptly.

"Frost, well ... ghosts usually suck up energy around them in order to manifest," Selene explained.

"So they absorb infrared light, and it makes things colder?" Jill suggested. "That makes sense."

"Yeah," said Selene. "But making it cold enough for *frost?* That's a seriously strong specter you got there. That, or ... Kati, who did you say lived in that house before you bought it?"

"Who?" said Kati. "No one. I mean, it was abandoned when the previous owner died. That was this old codger named Gibbons, and it's been empty for over ten years."

"Ten years is nothing to a ghost," said Selene. "Usually they get stronger over time, if they're not laid to rest."

"Is that what you do?" Kati asked hopefully. "Lay ghosts to rest?"

"Sometimes," said Selene, sounding evasive. "Look, what can you tell us about this Gibbons guy?"

"Not a lot," Kati admitted, trying to dredge up what little she'd bothered to read about the previous resident. It hadn't seemed very important at the time. "A farmer, I think? Oh, and he had a wife—Martha, that was her name—and she either died before him or got sent to an asylum. I . . . uh . . . didn't research it thoroughly. I didn't think the place would be haunted."

"To be fair," Selene said after a rather judgmental pause, "most places aren't."

"So where did the kid come from?" Jill asked.

"They had kids," Kati said. "I remember hearing that. But they all died young. It was really sad—one of them got run over by their dad's tractor."

"Ouch," said Selene. "What about the others?"

Kati frowned and rubbed her forehead. Her arm was getting a cramp from holding the phone up, so she put it on speaker and lay down on the bed, setting it next to her head.

"I don't know," she admitted. "Like, I've heard rumors—but that's all they were."

"Okay, so start with them," Selene suggested.

Kati sighed. "So, like—this is just stuff I heard about through people who didn't actually *know* the Gibbons. My agent mentioned that there was this rumor that Martha Gibbons had that—what do you call it when you get a kick out of caring for a sick person, so you try to make them sick?"

"Munchausen by proxy," Jill supplied helpfully.

"Yeah, that one," said Kati. "Well, supposedly Martha Gibbons had it, and that's why the two girls both died. They died of the flu—I think. This was after the boy got run over. Anyway, this was back in the sixties and no one really talked about it. I mean the local kids obviously think the place is haunted but I haven't talked to them. They think I'm a witch."

"Are you?" Selene asked with perfect sincerity.

"I don't think so," said Kati. "I mean, that's something you'd know, right? That you were a witch."

"Probably," said Selene. "I ain't a witch, so I couldn't say."

"We clearly need more concrete information on the Gibbons family," Jill said decisively. "Kati, do you have internet at your motel?"

"Yes," said Kati miserably. "But my computer's back at the house. Should I go back for it? It's getting pretty light."

"No," said Selene firmly.

"Well, I'll see what I can find out en route," Jill said. "We've got at least another, oh, I'd say another five hours. Where are we?"

"Just passed Abilene," Selene supplied.

"Yeah," said Jill. "So just another five hours. In the meantime—" she broke off. "Oh, Clara's calling back. Hang on, I'll merge her."

There was a faint roaring in the background, and Clara's clam, crystal voice intoned: "Faraday has no knowledge of a witch named Bonifaunt."

"Oh," said Selene, sounding disappointed.

"She did recognize the name, though," Clara continued. "She said she remembers buying whisky from an Alma Bonifaunt in northern Arkansas—Franklin County."

"Why would she remember buying whisky from someone?" Jill wondered aloud.

"Because it was during the Prohibition," said Clara.

Kati found herself rubbing her forehead again.

"I didn't think she was that old," Jill said.

"Appearances can be deceptive," Clara said. "I am going to turn north at Fort Worth and go straight up to Franklin. I want to find out what she is. Kati, can you describe her?"

"Sure," said Kati, and then wondered briefly where to begin. "She's an old lady—likes to wear lots of scarves and knitted hats—but her hair isn't all white. I think it was lightish brown? She's got greenish eyes and sort of grayish skin. Big, droopy nose and very jowly. Tall, for a woman, and sort of *thick*? Um . . .

and she's got this incredible scar. Like right across her throat and all twisted up on one side. Makes her look like she has a wattle—like roosters do, under their beaks."

"Thank you," said Clara. "That is very helpful."

There was another *boop, boop, boop,* and Selene sighed gustily.

"Well, there she goes again."

"It's good, though," said Jill. "I'm sure she'll find something out."

"Yeah," said Selene. "Hey, Kati, you still with us?"

"Yes," said Kati, rolling over to check the battery on her phone. It was at half, which meant she should probably go plug it into her car charger pretty soon. It was ten-thirty now, and though her eyes burned and her head ached, she was also ravenously hungry.

"How's it over on your end? Feel pretty safe?"

Kati wasn't certain about *safe.* But, she figured, there was none of the creeping, cold chills in her hotel room, and with the morning had come the rumble and bustle of other guests waking up and leaving, and it seemed impossible for her to be haunted when surrounded by so many living humans.

"Yeah, pretty safe," she said.

"Okay," said Selene. "Now would be a very good time for you to do what I can't, and get some sleep. Take care of yourself, and we'll be with you by the afternoon. Anything happens, you call us, got it?"

"Got it," said Kati, suddenly frightened of being alone in her room. But after Selene hung up nothing happened except that she got painfully hungry, and went out to the car to rummage for emergency snacks while her phone was on the charger. Then, as sated as stale granola bars and fruit leather could make her, she turned off the engine, grabbed her phone, and staggered back to bed.

It had seemed, before she had eaten, that she would never want to sleep again. But with a full stomach and the promise of help on the way, she collapsed onto the (big, soft, not-moldy) bed, and dove head-first into slumber.

*   *   *

Selene drove, and Arcana rumbled across the open highways of Texas like a dark red thundercloud, the trailer looming behind him. She had hoped Jill would spell her a turn behind the wheel, but the woman had promptly taken out her phone and started looking up Texarkana history—specifically anything having to do with a family by the name of Gibbons. By the frown on her face and unhappy twist of her mouth Selene guessed it wasn't going well. Then, when they were through the nightmarish interchange of Fort Worth and Dallas, she made a face and put away her phone, curling up against the passenger window.

"Anything?" Selene asked, hoping to at least keep her awake.

"Some," said Jill. "It's not nice. I'll wait until we meet Kati, so I only have to explain once." She pulled a pillow out of the back seat, and promptly fell asleep.

Selene gripped the wheel in frustration, and drove on.

Kati woke in the early afternoon to the disconcerting feeling that someone was calling her name. It had been clear as a bell in her sleeping ear, but now that she sat up and rubbed the sand from her eyes the room was dim and quiet and just a little warmer than was strictly comfortable. Still, the sensation of someone *needing* her lingered, and left a sour feeling in her mind that prevented her from going back to sleep.

It was one of the cruel ironies of life—sort of like the love of it getting diagnosed with stage-four lung cancer two years after you met him—that on the day when Kati could do nothing *but* lie around in her pajamas eating vending machine snack food, all she really wanted to do was get outdoors. Out . . . out *anywhere*. Mountains, deserts, swamps . . . even the uninspired stretch of highway on either side of the motel seemed more attractive than sitting inside it waiting for who knew what.

Clara had seemed competent enough, and Jill was likable in a sharp, energetic sort of way, and Selene clearly knew a lot about ghosts . . . but they were only voices on the other end of a phone, and Kati knew how easy it would be to simply take their word for everything and let them sort it out. It was torturously tempting, but she'd learned the hard way that the only person who really had her best interests at heart was *herself*.

She lay on the bed, a collection of Funyun crumbs growing around her. She tried to watch TV, but everything was either too grim, too dark, or too loud and flashy and shallow. Finally she switched it off and lay on her back, staring at the ceiling and feeling ill from too many Funyuns.

She'd roused herself to use the bathroom and drink a cup of water when there was the chuff and rumble of a huge truck pulling into the motel parking lot. Curious, Kati went to the window and saw it was one of those gigantic pickup rigs with double-stacked rear wheels. It was a rich, deep red that glimmered even under the overcast sky, and it was hauling an enormous trailer. The kind with a bit that extended over the truck's bed and had expanding compartments on either side.

Her phone rang, making her jump.

"Hi, Kati?" came a sharp, clear voice on the other end.

"Yeah," said Kati.

"It's Jill," said the voice. "We're here. Um . . . what room are you?"

Kati opened the door of her room for answer, and watched as a small, brown-haired woman with glasses climbed out of the passenger door of the truck, soon joined by a tall, black woman with her thick, wriggly hair in a bushy ponytail. She carried an olive-green duffle bag slung over one shoulder, and looked suspiciously around the sparsely populated parking lot as she followed her companion over. They were both somewhat heavy lidded and rumpled looking, and Kati guiltily remembered that they had been driving since the wee hours of the morning—all on account of her phone call.

"Hi," she said, waving awkwardly.

"Jill Hamilton," said the short woman in glasses, extending a hand. Kati turned her awkward wave into an even more awkward handshake. "Kati," she said. "Um, Clapham."

"Great," said Jill. She had a handshake like a cold wire— too small to be crushing, but severe and strong. "This is Selene Shields. She'll be seeing to your . . . uh . . . spiritual safety."

"Hi," said the black woman, hoisting the strap of her bag. Despite her haggard face and rumpled collar, Kati was impressed by her almond-shaped black eyes which seemed to look everywhere without actually looking at anything. She ushered them into her room, whereupon Selene pulled out a shotgun—a *shotgun*—and went around the whole place like she was checking for monsters.

"It's the *house* that was haunted," Kati said weakly.

"Yeah," said Selene from the bathroom. "But sometimes you take things with you. Seems clear, though. Jill, do me a favor and get the tub of salt. We'll want to do the doors and both windows and the heating vent in here."

"What about the one over the bed?" Jill asked, pointing.

Selene put her head out of the bathroom and frowned at it.

"Leave that," she said. "I'll cover it."

Jill nodded, and pulled an old jam jar out of the duffle bag. It was half full of white crystals which Kati had to assume was salt. Jill then went around sprinkling it under the door, on the window sills, and finally pushed some up between the vents of the AC duct in the bathroom.

"Okay," said Selene, appearing at Kati's elbow. She'd put away the shotgun, thankfully, and was holding what looked like a laser pointer. "Can I get you to have a seat—thanks—and let me see your hands?"

Bemused, Kati sat on the edge of the bed and held out her hands. Selene stuck the pointer in her mouth so she could take them in her own. She looked at Kati's palms, then turned them over, then she took out the pointer and turned it on.

It wasn't a laser—it was a blacklight. It made her skin look weird and rather blue, but nothing else.

Selene didn't react, she just moved on and checked Kati's nose and ears the same way. Finally she leaned back and said, "Could'ja say 'ahh' for me?"

"Ahhh . . . " said Kati. *Just like the doctor's office!* she thought.

"Huh," said Selene. And just like at the doctor's, Kati had no idea whether that was good or bad.

Apparently, neither did Jill.

"*Well?*" she asked, putting her hands on her hips.

"Everything looks pretty clear," said Selene. "'Sfar as I can tell from the blacklight."

"What does that mean?" Kati asked, bewildered.

Selene stuck the light pen in her shirt pocket. "It means you're not possessed, and it's unlikely you picked up a tail. You said you touched one of these ghosts?"

Kati nodded. "I mean, one of my hands went through it."

"Which hand?"

"My right, I think."

Selene looked pointedly down at it. "I didn't see any discoloration or necropsification, which is good."

"So we're clear?" Jill asked, almost eagerly.

"For now," sighed Selene, sitting heavily on the edge of the bed.

"Good," said Jill, and produced a slim laptop out of her own backpack. "I managed to do a little research on the drive over," she explained to Kati. "This Gibbons family . . . it's pretty grim, actually."

"Oh," said Kati. "Great."

"So, most of it we have to infer from old newspaper articles," Jill said, bringing up a web browser and typing in a URL from her phone. Then she had to wait for the motel's login page to pop up, click the "agree" button as soon as it loaded, and then go back to her original window.

"I had to work backwards," she went on, "since the more recent articles were easier to find. But . . . " She opened three more tabs and dragged them around. "Here's the series of events as near as I can figure.

"Martha and Fred Gibbons had three kids—Jeremiah, Dorothy and Rebecca.   Jeremiah disappeared when he was five.   The whole neighborhood looked for him, but he never turned up.

"So that kinda tipped the family on its head.   I mean, there's no more articles, but I can *imagine.* That left Fred and Martha with the girls—Dorothy was two and Rebecca was eight months—for the next ten years or so . . . " She switched tabs. "Until we get *another* obituary, this time for Dorothy, who it says died of complications from whooping cough."

"Whooping cough?" said Kati incredulously. "But she'd have been, like *twelve.*"

"That's what it *says,*" said Jill.

"And Rebecca?" Selene asked darkly.

"She . . . got run over by a tractor," said Jill heavily. "Which was pretty terrible—Fred was the one driving it. I got a couple of articles on it from the Texarkana Wire, but they say the same thing: Fred was taking out a blackberry patch somewhere on the property, Rebecca had a fight with her mother and ran off into the fields. According to Martha, the blackberry patch was one of her favorite places to hide and she was upset about Fred taking it out. So they think she went to hide there, but Fred didn't know and . . . " Jill pursed her lips and pulled a thumb across her throat. "Then nothing until the late 90's, when there was a little article about how Fred Gibbons was raising money to have Martha Gibbons sent to the St Francis Assisted-Care facility. That's the last I could find on them until Fred's obituary ten years ago."

"Ouch," said Selene, stretching her back.

"That's awful," said Kati.

Jill was frowning up at Selene. "What do you think?"

"I can't," said Selene. "I need food to do that. Like a real meal you eat at a table. Anyone else want in?"

"Oh *yes*," said Kati in relief, then realized she was still in her happy-pig pajamas. "Um . . . but I don't have any clothes."

Selene gave her an appraising look. Kati tried not to blush. The size difference between them was not comical, but it was significant. Then the woman grinned.

"Aw, don't worry. I bet Clara's got something you can wear. Hope you don't mind black."

Which was how they ended up piling into the big red truck—*Arcana*, Jill called it—and driving down the road to the nearest restaurant. This turned out to be a Pizza Hut and Kati forgot all about her awkwardly fitting shirt and trousers (Clara must have been some sort of giant, since her clothes could be convinced to span Kati's width in exchange for dangling off the ends of her limbs for miles) when the smell of cheese and pepperoni hit her nostrils.

It made listening to Selene talk about the Gibbons family all the more grotesque, however.

"Did I hear right, and it's thought Martha Gibbons had that monk-house by proxy crap going on?" she asked as she piled her plate with slices of Italian sausage and meat-lover.

"Munchausen by proxy," Jill supplied patiently.

"Yes," said Kati, dutifully taking a slice of the mushroom-and-spinach pizza Jill had ordered in the commendable hope that some vegetables might be consumed that night.

"Right," said Selene, eating nearly half a slice in a single bite. She pulled the string of melted mozzarella off with her fingers and stuffed it in her mouth. "So, say she did. Say she kept Dorothy sick for so long the kid eventually died. Then Rebecca. I suppose you could make an argument that she ran away, but it's just as likely her ma got her as well. And as for Martha Gibbons herself . . . it's possible she never made it to that asylum in Dallas."

"Why?" asked Jill.

Selene swallowed. "Because of the way the house is. What you're describing," she said, pointing at Kati with a piece of her crust. "Sounds like a classic case of vengeful spirits."

"Vengeful spirits . . . " Kati repeated, blankly.

"Basically," Selene went on, mopping up some extra sauce with her crust and then grabbing another slice of meat-lover. "Ghosts aren't really whole people. They're like echoes of a person. Memories and habits. Afterimages. If a person has a particularly strong character, they can seem almost alive. But it's different for every ghost. Anyway, if a ghost stays caught in the same place it died—and if there was a lot of trauma related to its death and that place—it can get a bit twisted. Infected, almost. They mutate into these things which aren't really ghosts anymore, since they really do have a life of their own. That's why we call 'em vengeful spirits. Spirits, because they're more than echoes, and vengeful . . . because that's usually what they're about. Only they're so messed up they kinda tend to take out their vengeance on whatever poor idjit wanders into their territory. In this case, you and that house."

She paused, in order to take another two bites of pizza, chew, and take a swig of soda pop. Kati envied her metabolism. Selene wasn't what you'd call thin—she was too solid and thick for that—but she certainly wasn't obese. Hunting ghosts must burn a lot of calories.

"Signs of a vengeful spirit haunting include cold flashes, surprise appearances, wildlife infestations, bleeding walls, screams coming from nowhere, telekinetic interference and in-explicable deaths," Selene went on, ticking each item off a cheesy finger. "Admittedly, you've only two—"

"Three," Kati said.

"Huh?"

"Three," she repeated. "On the second day, Alma was clean-ing out the attic. When I went up to check on her this big black bird flew right into my face, cawing and stuff."

"Mmm," said Selene, her mouth full of her third slice of pizza. "Raven or crow?"

"I couldn't tell," Kati admitted.

Selene shrugged. "This is just a theory—I don't have ir-refutable evidence—"

"Then it's not a theory," Jill pointed out. "It's just a hypoth-esis."

"Fine," said Selene. "I have a hypothesis, and I think its worth working on, that Martha Gibbons killed Jeremiah and Dorothy, and Fred Gibbons killed her, and the whole murdering lot of them have been haunting that place, slowing driving each other insane, for the last twenty years."

"What about Rebecca?" Jill asked.

Selene shrugged. "Violent deaths can create ghosts, too, but they usually fade pretty quickly. It's worth checking, though."

"And Bren?" Kati asked in a small voice.

"Ah," said Selene, leaning back in her hard plastic chair and folding her hands across her stomach. "That's probably a sepa-rate matter. You don't happen to have anything of his? Impor-tant keepsakes? Hair clippings? Ashes?"

"No," said Kati, suddenly feeling sore inside. "His mother got his ashes—she's in Chicago."

"Hmm," said Selene, prying a piece of chicken from between her teeth with her tongue. "Well, we'll work on that. It could be a separate phenomenon altogether. We'll have to see when we check the house tomorrow."

"We're going back?" Kati said. The words sounded stupid once they were out of her mouth, but she'd assumed they'd want to give the house a wide berth.

"First thing tomorrow morning," said Selene. "Which, by the way, you are going to take the watch tonight," she added, jabbing a finger at Jill. "Clara can ride all day and night and slay monsters in the morning, but I'm only human."

Jill looked put upon, but nodded. Selene eyed the three plates their pizza had come on, which had been emptied save for a lonely piece of mushroom and spinach.

"Is anyone gonna eat that?" she asked.

Silently, Jill slid it across the table to her. Kati didn't object. She wasn't hungry any more.

Ozark, MO

THE AREA WAS BEAUTIFUL, Clara had to admit, in a way that made you almost forget how dangerous it could be. Almost. Thick, forested hills that, even in winter, somehow managed to look lush and lively. Dramatic canyons with chattering rivers and the kind of narrow, windy roads that motorcycles like Unicorn rejoiced in. And lots of small towns where an odd-looking woman on a motorbike asking strange questions got a downright chilly reception.

Deciding she'd be better off seeking the sort of answers that didn't come from judgmental sources, she headed straight for Ozark and its public library. This was almost a disaster, since the assistant clerk on duty didn't know where they kept the town's citizen records, and wasn't willing to help Clara find them. Undaunted, she made a point of looming through all the likely areas (the dustiest ones) until the actual librarian turned up, and in the interests of making the uncomfortable stranger go away by giving her what she wanted, showed her down to the basement.

"Public records are that aisle," she said, pointing down a corridor of filing cabinets. "You can use this table," she added, kicking a dusty metal affair that looked like it had been dragged out of a Stazi interrogation room. "You're not allowed to take them off library property, but if you make an account with us we can give you photocopies."

Clara nodded, and waited until the woman retreated before heading into the trench of cabinets like someone stepping into a flooded sewer.

It was slow, tedious work. There were no official records of an Alma Bonifaunt from the 1930's, and moving backward there were no birth certificates either. There was repeated mention of an *Alfred* Bonifaunt, who might have been a brother or cousin, but nothing for Alma before her dustup with a gang from Fort Smith.

Three brothers had taken exception to her business as a bootlegger, as it brought her in direct competition with them. No one knew exactly what had happened except that the local deputies had found the three brothers dead from shotgun wounds to the face, and Alma with her throat torn open—but miraculously alive. Unsurprisingly, she hadn't been able to tell the officers what had happened, and by the time she'd recovered enough to speak, they had lost the nerve to ask. This, if anything, convinced Clara it was the same Alma Bonifaunt as the one currently frustrating Kati Clapham.

Clara set aside that article and continued searching for Alfred Bonifaunt, for lack of anything better to do. His trail was easy to follow: born in 1889 just outside Ozark, there were several citations for lewd behavior and inappropriate dress—whatever that was. Then he disappeared.

Or not quite. There was a newspaper clipping from what was obviously a different paper, stapled to the last chronological reference to Alfred Bonifaunt in Ozark. It was a Tennessee newspaper, and it was a profile of a sideshow performer named—yes, named *Alma*. A mysterious "southern belle" with a rich, auburn beard who charmed audiences with her throaty singing. In old, smudged pencil, a long-ago scholar had scribbled *Bonifaunt?* under the grainy photograph of a large woman wearing a gaudy dress and an impressive beard.

Clara stared at the picture for a few minutes, then went back and double-checked Alfred's birthdate. Then she skipped forward to the thirties again, looking for what had happened to Alma.

Alma had gotten shot in the chest during a raid on her distillery, but she survived. The article's headline was a notice that Alma "Ironheart" Bonifaunt had been released from the hospital. Afterward, no one wanted to bother her. There was nothing about her for the rest of the 30's, but in 1946 there was an article stating that three former marines had been detained for questioning regarding the disappearance of "Ironheart" Bonifaunt.

No charges were brought, but it was obvious to Clara that Alma had been the victim of yet another attack. One that, as far as the public record was concerned, had ended her life.

After that there was no mention of either Alma or Alfred Bonifaunt.

Which made sense, if they were the same person. Which Clara had no trouble accepting. It was the 1889 birth date which troubled her.

Because Alma might have disappeared from Ozark in the 1940's, but she was very much present in Texas now.

People who lived over one hundred and twenty years tended to have some supernatural aid. People who survived getting burned, beaten, bashed and shot, and people who could interact physically with ghosts were not strictly *human* any more. Not usually.

But if Alma was a ghoul, she was an exceptionally scrupulous, ethical one. If she was a lich Kati should have been able to tell by looking—and she was clearly too lucid to be a revenant or a zombie.

Which left one other option, which was so unlikely Clara's breath caught at the idea that it might actually be true.

Foregoing the hassle of making an account in order to get photocopies, she laid out all the relevant articles on the dusty little table and took photographs with her phone. Then she emailed them to Jill. Before it sent, her phone gave her a plaintive alert warning her that the email had no subject. Clara frowned at the empty field before typing in: "Alma may be an undying" and waited for the happy "whooshing" noise that meant the message had been sent.

Northeast Texas

IT FELT STRANGE RETURNING TO THE HOUSE IN BROAD DAYLIGHT, with a huge truck towing an even huger trailer down the narrow road. Despite everything they'd talked about, and despite how seriously both Selene and Jill took her claims, Kati couldn't help feeling a pang of nervous embarrassment as she pulled up in front of the house to find she'd left the door open in her hurry to leave. It was like the time when she'd been cat-sitting for her friend, Sue. Sue's cat had got a cough, and Kati had driven the animal down to the vet in a mad panic, only for the cat to stop coughing as soon as they got into the waiting room, and the vet couldn't find anything wrong with it.

Now she was wondering if her house would behave the same way. But she reminded herself that the vet had been delighted to find nothing wrong with the cat, and perhaps Selene and Jill would feel the same.

When they all trooped in through the front door, however, it was to find the kitchen a complete disaster: her camp stove had been overturned, food scattered about, and the refrigerator door was hanging open, its alarm bleeping forlornly.

"What do you call this?" Jill asked. "Poltergeist?"

Selene stepped nimbly through the mess and inspected the fridge. "Don't think so. Poltergeists don't eat," she explained, holding up a package of baloney that had been torn open and half eaten. "Unless this is your work?" she added.

Kati shook her head. Even at her most distraught, she didn't eat baloney straight from the package. That was what peanut butter was for.

"You mentioned finding some kids in the house earlier?" Selene suggested.

Kati shrugged, beginning to feel embarrassed.

"It's possible *this* is a conventional prank," Jill said.

Selene stuck the baloney back in the fridge and closed the door. She stood up and looked around the kitchen, peering down the hall to the living room.

"All right guys!" she shouted, so loudly it made Kati jump. "If anyone's in here who shouldn't be in here, now's a good time to *get out.*"

There was a rustling from above them, and the clatter and scratch of claws on wood. Selene leapt into action while Kati was still trembling from shock. She had an odd device in her hand— a taser, Kati realized—and she was pelting down the corridor, looking for the stairs.

"On your left!" she yelled after her, and saw Selene nod and dart out of sight.

Jill was only a few paces behind her, and Kati lurched into her wake, following Jill's light footsteps up the stairs with her heavy, pounding ones.

They arrived to find Selene had opened the window at the end of the hall and was leaning out, clearly looking at something. Behind her, the attic door was wide open—and Kati noticed there were now more scratches in the battered wood. Fresh ones. The sight made her stop dead.

"Just a raccoon," Selene was saying, turning away from the window. "Thought she'd be done for, busting out the window like that, but she made it—what?" She stopped, seeing the look on Kati's face.

Unable to speak, Kati just pointed at the attic door.

"Oh, dude," said Selene, inspecting the splintered wood. "Yanno, ghosts might not be your only problem here."

"That was where the raven came out of," Kati said weakly. "Before."

"Oh," said Selene in a very different tone of voice, and got the taser out again.

"Does that actually work on ghosts?" Kati asked as Selene disappeared up the stairs.

"The taser? Hell no. I use it to detect them."

"But what if you find one?" Kati asked, daring to follow— safely behind Jill.

"Generally speaking," Selene said, sounding a little distracted, "ghosts can't hurt you directly. That whole can't touch 'em thing? Works both ways. The way you handle a ghost is: find out who and where it is, then salt the place and clean it out. Huh."

She'd come up into the dim attic space where the ceiling beams provided the only footholds over the ancient insulation blocks.

"What is it?" Kati asked, trying to peer around Jill.

"It's clean, that's what it is," Selene said. "Except . . . oh, hold on here . . . "

Her voice moved off further into the attic, and Jill followed, allowing Kati to finally get a glimpse of the place.

Clean it was—Alma's work, undoubtedly—and completely empty . . . save a small nest near the southern gable end where

Selene was crouched, going over its contents with a long, brown finger.

"Funny she missed that," Kati wondered aloud. "Alma, when she came and cleaned up here."

"I don't think she missed anything," Selene said, holding up a strip of brightly colored nylon the same color as Kati's sleeping bag. "This is *new.*"

"Could animals have gotten in and made it?" Jill asked.

Selene frowned around at the attic. Despite the general dis-repair of the house, it was actually well sealed—again, probably thanks to Alma—and there were no obvious holes where an an-imal the size of a raccoon could have gotten in.

"Mice, maybe," she said. "But nothing the size of what made this. It's almost big enough for a kid . . . " She stopped. At her side, the taser had started to buzz and pop, little darts of electricity jumping across the head. Quickly she held it up and turned around, sweeping the blunt little gun across the empty space of the attic.

Only the attic wasn't empty. There was a child-sized shape standing in the shadows beside the stairs. Kati could see a pale hand clasped in a loose fist and the hem of a cream-colored gown. But there were no feet, and the child's head was just a dark outline.

"S-Selene," Kati whispered, not daring to move or even speak loudly.

"Someone there?" Selene asked, taking a step toward the child. The electricity at the end of the taser crackled audibly.

Kati nodded vigorously.

"You can see them?"

"Can't you?"

"Nope," said Selene, at the same time Jill said, "See what?"

Maybe I really *am* crazy, Kati thought for one mad moment. Then Selene chuckled.

"You've got some good eyes on you, sister. All right, where are they exactly—and can you describe them?"

"By the stairs," Kati whispered, and then shivered as she felt a wave of cold air roll over her. By the sudden intake of breath from her companions she guessed they had felt that, at least.

"It—I think it's a girl. She's wearing a white dress, and I can't see her feet or head."

"Headless?" Selene asked.

"No, just . . . in shadow. She looks kinda like she's floating, though."

"Okay," said Selene, and took a step toward the ghost.

Lightning arced from the taser through the air, striking the ground where the ghost stood. It briefly created an outline of a child, maybe five or six years old, with a mop of messy hair. There was a sound of screaming and a voice boomed out of nowhere:

"Where is Mama?"

There was a lump in Kati's throat, preventing her from speaking, but Selene answered, her voice calmly steady:

"Mama's not here anymore."

"Is it talking?" asked Jill. "I can't hear anything."

"Where is *Mama?*" demanded the ghost, and surged forward.

It wasn't a girl. It was a boy. He had sandy hair and a face screwed up in agony and fear, and he flew at Selene with his hands outstretched.

"Selene, d—" Kati began, and then the ghost had passed through her, turning to silver mist, and flattened itself against the roof beams behind her, leaving a circle of frost right above the animal's nest.

"Oh *bwwwwaah,*" said Selene, shaking out her limbs. "That's *never* fun."

"Are you okay?" Jill asked, looking between Selene and the circle of frost.

"Gimme a minute," Selene croaked, doubled over and beginning to shiver.

Clearly trusting the woman's word, Jill went over to the frost circle and poked it with a curious finger. It hissed as the portion she had touched turned to steam.

"Damn," she said quietly.

Selene unfolded herself slowly, experimentally shaking out her limbs. Kati noticed that her lips looked almost blue.

"Right," she said. "I need a cup of hot water—maybe two—and then we better do a full sweep. I don't know what's kept Jeremiah Gibbons here, but I'm bettin' he's not the only one."

*   *   *

Alma Bonifaunt sat on the front porch of the tired little house surrounded—and in places invaded—by pines and oak. With one foot she kept the chair gently rocking while she took sips from a Crown Royal bottle which held a liquid far too bright and yellow to be the liquor advertised on the label. The sun had reached the highest point in its shallow, winter arch, and the old woman tilted her gray face to better absorb its warmth.

Sunlight was about the only thing that made her feel warm these days. She didn't feel heat, fire didn't burn, but the sun—if she could just absorb enough sunlight, she thought, she might even come alive again.

There was a distant roar of an engine. She dismissed it at first, as she could sometimes hear traffic on the highway. When it drew closer she listened, curiously.

The back roads around her home were badly signed and maze-like. One of the reasons she had selected the house in the first place. That and the bitter old ghost she'd encountered had called her a she-male, and she'd taken deep satisfaction in burying him, and then proceeding to set up her home on his spiritual grave.

In any case, her house was hard to find. Especially if you were looking for it. Sure enough, the engine soon retreated.

Alma allowed herself the smallest inward grin.

Then it got louder again. Determinedly louder. Her inward grin vanished and her outward appearance bunched and sagged in displeasure. She took another sip of her brew, felt it tingle down her throat and into her veins, before putting the cap on the bottle and setting it beside her chair.

She was still sitting, hands folded neatly across her belly, watching the narrow gravel drive, when a motorcycle appeared in the middle of it. Big and black with a metal spike mounted above the headlight, it had the look of a machine more at home on the racetrack than the wilderness. The rider (also big and clad in black) handled it skillfully, and brought the bike to a controlled stop a respectful distance from her porch.

They dismounted, throwing a long leg over the back and then standing in front of the bike, regarding her inscrutably from behind their tinted visor. They had a sword—the long kind that wanted two hands to wield it—strapped to their back, and stood in the sort of way which would make it very difficult for anyone to knock them over.

Alma just stared at them. She'd found it advantageous to let other people talk first—it gave her a chance to take a measure of them—but this person seemed to feel the same way. They stood observing her for almost two minutes. Then with a faint twitch of their shoulders they reached up and took off their helmet.

Alma was not entirely surprised to find a woman's face staring back at her—though she was impressed by the intensity of the blue eyes and the pale nakedness of the shaved head. She didn't show it, of course, but she noticed with interest how the woman seemed neither frightened nor dismissive of her. It had been a long time since Alma had been looked at with such calm rationality, and she wasn't sure she liked it.

"Alma Bonifaunt," said the bald woman. It was not a question, so Alma didn't answer.

"I am Claymore Nordstern," she continued. "I wish to speak with you."

There was something not quite *on* about this woman, Alma thought. She wasn't a ghost or a spirit, but she registered in that part of Alma's mind that saw ghosts and felt spirits. And in what Alma thought of as her "backwards vision" there was a faint haze around her. As if, in the very immediate vicinity of her person, the rules of the universe *bent* to accommodate her.

Alma sucked thoughtfully on one of her better teeth. She reached into the pocket of her denim skirt and fished out a toothpick, which she began to chew.

"There's another chair 'round the back," she said, indicating the direction with a roll of her head.

Many people floundered against Alma's purposefully taciturn nature. They rained questions on her, and she soaked them up like a thirsty desert, never giving back so much as a drop.

Claymore Nordstern set off through the trees, picking her way carefully around the drifts of brown leaves and needles.

* * *

Selene frowned at the burned-out circle in the driveway, which Kati thought was unfair, considering she was the one who had made it.

"Huh," she said, in the way Bren's doctors had when they looked at his X-rays. She felt her heart sink.

"What's wrong?" she asked.

"Nothing's *wrong*," said Selene, crouching down to get a better look at the scorched gravel. "But, okay, you see this stain here," she pointed with a finger to the place that had burned green when Selene had lit the fire, leaving behind a flaky, white ash that stood out against the blackened stones. "That's Jeremiah. But over here," she pointed at a little fleck right on the edge. "That's not big enough to be a fully realized ghost, but it is *something*."

"How sensitive is this sweep?" Jill asked. "Maybe it's picking up a . . . maybe like an echo of some other ghosts?"

"You mean an echo of an echo?" Selene said cynically. Then she shrugged. "Could be. But it looks like there's just the one right now. Okay—Jill, could you get the box? You know, *the box.*"

Jill, who'd been frowning in confusion, suddenly perked up. "*Oh*," she said. "You're gonna try that?"

"Why not?" said Selene, and Jill took off for the trailer.

Kati sidled up to Selene and looked curiously down at the blackened circle.

"What are you going to do to him?" she asked in a small voice.

Selene twisted her mouth and rested her hands on her hips. "Technically speaking, I'm not gonna do anything *to* him. With ghosts it's easier to sever whatever material connection they have to this world and let them go on their merry way. Which connection is usually their body, but unless he's buried in the basement or something there's got to be something else that's anchoring him to the house. Ghosts usually stick close to their bodies, unless their death was really traumatic, in which case they can haunt that area for *ages,* even after their body's been burned and salted."

"Traumatic like . . . being run over by a tractor?" Kati suggested.

Selene shrugged and nudged a singed stone with the toe of her boot. "Usually it's the more emotionally traumatic deaths. But death by tractor might work. Which is why I'll be doing a purge of the place. Get rid of any physical anchors that might be keeping him here."

"Physical anchors?"

"Tools, toys . . . things he touched when he was alive," Selene waved a hand. "Things that were important to him. Take those away and clean them, he won't have any anchors to hold him here."

Kati swallowed. "You make it sound as if there's somewhere else he could go."

"Well, if he was a spirit, he could go to the spirit world—it's where those things end up, mostly," Selene said. "But if he's a ghost . . . ghosts aren't exactly people. Not the way you and me are. They're like, like a piece of personality that's just left, lingering. A lot of the time they fade away on their own. But if they've got a strong enough anchor, or a strong enough personality, they can last for years. Sometimes they get a bit twisted in that time, turn into something else entirely. It's usually not nice."

"Oh," said Kati.

A crunch of gravel announced Jill approaching, carrying what looked like the sort of metal case that might hold drill bits or wrenches. When she opened it, however, inside were three jars filled with a clear fluid and containing little nuggets of silvery-white metal. Selene grabbed each of them, and a pair of tongs from the side of the box, and marched into the house.

"Right," she said when they were gathered around the kitchen table. "This is the not-fun part. Kati, I'm gonna need to purge every object in this house that doesn't belong to you, since I can't know which of them might be Jeremiah's anchor."

Jill groaned, clearly anticipating an arduous task, but in reality it turned out to be fairly simple. Alma had been so thorough with her own cleaning that very little of the original contents of the house remained. Selene went through all the bedrooms, placing a nugget of silvery metal in the middle of the floor, and painting lines across the doorways with smears of the liquid—which seemed to be some kind of oil.

They worked from the top of the house down, after disman-tling the nest in the attic. The frost had vanished by then, but the room still felt colder than the rest of the house. There was no sign of Jeremiah. In fact, after Selene had been through, ev-erything felt stiflingly ordinary.

"What is that stuff?" Kati asked, indicating the bottles.

"This is . . . uh . . . sodium," said Selene, checking the label. "It was actually Jill's idea. See, we've been using salt for centuries to deter ghosts, and . . . uh . . . "

"Salt is usually sodium chloride," Jill explained. "I'm trying to determine what the active ingredient for the ghost-deterrent effect is. Because sodium iodide works just as well as sodium chloride I have a hypothesis that it's the *sodium* that's impor-tant, so we're trying the pure element. I'm also interested to learn to what extent this trait is shared with other alkali metals. Which is why we've also got some potassium"—she tapped the jar under Selene's elbow—"and lithium." She held up the third jar, which she'd been carrying for Selene.

Kati, who hadn't paid much attention in chemistry, was mystified. But Jill seemed to know what she was on about, so she just followed the two women as they slowly worked their way down through the house, dropping nuggets of greasy metal in every room.

"I've also got regular table salt," Selene assured her. "In case this doesn't work."

It seemed to, however. They didn't encounter Jeremiah (or Bren or anyone else for that matter), but Kati couldn't help feel-ing like every time they left a room that had been "purged," the rest of the house felt more charged. It was a subtle, creeping feeling that snuck up her arms and made her shiver, but since neither Selene nor Jill appeared to notice, she said nothing.

Finally there was only the basement left. Selene's jar of sodium was half empty, and descending the stairs felt like step-ping into a cold bath of pins and needles. It reminded Kati of the feeling she had gotten when she'd accidentally touched the ghost, only all over and less intense.

This time Selene did notice it. "Oh *jeez,*" she said, and as soon as she got to the bottom she unscrewed the jar of sodium and dumped the contents on the floor.

Kati did remember one thing about sodium. If you took a piece and threw it in water, it would explode.

Something like that happened when the oil-covered nuggets of sodium hit the dry, concrete floor.

Blue flame leapt up around them, and Jill shouted and took a step back. Selene, however, calmly stood in the middle of it, the fire dancing around her boots, until it died away.

"Ghost fire," she said, seeing their shocked faces. "Put pure sodium down as a yes, Jill. And hand me the potassium."

Kati sat on the bottom step of the stairs and watched in mute astonishment as Selene proceeded to go through the basement, carefully dropping globs of oil and potassium on the ground. It also burned—greenish this time—but never as brightly.

They were right around the back of the water heater, and Jill was suggesting Selene try the lithium next, when Kati felt a draft of cold air at her elbow and looked over to find the ghost of Jeremiah Gibbons crouched beside her on the stairs.

He had his knees up in his chest and his arms wrapped around them, his face twisted in unmistakable misery.

Kati suddenly became extremely conscious of every little movement she made, simply by being alive. Every breath, every pulse of blood in her veins was like a violent motion in comparison to the stillness of the dead child.

And he was, Kati realized, a child. Being dead didn't change that. In fact, Kati thought, it made him even more of a child.

Holding her breath for fear of scaring him, she slowly pulled her own knees up in mimicry, and tilted her head sideways so she could look at him out of the corner of her eye.

"Hi," she whispered.

"Where's Mama?" he asked, still not looking at her. But Kati recognized the waver in his voice from the many times she'd heard it in her own. He was on the verge of tears.

"I don't know," Kati admitted. She floundered for the right thing to say, and decided treating him like any other kid who'd lost his parents was probably the best thing. "When did you last see her?"

Jeremiah looked at her then, and his eyes were empty hollows. It made his face look all wrong in a nightmarish way, but Kati just swallowed and stayed where she was.

"I don't remember," he said, sounding so sad and lost Kati wished she could hug him—creepy face and all.

"First, it was me an' Mama and Papa and Dot and Rebbie," he went on, his brows crunching in concentration. "Then Papa got mad. He put me under the blackberry bush all night. When I got back he an' Mama and Dot and Rebbie were gone."

Kati swallowed. "You've been alone all this time?" she asked, while in her mind thoughts raced.

Papa put you under the blackberry bush? But the papers said you ran away . . .

"No," said Jeremiah. "I made friends. There was Raven and Rocky. And then Dot came back. And then Rebbie. And then Mama . . . "

A picture was forming in Kati's mind. If most living people couldn't see ghosts . . . maybe most ghosts couldn't see living people. Had Jeremiah been haunting his own house all this time, slowly joined by other members of his family as they died one by one?

"Papa was here for a while. But Mama said he wasn't our Papa no more. She say he the reason we can't leave the house anymore. We made him go away."

What if Martha Gibbons hadn't had Munchausen by proxy? What if Fred Gibbons had been a psychopath? Martha Gibbons never made it to the asylum in Dallas . . .

"Jeremiah," Kati whispered. "Where are Mama and Dot and Rebbie now?"

"Don't know," said Jeremiah. "They went . . . the Ammamonster got them."

"The . . . *Amma Monster*?" Kati repeated.

Jeremiah nodded jerkily. The motion left a faint trail of images in the air, merging together into a blur of faces.

"Ammamonster still out to get me," he whispered, leaning into Kati's side.

She felt him, like a cold fizzing and a spread of pins and needles up her side. She held her breath and tried to remain perfectly still.

"Jeremiah," she said. "What does the Amma Monster look like?"

"She big," said Jeremiah. "She wear a moldy hat, and has two mouths."

"Two mouths?" said Kati.

Another nod, which felt like a spill of soda water down Kati's side. "One of them is sewed shut."

Kati felt like her throat was drying up.

"Jeremiah," she said. "Do you mean the *Alma* Monster?"

"Yeah," said Jeremiah's ghost. "That's what I said. Amma-monster."

Around behind the water heater there was a *clang* and then Selene said "Oh holy *cows*."

Kati jumped, and Jeremiah evaporated into a thin, frosty mist.

"Is that what I think it is?" asked Jill.

"Yeah, pretty much," said Selene unhappily.

Kati pried herself up onto shaking limbs and hobbled off in the direction of their voices. She found the two women crowded around a dark hole in the wall, where a metal plate had been pried aside. Just peeking into view out of the darkness was a pale thing like a stick covered in white leather. Then Kati's mind caught up with what she was seeing and she realized it was the desiccated arm of a child's corpse.

"Which one do you think it is?" Jill was asking, then she noticed Kati.

"Oh, sorry," said Selene, shuffling forward to block her view. "Look, you don't need to see this . . . "

"I think that's Jeremiah," Kati said, feeling hollow and cold.

"What?" said Selene, looking at her sharply.

"Jeremiah," repeated Kati. "The one who ran away. I don't think he did. I think Fred Gibbons killed him. I think he killed them all. He must have hidden Jeremiah's body down here."

Selene raised an eyebrow, then looked down at the body, considering.

"What makes you think that?" Jill asked.

Kati took in a deep breath. "Because that's what he told me," she said.

*   *   *

The chair was old and plastic and sun damaged, but it held Clara's weight as she settled herself gingerly into it. She could feel Alma Bonifaunt's eyes on her the whole time, boring into her black leather armor like a pair of knives. In return, Clara allowed herself a frank appraisal of the woman, not caring if the scrutiny unnerved her.

Alma Bonifaunt was tall for a woman—though not as tall as Clara. Her skin was grayish and leathery, and there was a milkiness to the pupils of her eyes that suggested cataracts, though she appeared to see well enough. She was wearing clothes which, though worn, were well made and cared for. A denim skirt, an argyll sweater-vest, and a knit cap were the notable features, along with the impressive scar across her throat. She did breathe, Clara was interested to note, but so faintly it was easy to miss.

Minutes passed, and Alma Bonifaunt seemed content just to sit there and let Clara stare at her. To her consternation, Clara realized *she* would have to start the conversation. She cleared her throat in preparation, and Alma blinked. It was the first time she had done so.

"Do you know what you are?" Clara asked. It was perhaps the simplest question she had.

Alma Bonifaunt pulled the corners of her mouth down and shrugged.

Which was, as far as Clara was concerned, a perfectly fair answer.

"How many times have you died?" she tried.

This time Alma Bonifaunt frowned.

"Ain't never died, girl," she said. "Didn't hold with that bullcrap. Never did. Still don't."

"When did you know that you weren't going to?" Clara asked.

Alma looked at her critically.

"When did you know you weren't rightly part of this world?" she asked, and Clara felt like her bones had turned to ice. This woman saw. She saw *her*. In every way Clara had tried to hide . . .

"I'd say it was about like that, for me," Alma went on, uncaring about the internal turmoil she had triggered. Clara had to strain to hear over the roaring in her ears. "It's something one *knows*, innit? In your bones. Like you know you're thirsty, or hungry, or a woman."

Clara swallowed.

Alma Bonifaunt sighed, resettling herself into her chair and stretching her legs.

"Look," she said, rocking her head to one side. "You found me here. Means you already know everything you need to know 'bout me. What I'm wonderin' is what you're gonna do about it."

"Probably nothing," said Clara, honestly. The roaring was receding, and she was beginning to feel human again. "I am more concerned with your intentions toward Kati Clapham."

Two tufty eyebrows lifted in surprise, the first sign of emotion Alma had yet exhibited.

"I got nothin' but kindness for Miss K," she said. "She's a nice girl—I'm just trying to help her out."

"By exorcising ghosts from her house?" Clara pressed on.

"Oh, I ain't no preacher," said Alma with a touch of modesty. "I don't go in for those fancy rituals and jibber-jabber. But I don't like a bully, and that Martha Gibbons, she didn't strike me as the type to let the living live in peace, if you know what I mean."

"You mean Martha Gibbons's ghost?" Clara asked.

"No, I mean Martha Gibbons. Are those sails on either side of your head just for show? Martha Gibbons and her kids never so much as stirred a leaf until Miss K turned up. Then it's all hoollerin' and hollerin' such that I can't get no peace and I just know Miss K would up and leave if I didn't do anything. So I did what I do."

"Because you want Kati Clapham to stay?"

Alma hunkered down in her chair and glared at Clara. "She's a good girl," she mumbled, taking another sip from her bottle. "She got a shadow about her though, which I don't like. Don't like it at all. And I never did finish the job. She drove me off before I got Jeremiah sorted."

Clara leaned forward in her seat, clasping her hands together.

"And . . . how exactly did you 'sort' the others? Martha and Dorothy and Rebecca?"

"I just tidy things up," said Alma Bonifaunt, simply. "Clean out the cobwebs, dust off the shelves. You keep a clean house, you keep the spirits clean too. Sometimes they need a little convincing, but then I never been afraid to get hands-on if the need arises."

Clara let out a long, slow breath. Then she allowed herself a smile.

"You *are* an undying," she whispered.

"Say what?" said Alma.

Clara just smiled and shook her head. "I never thought I'd meet one—not in this world, anyway."

"I'm the only one of me there is," Alma declared, which Clara didn't doubt.

"Yes," she said. "But there have been others before you. Still are, by definition."

Alma regarded her cagily, her knobby fingers knitting together around the neck of the bottle.

"I am also concerned about Kati Clapham," Clara went on. "My friends are already investigating the house. I expect they will be able to handle Jeremiah Gibbons. What worries me is this shadow you mentioned. Can you be more specific?"

"You *talked* to the ghost of Jeremiah Gibbons?" Selene asked. Not as though she didn't believe her. More as though she wanted to make certain that was what had happened.

Kati nodded. "He was right there." She pointed at the stairs. "He kept asking where his mama was. I think . . . I think they all must have been here. Before whatever Alma did made the others go away."

Selene scratched her chin. "And he says his daddy killed them all?"

Kati chewed nervously on her bottom lip. "Not . . . not in so many words. But the way he talked about it . . . that's what it sounded like."

Selene nodded to herself. "Well, that makes sense to me."

"How?" asked Jill, straightening up from examining the withered arm.

"Man murders son," said Selene, spreading her hands out illustratively. "Hides body. Makes it look like a runaway. Little while later, kills daughter. Makes it look like an illness. Kills other daughter, makes it look like an accident. Wife finally catches on, he makes a big to-do about getting her committed. Then kills her."

She rubbed her hands together, as if cleaning them of invisible dust. "Simple as that."

Jill looked horrified. "But why would he *do* that?" she wondered aloud.

Selene gave her companion a heavy look. "Because there were voices in his head telling him to do it. Because he was possessed by a demon. Because he *liked* it. Lots of reasons people kill other people; none of them are nice."

"I'll say." Jill shivered.

"But what do we *do* about him?" Kati insisted. "Jeremiah isn't evil—just scared, and lonely."

"Right. That." Selene clapped her hands briskly. "For that, we just gotta send him home."

"Home?" Kati asked, frowning.

"Cut him loose," Selene elaborated. "Take away the source of the projection. In this case, I'm gonna make an educated guess and say . . . *that.*" She pointed at the body.

"And . . . how exactly do you do *that?*" Jill inquired.

Selene put her hands on her hips and gave Jill an incredulous look. "Believe it or not, this one is actually *really* easy. You remember the Gunn Classic?"

"Sounds familiar," Jill said. "I'd have to look at my notes."

"Not to me," Kati interjected a little desperately. "What are you doing?"

"Basically?" said Selene. "You cremate the remains, then bury them in salted earth. Or you salt them first and then burn 'em. Both work. Now . . . uh . . . you might wanna stand back. This won't be pretty."

And with a shrug of her shoulders, Selene turned and began prying the desiccated remains out of the crack in the wall.

*   *   *

"Ever since I first seen her, I knew she had a bit of the shimmer," Alma said, taking a swig from her bottle. Clara caught a scent thick and sweet and citrus-y, like lemon and honey and something else underneath she didn't recognize. "Thought it might have been a touch of the speaker's gift, or maybe the sight." Alma tapped her temple and gave Clara a meaningful look. "But the more I watch her, the more it seems to me her shimmer be too dim. Like there was a shadow, blocking it out. She buried under a mountain of grief, that girl. Tried to run away from it, I think, only brought it with her."

Clara was silent. Patient. A brief gust of wind tore loose one of the cobwebs decorating the roof of the porch, and it settled on her shoulder. After a moment she raised a gloved hand and peeled it away.

"This shade," Alma went on at length. Clara breathed out. "Looks to me like someone she lost. Someone she ain't ready to let go."

"Her fiancé," Clara said, before she could stop herself. She kicked herself internally for it, because Alma had to spend the next five minutes staring at the boards under her booted feet, sucking on her lower lip.

"That would explain it," she said after a while. "Ain't no shadow but a lack of light. He's feeding off her glimmer like a leech on a leg. *O*-kay then." With a decisive nod Alma set her bottle aside and pushed herself up out of her chair.

"What are you going to do?" Clara asked, standing as well.

"Can't let that clinger take away her glimmer, can we?" Alma said, stumping off the porch and beginning down the drive. "If we can't keep the line strong between the dead and the living then we're not much good, are we?" The old woman turned and gave Clara another one of her penetrating looks. Then she shook out her shoulders and walked off.

Clara stood and watched her go, her mind turning over the old woman's words until they fitted into place. The picture they painted was so alarming that she fairly leapt over the porch rail on her way to Unicorn.

Alma hadn't even reached the end of the drive when Clara pulled up beside her, Unicorn's engine growling like an angry beast. She was obliged to walk the bike along, however, as Alma didn't even so much as glance at her, let alone stop.

"I will go also," Clara announced.

"Oh, I am sure you'll do what you can," Alma said, rather condescendingly, not even turning her head.

"I would let you ride with me," Clara offered.

This did cause Alma to stop. She looked straight ahead down the road as if she was lost in thought. Then with the abrupt suddenness that seemed a trademark of her character, she turned and climbed onto the bike behind Clara. Clara felt the hard, cold arms go around her waist, and eased Unicorn forward down the rutty, dirt road.

The light was fading as they clustered around the makeshift firepit Selene had dug in the backyard of the house. She laid the shriveled remains of Jeremiah Gibbons in the center of it, setting them to rest gently on the pyre of mixed twigs and newspaper that had been hastily thrown together.

"This is *so* illegal," said Kati, beginning to shiver.

"Murdering your kid, *that's* illegal," Selene said. She stood up, dusting off her hands, and went over to the bag of salt that Jill had produced from the back of their large truck. Because apparently they were out of sodium.

"Actually haven't done one of these since I met you and Clara," Selene mused, pouring the salt generously over the body so that it fell in white drifts around it. Then she took an ancient hoe, liberated from a shed behind the house, and began scraping the salt into the earth until it was only faint white specks.

"Will it actually burn?" Kati asked.

"Eventually. The Gunns would use gasoline," Selene said conversationally, and rolled her eyes when Jill's head lifted in alarm. "Which, while flashy, is actually not all that great."

"Because of the hazard," Jill said.

"Actually, because it doesn't work," Selene said. "I mean, it'll get the thing on *fire,* sure, but it doesn't always purge the ghost. We don't know why, except you get better, more permanent re-sults, if you do it the slow way." She gestured at the pyre. "Jill, you got the matches, I think."

Kati shivered. It was too much like building a bonfire, which reminded her of the last time she and Bren had gone camping, which had been the last time they'd been happy together. Before the test results. Before the big decline.

She had to step away while Selene knelt down and put a match to the kindling, stuffing her hands into the pockets of her parka and looking down at her feet. She watched the warm light of the fire touch the toes of her Converses, staining the white with yellows and oranges and casting strong blue shadows to one side.

Like that she didn't see Jeremiah appear, though she felt his hand on her sleeve like a press of dry ice. When she raised her eyes to look at him she found he was staring into the fire with a confused, sad look on his face.

Like seeing yourself in the mirror from a weird angle, only a hundred times worse, Kati thought.

Neither Jill nor Selene noticed him. Jill was watching the fire as it slowly grew in strength and light, while Selene was prodding it critically with a heavy stick, coaxing the flames into nooks and crannies. She was speaking as she did so:

"The Gunns thought that it was the physical presence of the body that anchored a ghost," she was saying. "But it turned out that's not exactly right. You *can* have ghosts where there is no body, and you can have bodies with no ghosts. It has more to do with the specific treatment *of* the body. We're not sure why it works that way, but it just does."

"Fascinating," said Jill, taking notes on her phone. "It must have something to do with the sodium and the heat, if neither works on their own. Seems like alkali metals have a deterrent effect on ghosts, but at a high enough temperature the effect is intensified. Then—did it just get really cold or is that just me?"

She looked up and adjusted her glasses, squinting around at the darkening yard, and apparently didn't see the three shimmering figures which had appeared on the far side of the pyre.

Kati saw them, and judging by the tenacity of the grip Jeremiah had on her arm, he saw them too. But they seemed somehow more distant that he was—as if they stood behind a pane of smoked glass—and aside from the dancing firelight on their indistinct, gray faces, they didn't move.

She could still tell one was an older woman—as wide as Alma but not as tall—while the other two were children. One was tall with long hair, while the other was short with curly pigtails. Beyond that Kati couldn't make out their features, but she had no doubt it was Mrs Gibbons and her two daughters.

"That ain't just you," Selene said, stepping away from the fire and holding her hand out. She waved it back and forth, as if she were feeling for an invisible object, and paused when it passed between her and the three ghosts.

"Someone's there. Is it Jeremiah again?" she asked Kati.

"N-no," Kati stuttered. She was deathly cold, she realized. She hadn't noticed it so much, but Jeremiah was bleeding a deep chill clean through her clothes and into her body. Selene looked at her sharply.

"Jeremiah is h-here," Kati managed, jerking her chin down-ward toward the boy's ghost. "Th-that's Mrs Gibbons and the girls."

Selene looked around again, and Kati noticed that although she managed to point herself in the direction of the distant ghosts, her gaze passed clean through them.

"Talk to me Kati," she was saying. "What are they doing?"

"N-nothing," said Kati. "They're just standing there, looking at the fire."

"How do they look?"

"Sort of silvery. Not as clear as Jeremiah."

"Right," said Selene. "About that."

She turned, and began marching around the pyre toward Kati and the terrified ghost clinging to her arm. She'd gotten about halfway when the icy fingers on Kati's arm turned hot so fast she didn't feel the temperature so much as a sudden, harsh *pain*.

She yelped, but her voice was drowned out by a high, howl-ing scream. By the way Jill jumped and Selene honed in on Jeremiah's exact location, it was obvious they had heard him too.

For it was Jeremiah who was screaming. Screaming in pain and horror as a wave of golden fire rolled over him. He let go of Kati's sleeve (which wasn't even smoking, even though the skin beneath it was in searing agony) and batted at his own flaming arms, his ghostly mouth open in a dark, horrified O.

To Kati's astonishment, Selene didn't seem at all perturbed. Far from it: she gave a relieved sigh and said, "Oh good, it's taking."

"It's *hurting* him!" Kati shouted, trying to bat at the ghostly flames herself. Of course her hands went straight through them, but now, where it had been cold pins and needles, it was like putting her hands in boiling water.

"Yeah, it does do that," Selene said.

"Does it have to?" Jill asked, sounding more annoyed then anything. She had pocketed her phone and covered her ears.

Kati was suddenly supremely annoyed at them. Aggravated, even. Ghosts might be scary when you didn't know who they were or what they wanted, but since Jeremiah had sat with her on the stairs she realized she hadn't really been afraid of him. She felt quite sorry for him, in fact—especially now he was screaming and on fire.

So she did the only logical thing she could think of. Grabbing up fistfuls of blissfully cool, wet earth from the pile Selene had made digging the pit, she began throwing them onto the salted pyre.

Selene tried to stop her, of course. She said something like, "No, no, don't do that!" but Kati ignored her. Steam hissed and billowed up into the night as the wet earth hit the fire, but still Jeremiah screamed.

She saw Selene reaching for her, and braced herself to be pulled away.

Then Selene was shoved aside and sent sprawling on the ground. Kati didn't wait to see what had done that, but went on pushing dirt onto the pyre until the carefully nurtured fire had been stamped out, and Jeremiah's ghost was a small, smoking, miserable lump hunched on the ground.

Selene was up again, looking angrier than Kati had ever seen her. She swept the stick she'd been using to prod the pyre around, glaring into the night.

"All right," she said through gritted teeth. "*Who* did that?"

She seemed more offended at getting knocked over than at anything Kati had done, but it was still alarming to see her stomping around the yard, shouting angrily at nothing.

Jill, who'd covered her ears, lowered her hands and looked curiously at Kati.

"Why did you do that?" she asked.

Kati, chest heaving, hands shaking, skin still stinging from the cold and heat, found she couldn't answer. She walked back over to Jeremiah Gibbons and crouched beside him, gingerly extending a hand to touch his blackened shoulder.

Her own hand looked darker than it should have, but it was difficult to tell in the dying light. His skin felt like fizz on top of a glass of carbonated water, and when she gently stroked her fingers over the surface he looked up.

His face was a mess of black with streaks of pale silver where tears had washed the ash away, and he recoiled from her.

"Hush, it's okay," said Kati, even though she knew deep down that it was not.

Jeremiah looked like he didn't believe her either. He screwed up his face and shook his head, pointed with a hand whose fingers were shorter than they had been before.

"Wanna g-go h-home," he whined, and Kati followed his gesture to find that the silvery figures had faded to a mere smudge in the dark.

If he was going to go to wherever they were, he'd have to go now, Kati realized. She wasn't sure how she knew this, but the fact had settled in her mind, along with the knowledge that what she was about to do was probably quite stupid.

She didn't care.

She got up and walked around the ruined pyre, past Selene who had got out her taser again and was sweeping the area, to where the smoked glass seemed to come down between her and the other ghosts.

Martha Gibbons regarded her from the other side, her face blank and disapproving, while the two girls stared up at her with mixed fear and wonder.

Kati swallowed. She could barely feel her hands, but she was able to bring them up and push against the barrier that separated the Gibbons ghosts from the rest of the world.

To her surprise it tore under her numb fingers like old spiderwebs, and in no time at all she'd created a hole big enough for a large dog or a small child to crawl through. A silvery

light poured out of it, and Martha, Dorothy and Rebecca Gibbons backed hurriedly away.

It kept trying to close up, and Kati struggled with her grip
on the ragged edge. It felt like her hands were going to fall right
off. Desperately she turned around and called to Jeremiah.

"Come *on*," she said. "If you want to go home, do it *now*."

"What?" said Jill.

"Kati, what are you doing?" Selene asked sharply, wheeling
to face her.

Kati ignored them both. The cobwebby barrier was slowly
spilling through her fingers, the little hole closing up, and still
Jeremiah didn't move.

With a sound like sighing Bren walked out from the shadow
of the overhanging trees. He picked the child's ghost up, letting
him cling to his neck as he walked over to Kati and set the boy
down in front of the rapidly shrinking hole.

Still Jeremiah hesitated. Kati wanted to scream. Bren gave
him a little nudge, but it wasn't until Rebecca came right up to
the other side and reached through the hole to take his hand
that he stood up on shaky legs and stepped through.

The cobwebs felt like they had turned to razors by that point,
and Kati wasn't sure if she let go in time or if they ripped right
through her hands. She felt a *snap* like a rubber band breaking,
and a bolt of agony ran up both arms. It blinded her to everything, and all she could do was collapse on the ground, screaming almost as much as Jeremiah.

She thought Bren came to comfort her, but when she looked
up it was Selene. The woman must have put away her taser because she was using both hands to scoop up loose soil and plaster it over Kati's hands and arms.

The stars were coming out, Kati could see because she was
apparently on her back. She felt the aftershocks of pain—shivers
and cold flashes and a faint sickness in her stomach—but her
hands didn't hurt any more.

Her hands felt like nothing at all.

The ground beneath her trembled faintly, and in the distance
she thought she heard the sound of an engine approaching.

"Hey, hey, *Kati,*" Selene's voice said from somewhere above her. A hand, warm and solid, touched her face. "Stay with me, Kati. Kati, don't you dare . . . "

But her words were vague and distant, as if spoken from the other side of a spiderweb wall, and Kati couldn't for the life of her remember why they were important.

She was walking down a narrow, silvery path through a dark, hilly landscape. The stars above her were strange and strangely bright, but their light didn't reach the black earth.

Ahead of her on the path walked a woman and two children. The woman was carrying a third over her shoulder, and this one had his head turned into her cheek and his arms wrapped tightly around her neck.

"Where are they going?" Kati asked. She thought she only wondered it to herself, but Bren answered from beside her.

"Wherever people go when they are done with being."

It seemed so perfectly right that Bren was here that she didn't even question it.

"Where is that?" Kati asked.

Bren chuckled. "I wouldn't know," he said. She felt his hand slide into hers and when she turned to him he was smiling. "I'm not finished yet. And neither are you."

Then she woke up.

It took her a while to realize that was what was happening. At first it seemed like the world tipped sideways and Bren disappeared. Her hands went numb and the stars went dark. Her body filled with aches and pains, and real, living voices rang in her ears—even though their owners were speaking softly.

"Greatest damn fool in three states," Alma was saying. "Never did listen to me."

"Maybe if you'd told her the truth from the beginning," Jill suggested dryly. "People can tell when they're not getting the whole story."

"Never listened," Alma repeated bitterly.

"The woman is a god-damn medium," Selene snapped. "She would have understood."

"Hush," said Clara. "She wakes."

Kati peeled open her eyes and found herself on the futon in the living room, gazing up at three concerned faces . . . and Alma, who just looked resigned. Prying her jaw open—which felt like it had got stuck with dried spit—she croaked, "What happened?"

It took them a while to explain, since everyone's version was a little different. Selene said she was a medium—a word that hadn't applied to Kati since she was seven—and that she'd nearly walked into an early grave. Clara said she had a ghost shadow which had taken root inside her body and not even Alma could exorcise it. Alma glowered at her and muttered, "Didn't drink your brew. Too late for that, now. You've lost the hands, at least." She sighed gustily.

Eventually it was Jill who put everything together for her.

"The way I understand them," she said, pushing up her glasses as she sat down on the floor next to Kati. "You've got a natural sensitivity to ghosts. You can see and hear them when we can't. And you can feel their presence more acutely. Um." She looked awkwardly down at her hands, which made Kati look down at her own. She still couldn't feel them—not even as distant pins and needles—and all she could see were two bundles of white cloth, fastened together with safety pins.

"That means they can touch you back," Jill went on. "And when you grabbed Jeremiah, he burned you."

"He was on fire," Kati protested. "I had to do something."

"Yeah, that's what happens with a Gunn Classic," Selene said. She was sitting by the window where the wan sunlight gave her a pale, silvery halo. She didn't seem too upset, though. "It's easier for us. Most of the time we don't see the ghost—or if we do, it's angry enough we're happy to see it go up in flames."

Kati frowned. She was having difficulty remembering what came next. She'd pushed earth onto the fire until it went out, and then . . .

"What did I do?" she asked.

Selene shrugged and made a walking motion with two fingers.

"You escorted him out of this world," Clara said.

Kati wished she could rub her head, because her brain was beginning to ache, but she didn't feel strong enough to lift her arms. Jill must have understood her expression, because she clarified:

"Ghosts are echoes, right? Well, you sort of scooped up his echo—because your body has a special composition which allows it to interact with echoes—and carried it around to a weak spot in the inter-dimensional membrane that separates our world from . . . *whatever* . . . the afterlife or the spirit world. We need more data on that. Anyway, you opened up a little hole in this membrane, and he went through. Done. Simple as that. Only *you* nearly got sucked through with him. Alma managed to reverse the damage, however. Except your hands—they were too badly contaminated."

Kati didn't ask what Alma had done. Probably something involving that strange brew of hers. Now that she was coming further into consciousness, she could taste a faint trace of sticky-sweet lemon on her palate. With it came a memory, and the solid understanding that she hadn't done exactly as Jill said.

"That wasn't me," she tried to explain. "It was Bren who took Jeremiah through. I just held the thing open for them."

It was Jill's turn to frown, and she looked around at Alma.

"But you said the parasitic ghost was still attached?"

"She's still got the shadow, you can count on that," said Alma, settling further into her chair.

Kati found, now that she was thoroughly awake, that Alma looked different than she remembered. She had a bit of a glow about her—not quite like Jeremiah or the other ghosts, but it put her in mind of the silvery, cobwebby glass that had separated Martha, Dorothy and Rebecca from Jeremiah. What with all that had happened, she found she had no energy to maintain a filter between her brain and her mouth.

"You're not alive," she said, rather accusingly.

Alma Bonifaunt shrugged. "But I ain't dead," she said.

"You're a zombie," Kati sighed, leaning back on her pillow.

"She is an undying," said Clara gravely.

"How the hell does that work?" Kati asked, staring at the ceiling. There was a water stain in the shape of a heart in the middle of it. Unless it was a fat boomerang.

"Simple," said Alma. "You don't die. Get your throat cut? Don't die. Get the Spanish Flu? Don't die. Get shot in the chest

. . . well, that one laid me up a while. But I didn't die. Then one night you get your head knocked in by a pair of bastards and the next morning you decide it's time you got up outta that ditch and found you some breakfast. Only food tastes of nothing when you put it in your mouth, and what you do manage to swallow either goes right through you or sits in your stomach til you cough it up. You forget to breathe half the time and people ask if you have a skin condition. You move away. Find out the empty places in the world maybe aren't so empty. Maybe there's another world happening right alongside this one, and there you are with a foot on either side of the wall between."

Kati stared. Not only was it the most words she'd ever heard Alma string together, but the story they told was unbelievable. Well, would have been unbelievable, if she hadn't just helped a lost ghost get home. In the end she said:

"That doesn't sound easy."

Alma sniffed. "Never said it was *easy*. You try walking five miles with your throat torn open, or pushing your head back into shape after someone thought it'd be fun to use it as an anvil. But it is *that* simple: don't die."

"Then what about your brew?" she asked. "If you can't eat . . . "

"Can't eat living food," Alma corrected her. "Brew ain't that. Brew keeps you grounded. Gets into your veins, makes your body remember being alive. Like an anti-ghost. S'why I told you to drink it," she added bitterly. "Tryin' to keep you safe."

"Safe?" Kati demanded, so outraged that she managed to sit up on her elbows. "Safe from *what*? From a couple of sad, lost ghosts who just want to go home? Safe from *Bren?*"

Alma shook her head, and pointed at Kati's hands with a knobby finger.

"Safe from *that*," she said, dejectedly.

Almost as if in response, Kati felt a prickle of sensation in the place where she assumed her hands were, but it faded out almost at once. She felt a lump of panic rising in her throat. What if she could never feel her hands again? What if they had to be cut off? What if they fell off on their own?

"Oh, hey, easy now," said Selene, when she started hyperventilating. "Alma managed to save your hands—they just won't be the same."

"*How* not the same?" Kati wheezed.

Selene looked archly at Clara, who pulled her shoulders down and then up again, like a reverse shrug.

"Let me see them," Kati said, trying to get her breathing under control. If she could just see that she still *had* hands, she thought, she might feel better.

She was wrong.

Once Selene had reluctantly unwrapped the bandages Kati spent a good minute staring down at what looked like a mummy's hands, blackened and desiccated with the shape of the bones showing through the skin. Her wrists were still fully fleshed out, but the discoloration reached almost halfway up her forearms. With a mixed horror and fascination she found she could still move them—even curl and extend her fingers—but it felt more like operating a separate tool than a part of her body. Experimentally she tried rubbing them together, and though she felt the resistance of two objects meeting, that was all.

"Yep," sighed Alma. "That's what you get for reaching beyond the veil."

"I was just trying to help Jeremiah get home!" Kati protested, beginning to feel the panic rise again.

"You should have left him to me," Alma grumbled, folding her arms. "I took care of the other three, didn't I?"

"You attacked Bren!" Kati shouted, beginning, to her shame, to cry. Automatically she raised a hand to wipe her eyes, then remembered it was a dead mummy-hand, and threw it back down in her lap again and cried harder.

Above her, she heard Clara say, rather critically: "That seemed uncalled for."

"He's a shadow," muttered Alma. "He's holding her back. It ain't healthy, living with a ghost."

"*How* is it not healthy?" Jill asked, and there was a sharp edge to her words that made Kati squint up at her.

Jill was sitting on a stool in the corner by the woodstove, her knees folded up into her chest and her arms clasped around them. She was frowning at Alma and her lips were pressed into a thin, dark line.

"Do even *you* have to ask that?" Selene retorted, looking incredulous.

Jill's lips, if possible, got even thinner. "Yes," she said. Kati noticed that her knuckles had gone white from how hard she was gripping her knees. "Because Bren's never hurt Kati. It was grabbing Jeremiah when he was on fire and tearing open a portal that did that to her hands."

"Sure, he hasn't hurt her *yet*," Selene said. "But there's all sorts of problems you get, living with ghosts."

"Like *what?*" Jill insisted.

"Like . . . " Selene waved an arm in frustration. "*Things.* Clara, help me out."

"Ghosts are memory, echo," Clara said. "A manifestation in the present of something that no longer exists. Left on their own, they will fade. If given a source of energy—say, that of a living being—they will draw on it until it is exhausted. And because they are not alive, they cannot grow and change as we do. If their status is not maintained, they become distorted—like memory—and that distortion can twist into something malevolent, even if the original ghost was was benign."

"Poltergeists, vengeful spirits," Selene elaborated. "Lots of them started out as harmless ghosts who never went away."

"But Kati is a medium," Jill insisted. "You said so yourself. She's *different.*"

"Being a medium actually makes her more vulnerable," Clara pointed out. "She can see and touch ghosts—which means they can touch *her.*"

"But he was her *fiancé!*"

"And how does that make him less of a threat?" Selene asked, darkly.

Jill was outright glaring at her companions now, and Kati noticed her eyes were suspiciously bright and red. Then with an aggravated sigh she stood up and stomped off out the front door, slamming it behind her.

"Hmm," said Alma.

There was silence in the room after that, until Kati said, small and miserable:

"How can you exorcise Bren? He was cremated."

"Do you have any of his things with you?" Selene asked heavily.

Kati felt something tie up in her chest, and it took her a while to get it out.

"I have one of his shirts," she admitted.

"That's probably what's keeping him here," Selene said. "We can use that."

The thought of Bren—even a ghost of Bren—going up in flames like Jeremiah was too much to bear. Kati had to squeeze her eyes shut and bite her lip.

"You won't do anything like that," Alma said, firmly. "You let me handle it, like I handled Martha and Dorothy and Rebecca. I know how to be gentle with ghosts."

That made Kati open her eyes and look up, only to find Bren looming in the doorway behind Alma. He was looking down at her sadly, and when he sensed Kati's gaze he raised his head and shook it slightly.

Kati found herself nodding in agreement without even noticing.

"Right then," said Alma, cracking her knuckles.

But it wasn't all right, Kati realized, snapping her eyes back to the world of the living. Bren was *right there,* and he might not be alive, but he wasn't gone, and she couldn't—*couldn't*—let him go. Which was probably unhealthy, but then Kati had spent her whole life doing things people said were unhealthy—and it hadn't killed her yet.

"No," she said suddenly, making Alma pause. "No, I didn't mean . . . don't *any* of you do *anything* to Bren. I need to talk to Jill."

She started flailing her way out of the bed. It was significantly harder with numb hands, but she made it to her feet and tripped off through the living room.

Jill hadn't gone far; just out onto the front porch, where she'd wrapped a blanket around herself against the early morning chill and sat down on the steps. Kati stepped back inside to put on her slippers and grab her parka before joining the small woman on the porch.

Jill nodded in acknowledgement of her presence, but said nothing. They sat together in silence as the yard slowly grew into light, and a pale streak of gold appeared across the tips of the western trees. In their shadow Kati could glimpse a familiar shape, trying to look casual as he leaned against a tree, but she knew Bren was as anxious as she was, and it spurred her to action.

Or at least speech.

"Who did you lose?" she asked, rough and awkward.

Jill smiled, small and sad. "My boyfriend," she said quietly.

"Oh," said Kati. Somehow, she had thought the question might lead naturally to what she really wanted to ask, but in reality it only made her more nervous. Luckily, Jill was not the sort of person who, when she had an opinion, kept it to herself.

"I didn't," she began, stopped, frowned, and restarted. "When Christian died, it literally came out of nowhere."

"Car accident?"

"Monster attack. Long story."

Kati waited, but what Jill said next was entirely different.

"They don't know everything," was what she said. "They know a lot—more than most people—but the whole reason I'm here is because they *don't* know so much. So what I mean, I guess, is that you don't have to take anything Clara or Selene or even this Alma-person says as scientific *fact*."

"You don't think Bren's ghost is hurting me?" Kati asked, tight and breathless.

"*I* don't know," said Jill. "We don't have the data. There have been no studies of people living with ghosts long term. They might be perfectly right, and his presence could be a drain on your own life—however that presents itself—or they might be working from anecdotal evidence that comes from cases different from yours."

Kati hunched down on the porch, subconsciously mirroring Jill's own posture, and stared hard at the vision of Bren standing under the trees.

"Which do you think it is?" she asked.

"I think . . . " Jill followed her gaze, saw nothing but winter foliage, and looked away toward the pale sky. She took a deep breath. "Look, I'm not like them, okay? I never got into this to hunt things or even protect people. I'm just here to *learn*. But if I were in your place—if the person I loved had . . . stuck around—I mean . . . if he wants to leave, you need to let him leave. I don't think it's good to keep people around against their wills, dead or alive. But if he *wants* to stay then . . . then I don't see any good reason why you shouldn't let him. If he can help you, if he still loves you, then you should hold onto each other for as long as you can."

Under the trees, Bren had perked up and was watching them closely.

"It still doesn't feel right," Kati admitted. "Like I'm cheating, or something."

"Lots of people cheat," Jill said. "Life isn't fair. I don't see why death should be. I mean—hell—look at Alma! She just *won't* die. If that's not cheating, I don't know what is.

"But maybe that's how the world is supposed to work. Maybe ghosts and people like Alma play an important role in the balance of life and death. Like I said, there's so much we don't know. And we won't learn more by doing what's always been done and not looking at what's really happening."

The sunlight had reached almost to the base of the trees, and Bren had grown dim in the light. But when Kati concentrated on the shape of him, she found he solidified until he looked almost like a normal person.

Jill saw her looking.

"He's here now, isn't he?"

Unable to speak, Kati nodded.

"So go ask him what he wants to do," Jill said, and there was a wistful yearning in her voice that Kati couldn't allow herself to concentrate on, otherwise she'd start crying.

"He won't speak to me," she said. Then corrected herself. "At least, not when I'm awake. I don't think he can."

Jill shrugged. "Lots of ways to communicate besides speaking," she pointed out.

Kati nodded, then with a grunt she heaved herself to her feet and walked unsteadily down the steps and across the drive, toward the trees.

Bren came out to meet her. When he passed into the full sunlight he went almost completely transparent, but Kati could still see him like a shimmer in the air, and when she reached out, her cold, dead hands felt something warm.

The shimmer in the air grew a little brighter, and then for the first time since she'd woken up. Namely, she felt the rough, familiar scrape of Bren's calloused fingers over hers, and a moment later hands, warm and real enfolded hers. They felt as real and alive as anything she had ever touched, and when she tightened her grip they squeezed back.

That was all the answer she needed.

Alma grumbled ominously. Clara brooded. Selene looked up at the ceiling for a long time and then let out a massive sigh. But Jill set her jaw and remained firm, and Bren stood next to Kati the whole time, his hand warm in her cold, ruined one.

They left that afternoon; Clara on the big black bike, Selene and Jill in the huge red truck. Clara and Selene had spent most of the day asleep in the trailer, but Jill sat up with Kati in the kitchen, grilling her with questions. Ordinarily Kati would have minded, but Jill seemed to take Bren's invisible presence in stride, and went so far as to nod in his direction whenever a question remotely involved him.

Most of these were technical in nature: how opaque was he? Were there certain lights she could see him better in? Did the temperature of his hand change? Others related to Kati more closely: How did she feel? Did she have an appetite? Were their any other disturbances in her vision?

The answers to the latter set were: Good, yes, and no, which pleased Jill. The former required some amount of experimentation, during which Kati discovered Bren was generally pretty opaque when not in direct light, and was easier to see under the fluorescent lights in the house. His hands always felt warm to Kati, but she couldn't tell if that fluctuated at all.

Jill left her with a notepad mocked up as a journal, for Kati to record her observations, and an email address, for her to send them to. She also left her with the assurance that she would call back to check up on her the next week.

And then Selene had stumbled into the kitchen to say that Clara had created some food—whatever meal that was—and did Jill want any?

After that they had left, and Kati was alone in the house.

Only . . . not.

In a way it felt quieter, more peaceful. The rooms had lost their menace and even the smell of mold had abated. Now it just felt like a big, empty house, waiting for someone new to fill it with memory.

In this case, two someones, since Bren was sitting on the couch when Kati got in from seeing the three women off. He was looking at her expectantly, and even though he still didn't speak, Kati had a good idea of what he was thinking.

She got out her laptop and sat down beside him.

"I had an idea," she began, pulling up a window and typing "American sign language" into the search field. While the page loaded she glanced over at Bren, who was smiling and shaking his head.

"What?" she asked.

Bren raised a quizzical eyebrow.

Then he reached over her lap, just like he'd done a thousand times in life, when he was going to type something in for her. Only instead of going for the keyboard itself, he managed to slide his ghostly hands into her gray, solid ones.

It was like a switch got flipped in her brain, and suddenly Kati's hands felt normal again. Except she had no control over them. Gazing in amazement, she watched as Bren brought up a blank note and, through her hands, began to type.

"Yeah," Kati said a little while later. "Or we could do that."

Arcana rumbled east, and Selene drove with her chin almost resting on the top of the wheel.

"I just hope you know what you're doing," she said, rolling an eye at Jill, who was slumped in the passenger seat, pretending to sleep.

"I don't," she admitted readily. "But then again, neither do you."

"Girl, I know enough," Selene grumbled. "And I know there has never been any good coming from mixing up the living and the dead like this."

Jill's eyes came open, and they were surprisingly bright and steely.

"Then we'll find out, won't we?" she said. "This will give us an opportunity to collect real data on the effects of mediums and ghosts, so the next time we *will* know."

"Yeah, and how you gonna do that?" Selene asked.

"By email, probably," Jill said, and when Selene only stared at her, confounded, she clarified: "Kati's going to send me regular reports." And with a smug smile she leaned back in her seat and firmly shut her eyes.

Alma Bonifaunt sat on her front porch, feeling the late afternoon sun slowly seep into her cold, gray skin. A bottle of fresh brew sat by her foot, but she hadn't touched it. As a result, she felt the presence of the ghost prick her senses like a sharp pin, and she looked up to find the boy, Bren, standing in her driveway.

He was not such a bad-looking man, Alma had to admit. She could understand why Kati was so attached to him. And he was standing at a polite distance, his hands clasped behind his back.

He didn't speak, but Alma had spent a great deal of time working with ghosts, and she understood his meaning perfectly well.

"You do realize I don't eat," she said, harshly.

A nod.

"And neither do you."

Another nod.

"So, basically, you're inviting me over to sit there with you while we watch Miss K eat her dinner."

Bren spread his hands and smiled. Alma glared at him, but he was unaffected. If anything, his aura got brighter and he looked even more solid.

A strong apparition, then. He'd be around for a while. No one could say just how long, but then again, you couldn't say that for anyone, really.

"Let me just go get my boots on, then," Alma sighed, took a swig of her brew, and waddled into her house.

When she returned, booted and scarfed, Bren was still there.

They walked side by side down her leaf-covered drive, through the winter woods toward the big, rambling, legitimately haunted house.

*

You don't hear me even when I scream
I hear everything though I don't want to bleed

My mouth is empty, my hands are tied
All of my dreams can't satisfy

Oh, I don't see you
But I feel you

Oh I can't see you
But I know you're there

I can't see you
I feel your stare

I know you're there

There's so many things I wish I could change
The more I try the more things grow strange

I can hear your voice speak in my dreams
When I'm in your dreams I live and breathe

O-oh now I see you
and I feel you

Oh now I see you
and I know you're there

Now I see you
and I meet your stare

Oh now I see you
and I know you're there

I can see you
I feel your hand

I can see you

I understand

You can reach me
just take my hand

Just take my hand

and understand

Now I can see you

I'll never grieve

I'll never leave

—Now I See/*Rook Parliament*

The Arcana crew will return in
"Critical Magic"

The third and final novella of Bouragner Felpz *(as narrated by Cori-anne Birch), "The Peculiar Case of Professor Odd" serves not only as a bridge between* Bouragner Felpz *and* Professor Odd, *but also to fill in some of the gaps that remain in each. It is best to have read the first two volumes of* Felpz (A Study of Magic *and* Anatomy of a Magician, *both available from* Heliopause), *plus* Professor Odd Episode 6: "The Monster's Daughter" *and especially* Episode 3: "The Promethean Predicament." *It closes* The Adventures of Bouragner Felpz, *though Felpz and Corianne may very well go on to make appearances in other stories.*

THE PECULIAR CASE OF PROFESSOR ODD

Foreword: An Introduction to Mr Bouragner Felpz

WHEN I PRESENTED THIS MANUSCRIPT TO MY PUBLISHER it came back with a note to the effect that it had been so long since my last Bouragner Felpz tale that a great many of my potential readers would be encountering him for the first time. Rather than bring the two volumes of preceding stories back into print, they suggested I add a short introduction here, to welcome my new readers while reminding my old ones of the literary friend they had missed all these years. And though I was loathe to admit that they were right, you will notice that this is exactly what I have done.

My lifelong friend, the esteemed magician Mr Bouragner Felpz, is a man of many facets, but only one color. That color is purple. He wears it constantly, but through no conscious decision. Quite the opposite, in fact: the color sticks with him, staining his clothes and accessories, so that he must exert considerable effort in order to appear in something other than a shade of violet. It was not that he had an affinity for the color; rather, the color had an affinity for *him*. How exactly this came about remains a mystery to me, though I understand it had something to do with a fairy he dueled in his youth, and the legacy of the ancient color demons.

Felpz collects mysteries about himself, some of which—like the full extent of his powers—he guards carefully, while others—like his precise age—he simply neglects to mention. So of the former I can tell my readers only that he is the most skilled, powerful magic user not only in this country, but on this continent, and possibly the entire present world, and of the latter I must guess and say that he is somewhere in the vicinity of eight hundred years, though on which side I do not know.

If I make him out to be a formidable, unknowable man, it is because that is partly true. But for those such as I, who have spent the better part of their lives sharing a roof with him, a definite character emerges that is far from what one might expect of a centuries-old font of magical wisdom and power.

Felpz is dramatic, but only superficially so. At heart he is one of the more staid people I have known. Though he may fly into rants about the smallest of things, he shows great patience with what he deems important, and I have rarely seen him truly angry—and then only with the strongest motivations. He has an inverse sense of respect, being brusque with nobles and dignitaries, but showing the greatest care and sympathy to civil servants, craftspeople, and particularly sad, middle-aged, single women—as I can personally attest. Flamboyant and affectionate to his friends, I do not think he has demonstrated romantic attractions to anyone, and no mention of wives nor lovers has he ever dropped. Rather than take a single partner, Felpz prefers to cultivate a network of friends, to which he shows, albeit in a slightly different fashion, the same care and devotion as any man would his spouse.

His history, as I have said, is interwoven with mystery, so any attempt at giving a comprehensive biography would be frustrating, not to mention exhausting. A few facts about his activities of the last century, however, are perfectly clear, and as they are relevant to the following story I shall lay them out below.

Sometime in the 2240's he appeared in Redling and took a house between King's Street and Bridgeton Way that had the incongruous number 0000, where he set himself up as a consulting magician, assisting both other mages and the common populace in solving magical problems. It was in this capacity that he endeared himself to my father, who in turn made him my godfather. A little while after I was born, however, the two had a falling out—but the legal status between us did not change. So when my parents tragically died some thirteen years later, it was to Bouragner Felpz that I was sent, albeit against my wishes, and though I do not think he was any more glad to have me than I him, he performed his duties loyally, and contrary to our first impressions we became quite fond of one another. So fond, that when he inexplicably vanished in the spring of my twenty-first year I was utterly devastated, and saved from depression only by the birth of my own daughter.

It was to be another two decades before we would see each other again, but upon his return we picked up more or less where we had left off, save on more equal footing. Our bond has only grown stronger since.

Felpz still resides in his Redling house, which was my home as well until about ten years ago when, desirous of some real autonomy, I took myself away to Stanton Leaning to write the novels which would cause the gap in Felpzian stories that in turn necessitated this introduction. We have kept vigorously in touch, however, by letters and visits and most recently by telephone calls, and rarely does a Chandarmas go by that my little hamlet does not receive a visit from the great magician.

Of his time absent from Redling he has spoken very little; I know only that he was gone, not just from that city, but from our entire world, and that his travels in the great realms beyond ours were not easy; he was able to return only with the help of what he described as "unexpected friends." Though the state he was in upon his return—emaciated, weak, with half his hair long and tangled and the other half lopped off an inch from the scalp—begged an explanation, it was one I did not have the heart to drag out of him. So I added this absence to the other mysteries surrounding my friend, where I thought it would stay.

Which brings me to the present day, and this latest story, in which a little light is thrown onto that dark patch of my friend's history, and which was so madly entertaining (and, yes, *peculiar*) that I simply had to write it down and share it.

Chapter 1: The Student from San Randelfino

IT BEGAN, not in the smokey streets of Redling, nor in Felpz's sitting room—as had so many of our adventures—but on the platform of the Stanton Leaning train station, where I had gone to meet Felpz one fine day in May of 2342. The entire town was in bloom and thick with the sweet smell of roses and lilacs. The weather was pleasing, and Felpz had finally acquiesced to my perennial request that he come for a spring visit.

I was standing a little way from the coaches, being unsure which one my friend would emerge from, leaning on the birth-day present my daughter had sent me earlier that year. This was a perfectly ludicrous and nearly useless walking stick. A cane, really, of the sort with a hidden blade inside. In other words, ex-actly the sort of stick Milain would think I needed. What made it truly ridiculous, however, was the handle: rather than a sen-sible curve or even a straight grip, the crane was topped with an impertinent cast of a silver banana, which had the advantage of being perfectly unique and nothing else. I'd brought it that day only because I thought it would amuse Felpz; I am spry enough even now that I do not require a cane save early on very cold mornings.

Felpz appeared from one of the middle coaches, tall and el-egant with his dark hair swept cleanly back from his aquiline profile, and his reaction upon seeing the cane surpassed even my wildest expectations. He looked, eyes wide, and looked again. He missed his footing and nearly fell to his knees. Only a wild swoop with his arm saved his balance, and even so he nearly dropped his fine, purple top hat—had, in fact, to let go of his carpetbag in order to save it.

He was laughing as he straightened himself out, shrugging off the concerned porter who had made a beeline for him, and so I began to laugh as well. Our greeting was an exceptionally mirthful one, and the two of us were beyond speech for some minutes. We said our hellos in gestures and embraces, and con-tinued chuckling together—somewhat to the confusion of the other travelers—all the way through the station and half across the village.

It was only as we neared my cottage, passing behind the public house in whose backyard stood the namesake of Stanton Leaning (three obelisks, two at drunken angles and one flat on the ground) that Felpz finally regained control of himself enough to perform credible speech.

"Blushes, Corianne," said he, peering down at my cane with marked interest. "Wherever did you get a thing like that?"

"Isn't it peculiar?" I returned, wagging the stick at him so he could hear the sword inside rattle about. "Milain sent it to me for my birthday. I think it is her way of showing concern for my physical well-being in my old age. I understand she found it in a curiosity shop in Aldonica—she is living there now, with her husband and his family. They have been trying to get me moved up there, ostensibly so I may spend more time with my great-granddaughter—which I don't mind—but really I think it is because they believe I've gotten too old to be living on my own—which I *do* mind."

"I understand your irritation, surely I do," said Felpz, but he did not take his eyes off the cane. "Why, you haven't even reached your hundredth year yet! Still barely out of the shell, as far as a dragon would be concerned."

He spoke lightly, but I could see the topic made him uncomfortable. Though I knew I owed my good health in part to his subtle magics, the fact that he was functionally immortal and I was not was an unchangeable aspect of our relationship. Never openly discussed, I presumed the topic too painful for him, and so then as ever before I contrived to steer the conversation in a merrier direction.

"I honestly do not know what to do with it," I said, indicating my cane. "It is no good walking with, as you see it is more convenient to carry it over one's shoulder, as medieval soldiers did with their longswords. I bring it about with me mostly because it reminds me of Milain—and I thought you might get some joy out of it—but I expect it will spend more time upon my mantelpiece than in my hand."

"Oh, surely not!" cried Felpz, surprising me with the vehemence of his outburst. He sounded as though I had suggested something scandalous. "You must bring it with you, wherever you go. Such a gift, after all, should be treasured."

Again I caught him staring at the cane, as though it were the most fascinating object in all the realms of this world.

"Would you like a closer look?" I offered, and was nearly knocked off balance by the speed at which Felpz snatched it from my hands. My friend had to stop in his tracks to hold the thing up to the light, turn it around so he could observe it from every angle, and finally draw the blade from the shaft and inspect its edge.

All of which was made the more amusing by the fact that the cane was practically new—I myself had only drawn it once, just to confirm what was on the inside—and so there was nothing to see but a piece of bright, shiny metal and the black, lacquered shaft.

Then, with equal suddenness, Felpz sheathed the blade and handed the contraption back to me, as though it pained him to touch it. We continued on our way, and though Felpz went on to ask innocuously after my life—my cat, my writing, my neighbors—I felt that his attention never strayed far from the cane, and that his whole being was on alert, as if waiting for some surprising turn of events.

Such a turn we did have that very afternoon, just as I was pouring tea and Felpz was cutting into the apricot pie the girls down at Springdimple Farm had surprised me with that morning. There was the crunch of gravel in my drive, the jingle of a bicycle bell, and then a timid rap upon my door.

"Oh dear," I said, thinking it must be Nireen, the young woman who helped me with my cleaning and cooking once a week. It was her usual day, and though I had made special arrangements that week, it was not beyond the bounds of possibility that habit had dictated she pay me a visit.

When I opened the door, however, it was an entirely different young woman—one I had never seen before in my life. Her face was of a sun-ripened olive complexion, her hair glossy and black as a raven's wing, and her eyes like polished black stones. She had a strong, bony face—handsome, rather than pretty— which was a contrast to her comfortably rounded figure, which was rendered even more elliptical by the cycling dress she wore: baggy trousers buckled tightly around her ankles to keep them out of the chain, and a coat that fastened snugly around her generous waist yet flared out across her shoulders. She had a pair of cycling goggles pushed up onto her forehead, where they tangled with her windswept dark hair, and her cheeks were flushed from her recent exertion.

"Excuse me, mistress," she said, her voice deep and musical and indubitably Milanian. "I am here to beg pardon, and a favor. I am searching for *Signore Mago Aubergino*, and they say he can be found here. Oh, forgive me if I have intruded, but it is desperate that I find him!"

So effulgent was she that I had not the heart to turn her away, sore though I was to have Felpz's visit disrupted by his work. I might have been a shade gruff, but I stepped aside and showed her into my modest parlor, where Felpz was already setting a third place at the table.

"You find me on holiday," Felpz told her gently as the woman took the offered seat. "However, if the matter is serious enough for you to cycle all the way from Milany I can hardly deny you an audience. Now, will you take tea, or something stronger?"

"Tea is good, thank you," said the young woman deferentially. "And I do not cycle from *Milania,* never! Only from Grenchester, and then only because I took the wrong train from Redling, where I was looking for you. I come from San Randelfino, from the little town outside the monastery, but I was given scholarship to study at University in Baronia, where I have spent the last year. So I am not entirely foreign." She ended on a nervous laugh.

She was so inoffensively sympathetic that I was completely charmed and served her a generous slice of pie while Felpz pushed his own chair back so he could cross his legs and knit his fingers together, as was his manner when preparing to hear a client's story.

"Be at ease, my dear young lady," he said, causing the young woman to color even more. "Both Corianne and I have fond memories of your homeland, and I only keep to Kyrish on account that my *Ligua Milania* is so rusty that I fear I would butcher it terribly. Please, tell us who you are, and why you have been driven to such lengths to seek me out."

The young woman cleared her throat, suddenly overcome with self-consciousness. She took a polite sip of her tea and served a bite of pie onto her fork, but did not eat it. Setting the fork aside she folded her hands between the knees of her cycling trousers and knocked her heels together, worriedly.

"I apologize," said she. "How rude I have been. My name is Favulia Bragnana, and as I have said I am originally from San Randelfino, but for the past winter I have been studying at the University of Baronia. I came there by the grace of a scholarship granted me by their Astronomia College, for my work cataloging comets. The San Randelfine monks keep a small observatory, and as a young girl I was always climbing up to the monastery to attend their public demonstrations. I showed such a careful interest that the monks made exception for me, and when I was old enough showed me how to work their *Grande Telescopio*. Since then I have been enamored of everything that exists beyond the confines of our little world, and determined to make the study of stars and their brethren my life's work. It was a great honor to receive a scholarship from a foreign university, but I came because Baronia is also home to the Calameria Observatory, of which my monks spoke highly.

"So that is how I come to Kyreland. I tell you now, though it seems pointless, because it leads into the matter that has sent me here today.

"Arriving in this new country, though I thought I had a strong grasp of your language from all my correspondence with the Astronomia masters, I found it immensely difficult to speak—and even now, after half a year of solid practice, it be easier to read and write your language than to speak and listen to it. In my early days I found this barrier discouraging, and my social circle remained limited to my professors and tutors—who were patient with me—and a few of the older astronomers, some of whom spoke Milanian and were kind enough to coach me. It was one of these, a man named Giogiovan, who suggested I try making friends by letter with a fellow astronomy student he knew, who was currently studying in Fairbridge. I was too shy to take such a measure, but he must have said something to her, for around Chandarmas I received such a kind and interesting letter from this woman that I could not help but write back.

"This is how I came to be friends with Lilibell Donnet, who, despite being three years my senior and pursuing a doctorate in astrothaumaturgy at Dunchurch College, treated me as a perfect equal, and our friendship quickly bloomed. It was as though we were two kindred souls who had ever shared a connection, yet had never manifested it before. She was fascinated by the magic of the planets and how it affected our perception of them, while I was concerned with the more conventional elements of stars and other celestial bodies, but our mutual love of all things astronomical served to bridge the differences in our interests, and it seemed we each complemented the other's studies.

"We shared other, more mundane similarities: we had both found ourselves as young girls interested in a subject whose other students were overwhelmingly male, and still struggled with feelings of inadequacy on occasion. We encouraged each other, and by Midwinter it felt like we had been lifelong friends—being able to express things in letters which neither of us could have articulated in speech. We met in person for the first time when Lilibell came home to Baronia for a visit, and far from spoiling the magic of a friendship forged in paper and ink, it only served to intensify our relationship, and the letter exchanges became, if anything, more frequent. Lilibell even offered to buy me a lease on the college telephone, so that we might communicate more immediately, and soon we were exchanging weekly telephone calls in addition to letters. Though Lilibell lost her father in late February and was understandably subdued for weeks, our friendship sustained us through the hardship.

"I have not yet lost a parent, but I know well the grief of losing a loved member of one's family, and I offered what comfort I could, while remaining patient, knowing that it might be years before her spirit fully recovered.

"Imagine my surprise then, when last month I received a letter in which she sounded happier than ever she had been in all the time of our acquaintance. Gone was all sign of melancholy or introspection, and she could speak only of the peculiar new tutor who had inexplicably appeared, midterm, at her college. By all accounts they were the strangest person I had ever heard described, and yet it appears they had knowledge of the workings of the cosmos that astounded even the other faculty. Lilibell was practically infatuated with them, and promised that she would write more of them soon.

"However, the telephone calls ceased, and my messages to her went unanswered. When finally I received a letter it contained, not the usual musings and inquiries as to my studies, but a fantastic recount of her lessons under the mysterious tutor. These seemed to border on the insane—she claimed they had actually visited other planets!—and my replies requesting more information were similarly ignored. Finally, last week I received a letter so alarming that I telephoned the head of Astronomia and asked if he had noticed any changes in the behavior of my friend. Imagine my alarm when he admitted that he was about to contact *me,* since Lilibell had been missing from her classes for over a month now, and had not been seen since the 16th— the day after she posted her last letter. He'd hoped she'd gone to give me a surprise visit, since our friendship was well known among both faculties. I asked if he'd spoken with her curious new tutor, to which he expressed even more surprise: apparently Lilibell was not recorded as having a tutor since she began her post-graduate work, and asked who this mysterious person was. When I could only give him the most vague and inaccurate description he admitted it was impossible to tell whether such a person was employed by the college. He promised to make an official report to the police, after first confirming with Lilibell's remaining family.

"I was left to wait and worry myself into such a state that my own studies were irreparably underturned, and my tutor granted me a fortnight to put my mind in order. In that time I queried the head of Astronomia constantly, but no progress was being made. Lilibell had left her room in perfect order, with no note or sign as to where she was going, and there was no evidence that she had been abducted by force either.

"As the police had already been notified, I sought some other means of approach, which was when I thought of you, Aubergino. Tales of your exploits in Fiorino are still widely told, even as far as San Randelfino, and I thought if anyone could help it might be you. I went to your house in Redling, but found I had just missed you. Your kind housekeeper said that if I rode as fast as I could to the train station I might yet catch you, but alas I was too late. But the stationmaster, sympathetic to my plight, remembered the destination on your ticket and told me you might be found in Stanton Leaning. He sold me my ticket himself, but in the confusion I mistook the train, and got on the one to Standling instead, not realizing my mistake until the train pulled into Grenchester. Luckily I had brought my cycle with me, and so was able to ride the remaining miles under my own steam. So here I am, *Signore* Aubergino, to beg your help in finding my bosom friend."

In the time it took Miss Bragnana to relate her story Felpz had begun to lean farther and farther forward in his chair, so that by the time she finished he was perched at the very edge, elbows propped on knees, chin balanced on his tented fingers.

"And what," he said, his voice quiet but tense with pent up excitement. "What *was* the name of this mysterious tutor?"

"I am frustrated to say I do not know it," said Miss Bragnana. "Lilibell only ever gave the most rudimentary description of them—she would not even say whether they were male or female! Only that they were of medium height and slender build, fond of scarves and hats and long coats. She referred to them as the *odd professor*, and later on, as Professor Odd. Which, of course, means they could be anybody at all! Even a desperate villain!"

She took a sip of tea to prevent herself going on, but Felpz let out a long breath at the sound of the name and leaned back in his chair, uncrossing his legs and staring around my parlor as though he had forgotten he was in such a place. His eyes rested upon my ridiculous cane, which was leaning in a corner by the door, and he stared at it for so long that Miss Bragnana began eating her slice of pie almost out of self defense. This reminded me that she had been running and cycling about Stantondale all morning, and I cut her another slice as soon as she had finished the first.

"Get some nourishment into you, my girl," I told her firmly when she began to protest. "An active young person like yourself, goodness knows you need it more than I."

Miss Bragnana accepted my friendly admonishment, and as Felpz was still gazing distantly at my cane—had, in fact, begun to scratch his chin thoughtfully—she tucked into her second slice with a will.

"These letters," Felpz said, looking up just as our guest took a healthy bite. "Would it be possible for me to see them?"

Miss Bragnana chewed gallantly and swallowed, washed the pie down with more tea, and nodded vigorously.

"I expected you would want to," she said eventually, feeling in her voluminous top and producing a small bundle of papers. "You may keep them, if you feel it necessary."

"Please, might I beg you to read them aloud?" Felpz asked, kindly. "And Corianne will probably want them when you are finished, to make copies. You will assist me on this case, will you not Corianne?" He put this last question to me most earnestly, as though it were of the utmost of importance that I agree. So although I could not see what good my presence would do him, and though previously I had thought I was finished with his mad adventures, at that moment I felt the old stirring of excitement in my breast, and knowing that such an opportunity might not again present itself, I agreed without reservation.

Felpz clapped his hands in satisfaction and swiveled to face our guest once more, clasping his hands expectantly in his lap.

Miss Bragnana shrank slightly into her seat at the attention, but she straightened the papers briskly by tapping them on a corner of the table, and began to read clearly, if a little sedately. She did later allow me to copy the letters, so I have been able to include them within this narrative in their entirety.

Chapter 2: Three Troubling Letters

Dunchurch College, Fairbridge
Fifteenth of April, 2344
To my dearest Favulia,

Marvel of marvels, the world has exploded in color! No, I do not mean the spring—that is still but a promise whispered on the chill wind up here—but the world itself. I feel buoyed up with life and excitement, as it appears all my hard work is getting me somewhere at last!

I am ever so sorry to have been such a wet blanket these last two months. Thank you for bearing with my bleak, existential ramblings, and for suffering me in my blackest moods. I do not know what I have done to deserve such a friend as you, but your patience would do justice to a saint. Be assured that I am feeling much better now, and if you don't mind, I shall tell you the reason why.

I find that when I am sufficiently distracted from the present state of the world I become much happier with it, and therefore my life. Such a distraction has presented itself in the form of a new professor whom I recently met roving the Widder Clock. [*Note: this is student lingo for the Widder Camera, which houses the library of Dunchurch College.* —C] I had taken to going there on my darker days to sit and read in a particular chair on the second level which gets good sun in the afternoon, and where I can remain warm even when I stay still for hours on end, lost in a book. Imagine my consternation then, when on Monday I arrived to find that chair already occupied! And by a complete stranger, no less!

When I say "stranger" I do mean that I did not recognize them, but also that they were exceptionally *strange.* Sitting with their feet up on the chair and their knees in their chest, they were pouring over one of the library's bound journals—you know, the kind where the handwriting of some ancient scholar or scientist has been preserved by putting the original pages into a proper binding—and had obviously chosen that seat on account of the light, for I could see the ink had faded terribly over the years.

They were clearly faculty. Though I saw no insignia, they had the unmistakable look of a Dunchurch fellow: wild, unkempt silvery hair that fell around their ears in a cloudy veil; thick spectacles that distorted their eyes; and their neck was wrapped snugly in a wooly, brown scarf whose tasseled ends fell over the front of their black gown—which was dusty from chalk.

Since this is what most of the fellows look like, I was for a moment worried that I *had* met this professor before, and I simply did not remember.

Next thing, however, they leapt from the chair, stammering an apology in a raspy voice I knew I had never heard before, and this somehow put me at ease.

"Oh, please don't," I assured them, turning the collar of my coat so they could see I was merely a post-grad. "Besides, that is the best seat in the Clock, and your book looks more difficult than mine." I indicated Handelsohn's *Illustrated Galaxia* which I had tucked under one arm.

"You really don't mind?" asked the professor.

I really did, but I was not about to alienate a new professor by evicting them from what was technically a public chair. So aloud I said, "Not at all," and introduced myself.

"I don't believe I've seen you around here before," I said, casually, but I was already thoroughly intrigued. "Are you new? Which school do you teach?"

"New?" said the professor. "Yes, yes I am definitely new. And I do not teach any schools—not yet—which is likely why you haven't met me."

"Well, that sounds lovely," I said, because it did. To be a fellow at Dunchurch, with your income secured and access to all the best astronomic literature and implements, with no teaching to get in the way of your personal interests. "A pleasure to meet you, Professor, er . . . "

I had reached out my hand to shake theirs, and trailed off uncertainly when the professor neither shook it, nor answered the implied question. They stared at my hand for several moments, as though they had never seen anything like it before, and I just had time to think what a very introverted person they must be, and wonder if I should withdraw my hand, when they reached forward and shook it, tentatively, as though afraid my fingertips would bite.

"Odd," they said. "You may call me Odd."

"How suitable," I said, before I could help myself. I was mortified. I covered my mouth with my free hand and stammered an apology, but Professor Odd was not offended. I imagine they get remarks like that all the time.

We parted amicably from our first meeting, myself expressing a desire that we should see one another again, and Professor Odd cautiously reciprocating. For the rest of the day I could not get the thought of that peculiar person out of my head. It provided such a welcome distraction that I determined I must find out more about this Professor Odd, if only for my own sanity.

Luckily, they were to be found in the exact same place the very next day, and seemed to have been expecting me, for they had dragged a small, folding stool up from the common area and were sitting on that, as opposed to the chair, as if I were some timid, woodland animal which they were trying to entice into a trap. Only in this case, I was certain, the trap was in fact a friendship.

"I am sorry," said Professor Odd after greetings had been exchanged, "if I was a little brisk with you yesterday. I have not much experience dealing with other humans, and your customs are still largely unknown to me."

"No apology necessary," I assured them. "Many of the professors here are like that: too engrossed in their studies to bother developing social niceties. You'll fit right in. Not all of them are entirely human either—no one will say it to his face, but it's an open secret that Professor Starling's got elf blood in him, and my own tutor is half dwarf!"

"That is good to know," said Professor Odd, blinking at me from behind their huge glasses. They had strange eyes, though I could not quite pin down what it was. I assumed they were of mixed heritage, but since they didn't offer any explanation I didn't press for one. I asked what their main field of study was, and they admitted they had none. They were an omnivore when it came to knowledge, taking in all aspects—not just those of astronomy.

"I find myself flummoxed by certain areas, however," they admitted to me, almost with embarrassment. "The unconventional nature of this planet's atmosphere, the anomalies in its satellite's surface, the presence of life on one of the moons of the giant you call Amaugsamid—"

I nearly fell over right there in front of them, I was so astonished. Of course we have theorized that life may have been or will be possible on Kovor, but beyond that I had heard nothing more along those lines.

"There is *life* on Amaugsamid's moons?" I gasped, clutching my hands together in amazement.

"*One* of Amaugsamid's moons," Professor Odd corrected me. "Callanaph. I'm not sure about the others." They gave me an almost fearful look. "Why, did you not know?"

"*No one* knows," I exclaimed. "Not that I had heard, anyway."

"Oh dear," said Professor Odd, as if it was a secret they had accidentally revealed. "I'm sorry, I should not have said."

"Unpublished research, I *quite* understand," I assured them —so you must take care with this letter, dear Favulia, and not show this bit to anyone in Baronia.

"What are you studying?" Professor Odd asked me, to which I explained about my thesis on the theory of thaumaturgic gravitation, and all the problems I was running into on account of not having precise measurements of the magic present on other planets—let alone other star systems. Professor Odd was just as fascinated with my research as I was to hear about life on Callanaph, and we arranged that we should meet again—this time someplace more private—where we could discuss matters in detail. I suggested the professor's office, to which they confessed to not having one yet.

"Never mind," they said. "You can come to my rooms. You can find me in the basement of Dactidillian House. You might have to knock a bit loudly, but I'll be there tomorrow evening."

I cannot tell you how long that day was for me. I was on edge with excitement through my morning sessions and could not concentrate at all in the afternoon. I gave up around teatime and went down to the kitchens to bake some biscuits, as I had not done since Chandarmas, and the cooking did relieve some of the stress—sampling the batter as I made it helped as well. Bearing my freshly baked offerings I presented myself at the door of Dactidillian's basement and rapped quite hard, as instructed.

The door opened almost immediately and Professor Odd ushered me in. They seemed astounded that I had made biscuits, and ate them with great care and relish. It was most gratifying, and we spent the evening sunk in enjoyable conversation about each other's work, trading such stories and facts and research as would fill another twenty letters. Suffice to say we have arranged another meeting next week, and the anticipation has served as a welcome counterbalance to the black moods which still take me now and then. I expect I will have more stories about the peculiar Professor Odd when next I write, but I am also aching to hear how you are getting on. Don't feel pressured to write back—I know how busy you are—just be assured that I cherish your letters and the prospect of receiving one gives me strength.

Until next time, I remain faithfully yours,
Lilibell Donnet

Dunchurch College, Fairbridge
Twenty-eighth of April, 2344
To my dear, patient Favulia,

My deepest and sincerest apologies for not returning your calls or your messages, but when you have heard what I have to say you will understand. I promise this letter will more than make up for my previous reticence in communication, and I can only hope it will prove a sufficient apology.

First, let me assure you that I am physically well, and though I still feel as if I am walking on ice over a bottomless black hole, that ice has grown thick and sturdy beneath my feet, and I can tear my eyes away from contemplation of grim matters and appreciate the beauty of the world around me. It is all thanks to the professor, who has shown me wonders I could not have otherwise dreamed of, and who has instilled in me a confidence which I feel I must have once possessed, but somewhere over the course of my rigorous education and my recent loss, had all but deserted me.

One thing at a time and in the correct order however, or you will become cross with me for being unintelligible.

My second evening meeting with Professor Odd was as enjoyable as the first, as was the third. By this time we had enough trust in one another that the professor offered to show me some of their more sensitive research. I cannot tell even you what that was, save that it entirely changes my view of our world and the behavior of our solar system. In return I tried to explain to the professor the delicate way magic interacts with the laws of physics, which is something they continue to struggle with. They are of that particular mindset that abhors the arbitrary capriciousness of magic, and I think they may be one of those people who are magically disabled, as it were. They have no sense for magic or its workings, and everything about it puts them off. They are, however, fiercely intent on learning, in a way I have not known in any of my other professors, and that is both gratifying and inspiring to me. If such a learned individual as Professor Odd may admit that they don't know everything and put out the energy to actually *learn more* then it gives me hope that I will not become, in my old age, as stiff and arrogant as my tutors. Instead I can follow the path of Professor Odd, and be continually interested and open to expanding my knowledge.

Not that I am blind to their peculiarities. If I did not know them as well as I did, I might have been put off by their quarters, which as I have said are in the basement of Dactidillian House. I'm not sure what the rooms were originally for, only that they must have been built before the rest of the college sprang up around it, for they have *windows*. Professor Odd keeps the blinds always drawn, of course, since there is no view outside but packed earth, but it is a strange feeling walking into a room underground and seeing windows in the walls.

The room itself is drab, but not uncomfortable. It is mostly taken up by a table, with the area around the door draped in cloth—a grand project, Professor Odd told me, that could not yet be revealed—and a cozy station for making tea and a poky little toilet. The place is dim, and feels altogether out of place. Odd, just like its occupant. I asked if that was why it had been given to the professor, to which they looked surprised.

"You know, that might very well be," they said to me.

Before I go on and tell you *why* the place felt so odd, and what was under those drapes, I must swear you to secrecy. For what I am about to put on paper cannot be seen by other eyes, lest Professor Odd's research be copied and exploited before they have a chance to publish it. I feel a trifle guilty telling even you, dear Favulia, but I would feel worse if I kept this a secret from you. Besides, the experience was so incredible that I feel I must write it down, lest I come to doubt my own memory.

Favulia, Favulia . . . how do I say this without coming off like one of those muddled folks who have been abducted by fairies or wandered into Dream? I suppose there is no way but the most direct one: I have visited another world! Not a realm attached to ours like Faerie or the Dragon Lands, but literally another celestial body! You may recall I wondered how Professor Odd knew there was life on Callanaph? Well, now I know: she has been there and seen it! I know this, because now I have been there too.

The trip came about because I showed Professor Odd our diving bubbles—the magic ones undersea explorers use to study oceans—and explained how I had built one that would, rather than keeping outside forces *out*, keep inside forces *in*. She was most intrigued by my idea of using it to protect a soft, squishy object—such as a human body—in outer space. I told her how I had performed every test that could be run on the surface of a planet—putting it in a sealed chamber and vacuuming out all the air—and how now it was really only a matter of finding a way to shoot it—and a prospective occupant—into space.

Professor Odd went very quiet at that and looked tensely at the cloths draped over the objects by the door. These I could tell from their shapes included two chairs—one on either side of the door—some lumpish tables and things that bulged out from the walls like pipes and heavy picture frames. Occasionally I heard soft chirps and chimes coming from under the cloth, but as I respected the professor's privacy I had not asked what they were.

Now my patience was rewarded. Professor Odd leaned forward and told me, with barely restrained excitement, that they had a means by which we could test my exo-bubble. After making me promise not to breathe a word to the other professors, they got up from the table (where we had been sitting) and went to the front of their room and began pulling the drapes away.

This revealed two chairs, as I had expected, built of a greyish metal with a joint that allowed the seat to swivel around, but everything else took me by surprise.

How shall I describe it? Like a collection of fairy lights, with flat circular buttons glowing bright blue and orange and green and gold and red, and between them ran columns of filaments that pulsed with glowing liquid, again in all colors. Higher up, these widened into the pipe-shaped objects I had perceived under the cloth, and the picture frames turned out to be a uniform bank of squares which contained not paintings, but convex, glass windows through which I could see a constantly swirling mix of colors.

It was quite pretty in a way, but I had not the capacity to appreciate its looks, for Professor Odd had taken a seat in one of the chairs, where they began pressing buttons—rather like one would do with a typewriter. With each stroke a tiny chime sounded, seeming to come from beyond the walls of the room, from some echoing chamber.

"It's early days, yet," Professor Odd explained to me. "I cannot guarantee you the sights you wish for, but I might—*yes,* she is cooperating today!"

As she spoke these words Professor Odd looked up at the windows, most of which still showed the random swirl of colors, but a few directly above her head had transformed to a composite view (that is, each small screen showed a part of a larger picture, which was continued by their neighbors) of a dark field on which the graceful crescent of an illuminated planet glowed brightly. It was not Reanen, I can tell you that; nor was it Kovor nor Geda. Upon closer inspection I saw it was pale white in color, crisscrossed with veins of copper and blue, with splotches of brown here and there.

The view of the planet changed, coming around so we were looking at its face fully illuminated, and I had to admit it was no planet I knew.

"Professor," I asked. "What alien world is *that?*"

"Not such an alien world, to you," returned the professor. "That is Callanaph, the third giant moon of Amaugsamid, where, as I told you, I found the most intriguing form of life."

I was shocked. Amazed. Not even our greatest telescopes had produced such a clear picture, but if I had any doubts they were allayed when the view expanded, rendering the planet a tiny dot, and there, looming behind it like some great, godlike face, were the barred clouds and swirling storms of Amaugsamid's upper atmosphere.

"I believe we can see Orrus rising on our right," Professor Odd said. "Not as interesting as Callanaph—no life that I can recognize—but we could take a closer look if you like."

I felt like one who has wandered starving in the desert coming upon a hidden oasis filled with the bounty of a hundred kings' tables. If Professor Odd's machine could show us such an intimate view of Callanaph, what other worlds could it perceive? I regret to say my scientific mind, which wondered how her remarkable machine worked, was shouldered aside by my pure excitement.

"I found a possible anchor," Professor Odd was saying, though I listened with but half an ear. "The problem is I can't pass beyond. Callanaph's environment is deadly even to myself. I would need protection—protection not unlike your exo-bubble."

It took a moment for the enormity of her words to settle in my mind, and when they did I was so astounded I asked her to repeat the statement. Which she did, peering at me curiously.

Once I had ascertained that her device could in fact transport physical objects to the places it showed, my body could scarcely contain my excitement. I felt like I was beginning to glow, like a magic beast preparing to change shape. Professor Odd was surprised at my enthusiasm, but not in the least put off. We agreed that I should bring my exo-bubble the next day, and we would see if it was up to the test of Callanaph's environment.

Which was exactly what happened, and everything went perfectly. The manner by which their device transports objects is most marvelous, an amazing feat of magical engineering the likes of which I have never seen before. The door that nominally serves as a means to pass from the basement hall into their rooms is made to connect with some natural door or arch at the desired location, thus leading straight from their room to this other place. I have heard of magicians using a similar spell, in a more limited way, to fold space between two points so that one might walk a few steps and yet traverse many miles. Never did I imagine the theory might be stretched so far, however, and I confess I did not believe it possible until Professor Odd set all the chimes of their device ringing, and when they had quieted, went down to the door and opened it, not onto the hall of Dactidillian House, but to a bleak landscape of ice and rock, mounded with strange formations that created a maze of towers, arches and pillars. No breath of air nor sound came through the portal, for the professor's device was protecting us from the inhospitable environment beyond.

I produced my exo-bubble, and placed within it the little golem which I used when running my tests upon it, and sent it trundling out into the alien landscape.

We watched it as the golem, working under my instructions, took the bubble out to the nearest pillar and back again. By the time it returned the bubble was caked in ice that began to evaporate as soon as it passed through the portal.

We learned much from this short excursion: first that we had been lucky it was so short! My exo-bubble was on the verge of failure by the time the golem returned, and I was obliged to add several strengthening layers to the outside. I also constructed a thermal cloak, which would keep the interior temperature within a range comfortable to flesh-and-blood creatures such as ourselves. I also learned, from close examination of the golem, that it had suffered greatly from a force which I did not recognize, but that Professor Odd pronounced to be a specific type of unfiltered light, and under their advice I built a shield into the exo-bubble to protect its occupants against similar damage.

My golem's second outing was much more satisfactory, and with just a little further adjustment we determined the bubble fit for human occupation.

I can imagine how your fingers much be clutching the paper with nerves by now, so I shall come right out and say that everything went swimmingly, and neither of us suffered any ill effects! There. Now I have allayed your fears, I may take my time and tell you what transpired in more detail.

Since we could not agree on who should have the honor of setting foot upon Callanaph first (I insisted the professor should have that honor; they in turn wished that I should), we compromised by crowding into the little ball, and making our first foray together.

What a feeling, Favulia! Such delight tempered with care, and awareness of the extreme inhospitality that lay beyond the exo-bubble's shields, but also the sheer physical sensations that affected us, even protected as we were. With our first steps beyond the portal I felt as though I would float away clear into the dark, starry sky! Callanaph has significantly less gravity than does Reanen, and it took us both a little time to adjust to. Once I had a grasp of how much (or really, how *little*) effort was needed to propel the bubble across the smooth, icy surface, the sensation was a marvelous one.

We did not go far that first trek, being careful to remain within sight of the portal—which had anchored itself in one of the naturally occurring arches of icy stone that lay on the edge of the greater maze—but in that short time I observed more than I have in years of peering through a telescope. The composition of the ice was not unlike that of Reanen's polar regions, but I could see deep fissures in the smooth surface of the moon, with strange obelisks, like jets of water frozen in place, jutting out of them. By this I deduced that Callanaph possesses a hot and active mantle beneath its frozen surface.

Professor Odd was equally consumed with curiosity, and after our return we stayed up late into the night comparing notes and making plans for our next venture. Professor Odd believes their device can open a portal beneath the surface, in the subterranean ocean in which dwells the life they first observed. I am making the necessary adjustments to the exo-bubble, and we hope to make the expedition the day after tomorrow. I am so excited I can barely sleep; not merely for my own sake, but also for Professor Odd, who must, after they publish their findings, be hailed as the greatest explorer of our age.

I trust all is well with you, and I beg you do not fret over me. Rest assured I will write again with tales of new adventures. In the meantime, be well, and know that you are always in my heart.

Lilibell

Dunchurch College, Fairbridge
Fifteenth of May, 2344
Dearest Favulia,

It is past time I sat down and wrote to you, but so much has been happening I find myself so tired that the prospect of writing it all down discourages me, so I put it off, and so new things keep piling up! Well, I must procrastinate no more! Something has happened that entirely changes the nature of our explorations, and I simply *must* tell someone!

Firstly, life on Callanaph: it *does* exist! It is exists, and in forms that, I believe, have not been seen on Reanen since before the Dragon Age. Yet we discovered something further on Callanaph (or rather, *in* Callanaph, since all this took place beneath the cold, icy crust), that puts those ancient demons in the shade.

Of course, the whole place is in shadow, really. Only the very upper regions of the ocean get any light whatsoever, and that is so dim and filtered by the icy crust that it would take the eyes of an owl to pierce the gloom. Besides, Professor Odd said that what we were looking for lay near the bottom, in the inky depths.

To this end I reinforced the exo-bubble once more, this time to withstand outside pressure as well, and affixed to the bottom a spell of illumination. I shielded it with a steel plate, so that the light would be directed downward and not reflect upon the surface of the bubble, making it impossible to see out. Professor Odd was taken aback by such a plain use of magic, which surprised me, considering their device uses magic that is far beyond anything I have ever seen.

When we opened the portal—again, utilizing a fissure in the rocky bed of the ocean—it looked as though the doorway had been filled by a solid wall of water. It was perfectly still, and only the colored lights of the professor's device, reflecting off its surface, belied its presence. Otherwise, beyond, I could see nothing but blackness, and I would not have had the courage to step out into it—even safe within my exo-bubble—had not Professor Odd been by my side.

The engineer in me is delighted to report that the bubble, and the variable weight I installed to allow us upward and downward motion, performed beautifully, and never did I feel the slightest bit worried for my physical safety. We went drifting serenely over a rocky, desolate plain—but always with the little crack of colored light visible behind us—until we came to an underwater geyser: a great jet of inky liquid billowing up from a tower in the ocean floor.

I quickly lowered the bubble to rest on the slope below—for my outward sensors indicated such a drastic change in temperature that the bubble would likely be damaged—and from there we gazed up at what I began to realize was a city. This was no naturally formed volcanic cone. What the bubble rested upon, and what its light was illuminating, was a structure built of hard, rocky houses, rather like the ones built by coral in the warm equatorial oceans of Reanen. Above us I could see them marching away like a set of uneven stairs, and as we stood there, amazed, I saw a tiny filament extend from one of the nearer blocks, curling curiously around before unfurling like a flower, with tiny strands reaching outward, netlike.

They weaved gently back and forth, pushed by unseen currents, and as we watched, enthralled, more flowers unfurled from the surrounding rock, the jumbled mountainside practically blooming with them.

Pale white they were, with faintly glowing blue splotches. The professor bade me dim the bubble's searchlight, and as we watched the dance of bright blue dots upon the mountain I was so overcome by the beauty and wonderment of it all that it was as though the world filled with joyous music, though it was only the sound of my delighted mind.

It was then that we were visited by an entirely new form of life, one that neither of us were prepared to encounter. It began as a sour note in my internal melody, and strengthened to a buzzing pitch that filled my head and made my ears ache.

Professor Odd was more resistant, and for a minute was confused by my groans of pain. Then they too felt what I had, and covered their head as if to protect it from an unseen attack.

Which I soon realized was the case: the buzzing in my head was no internal phenomenon, but came from without. From something that drifted in the dark sea, coiling around us and pushing curious fingers clean through the surface of my bubble. I could not see it with my eyes, but sensed it as one senses malevolent magic, and by this sense I knew them to be no physical animal, but a beast of the spirit.

I do not say we encountered a demon, Favulia, for I do not believe it was any more related to the spirits of our world than the strange creatures with their rocklike homes are related to the sea life in our own oceans, but it was something similar. Similar enough that I was able to decipher a definite meaning from it: that it did not want us there.

Needless to say Professor Odd and I hastened back the way we had come, and the presence followed us—but at a distance, like a dog escorting an intruder off its territory. We dove gladly through the portal, and though the being did not follow we both had headaches for the rest of the day.

But I am not through with my investigations on Callanaph! Though I realize we have come to a point where more research is needed. It is one thing to go exploring unoccupied worlds—where the only thing you are disturbing are rocks and traces of atmosphere—but to go blundering about an alien realm which is home to intelligent, living creatures is quite another. Should Callanaph have an ecosystem as diverse and delicately balanced as Reanen, the last thing I would wish to do is upset it. Then there are the practical considerations for our safety: who could say what powers that strange being held, and what it might have done to us had we remained. I do not wish to imagine.

Professor Odd listened attentively to my reservations, and after some consideration declared that they agreed with me, and suggested a short holiday to help us recover from our unpleasant experience. When I demurred, pointing out that my studies would not allow it, Professor Odd told me the most astounding thing—even after all the astounding things we had already seen and done.

Favulia, can you imagine it? Their device does not merely open portals to different places—it can open portals to entirely different *worlds.* Just this morning we shared a breakfast of fresh bread and eggs in a land where the sky is ruddy orange and the grass is blue. We were served by a feathered, dragony sort of person who spoke a dialect of Milanian, and who, though surprised at our appearance, was nevertheless friendly and congenial. It was the perfect diversion from our stressful work, and we are going back for supper tonight. If all goes well, Favulia, I hope you can make it up for a visit, and I can show this world to you. It would be marvelous to have you by my side for these adventures, and I'm sure the natives would be delighted to speak with you.

Yours ever,
Lilibell

Chapter 3: The Mystery at Dunchurch

THOUGH WE SAT IN MY COZY PARLOR, filled with the strong afternoon rays of May sunshine and the smell of the honey I'd set out with the tea, I could not help the shiver that passed through me as I listened to Miss Bragnana read her friend's letters. They seemed incredible; highly upsetting if they were true, for it meant Miss Donnet had been courting extreme danger, but equally upsetting if they were a sign of deteriorating mental state. Such thoughts had obviously occurred to Bragnana, who cleared her throat nervously after she had finished and took a sip of her now-cold tea.

"You see why I am so fearful?" she said, gazing at us beseechingly. "From what I hear from the master of Astronomia, I think she must have imagined this Odd character, or been tricked by a malicious spirit."

Felpz, however, was shaking his head, an inexplicable smile creeping across his face.

"No, no," said he. "Professor Odd was no hallucination, I can assure you. Nor is she any spirit or mischievous demon. Yes, I say *she*—for Professor Odd is a woman, and an extraordinary one at that."

Bragnana nearly dropped her teacup, and I turned to Felpz in astonishment.

"You *know* this person?" I exclaimed. Not so surprised that he knew her—Felpz knew a great many extraordinary characters—but that he had admitted this knowledge so casually; I had known him before to go to extreme lengths to disguise the full extent of his knowledge, and it excited me that here was possibly an explanation ready and waiting.

I was to be disappointed, however. Felpz merely shrugged and said:

"I know of her." He gave me a twinkling glance. "Not well, I'm afraid, and it is likely she does not know me. But I do not see why we shouldn't be able to clear the matter up, and restore your friend in the process," he said, giving Bragnana a reassuring nod. "But first we must go to Fairbridge—there is nothing I can do from here. It is a pity—I had wanted to see a bit more of Corianne's new home—but it should not prevent us having our little reunion, provided I can convince her to take up her old mantle as my assistant and chronicler. Say you will ride with me, Corianne? If it is only this one, last time, I promise it will be a ride to remember."

He had no need for such sweetened words, however. Already I was intrigued by the case, and I scoffed at him as I rose to my feet.

"Count yourself lucky that I have not lost my knack for quick packing," I said to him. "I'll leave the pie for Nireen, and we can make a dinner of bread and cheese on the train—provided you allow it to take the ordinary amount of time to reach Fairbridge. Miss Bragnana can pay the visit her friend has been asking for, and she can leave her bicycle in my shed if she doesn't wish to take it with her on the train."

Miss Bragnana was most attached to her cycle, however, which proved advantageous as we were able to strap my trunk to the rack clamped above its rear wheel, and so rolled the whole contraption back to the station to catch the evening northbound train.

It was to be a long journey, requiring two transfers and a stop in Brittledam that I would not wish upon my worst enemy, and I was fighting off a snippish mood by the time we rolled into Fairbridge. It was long after the sky had purpled into night, and the faint, summer stars glimmered in the heavens over the spires of that city, now lit brightly yellow and orange by the electric lamps which had grown common in the last decade. It was a garish look, I thought, but they were to our advantage as we navigated the narrow streets and winding closes until we came to the gates of Dunchurch—whereupon Felpz turned away and led us across the street, to the doors of an inn at which we were able to secure lodging for ourselves and Miss Bragnana.

"It will do no good banging on doors and getting the masters out of bed," Felpz admitted with a sigh, and to my relief we were allowed one night's respite before the adventure truly began.

For an adventure it was, and one which I could not have imagined, even after my long career riding the coattails of Bouragner Felpz. Certainly it was not one I would have chosen, given my time of life, but in retrospect I am glad that it happened.

Here is how events transpired:

The next morning I woke with the sun as it crested the spiny horizon of Dunchurch Commons and the Church of St Mermund. It brought with it a hoard of madly singing birds which took up residence in a nearby tree and put up such a racket that I was roused from my bed having only enjoyed a handful of hours' good sleep. Turning to see what Felpz made of the morning I saw the reason for the volume of the noise: his bed was empty—had, it appeared, not even been slept in—and beyond that his window stood open.

I hobbled across to the offending aperture and pulled it shut, and in the relative quiet this produced I saw the note that had been left sitting on Felpz's counterpane. It was in my friend's own hand, and said:

Have asked our hosts for an early breakfast. Please bring Miss Bragnana and see that you both wear sensible shoes.

I snorted—as if I would don anything else at such a time!—but dutifully made my way to our client's room and knocked gently on the door.

Miss Bragnana had had a more restless night than I, judging by her tired face lined beyond her years. But she was glad of the prompt beginning, and I did not have to relay my friend's curious request regarding footwear: she had already laced up the neat, hardy pair of boots she wore for cycling.

We found Felpz in a little room off the inn's main dining area, seated at a wide, wooden table piled with such a breakfast as would befit a king—or perhaps a giant: racks of brown toast with pots of baked beans, trays of scrambled eggs and fried tomatoes, sausages, black pudding, jars of preserves and a crock of butter—not to mention coffee and tea and a small cake covered in fruit.

Most of the food already showed signs of having been partaken of, and I guessed the order had been largely for Felpz's benefit. He was in the act of cleaning his own plate when we arrived, but served himself a second helping to keep us company while we broke our fast.

"I realize that, despite your overwhelming competence in such matters, you had forgotten an important article," he said to me as I sat down. "So I took the liberty of returning to Stanton

Leaning to retrieve it," and here he produced nothing less than my absurd banana-handled cane, which I had purposely left at home.

"I cannot imagine what importance this could be," I said, a little peeved.

"Nevertheless," said Felpz, folding his hands under his chin and smiling at me, sunny as the morning, "I would rest easier with the knowledge that you were so equipped. Now eat, my friends, eat well, and then we shall begin our investigation of Dunchurch College. I have paid them a visit already, and they are forewarned of our coming. The Master of Astronomia was not awake when I first called, but by the time you have finished he should be available, and I propose that he is where we should begin."

Since neither myself nor Miss Bragnana had any idea where to start we were more than happy to follow Felpz's lead, though I for one could not fathom what importance my cane could be. I took Felpz's meaning, however, and dutifully kept it with me when we exited the inn and crossed the cobbled street to the gates of the college—which now stood open and inviting.

I read once that the colleges of Fairbridge began as feudal castles, built within the city and ruled by the five sons of the original lord. Of course there are more than five colleges now, and which ones began as castles and which were built to mimic them is a topic of some debate. Dunchurch might have been an original, if its high, studded walls were anything to go by, though it took its name from the flaxen bricks of St Mermund, which stood next to its common house and was a landmark in its own right. The college's defining feature, however, was the observatory at the top of the Astronomia Tower; a modern construction that, though it contrasted with the ancient stonework, was a remarkable feat of engineering, drawing visitors—both professional and amateur—from across the country.

Approaching as we did in the early morning we saw it gleaming above the walls of the college: a perfect white half-orb balanced at the top of the tallest tower, which was currently mired in scaffolding giving the impression of the observatory rising like the full moon over a tangle of spars and trusses.

We entered through the main gate, which led us to the green courtyard of the college by way of a short tunnel in which sat a booth manned by a neat, black-clad porter. He seemed young for his position, and though he called to us as we passed and asked us to sign our names in the college guest book, he did not demand our business but bid us welcome, touching his brow respectfully to the three of us.

After we were well into the courtyard, however, and I glanced back at him, I saw he had pulled out the mouthpiece of the telephone his booth was equipped with, and was speaking into it urgently. So I was not surprised when we were soon met by the Astronomia Master himself, having come directly from his own breakfast, if the crumbs on his black gown were anything to go by.

He was a hearty, white-haired gentleman of medium build but such good posture that I thought him a tall man until we drew near, and I found myself gazing directly into pale grey eyes with snowy lashes.

"Good gracious, you're actually here," he said, his voice a pleasant, husky Cairdrian brogue. "By Nuddic's Horn I thought the lad was joking when he said the Purple Magician had been asking after me this morning. But here you are! Forgive me, I am Professor Húron, the master of Dunchurch's Astronomia department, and I must apologize for the state of Evith Frell— but we are not allowing visitors up to the observatory until they've finished installing the lifts, which may not be for several months, considering the way work has been going. *Er-herm . . . "*

The professor cleared his throat nervously as we continued to stare at him through this long greeting, but when he finally halted, Felpz lost no time in reassuring the man.

"My dear Professor," said he, smiling warmly. "You mistake our intent—I am afraid I have no more idea what your Evith Frell is than what I would do if I was allowed to visit it. No, I am here at the behest of Miss Favulia Bragnana, of San Randelfino via the Astronomia College at Baronia, to ascertain the whereabouts of her friend, Miss Lilibell Donnet—one of your students. I was hoping you could grant us an interview and provide any additional information regarding events that have transpired since you last communicated with Miss Bragnana."

The Astronomia Master's face, which had first lightened at Felpz's congenial nature, shuttered visibly at the mention of Lilibell Donnet, and by the time Felpz had finished his mouth was twisting sourly.

"The case is in the hands of the Fairbridgedale police," he said, his tone gone tight and unfriendly. "Any inquiries you have must go through them. I have the detective's card if you wish a direct line . . . "

Felpz was already shaking his head, however, and held up a polite hand.

"We are conducting a private investigation," said he. "As I do not believe any criminal activity has occurred, I do not wish to put anyone—and certainly not a college master—into an unfortunate situation. By your own admission you know who I am; so you must also know that when I mean to do a thing I do it, but I would much rather proceed with your blessing that without."

The Astronomia Master still looked dubious, but he relented and took us up to his study, where he turned away the nervous first year who had been the morning's appointment, much to the boy's relief, and ushered us inside. When once we had settled into the aged chairs covered in leather so worn it shone, and the professor had swept aside the notes covering his desk, he clasped his thick hands briskly in front of him and regarded us expectantly.

"I can spare you twenty minutes," he said. "Ask what you wish to know."

Felpz replied, just as tersely: "Tell me of Lilibell Donnet."

The Astronomia Master shrugged. "A powerfully intelligent, motivated woman, if you had asked me a year ago. Bright girl, strong mind. On course to get her doctorate and even a junior fellowship, should her thesis live up to expectations. Took it hard when she lost her father, but who could blame her? She was given a week's full leave, which she declined, but the quality of her work . . . well, I do not like to speak ill of a person in front of their friends, but I have to say her work deteriorated sadly. Beginning in March she was missed from her Wednesday courses, and these absences only grew as time progressed. When, in April, it appeared she had abandoned her thesis entirely to drag out that ridiculous exo-bubble project she'd built in her second year, we attempted to have a consultation with her, from which she was again absent."

"You say this began in March?" interrupted Miss Bragnana, clearly having a little difficulty making sense of the professor's accent.

"Yes, I did," said the man, his pale eyes narrowing.

"That is when she began meeting with Professor Odd," Miss Bragnana said, speaking earnestly to Felpz.

"I had made that connection," Felpz assured her. "Do continue, Professor."

"Oh, do not bring up the blasted Professor Odd," said the Astronomia Master, leaning back in his chair with a groan. "They are the most frustrating character—no matter how many times I explain that he does not actually exist, the myth of his presence *persists*—"

"Professor Odd is no myth," Felpz said quietly, at the same time as Bragnana burst out:

"You mean that others have seen the Professor Odd?"

"No," snapped Professor Húron, apparently to Felpz, then, turning to Miss Bragnana, added: "Yes, apparently he is a catching delusion. But I will tell you again: we have no faculty members of that name in Astronomia, and neither do any of the other departments! We do not house our members in the basement of any building, and certainly not Dactidillian House—that place floods every winter."

Felpz gave Bragnana an arch look. "Did you show him the letters?" he asked.

Miss Bragnana looked horrified. "Of course not!" she declared.

Felpz turned his gaze back to Professor Húron. "Does Dactidillian House carry any additional detractions, aside from the annual floods?" he asked, innocently.

The Astronomia Master rolled his eyes. "Oh, it is only where most of these ghost-sightings have occurred. Third years playing pranks, I expect, only we haven't been able to catch them at it yet."

"And when was the last incident?" Felpz pressed on.

Húron shrugged. "Maybe two weeks ago? They are coming forward more frequently now that Miss Donnet has gone missing, but always the actual event happened much earlier."

"And, what is the date of the earliest of these events?" Felpz pressed on.

"Oh . . . it would have to have been in March," Professor Húron admitted.

"Which brings us back to Lilibell Donnet and her mysterious disappearance," Felpz said, smoothly. "Tell us about that."

"There is precious little to tell," said the professor, sounding peeved. "One day she is flitting about the college, head in the clouds, as the proverbial saying goes, the next she is gone. Her rooms have been searched—no signs of a struggle—a small number of her belongings are also missing, suggesting that she left of her own free will. Considering the mental upset she had been exhibiting since the loss of her father, we assumed this was a natural continuation of it; that she had gone back to her family in Baronia was the consensus, but when we received no word from her, and once we had ascertained she was not with her parents or with her friend, Miss Bragnana—by her own admission—we promptly put the matters into the hands of the police. The officer in charge of the case is one Inspector Lam, whose card I have—"

"Thank you, Professor Húron, you have been most helpful," Felpz cut in. Lowering his voice, he said, half to me and half to the professor: "I think we will be better served having a look at Dactidillian House—unless that, too, is closed for repairs?"

Professor Húron gave a long-suffering sigh. "I'll have Maggehrty give you the tour. If you have any further questions you can can find me in the Astronomia Hall this afternoon."

He stood, reached for the receiver of his study's telephone, and after a few short words there was a knock at the door which opened to reveal a squat young man in a black pillbox cap and matching coat with brass buttons. He seemed taken aback by both Felpz's authoritarian bearing and the striking appearance of Miss Bragnana, and could only manage a mumbled, "Maggehrty at yer service, mum," in my direction.

"Thank you," I said, putting my cane to use, for once, as I pried myself out of the chair. And with a nod to the white-haired professor, I led our little company from the room.

Dactidillian House was not in the main quadrangle of buildings into which one entered through the front gate, but lay beyond an archway that led to the circle in the center of which sat the Widder Camera—a squat, domed building whose sides were lined with windows and whose copper fittings had long since gone a bright, blueish green. Most of the ring was comprised of dormitories, though there were two distinctly larger, grander houses, which were used primarily as common study halls, though some resident tutors lived there as well. Dactidillian House was one of these, and had the distinction of a long, overhung stoa which faced the Camera. Here students lounged, some with books and notepads, others sunk in discussion with one another. A few sent curious glances in our direction, but for the most part we were ignored as we passed under the roof and into the building itself.

"Dactidillian is one of the oldest buildings in Dunchurch," Maggehrty informed us as we made our way down the long, interior hall—this one with windows on both sides, interspersed with austere portraits of the various masters who had once called it home. "You'll find it a bit dank, I'm afraid. That's on account of Professor Rivenstone, a fellow from the twentieth century who set the place up as part of a grand experiment to see whether a building's magical attributes could be enhanced by allowing it to fall partially into ruin."

"And did it?" Felpz asked, slightly amused.

"By the accounts of Rivenstone, no," said Maggehrty. "But you'll find there is many a student who's seen an odd thing or two in its halls, and I understand it's only the most desperate of tutors who will accept lodging here."

"Odd?" said Miss Bragnana, the word drawing her attention like a cat to a bird.

Maggehrty's round face colored a little, and he worked a nervous finger into the collar of his shirt.

Felpz, who had drawn a little ahead of us, stopped and turned back, fixing the young man with an intent look.

"You have heard of this mysterious Professor Odd?" he asked, his tone brokering no prevarication.

Maggehrty coughed. "Heard of him?" he said, his voice gone high and thin. "I've *seen* him."

Felpz raised his eyebrows, but did not correct our guide. "Where?" he asked instead. "Here?"

"Not precisely," said Maggehrty, now toying with the cuffs of his sleeves.

"Why have you not said anything?" asked Miss Bragnana. "Here is Professor Húron, thinking Professor Odd was a fabrication of my friend—a ghost story—but now *you* say you have met her as well?"

"I never said I met him," Maggehrty replied, a little defensive. "To own the truth I didn't know who it was I was seeing until after Miss Donnet vanished—I assumed he was either a legitimate aspect of Dactidillian or a prank by one of the students. The peculiarities of Dactidillian House are well known, you understand, and we have had more cases of students dressing up as ghosts or impersonating dead masters than we do of actual magical phenomena. I didn't feel that what I saw—"

"What *did* you see?" Felpz asked, wrenching the conversation back on topic.

"Only the back of him," admitted Maggehrty. "Just walking down this hall, as we are doing now. My only thought at the time was that he must be a tutor I hadn't met yet, but as I'm not even a junior porter it didn't seem appropriate to run up and introduce myself."

"That is perfectly understandable," I said, soothingly, for our guide was becoming flustered.

"Can you show me where exactly you saw her?" asked Felpz.

"Saw who?" Maggehrty looked bewildered.

"Professor Odd," Miss Bragnana told him, primly. "She is a woman."

"He is? *She* is? How do you know?" asked Maggehrty, his eyes gone wide.

"I know of her," Felpz said, with a secretive smile, and gestured for Maggehrty to lead the way.

"It was right about here," the young man told us, coming to stand at the far end of the hall, near two sets of stairs, one leading up to the floor above, the other down to the basement. "He—er—*she* was, anyway. I was down about two window lengths, running an errand for Professor Moss. I thought I heard a noise and glanced back, and I saw someone standing right where we are now. A stranger in a dusty black suit with downy, silver hair and thick glasses. I remember the glasses: they were at just the right angle to reflect the light, and shone like two lamps in the person's head. But as I was in a hurry I didn't stop to investigate, and when I turned again to leave the building he was—she was gone."

Felpz paced around the little area, touching the walls and the floor and sniffing the air, like a dog. Eventually he went to the top of the stairs leading downward, and glanced at Miss Bragnana.

"According to Miss Donnet's letters, Professor Odd's quarters were in the basement of Dactidillian House. Am I correct in assuming that is where these stairs lead?"

"They do go to the basement," allowed Maggehrty, dubiously. "But there is nothing down there but some half-flooded storerooms. Not used in decades."

"Then there will be no harm in our looking in on them," said Felpz, cheerily, and set off down the stairs.

Following my friend, I found the stairs descended sharply before turning left and continuing down, into the foundation of the building. No electric lights had yet been run down here, but Felpz conjured his favorite magelight: a warm, yellowish glow that spread from an orb that floated dutifully over his shoulder. It threw madly dancing shadows on the water-stained walls, so I had to feel my way cautiously, lest I mistake a step for a shadow and trip. Again my absurd cane proved useful, and I was revising my opinion of it by the time I came upon Felpz, stopped in the middle of the corridor leading off from the bottom of the stairs.

The passage was a short one, extending barely fifteen feet before opening up onto a long, low room stacked with broken pieces of furniture. The place smelled of mold, and there were puddles on the floor where the stone had crumbled away into the earth.

Felpz barely looked into the larger room; he had stopped at the single door that opened off the corridor, and was in the act of leaning forward to knock on it when we arrived.

"It would appear this is the door in question," he said, a slight upward inflection at the end of the last word the only suggestion that his own statement might have been one.

"How many basements does Dactidillian House have?" Miss Bragnana asked our guide.

"Just the one," said Maggehrty, looking around anxiously.

"This is the door," said Bouragner Felpz, taking a step back and looking down at his feet. Following his gaze I saw how, with the constant damp, a thin layer of lichen had grown over the stone floor. But under his feet this layer was worn away, leading clearly to the door in front of him. Evidence of frequent and recent traffic.

Felpz drew in a breath, and the magelight dimmed a little as he seemed to gather power within himself. Then it flared back to full strength, and he reached out and pushed the door open.

It revealed as dingy and mundane a setting as one might expect: broken chairs and tables and half a piece of mildewed scenery from some long-ago play or pageant. The floor was caked in dirt and similarly puddled, forming a soft, loamy layer above the stone floor. Which layer, it was clear to see, had not been disturbed in many years; I could see the tracks of worms and beetles clear upon it, and not a single footprint marred its surface.

"As I said," came Maggehrty's voice from behind us, sounding both disappointed and yet vindicated. "Nothing to see here."

Felpz did not reply at once, but remained, leaning into the room without actually setting foot inside, his body tense and his neck arched, for some moments. Then a small shiver passed through his frame and he withdrew his head and shoulders to give us a mischievous look.

"I would not go so far as to say '*nothing*,'" said he. "Come, I have a wish to speak with all the students who claim to have seen Professor Odd."

It was with no small feeling of relief that I climbed back up to the inhabited world above ground, finding the warm spring sun near its zenith and the noise from the camera's green redoubled as the morning classes had just let out.

Felpz settled himself on the railing of Dactidillian's stoa, and from there conducted an informal set of interviews with every student who Maggehrty could round up—and several more with those who chanced to pass by.

In this way we discovered that Professor Odd was in fact very well known around Dunchurch—especially Dactidillian House and the Widder Clock. Almost every student, when he or she learned of Felpz's purpose there, had some anecdote or tale concerning the mysterious person.

Professor Odd was a ghost, according to some; the spiritual echo of a long-dead professor, who could be found wandering the halls of Dactidillian House after dark.

Professor Odd was a guest lecturer from abroad (which country they hailed from differed between students, but the majority thought Elgany), and could be found most afternoons reading in Widder Clock's middle gallery. Which, to be fair, tallied with Miss Donnet's letters.

Professor Odd was the best person to ask if you had a problem in mathematics or physics, on which they were known to give impromptu lessons on the Dactidillian stoa, using a spare bit of chalkboard propped up at one end. They always managed to vanish when another member of the faculty approached, and so the students had taken it upon themselves to keep their presence a secret.

And while everyone gave more or less the same description: that of a tallish, thinnish person in a large overcoat wearing a scarf and dark glasses with light, feathery hair, no one was certain of their gender—though many defaulted to masculine pronouns, much to Felpz's annoyance.

Had she been seen recently? he asked them.

No, not for over a week. Either the ghost had been released, the visiting lecturer had returned to their home country, or their secret lessons had been found out and they had been forbidden to mingle with other tutors' students.

It was well into the afternoon by the time the stream of interviewees began to dwindle, and I was becoming distracted by hunger. Felpz treated us to an early dinner at our inn to make up for this oversight, and we spent the remainder of the day talking over what we had discovered. At least, I talked with Miss Bragnana; Felpz put his feet up onto the table as soon as the dishes were cleared away and stared off into gathering evening. Eventually he excused himself and went out, and we were left to our own devices.

After we had exhausted our combined store of theories the conversation lagged; the only discussion that bears repeating was an exchange we had regarding Felpz himself.

"What was that curious appellation by which you first called him?" I asked our client. "*Mago Aubergino*, I believe it was."

"Oh," said Miss Bragnana, coloring slightly. "It is the Milanian form of what you sometimes call him. The *Purple Magician* you say in Kyrish, I think. *Mago* is magician, and *Aubergino* is the color of the fruit of the *aubergine*. In this country they are white, and so you call them *egg-plants*. But in Milania we have a variety which produces a fruit of a deep, blackish purple. *Aubergine*."

Which explained one little mystery, but for the larger matter which had first drawn us to Fairbridge we were left to wonder. Eventually we gave up waiting for Felpz's return and retired to our rooms.

I had not been a minute alone in mine when there was a rustle outside the window above my bed, and the next moment the man himself was climbing in, sitting himself on the sill with his legs dangling out to kick the dirt off his boots, before swinging his feet inside.

"Ah, Corianne, you are not yet abed—good!" he said, before he was fully in the room. "I hope you had a restful evening? Yes? Good. Do you fancy an exhilarating night? Only I have a line of inquiry which, if it runs true, should set us on the right path for reaching the heart of this mystery, and I would very much appreciate your company."

So long had it been since I had been invited on one of Felpz's nocturnal adventures, and so jovial was his mood, that I spared not an instant to consider my flagging, aged body, nor the poor girl we were abandoning in the next room, and agreed at once.

"Splendid," said Felpz. "You may wish to bring an extra coat, oh, and your cane."

"But of course," said I, humoring him. "Though I still fail to see its importance."

"I am not entirely sure of that myself," Felpz admitted, pushing the window the rest of the way open. "Only that it may yet prove invaluable. Come now, Corianne, and put your arms around my neck. It is only a drop of thirty feet or so, and I promise to make it a smooth and pleasant one."

Tucking my cane through my coat's sash I put my hands awkwardly on Felpz's hard, angular shoulders. The man had gone to sit upon the sill as before, and now I felt us begin to tip forward into the night.

As a child I might have screamed in surprise. As a grown woman I might have chastised him in protest, to mask my own fear. But as a great-grandmother with almost eight decades of life experience I could only let out a mad, cackling laugh as together we dropped from the window and glided out into the fresh, spring night.

Chapter 4: A Strange Abduction

AFTER THE FIRST WILD RUSH OF NIGHT AIR—filled with the scent of fresh oak and distant lilac—I saw we were gliding over the walls of Dunchurch, past the prickly column of the Astronomia Tower, with its observatory dome like a ghostly earthbound sibling of the gibbous moon rising in the east. Felpz's coat billowed below me, a wind-filled sail or a flapping wing—I was not sure. And though I could feel his human shoulders through the cloth under my hands, he seemed at the same time to take the form of a great, dark bird, whose wings stretched out into the night.

Cresting a second line of houses we descended gently past the Widder Camera and landed with a whisper upon the wet green. Some lights still glimmered in the lecture halls and the dormitories—including a few on the upper floors of Dactidillian House—but the courtyard and the stoa were dark and deserted, and we made our way unimpeded into the house and along the corridor, until once more we stood at the head of the stairs to the basement.

"My friend, what is your intent?" I asked, speaking in a whisper out of habit; I doubted there were any nearby who could have heard us.

"My intent is simple," Felpz replied in a similarly low voice as he summoned a dim, reddish light and began descending. "To ascertain the whereabouts of Lilibell Donnet and see her safely returned. Since her actions have lately become interwoven with Professor Odd's, it necessitates I find her as well. Which she is a singularly difficult person to find, though in this case I am optimistic as to our chances. We are dealing with strange magic here, Corianne. Magic so strange and alien it almost isn't magic anymore. Yet what we saw today suggests that we have come at the right time, and with a few contrivances on my part, we should be able to achieve both our goals tonight."

"Is there going to be much waiting involved?" I asked, remembering our vigils of old; nights spent sitting up in cold stairwells, or hunched and silent in dark rooms. I looked around at the cold, wet walls of Dactidillian's basement, and wondered if the joyous night ride had been worth this end.

"Only a nominal amount," Felpz replied pleasantly. "I must perforce take my time, as this is a new piece of magic, and I am not certain where it will lead. But be assured, dear Corianne, I have as little wish to remain in this place as you do."

We had come to the single door which had so interested Felpz earlier that day, and now he motioned me to take up position on the far side of the corridor, so that he could stand directly in front of it. Again the light around us dimmed, but this time remained so—merely a faint, red glow that saturated the air around us and cast my friend as a black shadow.

I saw him raise his arms in silhouette, tracing the edges of the door, before opening it, briefly. I caught a glimpse of the same ruined interior as we had seen before, then the door shut again and my friend stepped back a pace.

Crossing his arms he stood, sunk in thought, for maybe a minute. Then he turned halfway towards me, his face a pale, reddish profile.

"It needs an anchor," he murmured, seemingly to himself. "And an anchor wants a chain. This will be like tossing the lead line over a tree's branch when setting up a child's swing."

"Will it now?" I asked, amused by his analogy.

Felpz nodded seriously. "I need a guiding weight. Your cane would do, if I might borrow it."

With much amusement I removed it from my sash and handed it to Felpz, who took it by the banana end and stood sideways in the hall to heft its weight. He made a noise of satisfaction and then smoothly drew the blade from the shaft, so he held two long, thin objects.

Pointing the ends of both at the door he pressed the blunt tip of the sheath against its center, while with the blade he traced an outline of the door's edge, where the rotting wood met the wet stone.

One whole circuit did he make and there was no sign or sound. He did it again, this time clockwise from the top, and now a thin trail of golden sparks followed the tip of the sword. Upon completion there was a short flare of golden light from between the cracks of the door and walls, and a smell of scorched earth filled the little corridor—though I felt no heat.

The shape of the light lingered on in my vision after it had vanished, and in the red dimness I had to blink and rub my eyes before I could make sense of what I was seeing.

Felpz still stood before the door. He had re-sheathed the sword cane but kept it close at his side, his free hand raised as if to touch the door, yet here he paused.

"The key," he said, his voce cutting like a knife through the silence, "is not to think of space as a cohesive whole. Nor as having a consistent size in regards to other pieces of space. It is not unlike the witch's house which is larger on the inside, or thin groups of trees which become an impenetrable wood upon being entered. Likewise one might draw a comparison to the fairy doors that sometimes open, leading to faraway places instead of, say, your pantry. This is no pantry, and I seriously doubt Professor Odd is any kind of fairy, but trust me when I say: what lies beyond this door is far beyond anything in our world."

With these portentous words Felpz lowered his hand and turned the knob of the door, pushing it wide open.

By this point I was expecting something downright marvelous, but what it revealed still took me by surprise.

Gone was the drab, ruined room. Instead, light streamed out into the passage from beyond. It was itself low, a mix of many colors which swam before my eyes, but in comparison to Felpz's magelight it was positively brilliant. It illuminated a flight of narrow steps covered in worn, grey carpet, and walls of flaking—but perfectly dry—plaster. The top of the steps were just visible under the lintel of the door, and through the crack I glimpsed a cavernous ceiling, black as night with colored lights blinking slowly in its depths.

"Now this," said Felpz, excitement thrilling through his low voice. "This is something truly *odd*."

"Incredible," I whispered.

Felpz let out a soft snort of laughter. Then he leaned inside and rapped, firmly, on the peeling plaster wall.

"Hello?" he called up the stairs.

There was a faint chiming from above, as of distant bells, but no voice answered.

Felpz shrugged, and stepped inside and up the stairs. I hesitated but a moment before following him.

The inside smelled a trifle stale, but not unpleasantly so. Closer to an old spice cupboard than an old dungeon. The steps were no more than half a dozen in number, and where they ended the carpet gave way to a scuffed metal floor.

The room we were now in had elements both familiar and alien to me: the huge, wooden table that filled most of it would not have been out of place in my own home, but the artifacts heaped upon it were unrecognizable—though I glimpsed something that seemed to be a sort of coffeepot.

To my right and left were minimalistic chairs of the sort with an articulated stem, so the person sitting in them could swivel around. Their squat, metal feet were bolted to the floor, and there were canvas straps that could be buckled around the occupant. Each one faced a sort of desk, but really it was just a flat space filled with colored buttons. Most of them were round, with a few rectangular ones down near the bottom. They were a variety of bright colors: blues and oranges, golds, greens and reds being the most favored, and all of them glowed faintly. From beneath the desks rose clear tubes and pipes, filled with a brilliant liquid which gave off more soft, colored light. These twined in and out of sight overhead, feeding into more slabs of buttons, and supporting a framework which held countless boxes with glass fronts. Currently these were all glowing a pure, sky blue, but occasionally one or two would darken, and flecks of color would whip across their faces.

The glowing pipes and buttons stretched away into the darkness above our heads, which lingered some twenty feet above—high enough that I could see there was another level to the place: a railed walkway stretched around the circumference of the room, which I could see now was shaped like a teardrop. We stood at the narrow, pointed end, while at the opposite, across the table, I spied a ladder by which one could reach the second level. Along that wall were little recesses—not quite rooms of their own, but clearly separate from the main area. One held a small washing station, a set of taps, and beyond that a cooktop and an impressive door which looked to be part of an oven of some kind. Another appeared to be a pantry. Another seemed to lead to a cool, blue cavern. The fourth was dark, so I did not pay it much heed. I was more interested in the rest of the room, which was lined with chipped, peeling cream wallpaper, and had—just as Lilibell Donnet had described—an incomprehensible set of windows. These were small, square things, each one covered with drawn curtains.

The entire place gave me a sense of imbalance—as though I was looking at something with my head upside-down—and yet it neither felt ominous nor sinister. Perhaps a little sad; I got the feeling it had once been a much-loved room which had been forgotten; but not bitter or angry for that.

It was also obviously the room which Lilibell Donnet had described as belonging to Professor Odd, and even as I gazed around in wonder I kept a sharp lookout for any sign of that mysterious character.

There was no one, however, and as I grew bolder I came to stand beside Felpz, who was himself staring rapturously at the colored display of buttons and lights.

"What a peculiar place this is," I said. "Was it here all along and we simply couldn't reach it?"

Felpz shook his head. "This place is outside of space as we know it. One could say that it is everywhere, and that it is nowhere. How else can you describe something that exists beyond the borders of the conceivable universe?"

"Beyond the borders of the universe?" I echoed. "Whatever do you mean, Felpz?"

For answer Felpz stepped around to the nearest window, and with a flick of his wrist flung the blinds aside.

At first I saw nothing. It looked like night outside, with the dim, colored lights of the place reflected in the glass of the window. Then I realized some of those lights could not be reflections, for they lay in Felpz's shadow. I thought them stars, and then realized what that meant: we had left behind the dungeon of Dactidillian House completely. Then, upon drawing closer, I saw that they were not the fine points of light I had first taken them to be. They were colorful swirls and spirals, twists and blobs floating in a void that was velvety black and blue. Peering closer, I saw that one of the larger patches of light held a circular object of blue and green, streaked with white. Not a star at all, but a *planet*. Our planet, I realized, as what else could have oceans so blue? I even thought I recognized a piece of Adamanta's eastern coast, much browner and lumpier than it appeared on maps, before it was obscured by clouds.

"Felpz," I breathed, struck dumb in my awe. "This is the most astounding thing! That is Reanen out there, or I am very much mistaken. And yet—"

I broke off to look back the way we had come, to point down the stairs to the door opening onto the dank corridor of Dactidillian's basement, only to find that it had been replaced by a blank, black wall.

I gave an inarticulate cry of consternation, but Felpz seemed not in the least ruffled.

"I did not expect the anchor to hold," he said, merely shrugging. "What with the inhabitant clearly elsewhere. If this place is at all considerate, it will not stray far from the world it was last set to visit. We need only wait until the door opens again, and then we may find the one whom we seek."

Pushed up against the wall, beneath the windows, were several armchairs, and Felpz now went over and pulled one out and sat in it, crossing his legs and resting his arm leisurely upon the table. The door remained a blank, black wall, but my friend seemed perfectly at ease, so I took comfort in that.

I was still ravenously curious about the place, and after a few minutes of waiting, with no sound but the faint chime of distant bells, I could no longer stop myself from asking questions.

"Stop withholding, old friend," I chided him. "Your manner tells me you know full well what this place is, and yet here I am with no more knowledge than what I might glean for myself— and that is confounding at best."

Felpz smiled apologetically. "I am by no means an expert. Like you, all I know is what I have managed to learn from my own observations. But I do have more experience with the ways of the world, and that allows me to make a better guess."

"I should be delighted it hear it," I pressed on.

Felpz leaned back in his chair and sighed, gazing up at the lighted racks of buttons and screens surrounding the door.

"What did I say before? That this is a place beyond space? That is a good beginning. Perhaps you have heard of somewhere called the *place between*. It refers to the murky area between the dimensions of our world, which I once likened to a tall, many-storied house."

"The floorboards and the stairwells," I said, nodding. It was, by Felpz's own admission, a simplified metaphor, but I found it to be a serviceable one.

"Yes," he agreed. "But those are, by definition, still within the confines of the greater house. What has been called the Wider Realm, by some. Now what you must introduce into your mental picture is the idea of *Realms,* plural. Not of a single house, but many houses. Perhaps an infinite number. Each one as intricate and complicated as our own."

Given what I knew of the nature of our own world, this was not a difficult concept for me to grasp, and I nodded my understanding.

"Where we are," Felpz continued, "if we can be said to actually *be* anywhere at all, is in this greater place between: floating in the space between these house-worlds. Only because these are actually *worlds* and not *houses* they are the only place where space has any meaning. So in a way we are out of space entirely. That is what you saw when you gazed out that window."

"But I saw worlds," I protested.

"*Windows* into other worlds," Felpz corrected me, nodding. "Yes, it is curious, and I think it may have something to do with this." He gestured at our surroundings.

"Then what is *this?*" I insisted, feeling ready to pull at my own hair, if not his.

Felpz shrugged. "A bubble," he said. "A twist in the nature of the void where space becomes real. An *oddity,* if I may use the term un-ironically."

"And this Professor Odd?" I asked, my breath catching as I realized what this entailed.

"A person not from our world, nor any world I have ever known," Felpz said, a small, dry grin creeping up one side of his face. "To think Miss Donnet was so entranced by the notion of seeing alien life, yet she had the best example of such right before her and did not notice."

"Poor Miss Donnet," I sighed. "What do you imagine might have happened to her?"

I was interrupted by the chimes, which had grown louder during the course of our conversation, crescendoing into a tumbling waterfall of sound which culminated in a loud *bonging* that reverberated up through the floor and shivered in my bones.

It faded away, and at first I thought nothing had changed, but then Felpz pointed to the boxes above the pipes and buttons, and I saw—as Donnet had described—that each one now showed a small piece of a larger image, and this complete picture was as incredible as anything else I had seen that night.

It put me in mind of the Frazian landscape I had seen when on holiday in Milany almost twenty years ago: rolling, rounded hills on top of which perched little villages or sprawling villas. Tall, narrow trees the shape of candle flames stood in avenues making boundaries across the hills. A dirt road cut through the grass and wheat, its surface pale and a little dusty, leading out of sight behind a hill. In the distance were mountains, rising up behind a cluster of houses crouched in the lowlands around a wide river.

It was also completely alien in that the colors were all wrong. The grass and wheat took me a little time to recognize on account of the fact that they were a deep, reddish-blue black. The hills were a dark, rustling sea, and the road, showing the pale face of the earth, stood out starkly against it. The houses had bright, sky-blue roofs, only that was probably not the word their inhabitants used to describe the color, for the sky itself was a warm orange, crossed by creamy golden clouds.

We had not stared at this astonishing sight for more than a minute, when there was a rasping from below and the door—now a rickety wooden thing—was dragged open. A streak of orange daylight flooded into the place, cut by a shadow which slowly advanced up the stairs, followed by its owner: a tall, slender person with shaggy, silver hair wearing a battered, brown overcoat and a ragged scarf wrapped snugly around her neck. She looked up at us in surprise when she reached the top of the stairs, and like the landscape, her face was familiar and alien all at once.

It could have been considered a beautiful face: fine-boned with a narrow chin and a sensitive, pointed nose. But the lips were very thin, and the eyes, though large, were also dark and not quite the right shape. It gave me a bit of a start when I realized I had seen those eyes many times before, peering up at me from the faces of all the cats I'd ever met. These were golden-brown ringed in black, and at the moment open so wide they reflected all the lights surrounding their owner, so it looked like they held a sky of colored stars.

Felpz got to his feet in greeting and made a short bow.

"Ah, Professor Odd," he said. "We have been expecting you."

The person—who must have been Professor Odd—gaped at him. She shot me a frightened glance, and then turned tail and ran: down the stairs and out the door, which she slammed shut behind her.

Felpz was after her like a shot, snatching up my cane and leaping down the stairs. I scrambled after him, certain I would be left behind, only to find him caught in the doorway, his hands braced as if to prevent some unseen force from pulling him out.

Around his limbs I could now see out the open door, and this showed me a narrow footpath leading between rows of black wheat, ultimately to join the dirt road I had seen on the image displayed inside. Professor Odd was a smudge of movement, brown and silver, down where it dipped out of sight around the bottom of the hill.

I could tell it took Felpz a great deal of effort not to give in to the lure of the chase, but he held himself steady in the door and cautiously put first the end of my cane, and then—when nothing ill befell it—his own hand out into the dim, orange world. When he pulled it back in he examined his fingers closely, even putting one into his mouth, before he gave a little shrug and stuck his head out of the door. He turned this way and that, sniffed, and then stepped bodily outside.

I hung in the doorway, still uncertain.

"Felpz?" I asked.

"This is no world that I have ever visited before," he said, his voice soft in wonder. He turned to me, and his eyes were dark and gleaming—not unlike Professor Odd's. He smiled. "Yet it does not seem to be an unfriendly one. Do step out, Corianne, the scenery is lovely, only stay close to me—I have only the magic I bring with me, so my powers are weaker here."

He did not have to repeat his last instruction. I had no wish to become separated from him in a world even he did not know. Yet, as he said, it did not seem an unfriendly one. The air was warm and soft and smelled of ripening wheat and moist earth— within minutes I was obliged to strip off my coat—and the sky above us, despite its fiery color, seemed not as bright as the sky of home. I thought perhaps this was twilight, and scanned the horizon for the sun. I found it almost above our heads, and while it was too bright to look upon directly, it was not the blinding disk of white light I had been expecting. There was a golden-orange halo about it, tinged with red. It reminded me of our star at sunset, seen behind a thin layer of cloud so that it appeared like an orange globe.

"Take careful observations, dear Corianne," said Felpz, laying a hand gently upon my elbow to guide me down the path. "We are not on any planet, and that is no star which anyone from our world has ever seen before. Any but one, I should amend: for I believe this is where we may find Lilibell Donnet."

I could sense the excitement in him, and an answering feeling ignited in my heart as together we walked down the path towards the road. Upon joining it, we turned right down the hill to follow in the Professor's dusty footprints. These were easy enough to trace: they were the only things recognizable as footprints, and the dirt was soft enough to hold impressions well. All was easy until we came to a place where some livestock had been driven onto the road, obliterating all trace of human passage.

We continued on the road, however, seeing no sign that our quarry had diverged into the thick crops to either side, until we came to a bridge over a calm, black river, and there discovered the source of the interfering tracks.

I do not know why I expected them to be sheep. The behavior of their tracks and the droppings they left behind suggested they were that sort of animal, but when all had been so different from our own world up to this point, I should not have been so surprised to find them, yet again, like nothing I had seen before.

They put me in mind of giant fowl at first, but I realized this was simply because they bore feathers, like a chicken. In size and shape they were closer to the hardy, Aldonican mountain sheep, being no more than waist high with four sturdy legs underneath a round, fluffy body. Their heads were naked and scaled, bright orange and blue, and almost half the face taken up by a huge beak like a pair of spades. Their feathers were a mottled assortment of iridescent blues and purples, and their naked legs, protruding from beneath the bush of feathers, matched their heads. They had feet with three stubby toes and one dangerous, hooked claw, which one was using to scratch under its chin as we approached.

If the herd was something to look at, their shepherd was even more incredible. As tall as Felpz they were, with long, double-jointed legs and feet like an ostrich. They had a long, graceful tail ending in a tuft of bright green feathers, and a long, graceful neck ending in a head covered in more green feathers, which formed a sort of frill around a flat, pale face with dark green scales around the eyes. These eyes were very big and dark, and a little slanted, and light from the orange sky glimmered in them as their owner blinked at us. They wore a simple, woven tunic and robust leather leggings, but hung around their neck was an intricate mantle of beads, strung together by a thin wire that glinted copper in the light. They carried a sturdy, worn staff, which they clutched in a hand that was not unlike our own, save that it had an extra thumb.

We had come upon them so suddenly that we had no opportunity to hide or otherwise mask our appearance. The shepherd, however, continued to let their flock drink from the river (which was the reason we had caught them at all), and only watched us with surprised curiosity as we approached.

"Good day, my friend," Felpz said in greeting. "I beg your pardon, but have you seen another of our kind? Almost my height, with silver hair and wearing a long coat. She would have been bound along this road not half an hour ago."

The feathered person started to hear this speech. Their dark eyes rolled sideways and down, almost as though they were ashamed. Then they answered, but in a language that was unmistakably *Milanian*.

Felpz actually gave out a short laugh.

"Now I regret my decision to leave Miss Bragnana safe in bed," he murmured to me, but managed to rephrase his question in what was, despite what he'd told the young woman earlier, a very capable version of her native tongue.

The shepherd was greatly relieved, and replied readily to Felpz's revised inquiry. By the nods and smiles and arm gestures I observed, I guessed we were being given directions.

I was correct. After the shepherd finished giving Felpz what appeared to be instructions for completing a maze, from all the angular hand gestures their conversation contained, they touched their feathery brow and shooed their flock aside so that we might pass.

"*Grazie, Signora,*" Felpz called back, giving the shepherd a wave after we had crossed the bridge and were standing upon the crest of the next hill.

The feathered person raised a hand in acknowledgement, and then a slope of black grass cut them off from sight.

"What an amiable person," said Felpz, swinging my cane over his shoulder and putting the other hand in his pocket. "She tells me that our Professor Odd can often be found at a particular bar in a village called *Montefaziano* which is not a long walk from here, but only if we take the *pecore* path by *Bonabagni*, which is the next village on this road. Ah, I think this must be it."

We had come to the top of a hill, and there found one of
the tiny villages with narrow, cobbled streets and blue-roofed
houses. A pair of feathered people sitting outside a café, who
seemed thicker and greyer and altogether *older* than the shepherd, deigned to give us lazy glances before turning back to the
board game set out on the table between them. They were the
only individuals we saw, despite the closely packed houses.

The road ran straight through the little town, but Felpz made
for a narrow animal track marked with a hand-painted wooden
sign that read: *Montefaziano, .25 ora, Abeterreni, 1 ora, Farraglio,
1.5 ora* with a little pictogram of a person with double-jointed
legs and a long tail walking beneath the letters.

Thus encouraged we took the path, and by it found ourselves
led around the village and on up the side of the neighboring hill,
which was considerably higher. Near its peak we found a helpful
sign that said *Montefaziano* with an arrow beneath pointing to a
branch in the path. This we followed up a last steep climb where
solid grey rocks had been wedged into the dirt to form a practical
stair, before we passed between high, stone walls and eventually
emerged into what I assumed was Montefaziano's main square.

It put me in mind of the little Elgan villages one sometimes
finds on postcards: quaintly cramped, with tall, leaning houses
decorated with streaming banners. There was a fountain near
the center, which was really more of a decorative watering hole,
if the copious droppings and livestock tracks which surrounded
it were any indication. Most of the buildings facing the square
appeared to be residences, with the exception of one towering
edifice whose front garden protruded into the square in order
to provide space for its patrons. Above the lintel of its generous
door was a solid block of stone onto which the word BAR had
been neatly chiseled, and through the wide windows I glimpsed
activity and warm, yellow lights. As before, a pair of older natives were seated in the front garden, though these were playing
cards. They both gave us mildly curious glances, and then returned to their game.

A great shyness overcame me then. I was intensely aware
that we were strangers in a very strange land, and that we were
here on pure speculation. Felpz appeared unfazed, however, and
walked up to the door of the bar as confidently as he would to

his favorite Redling coffeehouse. I followed close on his heels, and peering over his elbow to the interior of the place discovered that the shepherd had directed us well. Professor Odd was sitting at a small table near the back, almost entirely obscured by a huge map she had unfolded in front of her.

The place was otherwise crowded with members of the local populace. I was aware of a profusion of feathery heads in colors ranging from deep blue to bright red, of dark eyes glimmering and staring, and the awkward hush that comes from a dozen conversations abruptly cut off at once.

It was only for a moment, and then the patrons went back to their own business, just as the card players outside had done. But in that moment Professor Odd looked up, and her expression upon seeing us was of such dismay and outright fear that I immediately resigned myself to another mad chase. We must have blocked the only exit, however, for the peculiar woman remained frozen, staring at us like a wild animal, cornered.

Felpz raised his empty hand, palm up and open, and advanced slowly into the room.

"Please," he said. "I beg. Do not take flight again. This country is a delight, no doubt, but I do not think Corianne would thank you if she were made to trek to the next village. You have no reason to fear us—indeed, my only intention is to help you. That, and to locate a missing woman, whose disappearance has caused her friends and family much grief."

Professor Odd remained, pressed against the back of her seat, now glaring at Felpz through narrowed eyes. As his words sank in, however, her shoulders relaxed, and she leaned forward to blink at him, fiercely.

"Oh," she said, her voice light and a little hoarse. "So you're *not* the Oddity's owners, then?"

Felpz was so surprised he nearly tripped. "The Oddity's owners—" he began, then stopped himself. He looked again at the Professor, and an amazed expression dawned on his face. "Oh my," he whispered. "It *is* early days, isn't it? Well, things could be worse, I suppose. No, no I do not own that magnificent oddity—truth to tell I do not think it is a thing than can be owned. I am . . . how to say this? Call me an unexpected friend. Yes. And if you will but answer some of my questions, we might do as friends do for each other, and together we can put matters to rights."

Chapter 5: The Secret of Professor Odd

T HOUGH WE DID NOT HAVE ANYTHING resembling the local currency, the proprietor of the bar was more than happy to barter Felpz's silver crest, after he had transfigured it into a tiny model of the beaked sheep, for three small, strong coffees and a plate of savory rolls. These we spread over the neighboring table and there sat, drinking in small sips while Professor Odd continued to stare at us, arms crossed, out of her dark, feline eyes.

"I do not know you," she said after some time, as if just arriving at this conclusion.

Felpz paused with his coffee halfway to his mouth, the steam rising into the dark air of the bar like a pale wisp of smoke. Then he set it back down again, his hands going to smooth the tablecloth on either side.

"No," he admitted, curling his fingers in as he spoke. He sounded almost disappointed. "No, no you do not. Yet I know you, a least a little, and I hope you believe me when I say I am here to help."

Professor Odd unfolded her arms to lean them on the table as she bent forward to stare intently into Felpz's face. It was difficult to tell in the dim light, but I thought her skin had the faintest tinge of green around the corners of her eyes.

"Say that last part again," she whispered.

Felpz raised his eyebrows, but gamely he repeated: "I am here to help. We both are."

Professor Odd continued to stare at him, her eyes searching his face. Then she fell back in her seat and crossed her arms again, one hand coming up to cup her chin.

"You're telling the truth, I think," she said, her eyes narrowing slightly. She scowled and looked away. "I used to be able to tell, just by looking, whether someone was lying or not. Then they . . . well, I'm still not sure. Something happened. I got hurt. I forgot things. Things like faces. I'm better now, but there are still gaps." She moved one hand to tap the side of her head. "Is that why you know me and I don't know you?"

Felpz, whose expression had melted into something between concern and regret, shook his head. "I very much doubt it," he said. "One could say my narrative is more advanced than yours, relatively speaking. It gives me a certain vantage point over current events."

Professor Odd blinked at him, her face brightening. "Do you mean to say you're a time traveler? I've not met one of those, yet."

Felpz laughed at that but shook his head. "Not in the manner in which you imagine," he said. "Though you'll find time to be rather inconsistent when you begin shuffling between worlds. Not all rivers run the same, if you follow my metaphor, and moving about always shakes things up a little."

Professor Odd nodded, chewing on a finger. "An *unexpected friend*," she said. "That's what you called yourself."

"Yes," said Felpz.

Professor Odd grimaced. "I'm not good with friends," she said, sourly. "Haven't had any since before . . . before I got hurt. Nowadays I tend to lose them."

Felpz drew in a deep breath. "Which brings us to the matter directly at hand." He sighed. "Professor Odd, I don't suppose you have any idea what has become of Miss Lilibell Donnet?"

The Professor pursed her thin lips and looked unhappily down at her cup, which was cooling despite the warm temperature of the air. (Felpz and I had both long since divested ourselves of our outer garments.) With an almost petulant attitude she picked at the ceramic, as if trying to clean some invisible dirt from its surface.

"I don't know," she admitted after a time. "I mean, I've got loads of *ideas*, but none of them seem to be the right *one*. I've *been looking*, you understand. All over Niatano." She slapped the folded paper that she had been studying when we first arrived. "And I haven't found a single trace of her—which is impossible, considering I only left her alone for half an hour, and as far as I know she has no means of leaving this world. Then again, I didn't think anyone could *summon* the Oddity, like you must have done. Everything about your world puts me out of sorts.

Even when I come *here,* to a world I understand better, it still manages to confuse me."

Felpz blinked at her in surprise. He sipped his coffee and then settled into his chair a little more. The bar had emptied as we sat talking, and now the only other patrons were a pair of young-looking people with bright orange feathers wearing loose, robe-like gowns. Their table was covered in scrolls, and they were both busily writing away on one each. They hardly gave us any notice.

"I think it is past time we heard your side of the story, Professor," Felpz said. "If you would be so kind as to share the events of the last few months, from your perspective, we might come closer to an understanding of what has happened—and what has become of Miss Donnet."

Professor Odd looked uncertain, but as Felpz only continued to sit there, placidly sipping coffee in his shirtsleeves and looking as relaxed as I had ever seen him, she gradually appeared to unfold a little, loosening her shoulders and extending her neck.

"If you really mean to help?" she said, glancing between the two of us. When we made encouraging noises she sighed, then reached up and scratched her scalp. It caused her entire head of hair to move slightly, and with a jolt I realized it was a wig.

"I suppose I start," she began. "Yes, I should start by saying I'm not a professor. Not at Dunchurch or anywhere else. That was an assumption people made, and it was easier to go along with that than explain what I really am."

"And, what *are* you?" Felpz asked, sounding genuinely curious, but also somewhat hesitant. As though he expected the subject to be a delicate one.

He was correct. Professor Odd recoiled, drawing herself in so that she took up less space.

"I am not sure yet," she said, carefully. "Some of it I don't remember, and the rest . . . I don't like to talk about. I'm not human, in case you've been wondering, or any other animal you've met. Probably. Beyond that I'm not entirely sure *who* I am yet, because of my . . . because of the nature of my . . . because I was . . . well. I didn't grow up the way it appears most people do. That's all I'm really comfortable saying right now."

Felpz smiled, sad and fond, and nodded once. "Yes, and I suppose that is all I have a right to know, at this point. Very well, tell me as much as you can, with particular attention to your interactions with Miss Donnet."

Professor Odd seemed a little startled that Felpz would let the subject drop so easily, but she took the diversion gladly and began to talk, becoming more and more animated as she continued.

"I'm still learning," she explained. "Before, I was . . . well, I didn't get to move around much. Then I found the Oddity— or the Oddity found me, I'm not sure which way that goes— and since then I've been traveling *constantly.* The Oddity can go to many different worlds, you see. I didn't feel safe in my own any more, so the Oddity took me away. Turns out there are more worlds that I ever could have imagined, and they are all so *different* from each other it was a little overwhelming. I thought I was getting the hang of it, but then we sort of blundered into *your* world and everything went queer."

Felpz put his head on one side, thoughtfully. "How so?" he asked. "Is our world very different from yours? As different as this?" He indicated the bar and its colorful inhabitants.

"Goodness no," said Professor Odd. "Or perhaps yes. It's different in different *ways,* you understand. In my world, humans live on a planet called Earth, which is roughly equivalent to your home, Reanen—unlike Niatano, which is not even a proper planet—it's a moon orbiting a gas giant orbiting a red dwarf star—but the *universes* Niatano and Earth belong to are more closely related than either of them are to *yours.* For example, they haven't got probability fractures running *throughout* time and space *and* they haven't got naturally occurring splices *or* conglomerated realities. Also their laws of physics are pretty consistent. Whereas in your world it goes all over the place. It's all so *weird,* only I don't mean that in a bad way—*I'm* weird— but it is frustrating because it's so unconventional I simply can't understand it—"

"Magic," Felpz interrupted, so softly and gently that Professor Odd went on for a few words before she realized he had spoken.

"—I *try* to study it rationally but it keeps *slipping around* like . . . like what?"

"Magic," Felpz repeated. "What you are describing is my world's magical properties."

"Yes," said Professor Odd, bitterly, pulling her shoulders back and giving Felpz a narrow-eyed look. "That was what Miss Lilibell called it, and what all your native books called it: magic. Magic, magic, *magic.* As if it were one, tangible thing, and not a thousand different rules and peculiarities and constructs and forces all interacting together and contradicting each other half the time!"

"That is the nature of magic," Felpz said, smiling ruefully. "My people have been trying to make sense of it for the better part of the last ten thousand years, and I confess, though I make the practice of magic a particular specialty, even I do not fully understand it. Do not be discouraged if you cannot comprehend it after only a few months of study."

"Why shouldn't I?" asked Professor Odd. "I understand most other things in less time than that. Chemistry, mathematics, biology, *physics,* why, even quantum mechanics! They all operate according to natural laws and principles or at least hypotheses *based* on natural laws and principles that, once you've learned them, make perfect sense. And they all support *each other.* Whereas with . . . with *magic,* it can change its form and function seemingly at random—though that may have to do with the positive or negative charge of a given atom; that was one of the things I was investigating when Miss Lilibell distracted me."

I was utterly astonished at this outpouring of facts and names—some of which I only vaguely recognized—and Felpz seemed equally impressed, though for different reasons, it turned out.

"What is this?" he said. "Do you mean to say you come from a world with *no* magic whatsoever?"

Professor Odd gave him a wide-eyed look. "None that we could ever find tangible proof of," she said. "Most worlds—including this one—are like that. All natural laws and forces—conventional—no magic."

Felpz frowned and turned his head to gaze off into space.

"No," he said after a moment's thought. "No, there is magic in this world. It is old, and it is distant, and mostly it is asleep; but it is here, nonetheless."

Professor Odd gazed at him, stricken.

"Oh, do not be alarmed," said Felpz. "I assure you it would not interfere with the *conventional* realm in any tangible way—in that respect it might as well not exist at all. But I tell you that it does, otherwise I should not be able to while away the afternoon at such leisure. Take me to a world without magic and I am a sad thing; like a fish out of water. Literally."

Professor Odd continued to stare at him, now with a hint of grudging respect. "Perhaps it is something you must be born to," she suggested. "You and I are simply incompatible with each other's native universes."

"That's a rather defeatist attitude," Felpz chided. "I would not think of it so. Consider it this way: you have grown accustomed to worlds behaving in a certain manner, and part of understanding how my world works is *unlearning* the idea that there is any such thing as *normal* when it comes to the multitude of realms."

Professor Odd bit at her lower lip uncertainly, showing a flash a white, square teeth. Then she shrugged, as if conceding the point.

"Tell me what happened with Lilibell Donnet," Felpz urged.

Professor Odd tilted her cup of coffee, causing the liquid to swirl about, then she raised it to her lips and drank down the contents in a single gulp. She twisted her mouth to one side, and then began to speak.

"It was an accident," she began. "The whole thing. I did not intend to . . . to be so distracted. As I told you I'm not good with friends. They always seemed to be something that happened to other people. People in stories. So when Miss Lilibell discovered me in the library I thought she'd come to shoo me off. But instead she called me *professor* and started explaining how she was studying magic *and* science in a way that was almost comprehensible to me. I offered her some of my own observations, to which she was receptive, and when she kept meeting with me, day after day, week after week, I began to realize it wasn't just her insights that I enjoyed—it was her *company*. When she was around, my pleasure in learning increased, and my fear of the unknown diminished.

"I kept allowing her to assume I was some sort of professor, since it seemed to stop her wondering who I was, even though it felt wrong to do it. I guess I worried she wouldn't want to hang around me if she knew—which turned out to be a perfectly legitimate fear.

"Anyway, I showed her some of my own notes. She used them to help refine this amazing construction—sort of like a bubble one can walk about in—that we could use to explore inhospitable worlds. I'd managed to get a peek at Callanaph, which is a satellite orbiting one of the bigger planets in your solar system, and thought I'd seen some very interesting things. With Lilibell's help—and her bubble—we actually managed visit it in person. It was absolutely exhilarating. Also terrifying. There's life on Callanaph, you see. Not like life here or on any Earth I've visited. Reminded me more of really ancient, simple organisms. Maybe you still have some of that sort living at the bottom of Reanen's oceans, but I'm not sure. Anyway, that's not what was terrifying. What scared me—and Lilibell, too—was the . . . the other thing. It wasn't . . . it wasn't like any life form I'd ever encountered. It was more like a strange twist in the surface of reality. A bit of time and space that didn't behave as it ought to. I'd encountered things like that before in your world, but the difference here was that this one seemed to be *alive* in a way that those hadn't been. It had *thoughts* and *ideas,* and *opinions.* One of which, Lilibell was certain, was that it did not want us there. She called it a demon, but I'm not sure what that even means."

Professor Odd paused, turning her empty cup around on its saucer. Eventually she tipped it completely upside-down and clasped her hands in front of her. She had narrow, fine-boned hands, with long, strong-looking fingers. It might have been a trick of the dim light, but the skin around her nails looked greenish, too.

"After our encounter we were both a little put off. I was suddenly doubting everything I knew about your world, and Lilibell was pretty shaken up. I wanted a holiday, and I thought she could use one too, so I invited her along. I just told her we were going some place without demons, because I figured, what with all the strange creatures in your world, the Neätans must seem pretty mundane."

"I am sorry," Felpz cut in. "The *Neätans?*"

Professor Odd jerked her head at the orange-feathered pair across the room. "*UmanitÁ,* they call themselves." She grinned. "Roughly translated, that means *humanity.* But this satellite's name is Neä—though everyone here calls it *Niatano*—so I call them the Neätans. Nice people. Don't get flustered about strangers, and make excellent pizza. Where was I?"

"You took Miss Donnet for a holiday," Felpz supplied, readily. "Here, I presume?"

"Not *here,* here," Professor Odd said. "Originally I took her to Abeterreni, which has this marvelous gelato—that's a sort of extra-creamy ice cream—shop, but we wound up walking all over the hills, and when Miss Lilibell discovered that Niatano is a moon-world she insisted I take her planet-side so she could see Mandro, and *then* she wanted to take all these *measurements* and . . . well, she was getting on so well, and as I'd already made a thorough study of Niatano's orbital mechanics—which *are* fascinating, I'll grant you—that I'm afraid I sort of abandoned her. Not badly, mind you. I just went to the nearest village to have a nice, relaxing meal, like I'd always wanted.

"She finished earlier than I'd anticipated, however. It really upset her, going back to where she thought the Oddity's door was and finding it had gone perfectly ordinary. By the time I got back to check on her she was a nervous mess—she thought she was going to be stranded on this alien world for the rest of her life, and even though nothing actually *bad* had happened, it was still quite frightening. I found her in a concerned huddle of Neätans, who had wrapped her up in a blanket and were trying to feed her warm *caprini* milk. She burst into tears when she saw me, and I couldn't get anything coherent out of her until we were back in the Oddity.

"I was ready to take her straight home at that point, but she insisted that we go back to Abeterreni, since she'd dragged me off to go exploring before we'd had a chance to try any gelato. We went, and she tried to put a brave face on it, but I could tell her mood had changed. She was more quiet, more thoughtful, and as we were walking back to where I'd parked the Oddity, she started asking me all the questions I was afraid of answering.

"I guess she'd figured out I wasn't really a professor at Dunchurch a while back, but hadn't said anything because our adventures had been too much fun. Now that she'd had a not-so-fun adventure she was looking at the whole thing more skeptically. Funny, really, considering the conscious space-time anomaly on Callanaph was much more frightening—at least to me. But I suppose for her it was a little easier, since we were in *her* native universe, after all. There's a certain comfort—a feeling of belonging—that you lose when you go to another universe. Of course, I didn't belong very well in *my* native universe so it wasn't much of a loss for me, but to her it must have felt pretty sharp. And then thinking she was *stuck* here . . . well. Anyway. It was enough to get her thinking, and asking questions. Questions like, who was I, *really*? *What* was I? How did the Oddity work?"

Professor Odd hunched her shoulders, unhappily. "As I've said, I don't know the answers to some of those questions, and I'm afraid they made me withdraw into myself. Lilibell thought I was intentionally keeping secrets from her, and went all quiet and sullen. I thought she'd given up, when she asked me . . . she asked me what . . . " Professor Odd stuttered to a halt, her mouth working around words that didn't wish to be spoken. Despite my concern over the fate of Lilibell Donnet, I could not help the surge of feeling that rose in me at the sight of the strange woman, who really looked quite young under all that silver hair, struggling to relate an unpleasant memory.

"She asked me to take off my wig," she said eventually, pulling her chin right down into the collar of her coat. "And when I said no, she reached up and snatched it off my head. Clean off, just like that. The movement surprised me, and so I'm afraid I looked a lot more alarming than I do, er, normally. Anyway, she got one good look at me, her eyes went about the size of this coffee cup, and then she laughed. She *laughed* and said something like 'I *knew* it!' and then took off running."

Professor Odd stared miserably down at her upturned cup, her fingers twisting together and tapping at each other, restlessly. Eventually she shrugged, as if letting the event go. "I was so taken aback—and a little hurt, yes I was hurt too, though I suppose I deserved it—that I just stood there dumbly and watched her tear off down the *pecore* path. Even when I pulled myself together and followed I didn't try to catch her. I assumed she would go back to the Oddity, since she knew perfectly well where it was, and I figured some time alone to calm down would be a good thing.

"When I got there, however, she wasn't *in* the Oddity. I went back out and looked around, thinking maybe she was waiting nearby. Nothing. So I went inside and searched the place top to bottom—which is a lot of place, if you know the Oddity. Anyway, Lilibell wasn't there. So I retraced my steps, all the way back through Montefaziano to Abeterreni, and even on to Farraglio. Then I came back again by the road—which is a much longer way and takes you through San Castemagnano—and *still* no sign of her. I asked all the *caprini* herders I could find whether they'd seen her, and one of them said he'd spotted her off in a field near Montefaziano, so I've been concentrating my search in this area. But I've been looking for *days*—Niatano days, mind you, which are like six or seven days on Reanen—and I've found *nothing*. No sign of her. It was like she just *vanished*, but I know that can't be possible."

Professor Odd reached out and shook the piece of paper she had been studying when we arrived, which had been neatly folded and placed in the center of the table. "I was just plotting out where I'd looked on a proper map, to make sure I hadn't missed anywhere, when you showed up. Since I thought you were the Oddity's owners and that now we might both be stuck here I wanted to find her more than ever." She sat back and folded her arms—returning to the attitude from which she'd begun her declamation—and regarded us with a challenge in her dark eyes.

I could do nothing but gaze back in amazement. The Professor—I still thought of her as *Professor* Odd, even though I now knew this was incorrect—was unlike any person I had ever encountered, and there were gaping holes in her story that filled me with curiosity. What sort of world had she come from? What was the nature of the misfortune that had befallen her, which had so interfered with her memory? What sort of childhood had she experienced? What of her parents? What sort of people had they been, to bear such extraordinary progeny? Above all, how did she come to her current occupation as a traveler of worlds?

All these questions jostled in my head, threatening to spill forth, but I held my tongue as I did not feel it was my place to interrogate her. I left it to Felpz, who seemed to have some intimate knowledge of which I was yet ignorant, to ask what questions he deemed important.

For the moment, however, my friend seemed satisfied with the Professor's story. He nodded to himself and unfolded the map, which I now saw was a detailed rendition of the surrounding countryside. Though all the names were in Milanian, I found Montefaziano easily by dint of Professor Odd having circled the town in red ink. Another circle near Bonabagni, apparently in the middle of a field, marked the Oddity's entrance. Sections of the map had been circled, with notations inside such as: *"searched Domenig., Lumint."* or *"initial search Domenig., Albiat., re-checked Domenig., Penombrat."* or *"searched Lunedig., Albiat."*

I could not make sense of the words, though I guessed they were abbreviated dates of some kind. Felpz frowned at the map, briefly tracing over the Professor's marked-off areas with his finger. This covered almost the entire map, with only a small island of unmarked paper up on the other side of Farraglio, which I assumed had been foregone in favor of closer territory, as it was well out of the way.

"Well," said Felpz, after a minute of study. "This does not help us, I'm afraid." Briskly he folded the map and handed it back to Professor Odd, who took it and tucked it into the breast of her coat, looking a little sour. "Not through any fault of your own," he assured the strange woman. "It is exactly the sort of thing someone like you would do, and just so happens to be precisely the wrong way to go about finding someone like Lilibell Donnet. Come, there are other avenues we may pursue, which may or may not lead to success. One thing is for certain, we shall not find her sitting around here."

He stood up, scraping his chair back, causing the orange-feathered patrons to glance in our direction, but only briefly.

Professor Odd stared at him, unimpressed, while Felpz lifted my cane from the corner where he had stowed it, and tucked it neatly under one arm. When I clambered to my feet she turned the look upon me, an undercurrent of incredulity now present in her wrinkled brow.

"Just like that?" she asked. "You're *really* going to help me?"

"My services have already been retained to find this young woman and return her to her world," said Felpz, mildly. "But even had they not, I should consider it a pleasure to help you sort this mess out. After all, what are friends for?"

Still gazing at us disbelievingly, Professor Odd at last got to her feet, giving us both a searching look that put me more than ever in mind of a large cat. I wondered, briefly, if she had furry ears, like a cat's, hidden under that wig. But would that have frightened someone like Lilibell Donnet? I did not think so. But obviously her appearance was a sensitive subject, so I put that question away with all the others.

"All right then," said Professor Odd, a note of challenge in her husky voice. "Where to, now?"

Bouragner Felpz looked surprised. "Why, back to the *Oddity*, of course."

The sun—warm and orange with a red halo of clouds around it—was almost in precisely the same place as when we'd entered the bar. Perhaps it had sunk towards the horizon, but only a little. It surprised me, as I would have expected it to be full evening by now, considering how long we'd spent inside.

"Does time pass differently here?" I asked, directing my query in the general direction of both Felpz and the Professor, since I was unsure who held the answer.

It was the latter who enlightened me, and quite readily, at that.

"*Time* is consistent, as far as we perceive it," she said, coming out of her reserved shell, as the subject clearly interested her. She must have seen me glance questioningly towards the sun, for she went on: "You're wondering about the days, right?" A flash of white, square teeth. A smile this time, however brief. I nodded. "Well, remember how I said Niatano days last as long as seven of yours? It's because this moon is tide-locked with Mandro—that's the gas giant which orbits their star—so what we perceive as days and nights *here* is caused by the moon—Niatano—orbiting Mandro, not spinning on its axis, as yours does. The *UmanitÁ* don't stay active for all the daylight hours, though—they have four little rests between the *ottotaglia* to keep themselves going—and they don't sleep all through the night, either. They get up several times and do things in the dark. Planetside they're even more active, because of Mandro having its day and reflecting so much light onto Niatano. Everything's a bit quiet now because we're in the first hours of"—she pushed the sleeve of her coat back, revealing a pale, slender wrist. Around it ran a faint line of discolored skin, and the band of a watch, which she peered at before continuing—"*Caderataglia.* That's the last light *ottotaglia,* though it's *Lunedìgiorno,* which is the first of their summer days, so we'll have light all the way into *Penombrataglia.*"

"Summer days?" I echoed, cautiously.

This produced another burst of eager explication from which I gleaned that Niatano's years were so short—only twelve days—that the natives had done away with the concept of months entirely. Actually, had never had them to begin with, since Niatano was *itself* a moon, and had no way to reckon months, as we did.

"That must be trying," I said, looking around the countryside with new appreciation. "To have such short seasons."

Professor Odd laughed at that, high and cackling, but also full of warm humor. "Niatano doesn't have extreme seasons, the way Reanen does," she told me. "Remember, *it* is the moon, orbiting close to the equatorial ecliptic of Mandro, so the entire satellite has a seasonal shift closer to what your tropical environments experience. Oh, there's enough variation that they have their harvest days, and they've developed a midwinter light festival, but generally everything's pretty warm and comfortable. It's just a warm and comfortable world," she added, thoughtfully. "'Swhy I like it here."

I could certainly understand that, and admittedly, once one grew accustomed to the dark, blackish fields and the warm, orange sky, it was truly a beautiful landscape. We were on the path to Bonabagni now, and I could gaze out across the soft and gently rolling hills to where pale pink mist settled in the distance, turning them into dreamlike, floating islands, pricked with dark trees. I could hear the tinkle of bells, which Professor Odd had informed us were the herds of *caprini*—the beak-faced sheep we had encountered earlier—making their way in to be milked. I could smell their thick, pungent odor, but also a lighter, sweeter note, as of grapevines. It felt to me more than ever like Milany, but an older, sleepier, gentler version of that country.

I murmured a quiet agreement, and Professor Odd strode up beside me to give me a curious look.

"You're not like the others," she stated, in her abrupt, frank way.

I blinked back at her. "No?" I said.

Professor Odd shook her head, sending tendrils of silver hair waving. "Not like Miss Lilibell, and certainly not like *him*." She jerked her chin in the direction of Felpz, who was striding along in front, swinging my cane almost jauntily. He cocked an ear at us, to indicate he'd overhead, but said nothing.

My mind helpfully came up with several factors which distinguished me from both Felpz and Miss Donnet, not least of them that I must look far more grey and wrinkled, but Professor Odd did not seem to mean that.

"You're more ... well ... *solid*," she said, raising both her hands and arching her fingers, as if miming a hard object. "You haven't got that ... that *fidgety* sort of tingle. With Miss Lilibell it was barely a shadow, but *he's* practically *radiating* with it. In fact, I think he's mostly tingle, and if you took it away he'd wither up, like a mummy."

At this I finally grasped what she was getting at, and I very nearly laughed. "You must mean *magic*," I said. "You must be sensing their magic—I am sorry, I know you do not like that term. But the explanation is simple: you're not feeling it about *me* because I haven't got any."

Professor Odd stared at me, wide-eyed. "You haven't got magic?" she asked. "But you come from a world *full* of the stuff! How do you *survive?*"

"Quite comfortably, as it happens," I said. "With a little help from my friends. Magic is not the have-all, end-all, be-all, even in our world. Oh, certainly it is a major element—our world wouldn't be the shape and form it is now without it, I'm sure—but compare it to being blind, or deaf! It's not as though people without sight or hearing *or* magic cannot enjoy themselves. We get by just fine—even if we're inconvenienced now and then."

Professor Odd was nodding, but a frown kept creeping across her face. It was a peculiar, wrinkled expression, as she had no hair on her eyebrows—just bony ridges under her skin.

"No, there's more to it than that," she said. "I haven't got any magic. But magic doesn't make you *uncomfortable*, the way it does with me. And looking at you here, in this world, you seem somehow *even more* solid than the Neätans—who haven't got any magic either, as far as I can tell."

"Corianne simplifies," Felpz broke in, unable to restrain himself any longer.

"How so?" asked the Professor.

"She is not magically impaired, as some people truly are," Felpz explained. "It is rather that she possesses *inverse* magic; she is highly resistant to enchantments, and magical maladies which render me an invalid for days will leave her unaffected."

"Really?" said Professor Odd, peering at me with renewed interest. "How fascinating. I never considered magic to have opposing sides like that. Actually, that makes much more sense, now that I think about it."

"I am glad it clarifies matters for you," I said, magnanimously. "I still don't fully understand magic—mine or Felpz's—though I've lived with it all my life."

"Yes," allowed Professor Odd, inclining her head. "But I rather think you're acclimated to it, whereas I'm not. Not at all."

We had reached the path's terminus and emerged into the main square of Bonabagni. Here Felpz led us confidently down the road, back the way we had first come. The sun was low in what I had originally assumed was the west, but after the Professor's talk of orbits and moons and seasons, I wondered if Niatano even had a west—perhaps they called it something else. I was on the verge of vocalizing this query, when Felpz's voice cut across my thoughts.

"And yet," said he, "you make your home in one of the most eccentrically magical places I have ever encountered."

Professor Odd's head jerked up; she seemed affronted. "The Oddity's not *magical*," she said. "It's unconventional by nature, yes—that's why its *called* the Oddity—but it's not magic. Not like your world, anyway."

Felpz made a *hmm* noise, but didn't press the point. We descended the hill and crossed the bridge where we'd met the *caprini* herd—now empty—and trudged on up the other side. Now I could see, resting in the midst of a small field, a little stone house with a mossy roof made of black thatch. As we drew nearer I saw that the road passed by its tiny, battered door, and I realized it must host the entrance to the Oddity. I mentally chastised myself for not noticing it when we first arrived—I could only imagine that I had been too overcome with amazement to take everything in.

With the way things had been going, I almost feared that the door would no longer lead to the Oddity, but when Felpz gently pushed it open there were the carpeted stairs, and beyond them, the faint glow of lights.

Chapter 6: Lilibell Donnet is Found at Last

FELPZ STOOD ASIDE, HOLDING THE DOOR, and Professor Odd stepped cautiously through—no doubt feeling the same reservations I did.

All was exactly as we had left it, however. Professor Odd went over to the righthand seat at the blinking, lighted console, and ran her hands over the buttons—though she didn't actually press any. I settled myself into a nearby armchair, confident that any contribution of mine could be made while sitting down. When Felpz came up the stairs—having carefully shut the door behind him—he went over and leaned against the overcrowded table, dangling my cane between his legs, and looked at Professor Odd expectantly.

"Well?" she asked, a little impatiently. "I don't see what good being here does. Lilibell isn't *in* the Oddity—I checked!"

"May I ask how you know she has not returned while we were absent?"

Professor Odd blinked at him. "The Oddity would have told me. See, it says you were here." She pointed to a row of buttons which were noticeably fainter than the rest, save three; a green, blue and purple button were all glowing brightly. "Miss Lilibell's is this one." She indicated a button next to the green, which was so dark I could not ascribe it a particular color. "It's been that way for *days*. *Neätan* days, which worries me. She can't just be asleep under a tree somewhere—she'd have to have found shelter. And food. I made a point of coming back to the Oddity at the end of every *ottotaglia*, to see if she had returned on her own. Last time, I found you."

She straightened up, twisting around so she could glare at Felpz, but it wasn't a heated look.

"I thought you were the Oddity's *proper* owners. Maybe I said so before. But you're *not* the Oddity's owners. How did you wind up here, anyway?"

This caused me to look intently at Felpz as well, for even I did not fully understand what he had done. Under scrutiny from both of us, my friend merely shrugged, and smiled sheepishly.

"I *asked*," he said. "It was largely guesswork—I know even less about this place than you do. But I have an instinct for such things that has proven useful in similar circumstances."

Professor Odd turned her seat right around—it spun, like a top, upon the supporting column—so she could lean forward, facing Felpz.

"Do you think," she asked, her eagerness overwhelming her reservations. "Do you think you could use the *Oddity* to find Miss Lilibell? I know it can show pictures of different places within a universe—that's how I found life on Callanaph—but I can't control it very well. And I've never asked it to show something as specific as a *person*."

What I was more curious about was her allusion to the Oddity's "proper" owners. It raised the question of where she had got the thing in the first place, but Felpz seemed to consider this—like the Professor's identity—to be relatively unimportant.

He shrugged. "I might," he said. "It would be better for all concerned, however, if *you* did."

Professor Odd threw up her hands and let out a cry of frustration.

"What do you think was the first thing I *tried*?" she wailed.

Felpz settled himself more comfortably against the table, causing a grey, box-like contraption with lots of knobs and dials on its flat face to slide dangerously close to the edge. I reached over and pushed it to safety.

"Show me," Felpz commanded.

I could not fault Professor Odd for groaning and rolling her head back to gaze despondently up into the black expanse that served as the Oddity's ceiling. She rallied, however, and spun back around to face the array of buttons. These she pressed, one by one, in a careful sequence that meant nothing to me, but caused the Oddity to produce a simple note for each depressed button, and when she had finished I heard the distant chimes once more.

When they faded I saw that the array of windows above the pipes and buttons had changed, so that combined they displayed what I now recognized to be a typical Neätan landscape: rolling black hills lined with narrow trees, like spiky paintbrushes, cut by gold earthen roads. A herd of *caprini* rested in the bottom left, some grazing, others lying down, asleep. By their movement, and the subtle glimmering across the black sea of grass, I could see that the picture was not static, and therefore assumed it was showing us the landscape as it currently existed—not a snapshot of a single moment in the past.

"How marvelous," I breathed.

"It's *aggravating*," moaned the Professor, slumping forward in her chair. "No matter how many times I tell it to show me Miss Lilibell, *this* is what I get." She flicked a hand at the little windows.

"Is it always the same scene?" asked Felpz, who had leaned forward, resting his elbows on his knees to get a better look.

"More or less," said Professor Odd. "Sometimes it's different angles, but that line of trees on the hill over to the right is always visible, so I *think* it is the same place."

"Can you not convince the Oddity to open its portal within that area?" Felpz asked.

Professor Odd shot him a dubious look. "I can *try*," she said. "I'm not sure if the Oddity can—or, more accurately, if the Oddity *will*. When I tried to open a portal right next to the gelato shop in Farraglio I got that *caprini* herder's hut on the road to Bonabagni. Honestly, I've no *idea* where it would open up if I asked it to center on an empty field. The portals need a solid doorway—or something like a doorway—to anchor them in space. Otherwise . . . " she trailed off.

"Otherwise what?" Felpz inquired, leaning so far forward off the table that he looked ready to slide to the ground.

"Well, to be honest I've never seen the Oddity open an unanchored portal," she admitted. "I *hypothesize* that such a thing would be highly unstable and likely to collapse or detach at a moment's notice. Not something you'd want to go through, if you wanted to remain in one piece."

"I see," said Felpz, in a way that suggested he *really did* see, and in much more detail than I could ever imagine. "Then do you select the door, or, that is to say, the *anchor* of your preference, and then the Oddity chooses another?"

Professor Odd shook her head. "I haven't figured out how to be so *specific*," she said. "Usually I just input the place I'd like to go and let the Oddity pick the anchor. It's good about picking solid, safe, out-of-the-way anchors. Ones that locals would be unlikely to stumble into by accident. I guessed the hut was the nearest thing to Farraglio that it deemed safe."

Felpz nodded, tapping the end of my cane against the Oddity's wooden floor. Despite the high ceiling, the sound did not echo. In fact, I got a sense of the Oddity as being an inherently cozy place; if there were hidden spaces within it, then they were more like the burrows of a mouse, not wide, echoing caverns.

"I suppose I must ask," said Felpz. "How well can you communicate with the Oddity?"

Professor Odd twirled around and looked at him, puzzled.

"How well do you know its habits?" Felpz rephrased. "Its preferences? Its own desires?"

Professor Odd chewed her lip and looked at her shoes. They were worn leather, with golden, Neätan dirt caked on the soles.

"T'be honest," she said eventually, "I'd never really thought of it as being the sort of thing that *had* desires. I just assumed it was a highly advanced machine."

Felpz's eyebrows went up, sending waves of wrinkles across his high brow, and he gave a short bark of laughter.

"A machine?" he laughed. "No, the Oddity is far beyond a machine, though it has superficially mechanical aspects. Perhaps, Professor, if I may be so bold as to suggest: do not think of it as *inputting commands* but rather of *asking nicely*. As you would ask a person for directions."

Professor Odd frowned thoughtfully, considering. She slid around so she faced the console again and raised her hands, but left them hovering in the air above the buttons. Her shaggy, silver head cocked from side to side, as if she were taking in the array of colored circles for the first time. Then, slowly and hesitantly, she brought her hands down and pressed a few of them.

The Oddity chimed, and the screens flickered to show a large, blue-roofed house surrounded by tall, paintbrush trees, with what were unmistakably vineyards crawling down the hill below it. A herd of *caprini* raised a low cloud of golden dust as they ambled up the road toward the house.

"Oh, that's different," said Professor Odd, her voice blank with surprise.

Unable to restrain himself, Felpz left the table and went to stand behind her, keeping both hands clasped around my cane so he would not grab the back of her chair.

"Try asking," he said, his voice tense with excitement. "Ask the Oddity if it can open us a portal into the backyard of that house, but one of such a nature that anyone other than the three of us—or Miss Donnet—opening the anchor would not activate the portal. That is, the door would lead to wherever it ought, for them—and us."

"That's a lot to ask," said Professor Odd, uncertainly.

"Then ask graciously," suggested Felpz.

Professor Odd pulled the ends of her mouth down at Felpz in a dubious expression, but turned back to the console and put out her hands with a flourish. After a moment of thought she pressed another sequence of buttons.

Whether by chance or purpose, the notes these struck formed a lyrical melody, and the chiming when she had finished sounded louder—almost triumphant. I felt a tremble run up my legs from the floor which put me in mind of an eager horse, and then Professor Odd was out of her chair like a shot and leaping down the steps to the door, Felpz on her heel.

I followed at a more reasonable pace, and when I arrived it was to find their two tall, slender forms leaning eagerly out through a door that now led to a drowsy, crowded barnyard. I could glimpse a court paved with pale grey stones and scattered with stalks of coppery straw. A large handcart to one side was being slowly filled with rich-smelling manure from the stall beyond.

We slipped through the door, closing it carefully behind us, and I noted that it was a heavy, wooden one, set into the side of a house built of mortared stones. The small window beside it showed a dusty little room filled with crates and barrels, pitchforks and rakes.

Felpz quickly led us out into the center of the yard, so anyone encountering us would assume we had come by the nearby open drive that ran down through a field of vines, to meet the main road. It was just as well we did, for a Neätan came out of the barn pushing another cart piled high with dark, coppery hay, not a moment later. For the first time I saw a look of visible surprise cross the person's avian features, but this seemed more to do with the fact that we were on their private property, rather than any irregularities of our appearance.

I would have been at a loss, but Felpz swooped in with his indefatigable air of confidence and grace, speaking ingratiating Milanian, and soon the Neätan was quite at ease.

Unsurprisingly, Professor Odd had no trouble following the conversation, and darted in with her own questions as soon as it was clear we were not going to be chased off.

I stood behind and a little to one side, content to let the lyrical, flowing language wash over me. While my companions spoke with the Neätan, I took a closer look at our surroundings, and was comforted to find them as familiar as everything else about this world, apart from the colors. We stood in a small courtyard, flanked on one side by the bulk of the main house, out of which we had come; a barn with open-fronted stalls (where the manure cart sat) on another; the bare wall of another barn formed the third side of a horseshoe with the other two, and the final side opened onto the drive I have already mentioned.

The buildings were all mortared stone, painted mint green in some places, with the ubiquitous sky-blue clay roofs. These were constructed again after the Milanian fashion of laying tiles across the roof beams and then weighting them down with rocks. A creature that put me in mind of a large, furry wyvern was perched on top of the nearest roof, preening its leathery wings with a long, tooth-filled snout. When it sensed me looking it stared back, unashamed, before returning to its toilet.

"Well," said Felpz, coming away from the Neätan with the hay cart. "We are closer than we were, though no one at Casafiore has laid eyes upon our missing lady."

"They have noticed *something*, however," said Professor Odd, eagerly. "Our friend with the hay cart over there says that they have missed things over the last couple days. A barrel of grapes here, a bag of apples there; bread and cheese from the pantry, and a blanket from the stables."

"Signs," Felpz filled in, smoothly, "of either an extremely enterprising rodent, or perhaps the person we seek."

"Can you sense no other sign of her?" I asked my friend, knowing that he had an uncanny ability to detect a person's presence even when there was no visible trace.

Felpz screwed up his face in displeasure, however. "Not with my available powers," he admitted.

"If she has been here, then we may find evidence of where she has been hiding out," Professor Odd said, ignoring the reference to Felpz's unconventional abilities. "Now that we know we're close I am sure *someone* will have seen her!"

"I would not count upon it," Felpz warned. "Remember that Miss Donnet comes from a world with different rules than this one. Rules that, though she may be beyond their framework, still apply to *her.*"

"What do you mean, Felpz?" I asked.

"Do you recall what I said earlier? That the magic of this world is slumbering, distant? The only powers I have now are the ones that are intrinsically linked to my being—whereas in our homeworld I might call upon all manner of native magic to assist me. It is perfectly likely that Miss Donnet is in a similar situation."

"But she was no mage," I pointed out.

"Not in training to be a magician, no," Felpz conceded. "But she was making a study of astrothaumaturgy—she has *some* magical capabilities, of that I am certain. And when a person of that sort decides they do not wish to be seen, well, people quite literally *do not see them.*"

"What are you saying?" said Professor Odd, sounding off balance and irritated. "That Miss Lilibell has been going around *invisible* for the last few days?"

"Not in the purest sense of the word," Felpz said. "Making oneself properly invisible is a difficult achievement, even in our own world. In this one, I suspect she has simply cast a misdirection spell upon herself. It is easy enough to do, especially with strong motivation."

Professor Odd, who had been making strides towards the drive leading away from the villa, stopped in her tracks, and her shoulders sagged.

"Then what are we to do *now?*" she asked, turning to face us.

I in turn looked to Felpz and found him gazing thoughtfully down at my cane—which he still carried in the crook of his arm.

"There is something we might try," he remarked, taking the cane and turning it this way and that, so the silver banana caught the warm light and glimmered. "Any of us, in fact, it is so very simple. However, I think you should have the honor, Professor Odd. After all, Miss Donnet is *your* friend."

So saying he extended the handle of the cane to the Professor, who took it with a curious look.

I said nothing at this shameless exchange of my property, as I could tell it was significant to Felpz's plan. In fact I felt a warm swell of pride at having contributed, even indirectly.

Professor Odd turned the cane over, discovered the hidden blade, and started in surprise.

"What do I do with *this?*" she asked Felpz, almost accusingly.

Now that he had no object to occupy his hands, Felpz clasped them behind his back and rocked forward on his feet, looking as excited as child showing off their favorite toy.

"Even in our own world," he explained. "*My* world, I should say, there are what you might call 'realms' of reality, all stacked one of top of the other. Sometimes they mix, and that can be confusing, but it is not currently relevant. What is, and what

I will attempt to describe, is the affinity that things from the same realm have for each other. Take something as innocuous as a pebble from one realm to the next, and it will long to return home. Should another piece of that home be put in the same realm as our hypothetical pebble, the two will be drawn to one another, as if there were an invisible cord, pulling them together."

Professor Odd was frowning, but not in a way that suggested she was angry or frustrated; merely thoughtful.

"This sounds like more of your magic," she said, uncertainly.

"It might seem so, to you," Felpz allowed. "However, to people like myself, it is one of the natural forces that governs my world. What makes it important here, now, is that we three have all been removed from our home realms, and that two of us share an affinity with Miss Donnet. Now, I'm afraid Corianne's very nature prohibits her from sensing the presence of Miss Donnet on her own. I might, were I to extend a certain amount of effort. However it is *much easier* if one has an implement, a tool, which they can follow, like the needle of a compass. That cane, as it comes from the same world as our missing lady, is connected to her by this same affinity—the string I described earlier—and it takes only the barest magical sensitivity—which you have shown that you possess—to allow it to guide you to her."

Professor Odd, who'd been examining the banana handle curiously, looked up in surprise.

"What are you talking about?" she said. "That this *cane* knows where Miss Lilibell is?"

"It knows nothing," said Felpz. "It is a cane. Wood and metal—both of which, I might add, are excellent magical conductors—and it will naturally be drawn to people from its home realm. You will feel it, if you hold it loosely in your hands, as a faint tug. You will have to account for my presence, and perhaps Corianne's as well, but there should be a third. It might be quite faint, but have no doubt that it is Miss Donnet."

Professor Odd gave my friend a dubious look, but she took the cane and held it loosely in her hands. She made a sound like *humph,* and then spread one hand flat, palm up, so she could balance the cane across it.

All was still.

Then, slowly, the cane's tip began to move, sliding around until it pointed directly at Felpz.

Professor Odd made an irritated noise. She frowned, thoughtfully, and took a step forward. The cane turned on her hand, so it remained pointed at my friend.

"Miss Corianne," she said. "Could you stand in front of your friend? He's muddling with my readings. Like a magnet and a compass."

Obligingly I stepped around so that I stood between Felpz and the tip of my cane. At first I saw no difference, but when Professor Odd turned again and took a few steps away from us, the cane did not readjust itself.

"No, it still senses both of you," Professor Odd said, as if reading my thoughts of surprise. "But, Miss Corianne, he's got such a strong pull, I'm sort of using your reverse-magic as an insulator. *Ah,* there we are . . . "

The cane had not visibly moved, but now Professor Odd's open hand closed around it, and she held it aloft, perpendicular to the ground with the handle up, her arm extended rigidly in front of her.

Slowly at first, then gradually gaining speed, she began marching off down the road. We followed, with Felpz bringing up the rear this time, and walking carefully so as to keep me between himself and the cane.

We must have made a curious sight to any inhabitants of the villa who might have glanced down at their drive: Professor Odd with the cane held out at the end of one arm; myself following at a respectful distance, and Felpz practically tiptoeing behind me.

Down the drive and onto the road we went, descending the hill on which the villa was perched, and then winding along beside a sluggish, purple-black river. This color I now saw was not from any pollution of the water, but from the thick mat of floating plants, like our duckweed at home, that covered the surface. Here and there the current disrupted their ranks, and the clear water beneath shone a brilliant gold reflecting the sky.

The road was of the same golden dirt as the other, but here someone had been to great pains to shore up the riverside edge of it with closely fitted blocks of grey-blue stone. Nevertheless, a lush, almost purple moss had taken root in the cracks, and in places had succeeded in pulling the rocks apart. In one such place a herd of *caprini* had finished the work of the moss and torn a large portion of the road away as they trampled down to the river. Here Professor Odd paused, laying my cane flat across her palm once more, before slowly turning to follow the animal tracks down to the water.

I feared this would mean the end of our quest, but the river was rocky and shallow; a natural ford as well as a watering hole. From the string of boulders leading across, it looked to have been used as the former by both *caprini* and *UmanitÁ*. Professor Odd leapt from rock to rock with fluid grace, keeping my cane out in front of her, as if testing the air. I followed more cumbrously. The stepping stones had been erected according to the long, leaping gate of the natives, and my venerable human legs fell short of the task. Felpz of course had no such difficulty, and in due course we crossed the water and made our way on up the opposite bank, where the *caprini* had beaten a wide, golden track through the thick black grass.

Here the road forked and the fields ended, replaced by a wild orchard of sparse trees with silver bark and glossy, red-black leaves. These bore fat, shiny red fruit, which looked like apples until I got close enough to smell their sweet, spicy perfume, and realized they were something else entirely.

The *caprini* track turned right, to continue following the river, but a well-maintained road led off into the orchard. At their intersection was a small shrine made of piled stones, framing a painting so weatherbeaten only splotches of color remained. These suggested it had once depicted a portrait of some kind. A string of beads had been draped around the shrine, and a chipped, porcelain cup lay upended at its feet.

Before the shrine Professor Odd halted again, performing the same routine with my cane as before. This time it directed us up the road into the orchard, and with a sigh I resumed climbing.

It felt like a warm, humid afternoon, and though Felpz and I had had the sense to leave our outer garments in the Oddity this time, I was soon wishing for a light, cotton dress rather than my tweed traveling suit, or at least a drink of water. How Professor

Odd could stand it, bundled in her coat and scarf, I could not imagine.

Fortunately we had not much farther to go. Before us, against the deep orange sky, ran a line of tall, narrow black trees, like a fence cutting across the hill. Upon reaching it we discovered the orchard, and the road, terminated in another track that ran between the tall trees and those of the orchard. Looking out between their trunks I saw the hillside sloping gently away, with the fat, bushy crowns of things like oak trees dotting its face. Beyond that was a beautiful landscape filled with gold-orange light, the soft hills hazy in the distance and glowing from the light of the dim sun sinking towards them. The river curled into the distance, dark yet flashing gold. Sounds of clanking bells and the chirping of *caprini* drifted up to us, and a few dark shapes—birds, yet not birds—drifted through the sky.

Professor Odd did not stop when we reached the new road, but crossed it with confident strides and passed between two of the tall, narrow trees before forging out across the short-cropped grass of the field beyond. I followed in her tracks, and she led us to a large tree with spreading branches—like an oak— that put me in mind of a great and aged shepherd gazing out across their territory.

It was a splendid tree by any reckoning; old and gnarled with thick, pebbly bark of the deepest brown. Its leaves, like most plants in this world, were black, but clustered around bright blue nuts that stood out like jewels from the dark foliage.

We rounded the tree, and there, leaning up against its trunk so she could rest against it and gaze out over the landscape, was a young, human woman with dark, tangled hair. She sat thoughtfully with her hands resting in her lap, her legs stretched out before her, and I thought it was because she was half hidden by the grass beneath the tree that Professor Odd stopped and looked about in confusion.

"Hello!" I called, stepping around the Professor and waving at the young woman. "Hello, my girl, are you well?"

Lilibell Donnet—for it could only have been she—looked up in panic and astonishment. My first worry—that she had come to harm—was immediately allayed when she jumped to her feet with agility and vigor. Then I could see her more clearly, and the

The Peculiar Case of Professor Odd   287

signs upon her clothes of wear and weather suggested that the recent past had not been gentle with her. Her face was round and pink with emotion, and in build she was of the more solid and sturdy design than of elegance and grace. She wore a plain, white cotton shift with a wool skirt whose ends had been pulled up and tucked in at the belt, revealing limbs in stockings that were torn and streaked with dirt, and in one hand she clutched a small, leather satchel, which she was in the act of slinging over her shoulder when Professor Odd noticed her at last.

"*There* you are, Miss Lilibell!" she cried, darting forward with her arms outstretched.

Lilibell Donnet, however, shied away, her round, hazel eyes wide in fear, and Professor Odd nearly tripped in surprise. But she stopped, and conscientiously slid my cane through the belt of her coat. Then she looked again to Miss Donnet, but the young woman had retreated so that the tree was now between us.

"How did you find me?" she asked, her voice high and frightened, but also accusing. "You oughtn't be able to see me! I thought I made sure of that . . . "

"Yes, it was a fine piece of misdirection," said Felpz, who had still not moved from his rearguard position. "So fine, in fact, that you fooled one of the most perceptive entities I have ever encountered. Why you should do this, however, is still a mystery to us; are you in some jeopardy we are not aware of? Do you have any injuries?"

There was a flicker of movement from behind the tree, and Miss Donnet's disheveled head poked into view. She frowned at Felpz, as though she had not noticed his presence before, and then again at me. I saw her eyes flick towards Professor Odd, and caught a flash of what might have been fear.

"Who are you?" she asked, in the same accusing tone. It was clearly to mask her unease, so I did not let it disgruntle me.

"I am Corianne Birch, and this is my friend Bouragner Felpz, a magician of some skill," I said magnanimously.

"We have been retained by your friend, Miss Bragnana of San Randelfino, to find you, Miss Donnet," Felpz added. "You have been missed, and she of all people was the only one to think of asking me to find you. So here we are, and if you would but come with us we may all return home without further delay."

Yet still Miss Donnet hid behind the tree, though I saw her expression fall at the mention of her old friend.

"Oh," she said, her voice full of regret. "Poor Favulia . . . she *would* worry. But surely I've not been gone so long as all that . . . "

Felpz raised his eyebrows and glanced at Professor Odd, who shrugged helplessly.

"Time flows differently in different universes," she said. "Also, the long days here make it difficult to keep track of relative time streams."

"Miss Donnet," said Felpz, gently. "It has been over a fortnight since you left Dunchurch. Professor Húron has informed the police that you have gone missing. I am sure it would be to everyone's benefit if you came home and showed them you were alive and well. Which I take it you *are* well?"

Lilibell Donnet clutched the trunk of the tree as if steeling herself for a fight, but then all the tension released from her body and she let her hand fall.

"I am well," she sighed. "A bit sore and tired of the local fruit, but well. How are we to return home, though? Trust Professor Odd and her marvelous device?" She spoke the last words with such bitterness I felt a pang of sympathy for the Professor, who winced at them and looked down at her feet.

Felpz seemed astonished that such a thing should even be called into question.

"I fail to see a reason not to," said he. "Trust me, Miss Donnet, when I say it is far easier to let the Oddity bring the door to you than it is to walk the void between worlds alone."

At last Lilibell Donnet came away from the tree, so we stood facing one another unobstructed. She still did not approach, however, and by the fearful glances she gave Professor Odd I guessed the strange woman was the reason why.

"Mr Felpz," she began, uncertainly. "I trust you are an observant person. Have you not . . . do you not see?" She gestured, inelegantly, at Professor Odd. "She is not *of* our world, nor this one. I thought I'd know an alien if I ever met one, only to discover one had met me without my even suspecting. It was a . . . it was a shock."

Felpz looked disappointed. "I understand your surprise," he said. "However, I cannot see why it should be considered the Professor's fault."

"But it *is* my fault, sort of," Professor Odd cut in, still looking down at her shoes. She rocked forward onto the balls of her feet, digging them into the dark grass, before bringing her heels down and raising her face to meet ours.

"I am sorry," she said, turning to Miss Donnet. "For letting you assume I was . . . well, not what I am. You understand now, though, why it wasn't easy for me to put you right? I am a difficult thing for me to talk about—just ask them." She jerked her silvery head at us. "And I . . . well, truth to tell I was afraid of what you might do if you found out."

Miss Donnet got a strange expression on her tired face, a mix of surprise, consternation, pity, and a little embarrassment. The last emotion won in the end, and it was her turn to cast her eyes down, as though she could not ignore the truth in what the Professor had said. After a time she gave a deep sigh, heaving her shoulders up and down, and then a shaky little laugh.

"Afraid I might lose my senses and go running off into an alien world without a change of clothes?" she asked, a little humor flashing across her face.

Professor Odd blinked. "No, actually," she said. "I was afraid you'd do what the people in *my* world did. By comparison, you're taking it rather well, I think—even if you did worry me."

Miss Donnet stared at Professor Odd, as though seeing her for the first time.

"What *are* you, really?" she asked.

Professor Odd flinched at the question and looked away. Behind her, Felpz cleared his throat and stepped forward.

"She is Professor Odd, Miss Donnet," said he; "and more to the point, she is the one who can take *us* home."

Lilibell Donnet seemed to take the interruption with annoyance at first. Then, after considering Felpz's words, she gave a little shake of her head and began picking her way through the field towards us.

"I've acted a fool, haven't I?" she said, her pink face deepening to a dark rose blush.

"Like I said," Professor Odd repeated, bright and yet fragile. "Not as bad as the people in my world."

Miss Donnet gave her a look as though she desperately wished to know more, but bit her lip instead of speaking.

"The most important thing, as far as your friends and family are concerned," Felpz assured her, "is that you are safe and sound. I am sure their joy at your return will be sufficient to prevent them from finding fault with your actions."

The young woman laughed weakly. She was beside us now, and together we turned and began retracing our steps, back up the hill and down through the orchard.

"Which leaves no one but myself," she said, ruefully. "To own the truth I'm not rightly certain what came over me. I was more overwhelmed by this world than I realized, I suppose. These last few weeks I have pushed myself beyond what I could reasonably bear. I guess it was my way of running from the reality of my life. Which, I suppose you don't know, recently suffered a loss."

Felpz nodded, gently. "Miss Bragnana showed us your letters."

"Did she?" said Donnet, sad and fond. "The little traitoress. Well, then you know what we had been up to before coming here and I need not rehash. I suppose I'd become enamored of the idea of someone like Odd working at Dunchurch."

"*Professor* Odd," Felpz corrected her. We passed the shrine and started our descent to the river.

"I've no right to be called that," Professor Odd pointed out.

"Haven't you?" asked Felpz. "I think it suits you. Best keep it, if you want my opinion."

"Won't it give people the wrong idea about me?" Professor Odd asked.

"Pray tell, what would give people the *right* idea?" Felpz responded, but with a smile.

Professor Odd would not give an answer to that.

"I do like it," said Miss Donnet in a small voice. "All the professors I know are a bit odd in their own way—but not nearly so exciting as you. That, I think, was the biggest blow to me. I knew in my gut you were far too wonderful to be a real professor, but I held onto the illusion until faced with the stark reality.

Then, when all my carefully constructed delusions were brought crashing down, I suppose I must have gone a touch deranged."

Felpz gave her a curious look, but did not ask the question that was clearly on his mind. Nevertheless, after a moment of reflection the young woman continued.

"I remember running back the way we had come, or so I thought. I only meant to get away for a short while—to return to Professor Odd's device and wait there, and then demand she take me home. Only I must have made a wrong turn somewhere—I ended up in a field with no shepherd's hut, and when I tried to retrace my steps from *there* I found myself in the orchard yonder."

Her tale was interrupted for a spell as we navigated the river crossing, but after we had scrambled up the slope and rejoined the road, she went on.

"There I confess I had something of a nervous breakdown. It had been a long time brewing it my heart, and finding myself lost and alone on a strange world it was finally too much. I sat down next to the little shrine sort of thing and had a good cry. One of the locals nearly discovered me, but I was so frightened I scrambled away and hid myself. I do not hold with using magic to trick people, but in this case I felt justified. I cast the strongest misdirection spell over myself that I could manage, and when the local left I followed them. It was early twilight then, and I suppose I had some notion of finding a barn or loft to sleep in. I didn't realize just how *long* the twilight lasts on this world, but I ended up sneaking into a nearby farm and making myself a little nest in one of their barns. I confess I also helped myself to such food that they left unguarded, though for the most part I've been eating fruit from the orchard—which is not unlike our apples. Are we going to the farm now? Only we're all perfectly viewable, won't they take exception?"

Felpz smiled and shrugged. "It appears the locals are not put off by the appearance of aliens in their midst—though the inhabitants of the farm might be a little surprised to see us in their backyard. For this reason I suggest you all remain close to me—Miss Donnet is not the only one who can manage a keen misdirection spell."

Thus assured we began out climb up the drive to the villa, though Miss Donnet continued to speak until we were almost at the farmyard gates.

"That is all I have been doing, the past . . . oh, what has it been?"

"Three days," supplied Professor Odd, wearily.

"Only three?" murmured Miss Donnet. "It felt like a week. I thought I was stuck here for good, you know, and to my surprise I rather liked the idea. It feels peaceful here; relaxed in a way my world is not. Oh, I grieved for my friends and family left behind, and my work, and I wondered how I would get by when my magic wore out, but I was just coming to terms with all that when this lady"—she nodded at me—"came down the hill and spoke to me as if there were no magic at all between us. That is what so surprised me. I apologize if I acted irrationally."

We had reached the farm by this time, and anything Professor Odd or Felpz or I might have said had to wait while we hurried across the yard and to the little door—which opened at our approach and a small, shaggy Neätan with messy, purple feathers came out. They wore loose clothes and were sipping a large mug of steaming liquid that smelled of spiced coffee and seemed only half awake. We all drifted to one side to let them pass, Professor Odd visibly holding her breath.

The Neätan paused, sniffing the air with their noble, arched nose, and then peered about with bright, glittering black eyes. They were close enough I could see the definition of the scaled ridges surrounding their eyes, which moved across their face like human eyebrows as they frowned. Then they gave a little shrug, and walked gracefully out into the late, orange afternoon, their long, tufted tail flowing behind them.

They had shut the door behind them, but when Felpz reached forward and pushed it open, there were the steps to the Oddity, right enough, and it chimed happily as we all trooped inside.

Chapter 7: Arrivals and Departures

AFTER THE SURREAL, ALIEN LANDSCAPE OF NIATANO, the quiet coziness of the Oddity seemed almost homey. Almost, for now that I knew what lay beyond the curtains I could not shake the feeling of of being adrift in an endless sea.

I was distracted from such unsettling thoughts when Professor Odd seated herself at the swiveling chair and pulled the straps around her body, buckling them into place. Without instruction Miss Donnet went and sat in the corresponding chair across the aisle, leaving Felpz and myself to settle ourselves into the armchairs by the table.

"I'm afraid we might have lost a little time," Professor Odd admitted, tapping buttons. "There's always temporal slippage, passing between universes, and it seems yours runs a bit faster than Niatano's."

"Might you explain that in more simple terms?" I asked, though the prospect of losing time was not alien to me.

Professor Odd left off the buttons to turn around and face me, holding up both hands and moving them to one side.

"Pretend these are universes, right?" she said. "Or, *worlds,* as you like to call them. Each has their own internal, consistent temporal rate—that is, the rate at which *time* passes. The length of a second, a minute, etc." She began to move her hands crosswise in front of her, one slightly faster so it drew ahead of the other. "Which, you have to understand, *seems consistent* to the people in both universes. You only notice the difference when you have a place like the Oddity, which creates a means to pass between the two. The Oddity has its own temporal rate, but because it exists . . . " she paused, clearly wishing to add a visual aid at this point, but had run out of appendages. Or so I thought.

With a hunch of her shoulders and a wiggle of her neck, something slithered out from under her scarf, uncoiling so it hung in front of her, like the tail of a fat, pale snake, speckled with green leopard dots.

For one confusing moment I thought it *was* a snake, which had lain coiled around her neck all this time. Then I thought perhaps she was akin to the gorgons of Alturani myth, who had snakes for hair. But then the appendage curled, showing its underside to be comprised of little suckers, like those found upon the arm of an octopus or squid.

The tip of this strange appendage was bright green, and it waved gently between her two hands, and through my amazement I realized she had continued speaking.

" . . . *in the space between . . .* " Professor Odd continued, so intent on her explanation that she didn't notice our curious stares, or the way Lilibell Donnet suppressed a shudder. " . . . it won't retain consistency between universes. It *can't,* when you realize just how *many* universes there are. So if we leave one universe and spend time in another, if we were then to return to the original one the amount of time that passed *there* will likely be different than the amount of time that *we* experienced. Now, it's been *my* experience that Niatano's world moves more slowly than most others, so I expect more time to have passed in your universe when we eventually return."

I could only shrug at this, though Miss Donnet looked a little upset. I realized that we would probably have been missed in the time we were gone, but that considering we were returning safe and sound it was nothing to be worried about. Then again, I had more experience with this slippery aspect of time from my previous adventures with Bouragner Felpz, and could sympathize with the young woman, who had no such experience.

Felpz leaned forward eagerly in his seat, pressing his hands together.

"Are you certain it is so impossible to control?" he asked.

Professor Odd squared her shoulders and retracted the serpentine appendage. Now I knew where to look, I could see where it lay, curled around her neck under the bulk of her scarf.

"The passage of time? Yes I should say that's pretty impossible to manipulate—unless you're a gravitational singularity or something."

"No no, not the relativity of the time streams," said Felpz, shaking his head. "I mean the point at which you enter a world's timeline. Surely, if the Oddity exists outside any given universe, you should have some choice of *when* you enter it, just as you can control *where.*"

Professor Odd stared at him, her eyes blinking rapidly. Across from her, I saw Lilibell Donnet look between them in wonder.

"You know, I'd never thought of it that way before," Professor Odd admitted. Swiftly she turned back to the array of buttons and after some moments' thought began to tap out a new sequence.

The Oddity responded with an angry clanging in its depths, and she hastily pulled back a lever from the mass of pipes, letting it retract gently while she stroked the handle soothingly.

"Kindly now," said Felpz, his own tone low and gentle.

Professor Odd hissed in annoyance, but she tried another sequence; this one slower and with more repetitions. At the last instant she paused and turned back to Felpz.

"When?" she asked.

"I beg your pardon?" said Felpz.

"When would you like to arrive home?" Professor Odd asked, as if this were obvious.

"I don't suppose we can go back to a few minutes after we first left?" Lilibell Donnet asked, but she did not sound hopeful. Sure enough, both Professor Odd and Bouragner Felpz shook their heads vigorously.

"That would do unspeakable damage to the fabric of our universe," said Felpz, at the same time Professor Odd said:

"The Oddity can't cross its own tracks, timewise. It'd be like stepping on your own chin. Oh, but wait, you might have an idea . . . " She tapped a few more buttons, and the Oddity gave out a faint shiver all over, along with a cascade of chimes and bongs.

"*Yes,*" exclaimed the Professor, striking the air above her head with clenched fists. "I've *got* it! You were right, magician! It's all a matter of using the slippage to our advantage! Do you see, the Oddity remembers the last time and place it opened in any given universe and—oh, this is *brilliant*—I've *got* it! Same anchor . . . only, I'm afraid, several *weeks* after we left. Seems like the Oddity made additional contact while we were absent . . . " She turned to cast a look at Felpz, who just shrugged, smiling innocently.

"Nothing to be done about that, now," he said. "Take us home, Professor, as near to the last time the Oddity made contact as possible."

Professor Odd nodded, and this time her hands flew over the buttons with confident assurance. The Oddity chimed musically, the floors shook, but with a happy rumbling that put me in mind of a swiftly rolling train. Light flashed behind the buttons and flowed through the pipes, sending waves and beats of sound cascading into the little room. The volume rose with the intensity of the lights, until it sounded as if a small orchestra resided behind the panel of buttons, pipes and windows. It reached a climax with a small explosion of lights and chimes, and finally a deep, booming note that resounded from the depths of the Oddity.

We all held our breath as the sound died away, and when Professor Odd unstrapped herself and crept down to the door we leaned forward as one to watch.

It opened upon darkness and a rush of cold, moist air. With it came a smell of wet rock and mold, and I recognized immediately the aroma of Dactidillian's basement.

Professor Odd turned sideways and flattened herself against the wall, so that we might pass through.

"Here you are then," she said, her smile bright but a little sad.

I rose and put on my thick coat, then hesitated, unsure what to do. Felpz, as always, took the lead and stalked down the stairs and out into the passage. He'd given his own jacket to Miss Donnet, who lost her outer garments somewhere on Niatano, and who hadn't dressed for such cold temperatures in the first place. Together we crowded into the corridor, turning back to find that Professor Odd had remained in the Oddity, standing just on the far side of the door.

"An excellent job," said Felpz, positively beaming at her through the gloom.

Professor Odd's face, as she was silhouetted against the dim colored lights, was impossible to read. But her voice, when she spoke, was small and sounded a little lost.

"What will you do now?" she asked.

"Sleep through the remainder of the night, I should think," said Felpz, with a quiet laugh. "That, and I imagine Miss Donnet will be grateful for a hot bath. We shall reconvene in the morning, when we are better rested, to face whatever consequences await. Which, after all has been considered, should not be an unpleasant tune."

The shape of Professor Odd's head nodded.

ment of Dactidillian House led only to the grimy storeroom, and no amount of work on Felpz's part could bring the Oddity back.

"She's a better grasp of the thing already," he said ruefully, as we climbed back up the stairs.

We were met at the top by our old friend Maggehrty, who nearly fell over at the sight of Miss Donnet. The upshot was we were led without preamble to the office of Professor Húron, who was himself lingering over the remains of, it must be said, a poorer breakfast than ours.

What followed was a grueling interview which I need not cover in detail. Miss Donnet and Felpz both repeated their stories, but in a more structured fashion as Professor Húron called his assistant in to take notes once it became clear their narrative was no fabrication. For Miss Donnet had inadvertently brought home two of the strange Neätan fruit in the pocket of her skirt, and these, once examined, served to convince Professor Húron of the validity of her story. He had all sorts of questions which nearly derailed her narrative entirely—did she take a sample of the air? What did the constellations look like? How did Odd's device work? Could she build one?—and was understandably eager to meet Professor Odd himself.

Here Felpz was obliged to shake his head, sadly. The feeling appeared to be genuine as he said, in a melancholy tone:

"I fear that Professor Odd has moved on from this world, as indeed she moved on from her own. Be certain she is a wanderer at heart—though, as befits her name, an odd sort of wanderer; one whose home brings the places to her, rather than she making the journey to them."

"Oh, but she must return, surely," said Miss Donnet. "She did *say*—and besides, we've so much work yet to do! The things I saw on Callanaph, magician! The things I saw ... why, they alone will revolutionize our knowledge of the solar system! Think of what I could do if I had full access to her device!"

"Yes, and I believe that is precisely why you will not see Professor Odd again," sighed Felpz. "The Oddity is *her* device, if it can be said to be a device, or to belong to anyone. It is not our place to co-opt such a thing for the benefit of our world—it would be like the mortal who, graced with the weapons of a god, forgets their place and goes right on using them as if they were their own. It is no accident that fate turns sour for them, and it would just as surely have turned sour for us, if we attempted to chain the Oddity to one world. Nevertheless," he said, brightening. "Just as the mortal may benefit from borrowing a god's weapon, so too might we learn from the glimpse we have been given into the workings of our own world."

Miss Bragnana looked relieved at Felpz's words, but Miss Donnet sighed heavily, her shoulders heaving.

"But there was so much *more* to see," she moaned. "It shall drive me mad if I do not find out what it was we encountered on Callanaph."

"Then I would suggest you bend all your own power to finding out," said Felpz, giving her a piercing look from under one arched eyebrow. "Our world is not without its own resources—use *them*. I would recommend a visit to Syranna, as a starting point—Valsma, to be precise. Last I heard they were developing some very interesting engines that might, with the right modifications, be used to build machines capable of travel between our planets."

Miss Donnet fell back into her chair, her expression thoughtful, and nodded distractedly when Professor Húron declared that it was high time they notified the police of her safe return, not to mention her family.

"Yes," said Miss Donnet, coming back to the present reality from where her imagination had momentarily taken her. "My poor mother, and brothers. Oh dear—I had clean forgot about them. They shall be worried sick. Oh dear. Tell me, Professor, might I beg another week's leave, to see them?"

"Provided you remain in *this* world," said Professor Húron, his voice bitter but tinged with humor, "I cannot think of a reason why you should not."

"Never fear, Professor," said Miss Bragnana, squaring her shoulders. "I shall accompany her."

And though she still looked a little sad and lost, Miss Donnet laughed and clasped her friend's hand gratefully in her own.

"They will go far, those two," Felpz said as we ambled away from the meeting. It was getting on midday, and as we circled around the green surrounding the Widder Clock we found it littered with students taking a noon repast, some with books and papers spread around them, others with blankets and baskets, enjoying a picnic. Though they were all uniformly young and beautiful and filled with the nervous energy of people still finding themselves, the diversity in skin tone and hair styles came from all over the globe. There were fewer men than I expected; perhaps one for every two women, but that might have been an accident of timing and location, as Dunchurch had always accepted female students, even back in the days when few colleges who were not strictly devoted to them did.

"Better them than I," I said. "Strange demons and space travel and oh . . . it just makes me long for my own parlor, a cat, and a nice cup of tea."

"Oh, I do not think space travel will be incompatible with cats, or tea," said Felpz, mildly. "Though parlors may be lost, or suffer a redesign."

"Space travel," I murmured. "To think it may happen within their lifetimes. Certainly within yours," I added, giving my friend a sly grin.

Felpz did not return it. He pursed his lips and looked away, gazing out across the green.

Then he stopped abruptly, gripping the railing which separated the lawn from the cobbled drive. He stared up at the terrace which ran the circumference of the Camera, where a few tables had been set out under umbrellas. These were all crowded with students, save one which was occupied by a single figure with improbably bright, canary-yellow hair, wearing an equally bright, leaf-green coat. Despite the warmth of the day this was buttoned up to their chin, and they had a thick, blue scarf wrapped around their neck. Sensing us look, they turned and waved a long, pale hand in our direction.

Felpz tensed at my side, clearly repressing the desire to vault the railing and go tearing off across the green. He restrained himself, however, and we continued to walk leisurely on, turning in at the drive that led to the front doors and climbing the sun-warmed steps up to the terrace.

The crowd of tables was hidden from our view by the curve of the building at first, and as we rounded it I feared the figure in the green coat and yellow wig would have vanished.

They were still there, however, and had even set out two more chairs, as if in anticipation of our arrival. It was also unmistakably Professor Odd, though she had added a pair of round, dark glasses to mask her eyes. At our advance she looked around and smiled at us widely, gesturing towards the two empty chairs.

Felpz, his motions contained as if he were approaching a skittish horse, sat down a careful distance away and regarded Professor Odd curiously.

Apart from the change of clothes and wig she appeared no different than when we had seen her the previous night. She held her shoulders in a rigid square, making her frame look larger and more powerful, but this seemed to be a conscious effort on her part; she deflated a little as she took a breath and began to speak.

"I'm a coward, you see," she began, with no preamble. "Maybe that's not immediately obvious, because what frightens me isn't what frightens most people. Of course, *that's* pretty much consistent with most things about me, I'm coming to learn."

Felpz shrugged, and smiled understandingly.

"I am certain that Miss Donnet has suffered no lasting damage from her adventures with you. Quite the opposite, in fact," he said. "You need retain no guilt upon that point."

"I know," said Professor Odd, her mouth twisting uncomfortably. "I watched your meeting—from inside the Oddity— just to make sure everything worked out all right. But it is the principal of the thing. I'd much rather flee than fight. Easier to run away from danger than confront it."

"Sometimes running is, in itself, a form of fighting," Felpz remarked, serenely.

Professor Odd chewed her lower lip and did not look convinced.

"Yes," she said, but her voice was uncertain. "But only *sometimes.* And even then, eventually you have to stop, turn around, and look at what you're running from—otherwise you'll be running forever." She spoke the words as a statement, but I saw her glance questioningly at Felpz, who nodded assuringly.

"Running can be good," she went on, sounding more sure of herself. "It can give you time to think. Time to figure out who you are. So that when you *do* stop and turn around, you're actually ready to face the thing you're running from. As long as you do *stop,* eventually."

She raised her strange, smooth face to ours, the brilliant sun glinting off her dark glasses, so it looked for a moment as though her eyes were two huge, black orbs. I remembered the strange appendage, whose shape I could still just make out, hidden in the folds of her scarf, and wondered yet again what lay under the rumpled wig; what had frightened Miss Donnet so.

"That's why I came to say good-bye," Professor Odd said. "Properly, I mean. I left Miss Lilibell a letter, because I don't think it would do either of us any good to say our good-byes in person. She's still running herself, I think. And I . . . I just represent a door to her. A way to escape. It was unfair of me, taking her away. She needs to be here, and now she's back, she can face the thing she was running from. Seeing me . . . " the woman shrugged. "It would just be more temptation. But you, you I had to see, face to face. Because everything I've been doing up until I met you—the traveling, the wandering, the studying— was just what Miss Lilibell was doing on Niatano; running lost, without direction. I managed to bring her home, but only with your help. So I think . . . I think saying good-bye in person will help me to . . . er . . . get home. As it were."

She trailed off, running the end of her scarf through her fingers.

"I appreciate the gesture," said Felpz, with heartfelt gratitude. "If I may ask, where is it you are bound next?"

Professor Odd rolled both her lips inside her mouth and pressed them together, pulling them apart with a faint *popping* sound. She fidgeted, running her fingers along the rim of the table. "Back to where I came from, I think," she said at last. "I left . . . abruptly. So abruptly I wasn't aware I *was* leaving until I was very far away and then I was too frightened to go back. Now, however, I realize there are some things I can only learn *there,* and I need to learn them in order to keep moving on. Funny how that works, isn't it? You run and run, but at a certain point you have to go back to where you started if you're ever truly going to escape."

Felpz nodded understandingly.

"I am sure," he said, with a surprising amount of confidence, even for him, "that you will find what it is you seek, and that whatever destination you set your sights on, nothing will prevent you getting there."

At hearing the words Professor Odd's chest puffed up like a bird's, and she squared her shoulders once more, filling out her slender frame.

"You think so?" she asked, her voice bright and fragile and full of hope.

"Quite so," said Felpz, now smiling openly. The effect it had on Professor Odd was remarkable; her face split with the breadth of her grin, her teeth flashing white in the sun. She rose, and Felpz and I followed suit, my friend leaning over the table to shake her by the hand.

"If I may offer a small piece of unsolicited advice," he said, and the Professor paused as she turned to go.

"Yes?" she said.

Felpz took a breath, clearly choosing his words carefully. "When one has capabilities such as yourself, it is not always necessary to keep them solely for your own use. Perhaps you have helped Miss Donnet more than you imagine. And perhaps there are others, in other worlds yet unknown, who are in need of doors and unexpected friends. Do not wrap yourself in isolation, Professor. Friendship is, in its way, as strong as any magic or natural force, and we need it like we need air and light and water."

Professor Odd frowned, considering, but then she nodded.

"One more thing," said Felpz, and now there was a capricious light in his eyes, and they positively shone as he said: "Do not fear the unknown; for even magic, in all its contradictions and eccentricities, follows a course as strong and defined as the flow of the tides and the ways of the wind. It only needs a determined and impertinent mind to puzzle it out. And I believe yours is more than a match for that challenge."

Professor Odd colored slightly at the peculiar compliment, her chest expanding, if possible, even more. In lieu of words, she pulled off her wig, as one might raise one's hat, and bowed low to us.

I caught a glimpse of a perfectly bald head, as smooth and round as an egg, speckled with green leopard spots. A fleshy lump at the back hinted at where the appendage sprouted—in the lower center, just above her neck. Then the wig was replaced, and with a flourish, she spun on her heel, striding gaily off between the tables, before darting into the Camera by one of its side doors.

Yet I knew, as sure as I knew Felpz stood at my side in the bright, spring sunshine, that Professor Odd had not entered the Widder Clock at all. Likewise I also knew that even were I to run forward and throw the door open, no portal would await, and I would find only the interior of Dunchurch's iconic library.

It was not until almost an hour later, when we had returned to our room at the inn and begun to pack for our own journey home, that the full enormity of what I had seen came crashing down on me.

I had seen Professor Odd go striding off, yes, but what had given her gait its particular pomp and energy, was the way she swung the slim, black cane with the flashing silver banana for a handle, its metal-capped tip rapping sharply on the marble terrace as she walked.

"Felpz," I said, straightening up from where I was folding my crumpled clothes from the night before. "I do believe that Professor Odd has made off with *my cane!*"

Felpz looked up at me from across his own, closed suitcase (packed with magical assistance, I was sure), with such a look of chagrined guilt that I came very close to laughing, despite my annoyance.

"I hope you can forgive me," he said. "It was a presumptuous thing to do. But console yourself in the knowledge that she will undoubtedly put it to good use. A woman embarking on such a journey would be well in need of such an implement."

"Oh *Felpz*," I said, throwing down my clothes in a huff. "I had just begun to grow *fond* of the thing! And what *will* I tell Milain?"

Felpz, however, was smiling, and only that telltale glint in his eyes that spoke of some delicious secret yet to be revealed prevented me from snatching up my dirty laundry and hurling it at him.

"Why, Corianne," said he. "You may tell your daughter all about it, when next you meet. It is, I assure you, a marvelous story. And please, do not look so bitter. For I have something that, if you would be so good as to make a detour to Redling with me, will more than compensate you for the loss of that ridiculous cane."

And with that, at least for the immediate moment, I was obliged to satisfy myself.

I finished my packing in time to meet with Misses Donnet and Bragnana for an early tea, after which we bade them farewell and, leaving the two with their heads together, discussing the practicality of remote-controlled spacecraft, made our way to the train station.

Because these events happened so recently I have no satisfying retrospective with which to provide my readers with the historic context of this tale. I do know, however, that Lilibell Donnet did take up Felpz's suggestion of visiting Syranna, though she has since returned to finish her doctorate. Once she has, I understand she and Favulia Bragnana plan to build their very own spaceship, by which they might get a better look at what Donnet merely glimpsed during her time with Professor Odd.

What they will find is something I dare not guess. I must leave it to some other narrator to tell that story, with the expectation that, whatever it is, it will be an interesting one.

Chapter 8: Felpz Returns my Cane

M Y OWN NARRATIVE DOES NOT END HERE, but goes on a little further and contains the resolution to a mystery I had thought would never be revealed to me: that of Felpz and his twenty-year-long absence. For that reason alone I will tell you how Felpz returned my ridiculous, banana-handled sword-cane.

It had been over a year since I last visited Redling. That had been in winter, and was on the occasion of a friend's funeral, but the scenery was so changed from those grim, bleak days that I felt only a hint of melancholy as I stepped off the train at Redling Central—the very station that had welcomed me all those long years ago when I was but a tear-streaked girl with no possible idea of what lay in store.

Redling has changed a great deal in those years, and just as that girl is no more than the spark of a memory in the heart of grey, old woman, the Central station she had known is visible only in the overall shape of the building. Now, that dark and smokey cathedral to the steam train is full of shiny new ticket vendors, cleaner, quieter trains, and automated stairways joining it to the underground system which was only a stack of blueprints when she first set foot there. Gone are the clopping of hooves, horses having been replaced by motor-carriages within the city, and the porters and conductors wear bright yellow stripes on their uniforms, so that they might be seen more easily. But though the thronging crowd—thick, even at this late hour—was dressed in colorful new fashions that would have made that girl blush ferociously, the clamor and bustle remained as it had always been: just beside unbearable.

I followed close in Felpz's wake as we wove through the station, which was made easier by the plethora of electric lights which had been installed in the decades since I left the city. Still, it was a job to keep up, laden as I was with luggage, and I was relieved when Felpz turned towards the curb filled with waiting cabs upon exiting the building.

He must have been feeling a similar nostalgic melancholy as I, for he led us right to the end of the line, where the lone horse-drawn carriage waited behind a dingy, black motorcar. The driver seemed surprised that we should accost him, but then he looked again at Felpz's coat, and I saw a disbelieving smile cross his face.

"Bless your stubborn old soul," he said, hopping down to stow our bags for us.

The journey was more sedate, yet passed by quicker than I remembered. Within minutes we were turning off Bridgeton Way, and the cab drew to a halt outside the familiar, brick-fronted house with ivy up one side and the bright, brass number plate reading 0000.

Felpz paid the driver with a paper bill, then reached up and slipped a whole crown into his pocket. While the driver was still stammering his gratitude he took both our bags and carried them up the steps to the front door, which jumped open at his approach.

Inside I found my old home to be changed and yet even more the same as usual. In my absence Felpz's natural affinity for clutter had run unchecked; the stairs were decorated with piles of books, an assemblage of twigs and string lay in the hall, and the act of opening the door to the sitting room sent a river of loose papers slithering across the carpet.

"I'm afraid your old room has succumbed to a similar fate," Felpz said with a wry grin, seeing my expression of distaste when he raised the light. "I'd offer you my own bed for the night, only that room is in even worse condition. Nevertheless, I can make the sofa into the most comfortable thing in the world, and the curtains do a good job keeping out the morning light—I know from experience."

I could only chuckle tiredly at his apologetic tone, remembering what had happened the first time I had entered this room.

"Well, as long as you do not exile me to the closet I shan't complain," I said, and felt a warm swell of satisfaction at the scandalized look he gave me.

"Why *ever* would I do that?" he asked.

"You did," I pointed out with the magnanimity of sixty-six years removal from the event in question. "The very first time I saw you, you were with a client, and you put me in that closet yonder to keep me out of the way."

"I *did?*" said Felpz, looking aghast. "I must have been in a fit of pique; I do apologize. Well, the closet is out of the question anyway, I'm afraid; it was the first thing to fill up once the Great Organizer left me."

The Great Organizer, I should mention, was his affectionate term for the giant, intelligent spider who had stepped in to serve as his housekeeper after I had moved out. I met her only a handful of times, back when my room was still habitable and my visits to Felpz more frequent, and found that—once one got over the shock of speaking to a spider the size of a large dog— she was a singularly observant, thoughtful, and deeply competent person. She had left only a few months ago, I now recalled, and clearly Felpz had yet to find a suitable replacement.

"It has been my most persistent problem," Felpz moaned, gazing around at the clutter. "Finding a housekeeper who agrees with me. But I suppose as problems go it is not a very dire one." He snapped his fingers. "You'll be in want of a late supper, will you not? I'll send for it, won't be a moment." With these words he slipped out the door and I heard him padding lightly down the stairs.

He was gone for much more than a moment, during which time I made myself comfortable on the lone chair whose seat was visible. When he did return it was obvious he had not merely been out the door and back again: his face was streaked with grime and there were cobwebs in his hair. His hands were black with dirt and grease, and his fine purple coat was equally soiled. In his arms he carried a long, thin bundle of oilcloth wrapped with string so old and tight it had turned shiny black.

"Forgot I had it down at the back of the basement," he said by way of explanation, shoving a stack of books aside to make room on the tea table. I was momentarily struck by the similarity to Professor Odd's own, overcrowded table, and could only gaze in amusement as Felpz laid the package down and began working on the knot of string at one end.

"I don't suppose I might be treated to some illumination, before supper?" I asked, unable to disguise the mirth in my voice.

"And you shall, you shall indeed," said Felpz, his voice sharp with frustration. Apparently the knot was too stubborn for him, and he accepted my proffered nail scissors with gratitude. "This illumination in particular has been a long time coming. I must beg forgiveness yet again for keeping it from you for so long. You will understand, however, once the entire story is laid before you, why I was compelled to wait, and that the narrative, presented in its entirety, is worth it."

The black string came away from the bundle only reluctantly, leaving a deep groove in the oilcloth. This Felpz began to peel back with careful, if dirty, fingers. It revealed a relatively clean, white sheet, which Felpz used to wipe his hands as he pulled it away.

"You are perfectly justified in being cross with me," Felpz said as he bundled the cloth aside. "For giving away your cane so presumptuously. But see that I am nothing if not honest, and that I do return that which I borrow."

So speaking he flung down the bundle of soiled cloth, and lifted to the light a long, thin, familiar object.

I felt my mouth come open of its own accord, for just as sure as I had last seen my cane in the hand of Professor Odd, striding away through the tables outside the Widder Clock, now I saw it again—silver banana handle and all—laying across my friend's palms.

"Felpz," I said, gasping rather, unable to comprehend. "What is the meaning of—? How did—?" I was unable to even complete the questions bubbling up within me.

Then the obvious answer presented itself, and I mentally chastised myself for not seeing it sooner.

"Where on earth did you get one just like mine?" I asked. I narrowed my eyes. "Do not tell me you got the same idea as Milain, and purchased one as well?"

Felpz only smiled and shook his head.

"I did not purchase this cane, nor is it a duplicate. It is *your* cane, Corianne, though at the time I acquired it I did not know that. I have kept it safe, all these years, knowing that eventually its rightful owner would present themselves, and then I might return it to them. Honestly, until I stepped off the train in Stanton Leaning, I had no idea they would turn out to be you."

With hands that shook slightly I took the cane from him, and pushing my glasses up my nose I held it up to the light.

It certainly had the exact same weight and feel of my cane, but upon closer inspection I saw it was not perfectly identical: dents and scratches decorated the shaft, and the banana had acquired a faint tarnish in the crevices, while the outer edge was smooth and shiny from use. Drawing the blade I was shocked to find it a mere sliver of the one I had originally possessed, having been sharpened down to a narrow spike. Even so the edge was badly nicked, suggesting it had been put to hard use.

Sheathing it once more I laid the cane across my knees and looked up at Felpz, who still hovered over me.

"Explain," I demanded, my voice breathy and high.

"Ah," said Felpz, turning around with a flourish, so his coat-tails flared. He pulled out a nearby chair, moved the books which had rested upon it to the floor, and sat down, crossing his legs and clasping his hands over his knee. For a moment, his face darkened.

"You remember the . . . hmm . . . *leave of absence* I took from this world, oh, almost forty years past, now?"

"How could I forget?" I said. That leave had spanned the better part of my young life, and in the time I raised a child, lost a husband, and changed from a girl into a woman.

"Yes," said Felpz, having the grace to look chagrined. "If I have not spoken of my experiences during that time, it was only partly because they were singularly uncomfortable. I also held my peace on account of the fact that I felt events lay in a delicate configuration, and any presumption upon my part might bring about the gravest consequences. And, what you may not have noticed, or have understandably forgotten, was that when I returned I brought that very cane with me."

I could only stare in surprise, both at the cane and my friend.

"No," I whispered. "Surely, I would have remembered *this*." I raised the artifact in question.

Felpz shrugged. "As you may recall, the exact circumstances of my return were rather dramatic. I seem to remember being drawn to your residence by a timely spell performed by you, Abharus, and Milky. Upon arrival there was such confusion that I actually lost track of the cane myself for a few minutes. As soon as I retrieved my wits, however, I made sure to hide it in a safe place, and later removed, wrapped, and replaced it in my own basement, where it has lain for the past four decades. You likely only saw it once, in bad light, when there were much more important matters on your mind."

This I had to concede; I had been so overwhelmed at the arrival of my friend, and so distracted by his wild and disordered appearance, that I could very well have overlooked the presence of a cane—even one so extraordinary as this.

"May I take it that now, with its reappearance, events are stable enough to support you telling me all about them?" I asked. "What did you mean by saying they were in a *delicate configuration?*"

Felpz gave a great sigh and looked up at the ceiling, as if putting a complicated answer into order. When he lowered his gaze his face was fixed in concentration, and I leaned forward to listen.

"Do you recall how Professor Odd explained the discrepancy of time between universes?" he asked.

Slowly, I nodded. "Time flows at different paces, respectively."

"Yes. And keep in mind that the Oddity, existing as it does in the space *beyond* space, *between* universes, is capable of a certain amount of . . . the Professor called it *slippage,* I believe. It is an inelegant term, but not inaccurate. It is possible to slide about, time-wise, when crossing between worlds."

"That I can comprehend," said I, "but how is it relevant to your story?"

"It is relevant," said Felpz, a little sternly, "because, during my absence, I left this world—this *universe* as Professor Odd would call it—entirely. I was pulled through by that strange vortex into a world as far removed from this one as it is possible to imagine. This world is rich and textured, with a long, complicated history and many facets of reality; a towering house, to go back to my old analogy, with a deep, strong foundation. Winds may buffet it, storms may batter it, and strange things might creep through cracks in the walls, but the house is strong, stable, and resilient, filled with weights and counterbalances that keep it solid and grounded. The world I found myself in was hardly a farmer's shack, by comparison. It was all on one level, with none of the interweaving realities so common in our own. It was minuscule, as well: I felt as though I were shut in a small, cramped room, whose walls were riddled with holes and whose roof was on the verge of collapse.

"It was in this tattered excuse for a world that I became trapped; entangled, partially through my own actions, with the local inhabitants, some of whom were sorely lacking in the virtues of hospitality. They saw me as a means to sustain their world—which was not really *their* world, mind you, but they had wound up in it by much the same means as I had; sucked through by the vortex, which was that world's way of sustaining itself—feeding off other, stronger worlds. When I came through I sealed the vortex, as I told you I would. This quite probably saved our world a great deal of grief, but doomed the one I was now trapped in. Without the energy stolen from other worlds it could not sustain itself, and began to collapse. I endeavored to shore up that crumbling edifice using my own powers—an arrogant move, and one I paid for dearly. I had intended for the locals to use the time I bought them to discover a way out, as they had both the power and the ingenuity. However, the more violent half of them decided that they liked that world just fine, and as long as they could keep me there, holding it together, they need not find a way out.

"I should never have let it happen, only I was already tired from closing the vortex, and further stretched to the limit of my abilities holding that world's ceiling up, as it were. They invoked some particularly malevolent magic, and succeeding in binding me.

"It was one of the gravest situations I have ever found myself in. I saw that I would wear myself out, forced to go on past the limit of my powers, and then there would be an end to both the world and myself. I had just enough energy to call for help, but in that strange world, riddled with holes into the void, I doubted anyone would hear.

"But someone *did* hear. And not just any someone. *Professor Odd* heard my call. Thanks in part, I later discovered, to the very cane you now hold in your hands. Coming from the same world as myself, it resonated in sympathy with my magic, and led the Professor straight to me—just as we saw it lead her to Lilibell Donnet.

"At the time I was astonished to see such a thing in the hands of one so clearly alien as the Professor—who I had never set eyes upon in my life prior to that point. Even more astonishing, by certain hints and dropped words, I gathered that that was *not* the first time the Professor had seen *me*. I remember she mentioned Dunchurch in particular, but clammed up as soon as she learned I did not remember. She realized, before even I did, that somehow, in all our travels between universes and sliding around between timelines, our own lines had looped and crossed, bringing us to meet in that doomed world at a point where she was greatly advanced along her line with respect to me.

"Nevertheless, it was partly thanks to her expertise—and that of her companions—*and* that cane, that I was able to successfully extricate myself, her friends, and the remaining, decent locals, just as the world came apart completely. We parted ways when it became clear that her method of travel would compromise the temporal stability of my world, and so I was obliged to make my own way home through the void—helped once again by the very cane that now lies across your lap; for just as it led Professor Odd to me, it in turn led me home . . . to you."

My friend sat back, smiling wistfully at the cane, and I looked from him to it in renewed amazement.

"After my return, when I had time to think about things properly," he went on. "I realized what a delicate predicament I'd put myself in. For the cane had clearly come from a different point in time in this world, and by bringing it back I'd created the risk of a paradox. So I hid it away, so it would not interfere with what was, to it, the past. I had no idea when or how I would meet the Professor, or that *I* would be the one to give her the cane in the first place. Though the knowledge does soothe my conscience; I had felt a little guilty at walking off with what was certainly one of her prized possessions. Now that I know she did the same thing to me, I am sure she took it in good humor."

I could only laugh, a little incredulously. It was as fantastic a tale as I had ever heard Felpz tell, and yet it made a strange kind of sense.

"So when you arrived in Stanton Leaning and saw *me* carrying that cane," I began.

"It was not unlike the sensation of seeing a ghost," Felpz finished. "Though in actual fact I was seeing the *opposite* of a ghost, but that is not a feeling most people will recognize. I knew at the sight of it that something momentous was about to occur, but I still had no idea what or how or when. Then, when Miss Bragnana appeared so suddenly, I began to suspect events were moving close upon one another, and when *Dunchurch* was mentioned—*well.* At that point I was hardly surprised to hear that Professor Odd had appeared, though I was a little disappointed to learn she was yet at the beginning of her own journey. But the spirit, the character, was just as I remembered, and

I realized what a crucial role I was set to play—not only in regards to my past, but to her future.

"It's a delicate thing indeed, working with tangled timelines, and be sure there were many points where I feared I'd steered her wrong, or made some other blunder, that would jeopardize her future actions. I confess I was determined to give your cane away, dear Corianne, for my very presence here depended upon it. But now you know the whole story, I hope you can forgive me."

"*Forgive* you?" I cried. "Felpz, I *commend* you! I can only imagine what a complicated, difficult task it must have been, and it seems you have accomplished it beautifully!" I beamed at my friend, who for once could not meet my gaze, but turned his face aside and downward. Nevertheless I saw a faint blush darken his usually pale cheeks, and far from being embarrassed at causing such a reaction, I found myself inexplicably touched. Then, upon further consideration, I was struck by the enormity of what his tale implied.

"Why, Felpz," I said, amazed at my own words. "That must mean that I, without any knowledge or intention, albeit in the most indirect way possible, played a key role in enabling your return. Oh, do not chide yourself for a moment longer, my friend, for nothing gives me more pleasure than that thought. And, as you yourself said," I added, giving him a cheery wink and holding up the battered cane. "You did get it back to me."

Felpz smiled, and seemed to relax a little. I, too, felt a release of tension, as if the tangle of threads that had comprised the whole of his convoluted narrative had been suddenly pulled tight, forming into a strong, well-organized pattern. Now my thoughts turned to Professor Odd, whose presence I felt strongly in the room, as though she were just on the other side of the closet door. I even turned to look at it, half expecting it to open and reveal that mad figure.

No such surprise appearance was made, however, and when Felpz continued to look obligingly relaxed I gave voice to a question that had been pressing itself upon me ever since I first laid eyes upon the Professor.

"Felpz, does this mean you know what she is? Professor Odd, I mean."

Felpz propped his head on one hand and considered the question.

"I know little more than you do," he admitted, after a time. "Being, as I was, in a most compromised position when we first met, I did not have the time nor the inclination to inspect my rescuers more closely than was absolutely necessary. I am satisfied that she, though not entirely human, is not so very far removed as to merit some alienating term. Though I highly doubt that she belongs to anything as well-defined as a species—she strikes me as a too unique a character. If you must ascribe to her a pre-existing beast, consider her a most sophisticated kind of chimera; as she appears to be an elegant assemblage of several different animals. That interesting appendage, for example, looks like the arm of a cephalopod. Her eyes put me in mind of a large cat. And there might be other elements too, invisible at first glance. But as I was incapable of asking the relevant questions the first time we met, and she unable to give the answers the second time, we are left to speculate and wonder."

I found my gaze drawn, yet again, to my cane. This time I noted all over how banged and beaten it was, yet clearly well cared for. The sheath had been cracked at one point, and glued back together, and an extra layer of protective varnish applied. Something had caught in the varnish; a tiny filament, like the hair of a dog or cat. Removing the sword, I saw there were even more nicks and notches on its blade than I had first thought; many of them we so old, however, that they were almost worn away by subsequent sharpening.

"Ordinarily, I suppose, we might speculate and wonder what shall become of her now," I murmured, thoughtfully turning the cane over. "However, by the evidence here and your own experience, it is clear to me that she is bound for incredible—if sometimes perilous—adventures."

Felpz laughed, low and quiet. "That she is, dear Corianne," said he. "That she is indeed. Perilous adventures, magnificent friends, and a good deal—a *great* deal—of running."

The darkness of the evening pressed in on us, and though I knew we sat in Felpz's comfortable rooms, and that beyond the thick curtains lay the bustling metropolis of Redling—now more so than ever, what with the advent of electric lights and automobiles—I could not help but feel as though that infinite night, and that strange, marvelous place of colored lights and distant chimes, lay only a breath away; that we floated in an endless void, in the depths of which twinkled distant lights and faraway worlds.

"Do you fancy meeting her again?" I asked. "Now that she's met you when you didn't know her, and you've met her when she didn't know you, I'd say you deserve to meet when you're both more or less on the same page."

Felpz leaned back and smiled fondly at the ceiling. "Oh, Corianne, that I should like above all things. Just imagine the havoc we could wreak! But there is a danger that we may be forever out of synchronization; always one ahead or behind the other. Oh! I could not stand that. But then, in a multitude of worlds and endless possibilities, quite literally anything can happen. Indeed it must, yes, it must indeed. So it is not too much too hope. Not too much at all. And you may be sure that I do. In fact, I look forward to it. I have the time, after all. Ah, I hear a ring. That will be our supper. Do not trouble yourself, dear Corianne; I will step down and bring it up."

Postscript

W HEN I PUT THE RIBBON AND BOW on the second volume of my adventures with Felpz I thought that would be the end of them (the tales, if not the adventures), and said so. Then the events of *The Wolves of Riddlemoor* resolved themselves in the most spectacular manner, and I thought, this is too good a tale to leave in a dusty folder for some future biographer to puzzle over, better finish it off and put it out there for people to enjoy. It was an understandable exception. Then came the revolution in Suämiran and its neighbors, and I found myself once again hauling out an old story, as circumstances demanded its telling. As that was the only such narrative in my archive I thought, surely, this is the end. A strange, inside-out sort of end, but it stops here.

Now that I have come to the conclusion of yet another breach of intent, I feel any sort of farewell note to my readers cannot possibly be taken seriously. I am under no delusion of the onward progression of time, however, and so you will forgive me if I do not make any promises. Rather, I leave you with an open end—a loose, trailing tassel rather than a tight, neat knot—and the understanding that, though the players may change and the scene may shift, the great adventure continues, and surely will continue, for as long as there are people to laugh and dream and fight and love and do all the of mad things that make for good stories.

And if this does turn out to be the last thing I write in relationship to Felpz, let me say that, though we live in an eternally mutable and changing world, *he* will surely carry on. Go and ask him for more stories. For now I will rest, secure in the knowledge that I have done my part well, and that the future, as always, will take care of itself.

—Corianne Harper Birch
Stanton Leaning, Kyreland

About the Author

Goldeen Ogawa is a self-taught writer, illustrator and cartoonist. She has penned and illustrated dozens of short stories and novellas, three webcomics, and has exhibited her original art in shows all over the world. Outside of Heliopause Productions, she can be found online at *goldeenogawa.com*.

She lives in Bend, Oregon, where she enjoys biking, running, swimming, yoga, and the plethora of excellent restaurants.

About the Text and Design

The body of this book was typeset in Elysium using LaTeX. Cover art and design by the author.